FORTUNE IN BLOOD

PHIL PHILIPS

A cataloguing-in-publication entry is available from the catalogue of National Library of Australia at www.nla.gov.au.

Requests to publish work from this book should be sent to:
admin@philphilips.com

Philips, Phil, 1978-

ISBN-10: 0-9925345-0-X
ISBN-13: 978-0-9925345-0-9

Typeset in 10pt Sabon

For more information visit
www.philphilips.com

To my children, Alexander and Leonardo
this is a testament that you could do anything,
with a little hard work and determination.
My love for you is endless.

Chapter 1

Monday, 3:50 pm

Outside the California Bank & Trust, situated directly across the road from the famous beach strip, a white Ford transit-painters' van with dark tinted windows rolled up to the curb and parked. A logo with the words 'No job too big or small' appeared on its side. Inside the vehicle were four men dressed up in disposable head-to-toe white overalls. Young, inexperienced Joey watched on as his older brother, Phil, passed a 12-gauge shotgun to Victor, the eldest member of the crew, who had an ugly rat-like face, rough and mean-looking. He then handed over a Glock 9mm pistol to Matt, the designated driver, whose hair was as white as snow. Waiting for the go-ahead, they prepared their weapons and made sure their ammunition clips were full.

'Five minutes,' said thirty-five-year-old Phil Peruggia. He was raised to lead and he ruled with an iron fist; whatever he said went. Maybe it was his instinct for cruelty that made the others respect him … or fear him. He walked like a boxer and possessed a stare that could send shivers down one's back. He glanced over at his fellow compadres as he cocked his double-barrel sawn-off shotgun and said, 'One last time, boys.'

'Let's fucking do this,' replied Victor, an eager participant.

Under the wing of his brother was Joey Peruggia, the

1

youngest member of the gang. He was the complete opposite to his sibling: skinny, shy, with hardly any muscle definition. Blondish long surfer hair tucked behind his ears, his eyes piercing blue and his skin fair. He was nothing like his family, whose tanned olive skin showed they were of Mediterranean descent. This would be his first bank robbery – his first ever criminal experience for his father.

With arms folded tight across his chest, he tapped his foot with a nervous twitch, and all the while stared out of the grimy window.

'Are you okay, bro?' said Phil, sitting on the opposite side.

'Yeah,' replied Joey, but his knees were still shaking.

Phil reached behind him and took out a gun, a German-built 10mm Glock automatic. He made sure it was loaded and gave it to Joey. 'That's yours, all you need to do is point and shoot if you have to.'

Joey focused his attention on the gun; he weighed it in his hand, trying to find the balance between himself and his weapon.

'It's too late to bail out now,' said Phil.

'No, I'm good.'

'Remember you wanted to be a part of this.'

'Shut up, Phil, I'm good.'

'Okay then stop shaking and pass over the masks, time is ticking.' Phil held out his hand and received the plastic bag that was located under Joey's chair. He tipped the contents on the floor, over dried-up painters' trays.

Once he saw the masks, Phil smiled. 'You couldn't help yourself, could you?'

'What … You said any.' Joey observed the three men put on their individual face masks. His face lit up with a grin, unable to contain himself. One of the jobs designated by his older brother was to obtain four masks, any masks, it didn't matter as long as they would cover their faces. They were the exact same disguises used in his favorite movie growing up, *Point Break*, a nineties hit where the bank robbers wore masks resembling American ex-presidents – Lyndon Johnson, Richard Nixon, Jimmy Carter and Ronald Reagan.

'How do I look?' Phil asked, wearing the Ronald Reagan mask.

'Presidential,' joked Matt as he looked back through his rear-view mirror.

Joey placed his on last, revealing an old, big-nosed Richard Nixon. He raised his hands up in the air for all to see and said, 'I'm not a crook!'

Laughter erupted in the air-conditioned van that smelled of fresh paint. Victor, who sat to his side, slapped him over the head, while Joey continued to smile beneath his mask.

With his ex-president's mask on, white overalls, white gloves and a Glock automatic in his lap, Joey felt like a reincarnated member of the *Point Break* clan. He was living a dream he would never forget. An experience that would inevitably change his role in the family forever.

'Blood in, blood out, bro,' said Phil, holding out his knuckles.

Joey obliged by knocking fists. 'Blood in, blood out,' he replied.

Phil had begun repeating this phrase lately. It didn't mean anything; it was just a warm gesture of brotherly love and respect.

'Do as we discussed earlier and you'll be okay.'

'I will,' said Joey, happy to be part of this adventure.

Phil, Joey, Victor and Matt were all ready to go. Timing was everything – but one thing still remained to be accomplished.

Two minutes later a red Ducati Superbike 848 Evo with 140hp engine sped past the van. It came to a stop at the intersection of Wilshire Boulevard and Ocean Avenue and parked on the footpath between some palm trees that appear all over the city.

The man on the bike was none other than Alexander Peruggia himself, the most dangerous man in America. He was the grandson to Vincenzo Peruggia, most famous for stealing the original *Mona Lisa* back in 1911, described as the greatest art theft of the twentieth century. Now, one hundred years on, nothing had changed with his offspring ready to take on their own robbery. Theft was in their blood.

Alexander, helmetless, was in his early sixties. Although recently shaved, his face resembled a rasping board. He towered six-foot-three inches and had a solid, well-built physique and was without doubt a man you would not want to get into a fight with. He stepped off his bike, stretched his neck and glanced over at the van in position. He took off his black Oakley sunglasses, showing his brown eyes, and placed them into his inner jacket pocket, from which he extracted a cigarette pack.

He then bumped out a cigarette and lit up, as if in slow motion. He was the mastermind. Today needed to go without a hitch; too many things were at stake. After a few puffs, he flicked it in the direction of the bank and smiled. It was a wary smile – a sarcastic smile, to be exact. You could tell he was about to orchestrate something big. He whispered a sentence to himself theatrically: 'Soon I will possess all your treasures.'

In the confined space of the van waiting, Phil and Joey laughed at their father as he flicked a cigarette toward the bank.

'What a show-off,' said Joey, seeing his father in action for the first time. He had always envisioned what it would be like to be part of the gang, and now he was living it.

'He sure is something,' said Phil.

Turning now to face the beach, Alexander sauntered slowly across the pedestrian crossing on Ocean Avenue, leaving the keys in the bike's ignition.

'Keys are in place,' Phil whispered.

Dressed in his bike gear, Alexander pushed back the sleeve to his black leather jacket to uncover a shiny gold Rolex. A watch given to him by his sons on his sixtieth birthday. He glanced up in the direction of the Santa Monica Pier, in all its glory, then back down to the ticking hand.

The time was 3:59 pm, fifty-seven seconds.

Fifty-eight.

Fifty-nine.

KABOOM ...

A large billowing explosion erupted from the Santa Monica Pier. The detonation was the equivalent of an earthquake measuring 5 on the Richter scale. Fire and smoke consumed the Ferris wheel, or what was left of it. Fragments from the blast traveled long distances, some lodging in the famous Bubba Gump Shrimp Co. restaurant, named after the iconic movie *Forrest Gump*. Screams could be heard all the way from Wilshire Boulevard, as windows broke and shattered from the shockwave. People stopped what they were doing and ran in the direction of the beach to see the blaze. Dozens of tourists on the pier were instantly killed as a large section of it was annihilated. Around the pillars of the pier still intact, people hung on for dear life, while fire debris rained over their heads. Dead bodies floated on the beach, pushed in by the waves.

It was chaos. The explosion created panic, with people running everywhere.

It was the perfect distraction.

Chapter 2

Phil slid the door wide open and with his last words of encouragement said, 'Time to rock 'n' roll.'

The sizzling afternoon heat pressed in on them. Young Joey, Victor and Matt propelled out from the vehicle looking like they were about to fight a deadly airborne virus, dressed in what seemed to be white contamination suits.

They entered the bank's large double-glass doors and a wall of ex-presidents hit the security officer. The elderly man was the first to be disabled with a hit to the head from a Glock 9mm handgun. He had not been on guard, since he was too busy chatting away to a curvaceous young lady about the explosion that had just transpired.

The attractive woman wearing dark blue jeans and a pink striped shirt watched as the old man hit the hard surface. President Carter grabbed her by her long brown hair and hurled her to the floor. Joey could see her gritting her teeth. He could tell she wanted revenge, but a gun was waiting, so she turned away, defeated. There was no resistance.

'Everybody get down on the fucking floor, NOW!' yelled President Reagan, his voice strong and direct. 'Anyone still standing gets shot!'

President Johnson bolted to the surveillance cameras and sprayed them with black paint, while President Carter kept a keen eye on the tellers, making sure they didn't trigger the silent alarm that was located underneath their benches. Joey was the only inexperienced virgin at this heist; the only knowledge he'd acquired was from playing PS4 games and watching bank-robbery movies.

Eager to contribute and be part of the team, he had offered to formally introduce them, from up on the counter. He also wanted to fulfill one of his fantasies and re-enact a line from his favorite movie, a wish reluctantly granted by his brother.

Joey knew even though Phil was on the clock, if it gave his childish brother a laugh, he was going to let him do as he pleased.

Phil made sure the coast was clear, then gave him the go-ahead. Energetically, Joey jumped up onto the counter, waving his gun in the air, doing his Oscar-winning performance for every man, woman and child to hear.

'Hello, hello, hello. We are the new ex-presidents. All we need is a few moments of your time. We've been screwing with you for years, so a few more minutes shouldn't matter now, should it?' He emphasized the 'shouldn't it' like he was auditioning for a lead role in a James Cameron movie, and ended the speech with, 'I've always wanted to do that!'

Matt and Victor shook their heads and laughed at Joey's re-enactment, keeping a watchful eye, pointing their large shotguns at the terrified hostages, whose faces touched the cold marble.

'Thanks for that, Patrick,' said Phil. 'Now keep an eye on the front door.'

'You got it,' replied Joey, happy as could be, smiling from underneath his mask as President Carter's voice took center stage.

'One at a time, stand up and throw your smart phones in the bin, then move to my left away from the windows.' He had confiscated a small paper bin near the front counter. Dismantling all communications to the outside world was crucial for their robbery to be a success, especially before they had time to enter the vault, the main event. All the hostages obeyed and placed their phones one by one into the bin. One stupid man refused and copped the butt of Carter's shotgun to the face. Blood gushed from his mouth as his hands hit the marble first, followed by his overweight frame. Victor didn't like having to explain himself twice. He dealt with corrupt cops on a regular basis and was not going to take no for an answer, hence his first battered victim.

Joey did not agree with what he did, it was unnecessary. He had hoped they would take the money and leave without anyone getting hurt; he was so wrong.

Within two minutes, Phil was in complete control. He glanced around, faced his hostages and spoke to his shaken crowd in a calm voice. His calmness demonstrated his control and authority without the need to shout.

'As you may have witnessed, Mr. Nixon, my esteemed colleague had recited lines from a movie. Let me make something clear. This is not a movie, the good guy doesn't get the girl. We are the real thing, so listen to what we say or die, it's that simple.'

When President Carter strode by the hostages with his sawn-off shotgun, they stopped breathing. Up and down the floor he walked like a Russian soldier protecting his turf.

President Johnson emptied a large garbage bag. A pile of white painters' overalls, dark-framed glasses and backpacks massed the floor.

Phil ordered his new audience to suit up, strap on a backpack and put on a pair of glasses. The backpacks were to be filled with their purses, wallets and anything they were carrying, like jumpers so they could appear plump and full. That was Matt's role. He pulled computer keyboards out of their sockets, grabbed handfuls of photocopy paper and jammed them inside. No questions were asked, the hostages put on the overalls and dressed themselves. One lady's hands shivered so much she misjudged her step and fell over.

'Okay, time is ticking. I need Mr. Jason Smith, the bank manager. Please come forward and unlock the vault,' said Phil. 'Please don't hesitate or someone will be shot.'

No answer.

Everyone went silent, the only noise was coming from Matt, still shoving items into the last remaining backpack. Phil was not impressed with the silence. He shook his head and walked over to an elderly lady. She was one of the tellers, dressed in a conservative white top and black trousers. He touched her greyish white hair, tied back in a ponytail. It made her body shiver. He asked her, 'Tell me, how long have you worked for this bank, and how many children and grandchildren are in your family?'

Joey listened to his brother's bizarre question and paused to pay attention.

Trembling in fear for her life, the lady replied, 'I have worked for this bank for over twenty years. I have three kids, plus four grandchildren who I love deeply.'

Phil replied with a sarcastic tone, 'Ahh, that's nice.' He took out his Glock and without a trace of remorse fired into her chest from point-blank range. The bullet went through her old flesh like a knife through soft butter. She fell backwards from the force and the crowd frantically screamed in horror.

'What the fuck, man!' shouted Joey. 'I didn't sign up for this shit.' Joey grimaced at the sight with a hard expression underneath his mask. It was disgusting. He had not expected anyone to be killed, above all, not an innocent old lady. Seeing a woman killed in cold blood was not what he thought this would be like. This was wrong.

Joey approached his brother as the sobs echoed through the empty lobby of the bank.

'Go back to your position!' Phil ordered.

Joey shook his head.

'We just blew up the Santa Monica Pier to shit and you're worried about one old lady,' said Phil.

'Come on, that's not fair.'

'No, you come on, you wanted to be one of us, so fuckin' suck it up.'

'But …'

'No buts, move!' Phil bit out.

Joey moved back, while Phil scanned his terrified crowd, now giving him their full attention.

'I can do this all day long, people. Mr. Jason Smith, please.'

A frightened, frail older man in his late sixties, with a white beard and bald head stepped forward. He was a short man, who should have retired years ago.

'I am Jason Smith,' he said. 'Please don't kill anyone else.'

Phil nodded his head in his Reagan mask and pointed at the vault. 'You have thirty seconds to open the door, old man, or another person dies. Go – time starts now.'

Mr. Smith sprinted over to a section with its original wooden floorboards still intact. His hands trembled as he opened the first gated iron door in which he used the keys found in his pocket pants. The dark gate opened with a jarring noise. In front of the hatch was a heavy steel door, supported by a heavy steel frame, built into a wall and powered by a concealed hydraulic motor.

Mr. Smith punched a ten-digit code in the keypad, the door made a sound of hydraulic motors releasing air and the large impenetrable safe opened.

Matt and Victor did not hesitate. They ran straight inside and shoved the frail old bank manager. His elderly body hit the polished timber, where he knocked his chin.

Four backpacks a little larger than the ones given to the hostages were taken out. Their hands were a blur as fat stacks of hundred-dollar bills were shoveled straight into their bags. Stacks of hundred-dollar bills wrapped with paper bands sat on a grey steel shelving unit, eight million dollars in total.

While Victor pillaged away the last bundles, Matt checked his watch.

'Three minutes, man. We need to get the fuck out of here.'

'Don't worry,' Victor replied, 'this robbery couldn't have been planned any better.'

'Don't worry? Did you see what he did at the pier, killing all those innocent people – that's crazy, man.'

'Crazy yes, but not stupid: it'll give us enough time to escape while the police run around thinking it was a terrorist attack. Okay … let's go.'

The four backpacks were full, in the vicinity of two million dollars each. If successful, the heist would be a worthwhile robbery that would put Alexander back in business again and out from foreclosure.

Running out of the vault toward Ronald Reagan, they didn't notice Mr. Jason Smith crawl toward a counter nearby. Blood dripped from his head onto the shiny wooden floors. An emergency button in the ground was in sight. He pushed it and triggered the silent alarm.

Seconds later a call came in from a police scanner, in Phil's painter's pouch. 'All units in pursuit of the California Bank & Trust on Wilshire, possible robbery, proceed with caution.'

Phil began to laugh.

Joey and the hostages didn't know what to expect from this laughing lunatic, who was unpredictable. Perhaps it was a ploy to show he was a little crazy. No one would try to outsmart a crazy person.

'It's time to have some fun,' said Phil, turning to his younger brother. 'This is it, are you ready?'

Joey exhaled, the anxiety kicked in, knowing he needed to run for his life or face jail time.

'You'll be fine, just do as we planned. Now kill the lights.'

Joey flicked the lights off and moved in position among a bunch of people wearing identical white overalls. He removed his mask and replaced it with black glasses. His face still hidden by his hood.

The rest of the gang did the same. Their plan was simple: to blend in and not to be identified as bank robbers.

Phil stepped forward, his face in shadow, like the cloaked superhero 'Arrow.' 'I have one more favor to ask you all, and then we're out of your lives for good. What I need you all to do is run toward the beach. After crossing the road on Ocean Avenue run to your left. I repeat, to your left, until you see a bridge overpass. This will lead you over onto the sandy beach. Do not stop! I repeat, if you stop I'll kill you, just like the lady with the three kids and four grandchildren. Do not look back and do not stop, until you can feel the ocean water underneath your toes. When you hit the water you'll be safe, that's my promise, but you must do what I say if you want to live.'

Phil strolled over to a woman who had two young kids by her side. She tried not to look up at his face, only hidden with dark glasses and a hood covering his hair.

'Mommy, what are you going to do?' he asked.

'Run to the beach!' she replied swiftly as she shielded her kids behind her back.

'Good,' said Phil. 'I'll be watching you.'

He turned to a young man who was standing adjacent to the mother, pointed his 9mm at his neck and asked, 'What are you going to do?'

Shaking in his boots he replied, 'Run to the beach! Run to the beach!'

'Good, that's the correct answer. Do not disobey me and do not attempt to outsmart me, or I will not hesitate in blowing your brains out. If you want to live, it's simple: just do what I say. Now go ... RUN!'

Chapter 3

Police sirens on Ocean Avenue were close. Two veteran detectives weaved aggressively in and out of traffic, hurrying to be the first at the scene. Detectives Harris and Vancini were two of the police department's finest and most experienced older officers. In the car Leonardo Vancini hung onto the armrest and said, 'This smells like Alexander.'

'You think everything smells like Alexander,' replied Harris, overtaking another vehicle.

'I don't believe in coincidences.'

'What ... you think the bomb at the pier is related?'

'It's got to be,' said Leonardo, knowing his evil opponent so well and how he operated.

'But why?'

'Think of the diversion. It would allow them time to empty out the vault, while we're all running around trying to work out if it was a terrorist attack.'

'I guess we'll find out soon enough,' said Harris as he came to a stop at the corner of Wilshire Boulevard and Ocean Avenue, in front of the statue of St. Monica, the patron saint of the city.

To their surprise, from out of the bank a large cluster of men, women and children sprinted across the road. They all headed toward the left, wearing white painters' overalls, black glasses and backpacks strapped to their backs. The detectives watched as a swarm of people bumped and tripped over each other. The few that fell to the ground got back up and continued to run over to the left. A bunch of them headed for the patrol car. Some went left, some went right – they scattered everywhere.

Innocent people walking on the strip, still watching the fire burn on the pier, turned around and watched all this unfold, frozen to the spot. The detectives exited the vehicle, leaving the car in the middle of the street. They had no idea who were the bank robbers and who were the civilians.

'You go,' Leonardo screamed to his partner, as he was the fitter of the two.

Blue-eyed Harris began the chase.

Leonardo forced a handful of those running down on the asphalt, but unluckily for him there were no bad guys and no money bag.

Where were they headed? thought Harris, continuing the chase. Then he saw them turn on the concrete bridge overpass and knew they were advancing toward the beach.

The detective bolted and caught his first victim, tackling him onto the metal chicken wire that formed an igloo shape on the bridge. He pushed the man's face in the mesh and forced his arm backwards.

'I'm not a bank robber,' the man screamed. 'They told us all to run to the beach.'

Harris removed the glasses from his head and unzipped the backpack, but there was no money, just a pack of white copy paper.

'Shit!' he breathed, leaving the man handcuffed onto the metal railing, and sprinted across the overpass until his black leather boots hit the dry sand.

His next suspect was in sight. He seemed to be carrying a backpack slightly larger than the others, and as he continued to run he turned his head and glared at Harris with an intense expression.

'Stop or I'll shoot!' Harris screamed.

The runner kept going.

Harris had visited this three-mile-long beach with his wife and two kids on many occasions and knew it was a substantial ten-minute walk to reach the water's edge. He needed to make his move now. There were still fifteen or so people wearing overalls and running, but he was now conscious of the large crowds of people sunbathing that they were about to pass. If one of the runners decided to pull out a gun and start shooting, all hell would break loose and a lot of innocent people would get shot in the crossfire.

Harris could tell now that the suspect he was chasing was a bad guy as a hundred-dollar bill stuck out from the zipper, flapping in the wind as he ran. Going in for the tackle, he anticipated a gun swing back to take a shot. Harris responded with a dive on the sandy beach, followed by a commando roll to dodge the incoming bullets. Regaining his momentum, he came out of the roll and shot back at the perpetrator who had the sun in his eyes.

Screams erupted from a group of girls tanning as they heard gunfire.

The gunman took the hit in his chest, causing his painter's hood to fall back from his head, exposing his bleached hair as it hit the soft sand. His face closed in a grimace as his heart came to a stop, but not before squeezing his trigger one last time. Tragically, down went an innocent girl trying to run to safety.

On the horizon a thirty-foot speedboat waited. A man stood by waving his men to hurry up. It was their getaway vehicle. Harris needed to push on, or they would escape. Who was the man in the boat? thought the detective as he dug deep and powered on. Sweat poured off his aging face and trickled down his neck and back like warm soup, but he was not giving up. Dressed in his black suit with his 9mm by his side, he noticed two of the men divert from the pack and head straight for the boat, while the others stopped at the water's edge. They became his definitive targets.

Harris could now see the man in the speedboat. It was Alexander Peruggia. His partner was right in thinking he was behind it all – the bombing at the pier, the bank robbery and this eccentric escape.

Harris had caught up to his next target. The heavy backpack filled with hundred-dollar bills had weighed down the bank robber, who was peering over his shoulder to see that the detective had made tremendous ground.

All of a sudden Harris found himself in danger. The gunman stopped running, turned around and squeezed the trigger. Harris ducked instinctively just as two bullets zinged low over his head. All his years of target practice had to matter now and, lucky for him, he managed to shoot his next bank robber dead between the eyes in a single shot. His second victim was catapulted backwards by the bullet's impact as Harris jumped over his dead corpse.

Joey was the last to be chased down. He reached the water's edge with the fear he might not survive this. An onslaught of bullets made him trip over as he entered knee-deep in water. Bullets entered the water around him as he fell under an incoming wave. He gasped for air like a wounded animal as he emerged.

'Get in, Joey!' Alexander shouted. 'I've taken out the anchor.'

The current dragged the boat deeper into the ocean, making it harder for Joey to get a decent grip and force himself on board with the money bag on his back.

'I can't get up,' Joey yelled, in water too deep to stand in, while the waves came crashing over him.

'Hang on, I'll help you.'

Joey watched his father pull out a double-barreled shotgun from under his seat and shot twice at the man with the badge to help him, but the cop was too persistent. He continued to fire, like an unstoppable force.

'Throw the bag in the boat, son.'

Joey took the backpack off his shoulder while submerged deep in water. It was in his right hand, his stronger arm. He was ready to heave it over and into the boat, but was also trying to avoid the incoming bullets that scattered around his head. Having to move out of harm's way, he let go of the bag in the same instant that boat fragments chipped and flew all around him.

'Fuck!' yelled Alexander, ducking low inside the hull of the boat, protecting himself from getting hit. 'Stop, okay you win,' he shouted.

'Hands where I can see them!'

Alexander raised his hands high in the air and Joey, half-submerged in water, did the same as he waded ashore.

'Sorry, Dad.'

Alexander didn't reply and focused on the policeman's blue eyes, illuminated by the reflection of the crystal-clear water. 'Okay, you got me,' he said. 'Good for you.'

Harris caught his breath. 'You have the right—'

'Yeah, yeah, yeah. How about you let us go, Officer, and we'll be happy to give you a share of the money.'

'No thanks,' replied Harris. 'I'm not like other corrupt officers you have on your payroll. I don't make deals with criminals.'

A cold smile spread across Alexander's face. He would not allow any man to bully him, no matter what the situation. That included the officer who had a gun pointed at his head. Alexander stretched his neck with a crack and said, 'You killed two of my men and nearly killed my youngest son. You're like a cockroach that needs to be squashed, a pain in the ass, but one thing you don't seem to realize. I am Alexander fucking Peruggia! I will never be prosecuted and will never see the inside of a cell.'

After his melodramatic speech, he placed his leg on the

stainless-steel railing starboard side and smiled. His smile was toxic and mysterious. 'Looks like your backup is here,' he said.

'Then why are you smiling?' said Harris, who turned to face the sandstone cliff wall separating the beach and the city. He turned his head back and started to read them their rights again. 'You have the right to remain silent, anything you do—'

Alexander watched his son shut his eyes.

A shadow appeared on the detective's opposite side, and then a loud shot rang out.

Alexander grinned as the blood splattered out from the detective's skull, as if it had exploded out the other side. The officer fell to the ground limp, killed instantly, crumpling like a marionette whose strings have been cut.

'He should've taken the deal,' said Alexander, who had once again proved he was too smart for his own good. He had seen it unfold in his head.

One of the hostages who had run with the others had fired off a bullet to the detective's head from the left-hand side. She wore dark blue jeans and a pink striped shirt; she was the lady who had distracted the security guard when they entered the bank. She was Alexander's girl, and her name was Victoria.

'Let's go,' said Alexander with a wavering voice as they boarded his boat.

'Dad, what about the backpack that went under the boat?' Joey cried as he climbed on board.

Alexander looked up at the sandy beach to see a fleet of policemen. 'It's too late, we need to go now!' He pushed the throttle forwards and the speedboat knifed through the water and disappeared behind the distant mountains. Upset with the outcome, he kicked the booth from under the steering wheel and said, 'Let's hope Phil got away, because he's the only one with a fucking money bag.'

★ ★ ★

Three backpacks were recovered by the police. One drenched by the sea, the other two from the dead robbers' backs. Detective Joanne Brown was with a group of other officers who arrived a little too late to help Harris, who had been doing this all by himself. She closed his wide-open eyes, proof that he was killed by surprise, and touched his body softly, lovingly. The department had lost an experienced officer, mentor and friend. She stood up with her police radio in hand as a tear rolled down her check and announced, 'Man down, man down, Detective Harris has been killed. I need aerial units, choppers, whatever we have up in the air. Suspects off the beach in getaway boat, if spotted shoot to kill. I repeat, shoot to kill.'

Chapter 4

A million thoughts crossed Detective Leonardo Vancini's mind as he examined the situation on Wilshire. He thought about the explosion at the pier and all those dead innocent people. He thought about the bank robbery that had just taken place, but most importantly he thought about his partner on the chase all on his own.

Leonardo was the epitome of authority within the police department and his peers, even with his diminutive frame. This, however, was offset by his formidable bearing. He had thick jet-black hair and a goatee and spoke with a smoke-burnished voice. Considered the best detective in the force, he had a reputation for always getting the bad guy.

A battalion of police cars at long last arrived at the scene. He commanded the officers to run toward the beach to help his partner, not knowing he had been killed. As he instructed his fellow policemen, he caught a glimpse of a man walking past the front of the bank wearing faded jeans, a white t-shirt, black jacket, glasses and a backpack. He walked with his head held low to the ground as he approached a red sports bike parked up on the footpath. Leonardo's eyes narrowed as he shot glances at the suspect. Something was not right. Many years in the force had taught him one thing, to always trust his instincts, and his instincts were spot on most of the time. This was no exception.

Leonardo, now obsessed, ignored everyone around him

and slowly crossed the main road separating them. His walk turned into a light jog, his pistol hanging down by his hip. He couldn't see the man's face, only the back of his head and the backpack filled with something. He shouted, 'Hey, you on the bike, don't move!'

The man mounted the bike, turned the key and pressed the ignition. He ignored the detective and revved the throttle. It was obvious to Leonardo that he was doing it on purpose. The bike was running but not in gear. As Leonardo approached the suspect, a Beretta 38 was whipped out from the suspect's inner jacket. It all happened in the blink of an eye. Multiple shots were let loose at the detective's small frame.

'Aww shit!' Leonardo dived away from the gunfire like his partner had done on the sandy beach, but his dive hurt as his body hit the hard road surface. Pedestrians scattered and screamed as they heard the gunfire. Leonardo regained his balance and hid behind a parked car.

He had seen the shooter's face. It was Alexander's eldest son, Phil Peruggia. He must have been holding out, waiting for everyone to run to the beach, thought Leonardo. A simple misdirection that allowed him time to stroll out of the bank unseen and onto the Ducati for a quick getaway.

As Phil accelerated the 140hp engine between his legs, Leonardo leaned his elbows over the car's bonnet and fired off one single shot. It was only one, but that was all he needed.

Phil grunted as the bullet hit him in the abdomen. With one hand steering the bike and the other gripping a fistful of shirt, the bike propelled itself forwards on the council strip and onto the main Ocean Avenue.

Leonardo bolted to his patrol car and planted his foot down hard on the accelerator. The back tires skidded and the car drifted to the left, then it regained its grip and careered in the bike's direction. He swerved his way in and out through traffic, and then he overheard the bad news from the police scanner.

'Man down, man down, Detective Harris has been killed.'

He could not believe his ears: his partner and best friend was dead, murdered. Now he was more motivated than ever, steaming to ram this guy off the road. He knew his father was responsible.

'You're going down,' he said as he changed lanes at incredible speed. He turned into oncoming traffic and veered onto the footpath to catch up to this elusive bike. He picked up the CB radio on the dashboard as he avoided hitting pedestrians and ordered, 'All units I need help, block all freeways out of the city, do it now.'

The bike increased its speed and weaved through the traffic and gained a generous lead. He turned left and right through backstreets, but Leonardo was not far behind. Phil's body was hunched over with drooping shoulders, causing the bike to wobble.

Leonardo knew the pain to Phil's abdomen would be excruciating, having been shot before. He remembered how the loss of blood made him feel light-headed and dizzy. The trail of blood spread down his jeans and as the bike turned the next corner it lost control and skid in front of the famous Penmar Golf Course.

Leonardo watched Phil graze his right arm on the asphalt and struggle to get up, dragging his hurt hip and holding his bloody stomach. Exiting his vehicle, Leonardo jumped on top of Phil. He was not going to let him escape. His partner was dead and someone needed to pay. The two men rolled on the green manicured lawn and Leonardo tried to place Phil's arms behind his back so he could handcuff him, but realized the man he was fighting was weightlifting gangster Phil Peruggia.

Phil's jacket was removed in the struggle and in no time he had overpowered the detective. Now on top, he punched Leonardo in the head with a combination of left and right swings that caused blood to pool in his mouth. Leonardo felt the sharp pain of each blow, and when the ringing noise subsided he heard sirens that seemed to be getting closer.

Leonardo, bruised and battered, shook off the stars that burst in his vision. In a last desperate move to contain the fugitive, he dug his finger deep into the man's wound.

Phil let out a howling scream of unbearable pain and clenched his eyes in agony. The bullet had punctured his colon and was causing major internal damage. If he didn't get help quick, bacteria would spill into his abdominal cavity, causing infection that could result in his death. Getting bullied by an older, donut-eating policeman was not on his agenda. He did the intimidating, not the other way around. The veins popped out from his forearms as he moved Leonardo's penetrating finger and reached for his pocketknife in his jeans. It was a black Tac-Force spring folding pocketknife. Its carbon-steel blade was only two and a half inches long, but enough to cause serious damage. His father owned the exact same knife and never left home without it. He flipped it open and as he embraced the detective from the front, and pole-vaulted it deep into his back.

The detective fell to his knees as Phil took out his weapon, grabbed the money bag and darted into the golf course.

Located in the center of Venice, the Penmar Golf Course was an alluring, landscaped executive nine-hole golf course. Tiger Woods had given the course an overall rating of five stars the last time he'd played there. The perimeter was hedged with bushy conifer trees, giving you a feeling of being in another world, enclosed from the outside.

Two golfers who had teed off at the second hole were so into the game they didn't even see Phil sprint past them on the fairway. He soon realized he was trapped here, among a wall of manicured bushy trees. Once inside there was no getting out. But he needed to find a way out, or he was doing life in prison, that was a fact.

Now desperate, his search intensified. Then, near the ninth hole, he saw a small opening. It was only eleven inches in diameter, but enough to squeeze through for a quick exit unnoticed. His choices were limited: going back the same way he'd come was not an option.

He lay on his back and wove his way in. He brushed by the interconnecting branches and marked the leaves with his blood. On the other side, he wedged a fallen branch to conceal the hole and to hide any blood trail. He knew by doing so would prolong his chances of escaping and avoid the police from tracking him down.

He was now in the famous Marine Park, a large lavish playground for all ages complete with tennis and basketball courts, baseball and soccer fields, kids' climbing structures, barbecue areas, sandy play areas, cubbyhouses and swings, all of which were surrounded by a variety of exotic palm trees.

Phil's breathing intensified; he had run enough. He needed to rest somewhere and maybe think about hiding the money. As blood poured out from his wound his blood pressure continued to drop. Going into shock would be the next step if he didn't receive emergency assistance. He was strong with a high pain threshold, but knew if he didn't take home the loot to his father, all hell would break loose.

Alexander would not take shit from anyone, including his own son. From an early age Phil was brought up into the family business, surrounded by criminals and wise guys. At the age of six his father had put him to work as the delivery boy and sent him out with yellow envelopes filled with money: payouts to drug dealers, gangsters, cops, judges – whoever his father needed to use at the time. Everyone was bought out with a Benjamin Franklin.

Dotted around the park were excavators, lots of witches' hats, and builders' warning tapes placed around the perimeter. Phil spotted a small cubbyhouse in the far distance, away from the lights. It was a brilliant place to hide from the police and get some much-needed respite. He was tired and weak, his skin a pale yellow and was about to collapse. Using all the strength he could muster, he ducked his head, stepped inside and closed the swinging door shut.

He took off the money bag and threw it to one side. He needed to rest. His arms and legs weighed a ton. His eyelids heavy, he couldn't move a muscle and fought the urge to fall asleep. He blinked a couple of times and as his head moved forward, his eyes could not resist: too weak, they closed.

Chapter 5

With his eyes shut, Phil flashed back in time to a local cafe in the Santa Monica district, enjoying a cup of coffee with his girlfriend. Even though Monica Anton worked for the FBI as an intelligence analyst, their differences did not affect their love for one another. She was in her mid-thirties with mischievous green eyes. Her hair was honey brown and her figure was great, but it would never make the cover of *Sports Illustrated*, standing at only five foot four. Her voice was low and cool, and when she spoke it was obvious she had a quick intelligence.

She had once explained to Phil how anagram phrasing worked, made famous by the movie *The Da Vinci Code*, which used such phrases as 'So dark the con of man,' which translated into 'Madonna of the Rocks.'

'Come on, Phil give it a try, it's easy,' said Monica, who had demonstrated on a napkin the art form of creating anagrams.

'Babe, seriously, when will I ever use this shit?'

'You never know,' she hinted. 'Remember, knowledge is power.'

Monica was a passionate woman who other females loved to hate. She was the complete package in the looks department. But what drove them mad was her ability to walk the talk and always come out in front. She possessed a high IQ that most people found daunting. 'How about we start out with some simple food items?'

'Okay, let's see,' said Phil, grabbing a fresh napkin and pen, and glanced down at the table to a large bowl of fries. He thought for a moment, then wrote down the word 'fries' and rearranged the letters to make up the word 'fires.'

Then 'sauce' became 'cause' and 'salt' became 'last.'

This was too easy.

Monica smiled at him; he'd picked up the anagram phrasing effortlessly. To be able to say a word that could mean another using the same letters was one of the ways the intelligence agency communicated in code. 'Sometimes, in rare cases, a word could actually be described in an anagram.'

Phil frowned, not sure what she was talking about.

'I'll explain what I mean,' said Monica, who had devoted her life to this field of study. 'The word *astronomer* translates to *moon starer*, which is what astronomers do: stare at the moon.' Then she went through some other examples.

'*Debit card* translates to *bad credit*! *The eyes* translates to *they see*! And my favorite, wait for it: *mother-in-law* translates to *Woman Hitler*!'

Phil laughed when he heard that one. He was impressed by how clever the use of anagrams was and loved the fact that he was dating a woman who had taught him so much.

At this point in time a bill was placed down on their table by a waitress who wore a name tag that read 'Marie Philips.' Phil, now aware of any letters that could become an anagram phrase, began to un-jumble the name of the waitress on his napkin. He wanted to impress his teacher and show her what he was capable of. After a couple of minutes, while she finished her cold drink, he turned the napkin around in her direction, where an anagram had been created.

Phil blurted out, 'Marie Philips translates to Imperial Ship.'

Monica burst out laughing and clapped her hands with joy. 'You're a natural. That was a hard one – using the waitress's name for the imperial ship from the opening scene of *Star Wars*.'

★ ★ ★

Three hours had passed. Phil regained consciousness. His tongue rubbed his bottom lip in search of some water as he was severely dehydrated. A vibrating tingle was buzzing away in his pocket pants. He reached for his phone, which had been left in silent mode, and read the text message. It was from Monica. He had not called to let her know he was okay. It read, *Babe, it's been hours are you okay, call me, love you.*

The time on his phone was 7:15 pm. Phil pushed open the swinging door and crawled out of the cubbyhouse and peered around to make sure the coast was clear. He took in a few deep breaths and inspected his wound. He needed help, the wound was infected and his hands were colder than ever.

He attempted to dial her number, but his phone had only two percent battery remaining. He decided to leave a text message instead. He exhaled again and coughed, feeling as if he might go back into shock. After heaving a few much-needed breaths, he decided he needed to hide the money somewhere. He would have a better chance of surviving without the weight on his shoulders and he could come back to retrieve it later.

After considering his options, he disposed of the money. The hiding spot was clever and worthy of a clue. He decided he was going to send a cryptic text message in the form of an anagram, detailing the whereabouts of the two million dollars. Monica would be able to find the money; it would be his gift to her.

He studied his location and thought of numbers and phrases that he could use to throw off the common man if they did read the message. He put two and two together and came up with, *It lies beneath the third, P.ENIMAR GC.*

Then hit send.

Shockingly, after he pressed send, the message did not go through as the lack of battery turned off the antenna to the phone. 'Piece of shit!' he muttered. He shook his head and put the phone in his pocket. Day turned to night, 8 pm was fast approaching. Alexander always had contingency plans in case anything went wrong. Plan B was Trinity Church, 8 pm. It was Phil's only chance to get some help as he had lost way too much blood. His only priority now was to get to his father. He walked out of Marine Park unnoticed with a drag in his stride. He walked toward the main road, where he avoided some police cars that were parked nearby and hailed a cab. Having the weight of the money bag off his back helped him as he slid into the backseat and told the driver, 'Trinity Church please.'

The church was only a short ten-minute drive, but the driver did not stop scanning his rear-vision mirror as blood poured out of Phil's stomach and onto the high-grade faux leather upholstery.

'What are you looking at?' Phil asked, coughing out some more blood.

'Nothing, you're bleeding,' the driver replied with pursed lips, trying to avoid direct eye contact.

'I'm okay, just keep driving,' said Phil, dying with each breath.

Coming to a stop at the next red lights on Lincoln Boulevard three-quarters of the way to his destination, the driver decided to get out of the car and make a run for it.

'Hey, what are you doing?' Phil asked, shaking his head, too weak to do anything more. He laughed to himself as the driver raced to his freedom. 'Fuckin' cab drivers.'

Alone in the backseat Phil checked his iPhone again. The battery was completely drained out. It displayed nothing but a black screen. The pain that had burned like fire had faded away to an icy numbness. He was quickly losing focus as the blood drained from his head. Black filled the edges of his vision and the only thing he could hear was his own heartbeat. For a moment he blacked out and the phone slipped out from his hand.

A light from oncoming traffic brought him round. He blinked a few times and took a moment to recoup. All he had to do was drive over to the church unseen and his father would take care of the rest. His destiny didn't involve him dying in the backseat of this cab.

After a climb over into the driver's seat, he was en route and arrived at the Trinity Church at 7:45 pm. He parked the yellow cab up on the curb and left his driver's door open, marking the window with his bloody handprints. He forced himself up the last fifth concrete step to the church and reached for the door handle. Before he was able to pull it backwards, the doors swung outwards.

A beaten man stepped forward shadowed by another holding a gun.

Phil's smile turned into a frown and he stepped back. His face was puzzled. 'What are you doing?' he asked.

The person with the gun did not hesitate and two bullets were fired.

Bang ... Bang ...

Chapter 6

Monday, 8 pm

The Trinity Church was large and unique, constructed entirely out of white concrete and situated on a busy corner block. The front façade featured a large circular stained window, accompanied to the right by a large tower that held the sixty-year-old bell.

Alexander arrived at the church with his crew, muscles James, technician Frank, wise guy Tony, young Joey, explosives-expert Ian and crazy Marco, who parked near the abandoned cab. Monica was not far behind. She parked her Mercedes close by and jogged over to the team.

Joey pointed to the abandoned cab with its doors left wide open. On the driver's side window evidence of blood was everywhere. The person who had parked the cab there was in dire need of assistance. Worried it could be his brother, he rushed to the front door.

'What the fu—?!' shouted Joey, turning around to see his father stop and hold out his hands to warn the others.

Monica screamed in horror.

Phil was tied up against the large church doors' handles, strapped with an elaborate explosive device hanging off his neck. His hands were lifted high, while his head was weighted forward, facing the ground. In his chest were bullet holes, prominently showing on his white shirt.

'I don't know, boss, the bomb on his chest looks like C4, enough to blow this whole street,' Ian warned.

'I don't care,' said Alexander. 'I need someone to check.'

'I'll go, Dad,' said Joey.

'No you won't,' replied Monica. 'It's too risky.'

'Shut up and move back, you two, I'll go,' said fearless Marco, known for his bravery in the gang. He was in his early thirties, broad, with a clipped haircut and always wore a black leather jacket. Approaching Phil, he held his pistol up and ready to fire, just in case.

Joey decided he wanted to go, too, and as he walked forward, he was restrained and forced to the ground by Monica.

'It's too risky, wait.'

'Let me go, Monica, it's my brother.'

'Yes, but wait,' she said, holding onto his arm.

'Joey, Monica's right, shut up,' said Alexander with an increased awareness.

Joey watched Marco reach Phil's body. He walked up the fifth step of the cathedral, licking his lips, something he was known to do when he was scared. By the look on his face, Phil was a mess, barely recognizable, beaten to within an inch of his life.

He reached out his fingers to check the pulse on Phil's bloody neck.

Marco said, 'His skin is cold.'

'Is there a pulse?' asked Joey.

'I'm sorry, he's gone,' said Marco, turning around to face the shocked group.

'He can't be,' said Joey, sinking to his knees. With a rage that built, he forced Monica to the side. He needed to see for himself. As he stood up, ready to run to his brother's side, a noise of something breaking from within the church was heard.

'Someone's inside,' said Marco, cocking his semi-automatic pistol. 'I'm going in.' He opened the front door with one hand, holding his gun ready with the other.

'Wait, no!' Ian tried to warn him.

But it was too late.

An ear-shattering blast erupted.

The front section of Trinity Church exploded in a billowing cloud of concrete. Shards of the stained-glass window shot out with a deadly rainfall of knives. The tower, the bell, the walls just fell away beneath them. Large pieces of intact concrete scattered the site like the Roman ruins. There was debris and smoke everywhere. Anyone inside, near the back of the church, would have been killed instantly. Marco would have been incinerated. Alexander and his crew were forced backwards by the strength of the detonation, as the entire site shook.

Joey helped his father up and pattered down the flames still burning on his back. His expensive suit jacket was taken off and thrown away. Monica stood there in a daze, her body shivering, lost for words. 'It can't be,' she said, gasping for air.

Joey comforted her with a hug as he watched parts of the church that were still standing burn to the ground.

Alexander now jacket-less, walked forward alone. Out of the corner of his eye a familiar shiny object was visible. Near the steps of the church still intact, a gold cross was left behind. He walked over to the steps, protecting his face from the heat of the fire. What he saw next brought him to his knees, making his heartbeat pounce and his hands tremble. It was the gold cross his son Phil had been christened in, passed down from generation to generation. This cross was to be handed down to his own grandchildren one day, an event that would not take place now. He picked it up and read the inscription: 'In the end, it is between us and God, not between us and them.'

'James, get Alexander, we need to leave now,' Frank ordered.

Frank, Tony and Ian ran back into their car and grabbed

Joey for a quick getaway. Alexander was picked up by James and forced into the second four-wheel drive. They all needed to leave the scene before the police arrived.

Monica also got into her vehicle and left in a hurry, not wanting to have to explain herself to her superiors. Numerous rumors had circulated in the bureau about her loyalty. Many believed she had crossed over to the side of corruption, since she had been in bed with the devil for so long with nothing to show for it. No leads or illegal activities reported, nothing the FBI could use to bring down the notorious gangster. She didn't want to add more logs to the fire, so she decided to leave the scene, too.

Just like that, Phil was gone and one question would soon be on everyone's lips: who was behind his death and why?

Chapter 7

Reporters set up in front of the burning church and began to shoot video footage of the fire and debris that covered the entire corner block. It was dark, the stars were out, but a strong wind had risen from the south, causing havoc with the firefighters. They were trying to put out the fire and salvage the back half of the church.

Lead investigator Detective Luke Taylor arrived at the scene and parked his car up close to the action. He was a lanky man who slumped over when he walked. He was a family man in his early forties. The all-American good guy, a straight shooter who went by the book.

After his initial briefing by a younger officer, he was directed to the cab left abandoned on the curb. Using his smart phone as a torch, he peeked inside.

'We believe this cab was used by the bank robber, sir.'

'Sure looks like it.'

'Sir, bloodstains have been found in the backseat, the window and also on the steering wheel.'

'Okay, make sure the blood and fingerprints are tested.'

'Yes, sir,' replied the officer, taking notes.

'Hang on, what's that under the seat?' said Taylor, who leaned in, cautious not to disturb the blood on the vinyl seats.

'What do you mean?'

'I found a phone.'

'A phone?'

'Yes, a phone. Give me some gloves.'

The young officer passed over a pack of latex gloves that he had on his person. Taylor snapped them in place and reached inside the cab to pick up the phone from the edges in order not to smudge away any fingerprints left on its face. The phone recovered was a black iPhone with its screen cracked. The detective checked to see if it worked and pushed the circle home button, but nothing happened. Then he pressed the power button. No go, the battery was dead.

'I need this to be catalogued and bagged as evidence.'

'Whose do you think it is?' the young officer asked.

'I don't know, son, but it's the only real evidence we have.'

Teams of reporters were all over the story in front of the burning fire, like a fat kid eating cake. It was the most talked about news all over the country, on every channel. One reporter linked the explosion at the church to the one at the pier, due to the same explosive device used in both.

Another female news reporter from CBS had her own theories and questions as she delivered her speech live on air.

'*Today has been a busy day for the Los Angeles Police Department. At 4 pm an explosion erupted at the Santa Monica Pier, killing eleven and injuring over twenty people. Soon after this, an attempted robbery was staged at the California Bank & Trust on Wilshire Boulevard, where eight million dollars was taken. Veteran Detective Peter Harris managed to kill two of the suspects, recovering six million dollars, but was sadly killed in the line of duty. And now there's been the Trinity Church explosion behind me, all happening on the same day. The question on my mind leads me to believe one thing. Could all these three events possibly be linked in some way or form to one man or group? If I am correct and there is a connection, do the police have any suspects? It has been reported that two of the robbers killed this afternoon were linked to the infamous Alexander Peruggia. Could he be involved or be behind this?*

'Is he the number-one suspect? And where is the missing two million dollars? There are more questions than answers. Coming to you live, I'm Tracey Henderson, CBS news.'

Chapter 8

The University of California, Los Angeles, otherwise known as UCLA, is the most applied-to university in the nation, situated in one of the most influential cities in the world. Some of its buildings are extremely old, mixed in with contemporary new structures that merge together in unity. The campus is well landscaped and designed, without the use of the same trees or flowers, but rather an abundance of different plants so that each area has an integrated architectural style with its own color scheme. Historical landmarks occupy the entire site, built high up on a hill. There are endless amounts of places to sit, read a book or enjoy the sunny outdoors from one of the many water fountains on the campus.

The first classes of the day had commenced. All students were in class – except for one. Vince Vancini was still fast asleep in his Sunset Canyon dorm room, located in the midst of it all. Running late was a regular occurrence for the twenty-two-year-old senior completing his fourth and final year.

He was not conspicuously tall, his features striking but not obviously handsome, and he was seldom without his necklaces and bracelets that gave him an artsy look. His hair was short, dark and coarse, and he kept it brushed backwards from the temples. He had brown eyes with a tanned European complexion, like his detective father,

Leonardo Vancini. Dark circles shadowed those eyes, caused from long hours at Terry's Bar, where he worked. To be able to afford his education at this prestigious college, he needed to work the night shift Monday to Friday. In between lunch breaks he finished his homework and studied for upcoming exams. It wasn't the best way to study, surrounded by smoke and alcohol, but he had no choice.

Vince's friends at the campus were from wealthy families with large trust funds. He grew up in a middle-class family, having to pay his own way. When he was twelve, his mother left because of his father's workaholic habits and moved to Chicago to start a new life. She said he neglected his family and paid more attention to his work. Vince had never known any differently. His father had devoted his life to catching bad guys, and though there were times when Vince needed a father figure, Leonardo was never around.

With no financial support from his parents, Vince had to pay his own way through college using financial aid provided by the campus. In a way, he was proud he was doing it alone. No one to rely on, and no one pushing him to do a course he didn't want to do, like his college friend Peter Chang, who was studying to be a doctor to please his parents who were also doctors.

Vince had enrolled in the school of Cinematic Arts, graduating with a bachelor of arts degree that covered all aspects of CGI, animation and the digital-arts industry. He was passionate and determined, with the talent to make it big as an animator or digital-effects expert. The top three percent in his year would be chosen to have the privilege to get their feet wet in the film industry. Vince was at the top of that three percent, he just had to do one thing: arrive at classes on time. Attendance was his Achilles' heel.

A loud car horn outside his room woke Vince up. He struggled to lift his heavy eyelids, having only slept a couple of hours after last night's busy shift. He stared at the clock until both his eyes focused on the red numbers. His eyes were wide open now. Late, yet again.

'Aww shit … Aww shit … not again!'

His professor was not going to be happy. Up in a flash he jumped out of bed, his Autodesk Maya texturing class having already started. He was half an hour late. He put on yesterday's clothes, blue jeans and a black shirt, which reeked of cigarette smoke. His jeans had a slight weight to them, as his cell phone was still inside. Anxiety hit him like a rollercoaster ride. He was fearful about his attendance record this year, scared he would not graduate, as he had been warned. Even though he was still sleep deprived, the adrenaline from running woke him up as he sprinted to class, holding his laptop.

He promptly walked in and placed his laptop on the desk, the same desk he used and sat at throughout the year.

'Hey,' a friend to his left said.

'Hey,' responded Vince, catching his breath.

Vince smiled at his teacher, hoping to not receive a lecture again. Mr. Tom Jefferson resembled KFC's Colonel Sanders and wore thick, black reading glasses. He was short with healthy straight snowy hair parted to one side, accompanied by a matching beard. Before deciding to become a teacher, he'd worked on many motion pictures. He was known to be strict but fair and hated when students arrived late to his class. On occasions he joked openly that his lessons were an experience not to be missed – but Vince was a student who kept breaking the rules.

'Late for class again, Mr. Vancini. Please enlighten us as to why, it must be important,' said Mr. Jefferson, his tone heavy with sarcasm.

Vince was out of excuses; he couldn't use the working late excuse again, that was not going to cut it.

'So tell me, were you lining up to buy tickets to see reruns of *Twilight*?'

The students erupted with laughter and threw papers at Vince's head. He flashed a smile and dodged the onslaught of scrunched paper and quickly responded, 'That's a good one, sir. Go team Jacob!' He continued with a wink at the girls in his class. 'No, actually, tickets to see *Fifty Shades of Grey*.'

'Okay now, calm down,' said Mr. Jefferson with a smile. 'Enough fun and games, let's get back to the reason you're all here. Let's start with texturing your model, don't forget to UV unwrap your character first. Vince, see me after class, please.'

Vince nodded. By the time he logged into the school server on his laptop and began to do work, it was time to leave. The bell rang. Students evacuated the room, like a herd of horses entering a paddock. Vince was the last to walk out the door. He approached his teacher like a dog with its tail between its legs.

'Vince, you need to do something about your absence and lateness.'

'I know, sir, I'm trying. These long hours at work are killing me, but I have no choice if I want to stay at this college.'

'I understand, believe me. I was in your shoes once, too. I need you to try harder this year. Please, you have an opportunity – don't throw it away.'

'I will, sir.' Vince stepped out of the classroom. Minutes later a message beeped from his pocket pants; he had forgotten he had his phone with him. Digging into his pocket, he took it out.

The message read, *Bella time*.

Isabella had programed into his calendar the times she would be free so that they could meet up. He read her message. A picture of his gorgeous girlfriend displayed on his phone. He decided to pay her a visit and ran across the manicured lawn in the direction of the drama department building, a good ten minutes away.

Isabella was exceedingly attractive, with long wavy dark

hair that draped over her shoulders like a Greek goddess. She had the looks but also the brains to become a famous actress one day. Her green eyes told a story of someone who'd had a rough childhood back in the Ukraine, where she was born. Her frame was small but strong and fit, and she spoke with a sexy, husky voice. Isabella was also in her last year of school, studying acting and film production. Vince's best friend and roommate, Gary, would always state openly to Vince, 'How could someone like you get someone like her?'

One thing Vince did have over his friends, though, was his confidence. Known as the comedian on campus to Isabella and her friends, Vince knew his confidence and humor had sealed the deal for Isabella. She had told him about the asshole of a boyfriend she had back at home in the Ukraine and that she had struck gold with him.

He approached the large white-framed windows of Isabella's classroom. He faced up sideways onto the window and walked across it like he was walking down a flight of stairs, lowering his body so you could only see his head moving downwards. All the students in the drama class laughed and were distracted from what they were doing, including Isabella.

The female teacher strolled over to the window and closed the blinds, so no student would get interrupted by the idiot outside. The students laughed a little more, then continued to listen to their teacher.

The bell rang and the drama class was over. Vince entered the building and waited for his girl at the classroom door painted blue. Raising his hands in the air, he waited for her with a smile.

'There's my girl,' he said, picking her up off the ground with a warm hug and kiss. Isabella's friends laughed as they walked by. Someone said, 'Get a room.'

Vince laughed and replied sarcastically, 'Get a boyfriend.' Then wrapped his arm around Isabella's shoulders. They strolled past the manicured gardens exchanging sexual innuendos, when they were unexpectedly disrupted by two uniformed officers. They held their police hats to the one side, a sign of bad news to come.

'Is my father dead?' Vince blurted out.

Isabella's eyebrows lifted, waiting for the response. A short, stocky man said, 'Your father was stabbed in yesterday's bank robbery and rushed to hospital.'

Vince asked, 'Is he okay?'

'He's fine, son, but we need you to come to the hospital, discharge him and take him home.'

Vince turned to face Isabella's exotic green eyes. 'Babe, I'll call you later.'

She embraced him with a kiss. 'Of course, take care of your father.'

Vince left with the two policemen, who dropped him off in front of the Ronald Reagan UCLA Medical Center, a short stroll away. 'He's in room twenty-six, on the second floor,' said one of the officers as he exited the car.

After taking a lift to the second floor, Vince entered his father's room. Leonardo was in bed reading the local newspaper. Before any words were spoken, Leonardo said in a corrosive tone, 'What fucking took you so long? Get me out of this place.'

Vince sighed and replied, feeling unappreciated as always, 'Nice to see you, too, Dad. Let's go.' He signed all the release forms and as they walked out of the hospital's outer sliding door, Lee Davis, the Chief of Police, stood there waiting with his arms crossed.

Lee knew Leonardo was not just going to do nothing; it wasn't his style. He needed to reinforce the consequences of his actions and acknowledge that he was off on sick leave.

'Hello, Leonardo, good to see you up on your feet,' Lee said with a grim smile.

'Hey, boss, what brings you here?'

'You're going to look after yourself, right?'

'Of course,' Leonardo said, pointing at a waiting cab.

'I know you want to get the fucker.'

'What?'

'Don't what me, you know what I mean,' Lee said in a furtive manner, moving closer.

'Who's leading the case?'

'I put Taylor on it. It's in good hands. Let it go.'

Leonardo stared deep into the chief's brown eyes and said, 'You know it was Alexander Peruggia.'

'We can't prove shit, stay away,' said Lee, lifting his index finger. 'I mean it.'

'If his son Phil was involved, believe me Alexander was behind this.' Leonardo ignored his boss and entered the cab. Vince followed, but was grabbed by his left arm as he ducked down.

'Take care of your old man. Keep him out of trouble.' Lee knew he was going to become a problem, this was personal. He hadn't been made the Chief of Police because he was stupid.

Vince replied, 'I will, sir.'

The cab sped away, leaving the chief in the distance.

The first ten minutes of the cab ride proceeded in complete silence. They were like strangers sitting at a bus station. Vince had learned from his previous conversations with his father that they always surrounded his work life, so he tried an opener: 'So did the bank robbers get away with any of the money?'

'Two million,' replied Leonardo, now interested.

'Two million!' Vince said, lifting his eyebrows.

'Actually, the money was never recovered. Phil managed to hide it somewhere.'

'Are you serious?'

'Yep.'

'Wow, I can't believe two mill is out there somewhere.'

'It would have been eight mill, if it wasn't for Harris.'

'Champion. Where is Uncle Harris?'

Leonardo placed his right thumb and forefinger on his temple. 'Harris is gone.'

'What do you mean *gone*?'

'Harris was killed yesterday, on the chase.'

Vince's shoulders shook in disbelief, his eyes now watery. A single tear slid down his cheek. He turned away from his father and sat still, taking in the bad news. Detective Harris, otherwise known as Uncle Harris, was part of the family growing up, and now he was dead. He had a special bond with his uncle and considered him like a father figure, even more than his own dad. He was a family man who loved his family and always put them first. Not like his dad, who was obsessed with only one thing, his work and getting the bad guy, like he was the only one on the planet with this task.

'Vince, the funeral is tomorrow. The police force has organized a traditional ceremony. I need you to come with me. I don't know how I'll cope seeing Nadine, Justin and Maria alone.'

'Of course,' said Vince in thought, as the taxi pulled up to the Vancini residence. This was going to be a long week.

Chapter 9

Tuesday, 10:30 am

Sitting underneath a large umbrella outside his father's beach club, Joey dug and buried his toes in the cold, soft sand. This was one of the spots he and his older brother, Phil, used to come to unwind and relax. He missed his brother's company. He looked up to him and now he was gone forever. Phil's death played over in his mind, again and again, until he could do nothing but crouch low and stare into the sand.

Generally, Joey was a happy young man. He'd never worked a day in his life, just lay around all day, surfed and partied with girls. But now another family tragedy had hit home. The first death in his family hadn't affected him as much as this one. His mother had died giving birth to him, as a result of complications. The only memories of her were through pictures his brother had shown him. Phil would always say, 'You look like Mom,' as his blond hair, blue eyes and pale skin were definitely not from his father's side. Today his sadness overwhelmed him.

He had not spoken to his father. He, too, was not taking it well, locked away in his penthouse suite, dealing with it in his own way. Everyone needed time out. Joey sat there thinking about what had gone wrong and grabbed a beer from the cooler by his side. He flipped the lid off and began drinking. It was still early in the day, but it helped him to relax and think.

To his surprise, a friendly face approached, carrying a large plate with a burger and fries. The lady carrying the food was Monica Anton, the FBI agent his brother had fallen deeply in love with, who was still residing in Phil's old room.

'Can I join you?' she asked.

'It depends, is that for me?' Joey said in a dull, unassuming voice. He knew she was probably sent out to make sure he was okay.

Monica handed over the plate and sat down in the chair to his right, where his brother would have normally taken a seat. She was a good-looking woman, but only a few people had the pleasure of seeing her warmth and compassion. It was one of the characteristics Phil loved so much and was constantly bragging about.

In the short time Joey and Monica had known each other, a strong bond had formed between them. He was comfortable around her and treated her as if she was his adopted older sister. She'd told him she felt the same way: Joey was the first person to accept her into the family when Phil had brought her home to meet them.

Joey asked her openly, 'You're FBI, what's your outlook on all this? Who do you think killed my brother?'

'Who the hell knows?' said Monica, shaking her head.

'I know how analytical you are, you must have suspects in mind.'

Monica paused. 'Look, I'll tell you, but eat. Tony is worried you haven't eaten. His fat head is probably fixed at us now through the window.'

'Tony's a good man.'

He took a bite from his burger and some of the lettuce fell off to the side. He hadn't realized how hungry he was until he'd dug in.

'There are many people who could have been involved in your brother's death: he had many enemies, and so does your father.'

47

Joey shook his head. 'That's true, but why not go after my father if it was about him?'

'Maybe it's personal. Having to bury your own child would be the worst thing for any parent to do. Maybe they wanted Alexander to suffer, killing what he loved most.'

'It must be hard for Dad,' he said, his voice trembling.

'You think?'

'Yes, I do.'

'I don't see your dad starving himself though.'

'How am I starving myself? Only yesterday we found out Phil was killed,' said Joey as the wind blew his sun-bleached hair over his stark blue eyes.

Monica gave him a small smile; he had eaten half the burger.

'I have two suspects in mind,' she said.

'Go on.'

'Here it goes: the first is your father himself.'

Joey's unease sharpened. 'What! That's absurd, why would he kill his own son?'

'That's the question you should be asking yourself.'

'I know they had their issues, but—'

'Listen, Joey, Phil confided in me, and he was very upset with your father. A week before the robbery, they had a big argument. Maybe your dad felt disrespected, distraught that his eldest son was planning to leave the Peruggia clan for good.'

Joey's demeanor thawed instantly with the possibility that she could be right. Phil was open about leaving and starting a new life. Maybe it did upset his dad – but killing him for that seemed somewhat extreme.

Joey started eating the chips now, his eyes focused on Monica. She paused and let him finish.

'Dad did put all the emphasis on the distractions and not enough on the actual escape,' he said after a few moments. 'Was he setting him up to fail?'

'Just speculating, Joey, keep it between us, okay?'

'You said you had two possible suspects. Who is the other?'

Monica's expression turned leery. She opened her mouth and said, 'You.'

Joey spat out the chip and wiped his mouth. 'Me? Why would I want to kill my own brother, Sherlock Holmes?' Joey said, wincing at the thought. 'I love – loved my brother.'

'You could've easily arranged the explosion. As for a reason why, it's simple. Your father has always favored Phil. Maybe you were jealous. People have killed for far less.'

Joey stared down at her like she was the enemy, not liking what he was hearing. She stood up and leaned in for a hug. He reluctantly reciprocated.

'I don't believe it was you, Joey,' she whispered into his left ear.

'Of course it wasn't me, smartass.' He was upset that she'd even mentioned him. 'Maybe it was you?'

'Ha ha, I think you've had too much to drink.'

'Yeah, you might be right.'

'I promise you I'll find the person involved,' she said.

'I know you will.'

Monica grabbed the empty plate and walked back to the beach club, also taking away his cooler container filled with German beers, his favorite.

'No more drinking. Your brother wouldn't have liked seeing you like this.'

'Ah, come on!' Joey said, knowing she meant well, but he wanted to drown his sorrows a little more.

The jealousy assumption made by Monica was not one hundred percent untrue. He did feel like the odd one out, but he loved his brother; he never would have killed him.

Joey had always applauded his father for his brilliant mind, but now at the age of twenty-five he found himself questioning his father's actions for the first time.

'What if it's true?' he whispered to himself, alone on the beach. Maybe his brother's killer was closer than he anticipated. Monica had opened his eyes to the possibility that it could have been orchestrated by the mastermind himself: his father.

The seed was planted.

Chapter 10

Tuesday, 1 pm

Vince watched TV in the house he'd called home for the last eighteen years of his life. The decor was old and dated, with a distinctive smell to it, but it was comfortable. Leonardo was in the kitchen on the phone that was put on loudspeaker. His father's booming, unique voice could be heard through the dry walls, chatting away to his closest friend on the precinct, Detective Luke Taylor.

Vince remembered having him over at the house for a barbecue a long time ago. This was a time before his parents had split up and his Uncle Harris was still alive, telling rude jokes to make everyone laugh.

The chief had said Taylor has taken the lead to investigate the bank robbery on Wilshire, plus the two explosions that happened on the exact same day. Vince knew this was no friendly catch-up call.

'Can you come over?'

'If the chief finds out …' said Taylor, clearly nervous.

'He won't.'

'He warned me you might call, he's not dumb.'

'He won't find out.'

'You know my job's on the line?'

'Don't be a pussy, trust me,' his father said.

'Look, Leo, I know you want answers, but I'm under strict confidentiality—'

'Come on, goddammit,' hissed his father. 'Harris is dead. I'm not going to sit on my ass while the fucker who killed him gets to roam around the city doing whatever the hell he wants.'

'Alright … alright … I guess I can give you a rundown.'

'That's all I want. You're a good man, Taylor.' Vince heard his father's gruff response.

'Okay, I'll be there after my shift, around six.'

At six o'clock Detective Taylor pressed the doorbell, followed by a tentative knock. Vince greeted him with a friendly handshake. 'Hey, come in. Pizzas are on the table, plenty to go around.'

Taylor stepped in and surveyed the premises, a skill embedded in his subconscious. At the academy the cadets were taught to be able to walk into a room, close their eyes and after a few seconds recollect anything they had seen. He remembered what the house had looked like when Leonard's ex-wife was still around. Antique wooden furniture, brick-featured fireplace, and plush fabric lounges with sumptuous rolled armrests, complemented by plump cushions. Gemma had always kept the residence in a clean, organized fashion. It was a different story now. One thing was certain, the house lacked the female touch. A vacuum here and there wouldn't have hurt, either.

Taylor sank into the couch and helped himself to a slice from a selection of three pizza boxes that had been left wide open. Leonardo entered the room holding two Coronas fresh out of the fridge, a slice of lime inserted in the top of each bottle. He handed over the beer bottle and thanked Taylor again for coming.

'How are you feeling?' Taylor asked, sitting back into the deep couch.

'So tell me, what do you have?' Leonardo asked. He was never one for small talk. All work and no play. His stubbornness was rude and unnecessary, but Taylor knew he didn't mean to be disrespectful, it was just his nature.

'Okay, we know Alexander's son Phil led the robbers into the bank. The two men killed by Harris were Matt Stevens and Victor Matino, known members of the Peruggia Blood.'

Vince interrupted. 'What's Peruggia Blood?'

'Peruggia Blood, son, is what Alexander calls his gang members. Every member has a Peruggia Blood tattoo on their arm. It symbolizes unity, respect and a protected blood brother. He created his own family of soldiers. He's like any other smart leader in the past. Take Julius Caesar or Alexander the Great, for example: they were intelligent, strong and ambitious men, but if they didn't have a large army marching behind them, they were nothing.'

Vince seemed to have understood the analogy by the way he moved his head. Taylor, on the other hand, was surprised with Leonardo's knowledge of ancient history. That was a first, but he was spot on.

'So what's the tattoo of?' asked Vince.

'It's the Vitruvian man,' said Taylor.

'Yeah I know the one. The man who's superimposed with his arms and legs apart in a circle. What's the relevance of it though?'

Taylor stepped forward. 'It's relevant to them as Alexander's grandfather Vincenzo Peruggia was the man who stole the *Mona Lisa* back in 1911. Look it up, kid, it's a cracking read.'

'Wow ... what a connection!' Vince said, sounding impressed.

'Even though we know Alexander was involved, knowing isn't enough: we have nothing on him,' said Taylor.

'But weren't two of his men found dead at the scene?' said Vince, eager to contribute to the discussion.

'If we tried to convict with only that,' said Taylor, 'we'd have no chance. We'd lose. Alexander would play the dumb card and be excused, as he's not responsible for his friends' actions.'

'What about Phil?' replied Leonardo, entering the conversation.

'Another dead-end. He was killed in the explosion.'

'Did you find his body?'

'The only remains found were two of his teeth confirming his identity through dental records.'

'So nothing.'

'Hang on, I didn't say we found nothing.'

'What did you find, then?' Leonardo said, his eyes glinting with anticipation.

'In front of the Trinity Church we found an abandoned cab with traces of Phil's prints everywhere: smeared on the seats, the tinted windows and on the steering wheel.'

'He used the cab to get to the church.'

'Yes.'

'Is that it?' Leonardo replied, unimpressed.

'No, we also found a phone.'

'A phone?'

'I found it on the floor of the cab. Its screen was damaged and the battery was completely drained.'

'Who does it belong to?' asked Vince.

'Phil.'

'Big deal,' said Leonardo. 'How's that going to help us?'

'At first I thought the same, but after a little digging we found something.'

'Tell me you have a voicemail identifying his father as the mastermind in yesterday's hit.'

'I wish. No, but we did find a text message sitting in the outbox folder, sent to FBI Agent Monica Anton.'

'FBI ... What? Why?' said Leonardo.

Taylor could see Leonardo's forehead crease in a frown of concentration. 'The text message is interesting, we believe it tells us the location to the two million dollars unaccounted for.'

'But don't you think Monica would have it by now, if he sent her the text message?' replied Vince.

Taylor smiled at Vince's curiosity and cunning, he was

just like his old man. 'Actually no, Vince. Here's the kicker. Unlucky for Phil and his girlfriend, the message didn't reach its target. Who knows, bad reception or no battery life most likely caused it to fail.'

'What about the time it was sent? Can't the police trace where the phone was last used?' Vince asked.

'The message was sitting in the mail outbox folder, marked with a red question mark, to show it didn't go through. Sent at 7:35 pm, twenty-five minutes before the explosion at the Trinity Church.'

'It's got to be just after he hid the money,' said Vince.

'So what did the message say?' asked Leonardo.

'Actually, it's more of a clue or riddle.'

'Clue? Can you read it out to me?'

Taylor pulled out a piece of paper he had transcribed it on. He glanced up at Vince and Leonardo and said:

It lies beneath the third

P.ENIMAR GC

Vince repeated the message. 'It lies beneath the third … So he buried it somewhere under the number three.'

'That's good, Vince. We believe P.ENIMAR GC is referring to the Penmar Golf Course. The last place your dad had an altercation with Phil and was stabbed.'

'The fucker got lucky,' responded Leonardo abruptly.

Taylor laughed and repeated the first line of the message. 'It lies beneath the third, as you said, Vince. We think he buried the money around the third hole of the golf course.'

'Clever,' said Vince.

'I closed down the golf course and digging around the third hole has begun.'

'Find anything?' Leonardo asked.

'Nothing as yet. In the next couple of days, I might need to obtain a search warrant for a full perimeter search if nothing is found.'

'That sounds like a lot of fun,' said Leonardo, 'but the

question you should be asking yourself is why did Phil send the text message to his girlfriend and not his father or his brother? Who is this lady? What does she do at the FBI and can she be trusted as an ally? If I was you, I'd keep all findings to myself, which includes the discovery of Phil's phone and the message, until you know who to trust.'

Taylor shook his head. 'Good point.' He had not met Monica Anton before and didn't know her intentions. All he knew was that she was a special-intelligence agent for the FBI in deep cover, and was involved sexually with Phil Peruggia.

Vince made a suggestion. 'What if the clue was not so straightforward? Maybe you haven't found anything because it was meant to trick the police?'

'What do you mean, Vince?'

'Well, Monica works for the FBI. If intelligence is her specialty, perhaps it's an anagram of sorts. Have you tried rearranging the letters?'

Taylor smiled at Vince's theory. 'Your son's a regular Columbo. We considered that, but we're looking at the obvious first and if nothing gets found at the golf course, we'll re-evaluate the SMS and consider other avenues like anagrams. For now, that's the plan.'

When the detective left the house, Vince slumped onto the couch opposite his father and finished his beer. 'I can't believe there's two million dollars buried somewhere. We should try to find the money for ourselves, Dad. Can you imagine what we could do with two million dollars? Pay off the house, pay off my school fees, buy whatever we want and live like kings.'

Leonardo flashed a smile. 'That money belongs to the bank. I believe in karma, kid, and it'll end up biting you in the butt, not to mention a life sentence in prison. Do you know what they do to corrupt cops in jail? No thanks.'

'I know, but it'd be awesome not having any debt. I sometimes dream about winning money and what I'd do with it. When I've asked my friends in the past what they would do, they say buy a Ferrari or go on a big holiday – spend it all. I'm different. I'd rather not tell anyone and just live comfortably, pay off my schooling, buy an investment property or two, be smart with the money.'

'Vince, I'm proud you have your head screwed on right. I know I haven't always been there for you, but I'm going to give you some advice your grandfather gave me.'

Vince waited in anticipation.

'Be the captain of your own ship; chart a course and navigate with determination in the choppy waters. You alone are the master of your own destiny in the harshness of life. You can have anything you want if you just work hard for it. Money is not everything in life, believe me.'

Vince rarely got a compliment or any fatherly advice growing up and was taken aback by it. Maybe his father was a changed man? Only time would tell.

Chapter 11

Wednesday, 8:30 am

Vince was wide awake with a fresh face and there were no dark circles under his eyes. It was the first time in a long time that he had enjoyed a full night's sleep uninterrupted, with no assignments due or shift to cover at the bar.

Today's agenda was Uncle Harris's funeral. First he needed to leave the house and pick up a black suit, hanging in his dorm-room closet. After extracting his father's car key from a hook mounted near the front door, he was on his way.

Not long after, his cell phone rang. On the screen the name Terry Woods was displayed. Terry was Vince's boss, bar owner and friend. He was the old Australian guy at the bar that everyone loved. In his mid-sixties, tall with a full head of hair, Terry was an energetic businessman who loved his job and knew how to have a good time. Vince had learned the art of bar tending and landing the ladies from this man.

In a cheery voice Vince answered, on speaker phone, 'Hey, Terry, what's up?'

'What's up? Where the hell were you last night, mate?' Terry's angry tone tempered Vince's ebullient mood.

'What?' Vince gazed absently out the window.

'What do you mean what? I was short-staffed.'

'Aww shit.'

'Tell me why I shouldn't fire your arse?' Terry always

said 'arse' even though he'd lived in the US for years. His Australian accent was as strong as ever.

With all the commotion going on with his father, Vince had forgotten to call Terry to explain his current situation. 'Shit, Terry, I'm so sorry, I totally forgot.'

'Flaming hell, mate, I hope you have a good reason?'

'My father was stabbed yesterday.'

'Stabbed? Fuck, is he okay?'

'Yeah, I'm taking time off college to take care of him.'

'I'm sorry to hear that, Vince. So does that mean you're not coming into work tonight and the rest of the week, too? Because I need to organize someone else to cover your shift.'

'I just need a couple of days off. I can be back Friday. I'm so sorry, Terry. I need to help my old man, he's going through a tough time. I'm on my way to pick up a suit to go to his partner's funeral right now.'

'Okay, Vince, next time call me, okay?' said Terry, wishing his father the best and ending the call. Terry employed new students from the college every year. He had queues of students needing work. Vince was lucky Terry was a sympathetic man and a good friend as, without a job, he wouldn't be able to pay his tuition fees.

After a fifteen-minute drive, Vince arrived at his campus and entered his dorm room. Two brown eyes raised from a laptop screen. It was his roommate, Gary, who was surprised to see him. Gary was the typical college student who went to college to party. He was tall with bushy brows and an edgy handsomeness to him.

'There he is. How the fuck are you?' Gary said. 'Isabella told me what happened. Thanks for letting me know. A call would've been nice.'

Vince smiled at Gary, who sounded like a worried parent, waiting for his child to come home after a big night out. 'You're not the first person to tell me that today,' replied Vince.

'Dude, how's your old man?'

'You know my dad: a dagger could be in his back and he'd say he was fine. I'm here to pick up my black suit. The funeral is in an hour.'

Gary nodded with a serious expression. 'So when are you back?'

'I'm going to stay with Dad for a few days, keep an eye on him.'

'Of course, bro. Just remember Friday night at Terry's Bar. A lot of hot girls are coming, make sure you're there.' Gary was a simple man. He only concerned himself with two things in life: girls and cars.

'That's right, your birthday. Don't worry, I'll be there. I'll be the one providing you and all the hotties free drinks.' Once Vince changed, he smiled at Gary and left in a hurry.

The time was 10 am. Vince and Leonardo arrived and parked at the Woodlawn Cemetery. They stepped out of the car with dark sunglasses that framed their faces. Leonardo was dressed in his blue police attire. They proceeded toward the front of the mausoleum where the service was taking place. Leonardo gazed around the twenty-six acres of tranquil manicured lawns and gardens. The mountains and the Pacific Ocean could be seen in the far distance. He felt calm: his partner and best friend was going to rest in a peaceful environment.

The ceremony was held at the mausoleum adorned with handmade stained-glass windows and ironwork. It featured two distinct chapels that offered a special setting. A flood of navy-blue uniforms occupied the area, all here to pay their respects for their fallen officer and friend. White lilies engulfed the site with pockets of blue hydrangeas hung up on the perimeter wall.

Leonardo approached Harris's wife, and good friend, and embraced her with a warm hug and kiss. There was no need to say anything: no words could describe how they both felt at this moment. Nadine returned his embrace with equal warmth.

Leonardo stepped to the side to see his son hug the lady he knew as Aunty Nadine. They had spent many Christmases together and had grown up with her kids Justin, who was the same age as Vince, and Maria, who was three years younger.

Leonardo moved over to Justin, whose sunglasses hid his bloodshot eyes. He could tell the kid was trying to be strong, trying to be the man of the house now. It nearly put a tear to his eye when he turned to see Harris's daughter break down when Vince hugged her. The two were like brother and sister.

Justin approached his sister strapped to Vince's shoulder, gave him a nod and helped direct her back inside the chapel for the start of the service. The emotions flying around were too intense for Leonardo so he decided to stay outside near the door and get some much-needed air.

The procession began and the priest could be heard through the amazing acoustics created by the mammoth marble and granite walls. It was only five minutes into the service when Leonardo spotted in the far distance a plethora of black limousines roll in and park, one after the other. The entire strip of road was filled by them, back to back. Someone special must have also passed away; it was like a celebrity's funeral. He was curious, always on the lookout, always being a detective and a little bit of a sticky beak. One limousine had two men standing over it like bodyguards to the president's car. *The person in that limousine must be important*, he thought. They opened the door and, to his surprise, out walked a tall, olive-skinned man. Alexander Peruggia in the flesh.

Dressed in another one of his expensive suits, no creases in sight. He approached his gathered family and friends. Leonardo wondered why he would choose today of all days to bury his son. He would have known the detective's funeral was on today, and if this was for his son, what was the point? There was no body to bury anyway. This was no coincidence for the so-called genius. Alexander didn't do coincidences.

What was he up to, he thought, standing there with Vince, who turned to see what had drawn his dad's eye like a hawk.

Leonardo recognized the men in his crew from a wall of photos he had built up over the years back at the precinct. He watched Alexander move over to his youngest son, Joey, who was a couple of years older than Vince. He hugged and lightly tapped him on his right cheek, before gazing over to see Leonardo peeping in the distance. Their eyes met. It was like looking into the eyes of a rabid dog. Neither one wanted to look away to show fear or weakness. Hatred glowered between them.

Alexander leaned over to a tall, tanned, overweight but extremely muscular man with a shaved head and whispered something in his ear. James was known to the police as a serial killer, and was as crazy as they came. James turned and focused in the detective's direction with a smirk and continued to stare back at him intensely.

Leonardo was disturbed and agitated, like the hurricane winds stirring the sea. The man responsible for his partner's death was in sight.

Vince could see his dad's discomfort and indecisive mannerisms and asked, 'Dad, you okay?'

'Ah, stuff this,' whispered Leonardo to himself. On impulse he walked out of his partner's service and headed up the hill. He couldn't stand being so close to this animal.

Vince tried to follow, but his father's walk was too fast. Detective Taylor, who was also outside the mausoleum, jogged to keep up.

Leonardo was very close now. Restlessness was felt and heard by the Peruggia men as a police officer interrupted their funeral proceeding. Alexander calmed his men down with a hand gesture. Leonardo's intentions were clear and transparent: he wanted to face up to his enemy and have a word.

Only moments from confronting Alexander, an intriguing

woman stepped in his way. He had not seen her before. 'Now's not the time,' she said in a calm voice, placing her palm on Leonardo's chest.

'No, now's the perfect time, miss,' he said, ignoring her and stepping in front of the much taller Alexander Peruggia.

They were like two schoolkids trying to stare each other down. It was a standoff. The staring went on forever. There was so much hatred between the two, anything was possible. Leonardo's actions could put many people in danger if he didn't watch himself.

Alexander was the first to open his mouth.

'If you don't mind, pig. I'm trying to bury my son that you fucking shot, so get out of my face before I squash you like a bug.'

'What with an empty casket?' mocked Leonardo.

'My son deserves a proper burial and a blessing from the priest.'

Three of Alexander's men surrounded the detective, handguns visible underneath their suit jackets. Leonardo was not in the best situation, but he didn't care. He was a much smaller man and the weaker one, but had acquired a street-smart toughness long ago.

'You killed my friend, my partner. This is personal. I will not rest until you are behind bars for life. Where you'll be fucked by a three-hundred-pound Mexican and love it.'

The crowd of people around Alexander's funeral sighed out loud. Alexander moved his face even closer, bending his knees to get to Leonardo's height, way down, practically touching nose to nose, and said with a smirk, 'Listen, you can do whatever you want, but you have no proof of anything. You think you know pain, losing your friend? How about losing your son? My own flesh and blood, the one who was going to take over the family business.'

Leonardo could see Alexander heating up by the throbbing vein on his forehead. He knew he wouldn't react due to the circumstances. He was too smart to.

'Come on, I dare you,' said Leonardo. 'Hit an officer.'

'Listen, midget, you had your fun, now go.'

Without warning, Vince grabbed his dad on the shoulder and pulled him backwards. 'Dad, let's go,' said Vince, yanking on his shoulder that would not budge.

Alexander froze and looked down at Vince with a sarcastic smile. His face lit up, noticing the resemblance. 'Oh, you have a son? He's a little taller than you, he obviously got his good looks from his mother.'

'Be careful,' said Leonardo

'I never pictured you as a family man. It's good to know you have a weakness, an Achilles' heel. Now get out of my face, before you're not the only father grieving his dead son today.'

'What did you say?'

Leonardo was not going to take any threats to his family, and with a quick step, he punched Alexander with a right hook. Alexander fell to his knees. Leonardo continued with the momentum and jumped on top of him, grabbing his suit collar by the neck and shouted, 'Don't you ever fucking threaten my boy.'

Muscles James retaliated and pulled the detective off, and threw him hard onto the grass like a rag doll.

'Stop!' yelled Taylor. 'Everybody stop.'

'Leave him alone,' cried Vince, moving forward to help his father.

Joey stepped in his face. 'And what are you going to do about it?'

Vince backed away.

Detective Taylor was all over his friend and stopped him from reacting again.

Alexander picked himself up and dusted the dirt off his hands. He readjusted his jaw and commanded his men to back down and let the others go. Alexander, though visibly shaken from the punch, smiled. He was unnaturally happy for someone who had just been physically assaulted.

It was as if he had taken his opponent's queen in a game of chess.

Leonardo was forced away by Taylor, who screamed, 'Are you crazy? You don't want to provoke this man.'

'He's planning something, Taylor, I can feel it.'

'Dad, you're crazy! And you call me stupid.'

Leonardo was unimpressed with Vince, as he had almost gotten in an altercation with Joey Peruggia. 'Now he knows I have a son. That's why I keep my work to myself and don't involve my family.'

'What family, Dad? I never saw you growing up. Even poor Mom didn't want anything to do with you. You were never there for us. Maybe you should've thought of the danger you were putting me in before reacting and putting your selfish needs first, as always.'

Vince walked back to the mausoleum, kicking the dirt on the way, clearly upset.

Leonardo's demeanor changed to guilt, his head bowed down to the ground and he placed both his hands over his head.

'Are you okay?' Taylor asked.

Leonardo nodded and said nothing, upset with how he had acted. This was his friend's funeral and he needed to head back.

It was time to lower veteran Peter Harris six foot under. Leonardo held in his hands his partner's badge. Looking at it, he rubbed it with his thumb, then positioned it on top of the closed wooden casket. He made the sign of the cross with his three fingers and paid his last respects to his fallen friend. 'See you in the next life, brother, rest in peace.'

Alexander's procession had also finished and everyone went home. He climbed into the backseat of his limo and faced Ian and James. 'We can now organize stage two of my plan.'

'What's that?' asked Ian, the explosives expert responsible for all his destructive needs, which included the bombing at the Santa Monica Pier.

'Well, Ian,' said Alexander in an excited manner. 'This afternoon we're going to walk straight into the police department, like we own the place. I'm going to lodge a formal complaint against the detective and his department for their constant harassment.'

'I love it,' said James in his deep voice.

Alexander smiled and continued. 'The police have no option but to follow the law and oblige this time. There were far too many witnesses, including some high-ranking officials who are on my payroll. I want Leonardo out of the way before stage two takes place next week. It'll help not having him sticking his nose where it doesn't belong.'

'Sounds good,' said Ian with his subdued personality.

'Imagine their faces when we walk into the station,' said James.

'Precisely,' said Alexander, satisfied. 'After that is all done, Ian I have a special job for you. The kind that doesn't end well for the victim.'

'What's that, boss? Who's the target?'

'All in due time, my friend,' responded Alexander as the limousine drove off into the distance.

Chapter 12

The smell of fresh cinnamon donuts was in the air, a regular scent at the Santa Monica Police Department. The windows around the office were large, and allowed lots of natural sunlight in the open-plan space. Modern furniture and decent-sized cubicles were designated for each officer to work in. It was Los Angeles, after all, considered as one of the best police bureaus in the world to be a part of. Some officers were getting their afternoon coffee from the shiny two-thousand-dollar coffee machine, while others were attending to their police reports.

The chief was situated in a large glass-walled office, to the far back end of the room. Three days a week he spent there, while the other two days his office was at the newly built headquarters downtown. Lee Davis was in his mid-sixties. He was diminutive with pitted scars on his skin, a sign that he'd suffered from acne as a kid. Not a tall man, with a large forehead and a recognizable drawling voice, in which he spoke in a distinctive clipped manner. He was deceptively intelligent and ruthless if he needed to be.

He was on the phone to the commissioner. Irritable and apologetic, he walked back and forth. He was responsible for all his men's actions and the events that had taken place this morning at the cemetery were reprehensible, needing to be dealt with now. He raised his right hand in a fist, like he wanted to punch someone, but at the same time replied back in a calm tone. 'Yes, sir, yes, sir … you realize he's one of our best detectives? … I can't believe I have to do this.'

The commissioner gave him strict orders to follow and alerted him to expect a visitor that needed to be treated with utmost respect, no matter what. Lee hung up the phone and kicked a chair off its current position to the floor. He was not happy with what was about to happen and who was about to enter these walls.

Detective Tarn Mostrom, the known bad boy in the department who wasn't a stickler for the rules, looked over to his right where Detective Taylor was sitting and said, 'I bet any money this has to do with Alexander Peruggia. Who else could piss off the chief like that?'

'I bet this is about the funeral this morning,' said Taylor. 'Leo shouldn't have punched him in the face.'

'Alexander's fucking untouchable,' said Tarn, with his legs up on his desk. 'How many years have they gone after him?'

'His time will come.'

'You reckon?'

'What are you, a fucking fan now? Don't worry, he'll make a mistake. They always do, and when he does I'll be there.'

Detective Taylor admired men like Leonardo who had the balls to walk up to Alexander at his son's funeral and punch him straight in the face. Taylor could not have done that in a million years; it meant breaking the rules, and that was not his style.

To go after a man like Alexander you needed to understand how he worked and why he was considered the most dangerous gangster of his time. He hid behind his multimillion-dollar businesses and real estate developments. He was also the owner of the famous Alexander Beach Club, which he used to solicit his corrupt deals. For him to be able to stay on top of the game without getting arrested or caught, he surrounded himself with people he called his family. He was an intelligent and calculating man, always one step ahead, with corrupt officers high up in the police force helping him to escape convictions. Even good cops had to obey and accept his bribes or their families were threatened and targeted. The one thing that set him apart from any other criminal was his way of thinking, his mind. This afternoon was a perfect example, planned to perfection.

All of a sudden the chief's door swung open. Taylor could tell by the look on his face and how he dragged himself out of his office that he had something important to share. Everyone glanced over to the chief with a bewildered look on their faces.

'I need everyone to stay calm, not to react,' he said.

'What's up, boss?' Taylor asked.

'We have a visitor entering the department, any minute now.'

'Who is it?'

'It doesn't matter, just stay calm. I have orders from the commissioner to let this person in unscathed.'

'It's Alexander, isn't it,' said Tarn.

Lee didn't respond, he didn't need to. He clapped his hands and ordered everyone to go back to work.

The time was 3 pm. Taylor dug into a jam donut from a box that was left on his desk. Cleaning off the excess sugar from his lips with the back of his hand, he spotted five men entering the office. The man in the middle was none other than Alexander Peruggia, dressed in another one of his expensive Armani suits, shiny pointy leather shoes and a pair of Versace glasses. Now that Taylor was leading the case, he had studied and learned the faces that were in Alexander's crew from photos on a wall created by Leonardo. The younger male to his left was his son Joey. To his right Frank and James towered in the back as the protectors. Leading the way, they were accompanied by a frail-looking man with glasses, who carried a briefcase. If Taylor was to guess, he was the high-priced attorney.

'Here we go,' said Tarn. 'The dickhead is here.'

Taylor stood up. His hand instinctively reached for his gun in its holster. Alexander walked by and eye-balled him through his penetrating eyes and refined carriage, smiling as he noticed the box of donuts on his desk: a stereotype with some truth to it.

Tarn stood in his path and held his ground.

'You have balls,' said Alexander in Tarn's face with a smirk.

'Big enough to hang around your neck,' replied Tarn, showing he was not afraid of him.

Alexander cheekily smiled and walked around him, and his men followed.

Laughter erupted when they discovered a picture wall of the most wanted criminals. Alexander, of course, was at the top. Underneath his surveillance photo, like a family-tree diagram, were his known associates. He leaned over to his left and said to Joey, 'Look, you're famous, too,' pointing at a picture of his son's face. The chuckle continued from James and Frank, who admired their mug shots as they stepped into the chief's office.

'The balls on this guy,' said Tarn. 'I can't believe he has the audacity to walk into the building without a worry in the world, like he fucking owns the place.'

Taylor glared disapprovingly.

Alexander was greeted by Lee with a friendly handshake and their meeting began. The door to his office was shut. All the men were seated and the lawyer began to speak, handing over the legal protective-order documents that had been issued by a judge. Alexander was quiet and let his lawyer do all the talking. He sat there and smiled as Lee read the documentation. Due to the thick soundproof walls, no officer outside could hear a word spoken from inside the chief's office.

Ten minutes was all it took. The meeting was over. Alexander readjusted his suit tie and walked toward the front door followed by his posse. The chief was left alone at his desk, slumped in his chair.

Taylor blocked Alexander's path. He placed his hand on the other man's chest and said, 'I'll be watching you.'

Alexander stifled a smile. 'Get out of my face, before I put a restraining order on you, too.' He pushed the detective's hand away with his forearm and stepped outside to a parked Bentley, where the driver sped off way over the speed limit; another sign to show the police who was in control.

Lee had some explaining to do. He exited his office and gained everyone's attention with a loud whistle and with a loud voice said, 'The Feds are on my back. It's official, people. We cannot touch or go near Alexander Peruggia, period. He has filed a restraining order against Detective Vancini for punching him at his son's funeral, as well as the police department for the constant harassment over the years, causing him to lose an abundance of new business.'

'What?!' shouted Taylor in disgust. 'I can't believe this guy.'

'We all know it's bullshit,' said Lee. 'But it's final. To go near Peruggia we need solid evidence, because if we don't the mayor and the commissioner will be on my ass quicker than a fly on shit. I don't like getting my ass fucked, so please get me something I can use or stay away, *capiche*?'

Taylor nodded his head.

Tarn smiled wryly.

The chief ordered for all the pictures to be taken down. The high-priced attorney had had all the angles covered. The police had been warned: if this continued they would have a hefty lawsuit on their hands, something the commissioner tried hard to avoid.

Knowing someone was guilty of a crime, or crimes, was not enough. Solid evidence was needed to continue any long investigation or surveillance on a suspect. These investigations and allegations on Alexander were long overdue. Knowing that Phil and his alleged associates were involved in the bank robbery on Wilshire was never going to be enough to arrest the father.

The paperwork and the ban were official, stamped and finalized. Mr. Peruggia was free to do as he pleased. He was legally protected by the law, a fantastic position to be in. Which went some way toward explaining his wide grin.

Chapter 13

Wednesday, 4 pm

Back at the Vancini residence Leonardo prepared Vince a late afternoon snack. It was his famous grilled sandwich, which was a regular meal in the household. The term 'famous' was used by Leonardo, even though Vince was the first person he'd ever served it to. Smothered in avocado, sliced tomatoes and a slice of American cheese that melted over the entire sandwich, bonding it together.

Leonardo was old-fashioned; he never showed his affection with words. The phrase 'I love you' did not exist in his vocabulary – it was never said or spoken. He preferred to allow his actions to speak, like making someone a cup of coffee or, in Vince's case, making him his famous grilled sandwich. This gesture was his way of showing Vince his love and how much he cared for him.

Leonardo came to realize that Nadine, Justin and Maria were going to eat dinner without their father tonight for the first time. He was a lucky man to be able to enjoy this moment with his son. He wanted to try to make amends and make an effort this time, wanting to be in his son's life. He plated the sandwich and acted like there was no bad history between the two of them and tried to begin a conversation. 'So how's college going?'

Vince stared at his father, perplexed. This was the first time he'd ever showed an interest in his schooling or his life and didn't know what to say, or where to start. His father was never there for him when he'd needed a male figure growing up. He'd missed many important events, like graduating high school, art accomplishments and the day he'd received his all-important acceptance letter from UCLA.

Vince took a bite from his dad's sandwich. 'School's good, one year left to go,' he said, breaking the silence.

'One year left? That's great,' replied Leonardo with a smile, having nothing else to say or add. The awkwardness at the dining table was apparent; the silence stretched. It had been years since they had spent this much time together in the same room. Vince loved his father, his blood ran through his veins, but he didn't know him at all. As a young teen, he'd asked his mother one day as they drove to a soccer game, 'Why doesn't Dad ever come to see me play?'

Vince's mother had explained as best as she could. 'You have to understand, Vince, how your father was raised. He grew up in an old village in the mountains of Tuscany. He didn't even finish primary school. He was put to work at the local farmers' market at an early age to support the family. That's how it was back in the sixties. So now your dad works hard because that's all he knows. Like the saying goes, you can't teach an old dog new tricks.'

'It's not fair, Mom.'

'I know, Vince,' his mom had said with a shrug. 'That's why I want you to promise me that you'll get an education. I want you to live by the motto: work to live, not live to work.'

As a young boy Vince had just accepted it: that's how it was. He was never going to have the same relationship his friends at school were having with their fathers.

The cordless phone resting in the middle of the dining table broke the silence. Leonardo shoved the last bite of his sandwich into his mouth and leaned forward to pick it up.

'Hello, Vancini here.'

It was the chief. He was quick and precise with his words. 'Leonardo, I need you to come into the department ASAP. Bring with you your badge and gun. I'll explain everything when you get in.'

The phone was disconnected before Leonardo had any time to ask why or respond. This didn't sound good.

'Who was that?' Vince asked.

'I'm needed urgently at work for something.'

'Do you need me to take you?'

'No, Vince, I'm not disabled. I won't be long.'

Leonardo walked into his bedroom walk-in closet. A large metal safe was tucked away in the far left corner. Above the safe all his police gear and clothing was lined up like an army cadet's closet. After punching in the four-digit combination, the safe opened. He extracted his firearm and badge, then put on a clean shirt. His eyes closed and his mouth tweaked as he threaded his arm through the sleeve, careful not to press on the fresh stitches.

Vince was not far behind. Leonardo turned to see his son staring at his stab-wound patch, where a dark stain of blood was noticeable.

'Vince, I don't need you to babysit me.'

'I never said anything,' said Vince with hands up high.

'I'm okay. I'll see you in a couple of hours,' said Leonardo.

Vince shook his head and gave him his space.

It was 5:30 pm. Many police officers had logged off work and were heading home as Leonardo walked into the department. The atmosphere was different today. Officers' heads hung. They looked deflated and troubled and they kept a safe distance from Leonardo. Everyone knew he was going to be suspended this afternoon. Even his old friend Taylor was distant and walked in the other direction. No one wanted to confront the veteran, working on the assumption that he was going to erupt with frustration. He entered the chief's office feeling anxious, knowing something was up.

'What the hell is going on in this place? Everyone is acting weird.'

Lee sat down in his chair and took a breather, preparing himself for the information he was going to reveal and avoided eye contact.

'Now you're acting weird. What in the hell is going on, Chief?'

'Alexander Peruggia came here this afternoon with his lawyer.'

'What?' said Leonardo, surprised.

'Yes, it's true. He filed a restraining order against you for physically abusing him at his son's funeral.'

'Come on!'

Lee continued, 'And also the department for ongoing harassment.'

'Boss, seriously?'

'Yes, Leonardo, this is no joke. If the harassment continues, he'll sue the police department for millions.'

'Is that why I'm here?'

'The commissioner is trying to avoid getting sued. I've been warned, and I'm warning you now.'

Leonardo shook his head, muttering with disgust, 'How can we allow this to happen? We're supposed to be the good guys.'

Lee apologized to Leonardo. 'I need your badge and gun. You are suspended immediately until further notice.'

'Think, Lee, you're a smart man. Alexander would never have gone to all this effort for nothing. Something is going down.'

'That may be true, but I need you to stay away. You're suspended. This is the restraining order I need to give you.' Lee held out the Penal Code 273.6pc letter, which stated that if it was broken the punishment would be a hefty fine and up to one year in jail.

Leonardo exhaled in disbelief, wrinkling his nose. Then he took out his badge and gun and left them both on the chief's table, walking out, leaving the letter still in the chief's hands.

'Make sure you stay away. Don't make me suspend you permanently,' shouted Lee to his retreating back.

Walking toward Taylor's desk, Leonardo thought how Alexander used the system to secure his immunity against any further cases against him. He was a big believer in the justice system, but today proved how unjust and flawed the justice system was. He approached his friend who was knee-deep in paper work and asked, 'What's the latest on the case? Any leads?'

'Leo, let it go,' said Taylor. 'Didn't you hear the chief? We can't investigate or even seem to interrogate Alexander. Besides, Peruggia isn't the only rich person who is filing against the police department. It's a touchy time.'

'What do you mean?'

'The Penmar Golf Course owner is up my ass since we dug up his entire course looking for the bank's money. He claims he's lost thousands of dollars and we've upset his regular customers. He wants compensation for his losses. Fuck, if I was him I would, too.'

'So the money was not in the golf course?'

'Looks like it.'

'So that's it?' said Leonardo. 'We're just going to give up and let him walk?'

'For now, yes,' said Taylor.

Leonardo shook his head and left the department upset with this afternoon's outcome.

'Don't do anything stupid,' said Taylor as Leonardo disappeared out of sight.

With or without a restraining order, nothing was going to stop him: Leonardo was a man on a mission.

Chapter 14

Wednesday, 6 pm

'Hey, Lex, what's up?' Tony said, having been sent for.

He was the only one who called him Lex, and had done so since they were kids.

'Look, about the plan,' said Alexander, touching his trusted friend's shoulder.

'I know, Lex, I know.'

'Make sure you don't miss.'

'Don't worry, Lex, I won't.'

'You only get one chance at it, one shot.'

'Don't worry, I'll make it count,' said Tony. 'Leonardo Vancini is going down, trust me.'

Chapter 15

Wednesday, 6:25 pm

'Hello, Mr. Vancini, I confronted you at the Woodlawn Cemetery,' said an anonymous caller as Leonardo stepped into his car.

'Who is this?' replied Leonardo, trying to put a face to the voice.

'My name is FBI Agent Monica Anton. I infiltrated Alexander Peruggia's crew and maintained a relationship with his son Phil.'

'Good for you. Why are you calling me?'

'Leonardo, I know about your situation. Even though your department closed all surveillance on Alexander, that doesn't mean we have. On the contrary, I have information you might be interested in.'

'I'm listening.'

'Today at the funeral I overheard a conversation between two of Alexander's men about a transaction taking place tonight at his beach club.'

'Why are you telling me this? Why don't you organize a team and intercept the transaction?' asked Leonardo, doubting Monica could be trusted. Who was she anyway and why was she giving him this information?

'The FBI will get involved in due time. I just wanted to keep you in the loop, since I know you're a man who's after retribution.'

Monica paused for a moment and hung up the phone.

Leonardo was headstrong and impetuous. He wasn't going to ignore vital information like that, even if it was coming from an unreliable source. He started the car's ignition and headed toward the club. The chief's voice echoed in his ear. 'Stay away from Alexander.' It was like telling a child not to touch candy: he didn't care.

Alexander's Beach Club was on Palisades Beach Road, Santa Monica. An extravagant club owned by its namesake, Alexander Peruggia. It was his largest and most successful business, fronting the beach and the Pacific Ocean. The tranquil setting was a keystone of a vista stretching from Malibu to Palos Verdes. Members of the club were welcome to indulge in the many amenities it had to offer, including the large swimming pool and gym.

On the way, Leonardo called Vince to inform him he was going to be late.

'Hey, Dad, what did the chief want?'

'Nothing. Listen, I'm going to be home late tonight, don't wait up.'

'Where are you going?'

'I'm meeting up with some work colleagues for a drink at the Sapphire Bar, to toast Harris.'

'Okay, Dad. See you in the morning. Don't forget to grab a cab if you drink too much.'

Leonardo smiled at his son over the phone for playing the role of a worried parent.

Day turned into night. Leonardo parked his car in one of the many spots provided by the club at the rear of the building. He opened his boot and picked up a backup 9mm handgun and concealed it in an ankle holster.

As he walked down the side entrance from the parking lot, the sandy beach could be seen. It was the entrance people took to the beach, where a group of tennis courts were located. Leonardo used it to walk through unnoticed, without the need to use the front door. He approached the clamorous wing of the club that was used for parties and events. He gazed around the site, ducking and weaving in the shadows, searching for anything out of the ordinary. To his surprise, a surveillance camera was aimed straight at him. He had been detected on the premises.

Within minutes, a large muscular bald man with tattoos covering his arms approached the detective. It was muscles James, known to the police as the Hulk because of the many victims he had crushed dead – literally. He took enormous pleasure in breaking his enemies' bones with a brutal bear hug.

Leonardo retrieved his ankle gun and pointed it at James, in fear of his life. James, in a calm, deep voice, told the cop, 'We've been expecting you. Please,' gesturing the way inside to the club's back entrance door. Leonardo had to think fast, still pointing his gun, ready to fire all the rounds into James's broad frame.

'Mr. Peruggia has requested a meeting with you,' said James again, trying to sound friendly, but his size was intimidating.

Leonardo agreed hesitantly and walked cautiously inside the club with James at his back. Once inside, he was stopped by a strong hand on his right shoulder and he could not move: it was like an elephant's trunk was holding him dormant. Young Joey confronted him with a pat-down and removed his concealed weapon.

'Sorry, I know you're a man with a badge, but there's no way I'm letting you walk in here armed,' said Joey, who leaned in and punched the detective hard in the guts, causing him to fall to his knees, letting out a whimper.

'What was that for?' Leonardo asked, caught off guard.

'That's for my brother, you fuck.'

Joey walked back to the booth Monica was occupying.

Leonardo stood up after he'd regained his breath and

recognized the agent, who he had seen once before at the funeral. The same FBI agent who was supposedly on his side. This meeting was too orchestrated, it had been planned, and he felt lied to and tricked. She was a deceitful dog in his eyes, never to be trusted again.

James nudged him to continue inside; the further he went, the more he realized he was putting his life at risk. Then he spotted Alexander sitting in a booth, in a private room decorated in yellows and browns called 'the gold room.' He was not alone. He was with his girlfriend, Victoria. As Leonardo approached, she kissed her man on the cheek and evacuated the booth so they could have their meeting.

Leonardo sat down, rubbing his stomach from the previous unexpected punch and said to Alexander, 'Is that how you treat all your guests?'

'Joey is the least of your worries, believe me.'

'So tell me, why the setup?'

'Before we get into our meeting, eat something,' Alexander said, waving his open hand over a spread in front of them. He almost sounded magnanimous. 'Can we offer you some champagne? We need to celebrate and raise our glasses.'

'And what are we celebrating?' Leonardo asked, as four of Alexander's men stepped into the room.

'Our new arrangement.'

Leonardo laughed; it was like negotiating with a terrorist. No arrangements with this man were going to do anyone any good.

'Sorry, I don't make arrangements with criminals.'

'You have balls walking into my domain. I could kill you right now. But I won't, it's too easy. I would like to make a truce with you. I have a proposal I hope you will consider,' said Alexander, as the waiter poured a Château Clos Puy Arnaud 2009 into two chilled flutes.

Leonardo smiled and replied in a calm voice, as if they were best friends having a casual conversation over a drink.

'You won't kill me. I know this because you're a smart man, you wouldn't take a chance like that, without knowing if I was alone. Maybe there's a second police unit outside.'

Alexander returned the smile. 'All I want is for you to look the other way. Stop trying to come after me and you'll be rewarded generously with $250,000 in cash. You're not the only police officer I have on my books, so why not help your son pay off his school fees, pay off your home loan, and retire with a reasonable sum of money in your bank account?'

It was a generous offer that many people would have accepted. Leonardo glanced around the room, overlooking the beach and the tennis courts and changed the subject. 'You have an incredible club.'

'You should become a member,' replied Alexander. 'No more donuts, though.'

Leonardo smiled: like that was ever going to happen.

'Thank you for your offer, but I will graciously decline. I will continue to play this game, whatever it is we are playing. The money you're offering me is blood money. Money that was inherited from drugs and corruption. I will not stop until you are behind bars where you belong. Sooner or later you'll make a mistake and I'll be there to get you.'

Alexander frowned, agitated with his answer. He looked like a man who didn't take rejection well.

'It's up to you, my friend,' said Alexander, focused on Leonardo's sad brown eyes. 'But if I was you I would take the deal I offered you and everyone will be happy. Don't be stupid. If you continue playing games with me, you'll lose. I can turn your life upside down, so don't tempt me.'

Leonardo stood up and looked down at Alexander, something he rarely did, being considerably shorter. 'Do what you like,' he said. 'Remember, even the best chess players make mistakes, and I'll be there when you make yours.'

Leonardo's pleasure was short-lived as Alexander stood up and reversed their roles. His annoyance was palpable. 'So you want to play games, huh? Okay, let's play: do you realize I have a restraining order against you and you're technically not allowed to come within three hundred feet of me?'

'Ah come on,' said Leonardo, knowing where this was heading.

Alexander glanced over to wise-guy Tony, who had positioned himself behind Leonardo, wearing latex gloves, holding Leonardo's gun that was retrieved earlier.

'What are you doing?' Leonardo asked.

'Shut up,' said Tony.

Alexander gave a nod, as if they had planned something ahead of time. Leonardo watched Monica and Joey leave the scene. Out of the blue, two of Alexander's men grabbed Leonardo's arms and faced him to their leader.

Tony pointed the gun straight at the detective's chest.

Leonardo bit his lip and shut his eyes. He was pinned down, this was it. He was joining his best friend on the other side. Then it came quick.

A single shot was fired.

Nothing happened.

Leonardo exhaled heavily, feeling his chest for a bullet hole. No hole, no blood: he was still alive. The sound of the gun echoed in the room. His mind raced as he looked up in horror. If he hadn't been shot, then who had? He flashed over in Alexander's direction and realized that he was the victim with the bullet wound.

'What kind of bullshit is this?' Leonardo asked as customers in the restaurant dived to the floor and hid under their tables, in fear of their lives. Tony dashed over to make sure his boss was alright and placed a small towel over his shoulder wound.

Alexander seemed to have taken the pain well. He walked over to Leonardo, who was being held, and smeared his blood over his clean shirt. 'I warned you not to fuck with me. If we were playing a game of chess right now, I would've just taken your queen.'

Leonardo was lost for words, realizing the situation he was in.

'Call the police,' ordered Tony to the bartender. 'Tell them a shooting has taken place at Alexander's Beach Club. Tell them Alexander Peruggia was shot by Detective Leonardo Vancini ... Go do it now.'

Leonardo, entrapped by his own stupidity, was forced down on the floor while the men in blue came to arrest him for the attempted murder of Alexander Peruggia and took him into custody. His rights were read as he was escorted into a police vehicle.

Two police detectives questioned some distraught witnesses in the restaurant and were asked to explain what had transpired. They all gave the same answer: it was as if it had all been scripted.

'This man came into the restaurant trying to kill Alexander.' They all knew what to say, if they valued their lives. Alexander had once again outplayed Leonardo, but he wasn't finished with him yet. This was just the beginning. Inside the ambulance, Alexander flashed a smile over to Ian, who was standing in the doorway.

'It's time to do that thing we discussed at the funeral.'

After a quick brief, Ian nodded and then walked off. He had a job to do.

Monica squinted her eyes like a hawk at Alexander, while his wound was being treated in the ambulance. Leonardo, cuffed inside the police car, saw Monica standing outside Alexander's ambulance as he was being treated. Her facial expression showed her disgust with herself and the situation. She mouthed the words, 'I'm so sorry' at Leonardo as he was taken off to the police lockup cell, where he would remain incarcerated until his court hearing in the morning.

This was not going to end well for the detective. He had

a motive, and he knew the lawyers were going to play the revenge card, summoning the specter of his partner's death as his reason for having attacked Alexander.

Chapter 16

Wednesday, 7:30 pm

Vince had the whole house to himself, but he was bored. There was only so much TV one could watch. He called Isabella, who agreed to visit the house after she finished a few errands. Awaiting his girlfriend's arrival, Vince took out some scented candles that were stashed in the pantry. The scent of lavender was a regular smell in the household when his mother was around. She had loved her candles and always had backups just in case. As he lit them, a familiar perfume filled the room and childhood memories flooded his mind.

Wanting to set the mood, he dimmed the lights and removed his father's dirty laundry that draped the lounges and the staircase balustrade. Within minutes the house was tidy, the smell was improving and the lights were dim. Background music was the only thing missing. He opened up the tinted glass doors to his father's old Sony stereo unit. In its day it had been supreme, the best, but now it was a little outdated.

After dusting the old stereo unit, he switched on the radio. The first song he tuned into was by Motley Crew. The song was called 'Too young to fall in love,' which was loud and upbeat. He smiled as he turned up the dial and rocked his head up and down like a headbanger to the music. He didn't keep it up for long, though, stopping due to a developing headache building from the erratic movement. Motley Crew did not fit the mood, especially with that chorus. He wanted to get into Isabella's pants tonight; heavy metal was not the answer.

He searched the station and landed on something by Eminem. 'No … no …' said Vince as he continued his search. He then found a radio station that was celebrating the best of George Michael, a collection of his greatest hits. 'Careless whisper' was playing. He knew the lyrics to the song and began to sing it out loud.

'Surprise!' A loud voice shouted, jumping out from behind a wall.

It was Isabella, who let out a wild, uncontrollable burst of laughter. She had let herself in and had waited for the opportune moment to reveal herself.

'I nearly wet my pants,' Vince said, startled at first, flashing a million-dollar smile.

'You're crazy you know that?' said Isabella. 'But that's why I love you.'

Vince approached his girl, pulled her close to his body and told her that he missed her and that he was going to try out for *American Idol* next year.

Isabella laughed again.

'So this is where you grew up?' Isabella said, her eyes glancing around the room. 'This place reminds me of a holiday house my parents once owned in the woods.'

'Yeah I know, the decor is a little outdated.'

'So how's your dad?'

'He's okay. He's gone out drinking so we have the whole house to ourselves,' said Vince with a smile, having one thing on his mind. Standing there in the middle of the room, he decided to tickle her, knowing she was extremely ticklish. Isabella moved out of the way and a chase around the house ensued that ended with her running upstairs. Vince laughed as he viewed her perfect behind from the bottom of the staircase and followed without the need to rush.

Giggles could be heard coming from his bedroom. What was she up to? he wondered.

Then at the entrance to his room, he was struck by her beauty. He stood agape as he saw Isabella silhouetted by a desk lamp situated behind her. She stood in her sexy red lace panties and matching bra, which showed off her perky breasts. Vince could still not believe he had scored a girl like her; he sure was a lucky man. He approached her and obliged by taking off his own shirt. Their warm bodies touched as they embraced passionately, moving first toward the bedroom wall then onto his old single bed. His heart raced as he leaned over her, touching her skin. The rest of his world became an unimportant blur that was banished into the far recesses of his mind. As she lay on the bed, he removed her bra with one hand and licked around her hardened nipples. His tongue moved down, caressing her toned stomach until he could feel her shiver. She raised her head as he moved further down between her legs. Even though they had slept together before, this was going to be a night of passion they would never forget.

Just as they were both caught up in the heat of the moment, Vince heard a sound coming from the hedges outside his bedroom window. It sounded like branches being moved or pressed onto. He reluctantly detached himself from Isabella's warm body to take a quick glance from his window, hoping it was nothing. But what he spotted was a man standing there dressed all in black, holding what looked like a silver briefcase.

Vince knocked on his window to get his attention. But all that did was frighten the man, catching him off guard. He reacted and threw the briefcase under the house, then sprinted down the street to a black sedan.

This was not a good sign. Vince needed to act.

'Babe, quick, get up now!' shouted Vince, worried the briefcase was a bomb.

Isabella obliged and pulled up her skinny jeans and slipped on her diamanté-detail pink top while searching for her bra.

'There's no time for the bra,' Vince warned. He had his jeans and top on in seconds. Just as Isabella grabbed a shoe, an explosion erupted from underneath the house, forcing her face first onto the carpeted floor. The entire house shook as if in an earthquake and parts of the second level collapsed to the first level. If anyone was downstairs, they would have been killed instantly. Vince hovered over Isabella's body to protect her as the walls caught on fire. He shielded her as best as he could, not wanting anything to happen to her. They had seconds before the house was consumed and burned to the ground. Fire and smoke rapidly filled the room, chewing up all the oxygen. They needed to get out before it killed them. As the fire grew it destroyed everything in its path, spreading out of control all around them. The staircase collapsed like toothpicks. The only way out was through the bedroom window. Vince kicked out the glass which fell and shattered on the ground below. He grabbed Isabella by the hand and forced her outside the window ledge.

It was a long way down.

The reaction on Isabella's face was one of horror. 'I can't! I'm scared of heights.'

'You need to trust me, we're going down this tree,' said Vince, who had done this many times before. They had seconds with the blistering heat increasing with each second.

His father hated the camphor tree – it always caused major pipe damage from its roots that were constantly searching for water – but the council never allowed him to cut it down, since it was in a beautiful tree-lined street. It was not a hazard in their opinion. Vince, as a teenager, had used it many times to sneak out of the house. Lucky for them tonight the tree was still there. It was their only way to safety now.

The hardest part of the climb down was the initial reach over to the first branch, a small leap. Once that had been done the rest was easy, but they needed to hurry since the tree's canopy had caught fire, as its dense evergreen foliage rested on the roof. Burnt leaves from above rained down over them. It was now or never.

'Trust me, I'll go first, do what I do.'

Vince jumped and grabbed the first branch with ease.

'Okay, your turn,' he said, hanging on, looking back at his bedroom window.

The room behind Isabella was now completely on fire. The ledge of the window was giving. 'You need to go now,' he shouted.

She threw herself in the direction of the large branch and stretched for dear life. It was a small leap, but it looked as though she was suspended in the air for an aeon. As she grabbed the branch Vince felt a sigh of relief. A thought crossed his mind: if she had mis-jumped or lost her grip, it would have been her death sentence. As she held on, Vince was there to help by placing her right leg onto a lower branch to give her a strong footing.

'You did it!' he said.

Isabella flashed a smile, her teeth were visible against her smoke-blackened face and clothes.

'Now follow me down.'

One branch at a time, they climbed down as the fire engulfed the house. Vince walked around to the front to see the structure burn and collapse in flames, like kindling. All the memories and family possessions now were turned to ash. Isabella comforted him with a warm hug as the sound of sirens approached the house.

It was an inferno, black smoke billowed into the heated air, sending its distinct aroma over the neighborhood. Vince could feel the radiating heat on his face even from a safe distance, as the orange flames continued to burn.

The fire brigade was quick to react with their water hoses. There was no way they were going to salvage the house – it was too far gone. All they could do was stop the neighbor's house from burning down as well.

A man with a lieutenant's helmet stepped up to them and asked, 'Are you two okay? Was it just the two of you in the house?'

'Yes, sir, just us,' replied Vince.

Happy with the response, the lieutenant left the students and went to work, giving his men tasks to be carried out to contain the fire from spreading.

'Isabella, we need to find my dad. He needs to know.'

'The place he went drinking tonight, is it far?' asked Isabella.

'No, let's go.'

Vince got into the driver's seat of Isabella's Toyota Corolla and watched the fire brigade do their thing as they drove away.

The Sapphire Bar was a short ten-minute drive, known to many as a police hotspot. It was a bar with character, inspired by the 1980s. Large movie memorabilia posters filled the room, the jukebox was always playing classic songs and above the bar were colorful neon lights. In the far back of the room a couple of pool tables sat, with some wall-hung TVs that showed whatever sport was playing. At the moment the NBA was playing and the New York Knicks were up by three, a close game.

Vince and Isabella entered the bar. Many eyebrows were raised as they looked like shit, to be frank, covered from head to toe in black smoke, like they had been to war. Vince scanned the room for his father, but only spotted Taylor, who was standing next to two others. They all seemed to be enjoying themselves with a few cold beers. Once Taylor crossed eyes with Vince, he immediately walked over and so did the others.

'What happened to you two?' Detective Taylor asked, patting Vince on the shoulder, which sent soot and ash into the air. Vince coughed, having inhaled way too much smoke.

Vince spoke rapidly, unable to hide the lingering fear of what they had just escaped. 'Is my dad here? I need to talk to him.'

Taylor calmed him down with a hand on his back. 'No, why? What's wrong?'

'Dad told me he was going to be here tonight.'

'That'd be a first,' said a female who slurred her words, having had a few too many to drink. 'Leo joining us for a drink? Ha, that's funny.'

'Sorry, Vince, if you haven't met before, this is Detective Joanne Brown and Detective Tarn Mostrom, we all work together at the bureau.'

While Isabella stood there and listened, Vince noticed one of the detectives he had just been introduced to, gazing down at his girlfriend's breasts. Due to her not wearing a bra, her nipples were showing through her shirt. Tarn sleazily looked up, caught his eye and smiled, which forced Vince to step in front of his girl to cover her from his prying eyes.

'Hang on, that might be him,' said Tarn. His phone was ringing. He retrieved it from his inner jacket pocket and Vince noticed his police badge out in the open, tucked in his pants. A four-digit number was visible: 2426. Everyone gazed up at Tarn as he answered his cell. Within seconds, Tarn's facial expression had turned serious. His eyebrows pulled into a frown; it was definitely bad news.

'He did what?' Tarn shouted.

'What is it?' Vince said, now fixated on the detective and what he was about to reveal.

Tarn blurted out, 'Your dad is being charged for the attempted murder of Alexander Peruggia. He has an expedited court hearing first thing in the morning.'

Vince shook his head.

'That explains tonight,' said Isabella, holding Vince's hand.

'What happened tonight?' Taylor asked.

Isabella answered, 'They blew up the house, we were lucky to survive.'

'This has to be a revenge attack,' retorted Vince.

'You're safe now, do you have a place to stay?' Taylor asked.

'Yeah, my dorm. I was only staying with Dad because of his injury.'

'Okay, go get some rest. I'll pick you up in the morning.'

'Do you think my dad went to kill Peruggia?'

'Anything is possible, kid,' said Tarn in a negative tone.

'Shut up, Tarn,' said Taylor. 'Leo is not a killer.'

'I'm just saying.'

'Well, don't,' Taylor said. 'Vince, you can ask him yourself tomorrow morning.'

'Yeah, I want to find out what the hell is going on,' said Vince.

'Me, too, Vince,' said Taylor. 'Me, too.'

Walking away with his arm around Isabella, one thing was certain in Vince's mind: he needed to distance himself from his father or he could end up dead in the crossfire.

Chapter 17

Thursday, 7 am

Leonardo endured his first night locked up in the police department's holding cell. Being one of their own, the fellow officers and the janitor, Nick, made sure he was comfortable with ample amounts of pillows, blankets and a decent meal to eat. Also, a small TV was rolled into the cell to get him through the night, compliments of the chief. Even though Leonardo was labeled a killer by witnesses at the restaurant and Alexander's men, including Mr. Peruggia himself, his fellow officers did not forget who he was and what he had done for his city.

The cell was situated on the lower level of the police department. It was old, neglected, and maintained like the rest of the building. It had become a lock-down area where the police stored their evidence, confiscated drugs, or anything relating to an acting case.

The fluorescent lights from above flickered as they turned on. Leonardo readjusted his eyes to the bright light. The entire storage floor was lit: he could see long rows of orange metal shelving units displaying boxes in chronological order. Each box had its own tag and number, which gave a brief description of the case in question and the evidence inside.

Noises of people talking echoed from the outer door. Someone swiped a card and punched in the six-digit access code. The door swung open with a jarring sound and in walked Detective Taylor, Vince, two officers and an old janitor who maintained the evidence room meticulously.

Leonardo wanted answers. He believed he had been set up by FBI Agent Monica Anton. Her call informing him of a transaction was complete fiction. Alexander had pre-orchestrated their meeting, with his own objectives to try to buy his way out. Knowing he was going to refuse his offer, plan B was carried out to perfection. All in all, Alexander won either way you looked at it.

Detective Taylor and Vince entered the storage room behind seventy-year-old Nick. His role was to organize and catalogue all evidence brought into the department.

'What was your name again?' Taylor asked as they approached the cell, walking by the elevated shelving units, resembling a storage factory.

'Nickos is my name, but everyone calls-a me Nick.'

'Nice to meet you, Nick. Looks like they've kept you busy down here.'

'Yes, a-very busy.' Nick smiled.

'So, Nick, anything valuable down here?'

'Nah, just small things. Maybe some cocaine if you're lucky. Small stolen items not yet to be collected, case files. Things like that. All the good stuff is sent to downtown headquarters, the new facility. The storage space there is gigantic and the security is state of the art. They have machines that catalogue and organize all the evidence, no need for some old fart like-a me anymore, goddamn computers have taken over.'

Leonardo stood upright, ready to be detained. He hadn't expected to see Vince; he didn't want him to see him this way.

'Good morning, Dad,' said Vince with a smile. 'This is not what I call being a good role model.' His joke was ironic but true.

Taylor laughed.

'Ha, ha, get me out of here,' said Leonardo.

Nick unlocked the cell door, his old hands found the key hole. 'I'm sure this was just a big misunderstanding, sir,' said Nick. 'I've seen you take down some of the biggest criminals off the streets and I know you're a good man.'

Leonardo smiled and thanked him for last night's hospitality. He was then escorted to an elevator, since they were technically in the basement. Arriving at ground level, Taylor led the way and walked his friend through the department's floor, where all sympathetic eyes were on him.

Leonardo glanced over at the chief's office, only to find him in conversation with the deceitful FBI Agent Monica Anton. His blood began to boil as he paused, twitching with anger. He wanted to confront her and give her a backhand, treat her like the bitch she was.

'What's she doing here?' Leonardo asked, clenching his jaw. What did she want with the chief, and what was she up to?

In the chief's office, Monica's body language and tone exuded authority. If one didn't know any better, they'd say she looked more like the boss than Lee did. She was definitely the aggressor in control, a woman who could not be trusted.

'Come on, let's go,' said Taylor, resting his hand on Leonardo's right shoulder.

As Leonardo continued to walk, he kept his eyes on her.

Taylor did not say anything, but it was clear he didn't like her, either.

Vince followed and they exited the building.

The two detectives and Vince reached the car. Taylor hated what they were doing to his friend; the accusations against him were incomprehensible. Leonardo was one of LA's finest detectives. He was a legend in his field, whom everyone idealized. Every officer knew he was a good man, and if the allegations were true, then there must have been a valid reason for his actions. The countless number of criminals he had taken off the street and the numerous families he'd saved were testament to his character. Such actions could only have come from a man with a good heart. He should be praised and given the benefit of the doubt, not sent to court.

Inside the vehicle on the way to the courthouse, Taylor asked straight up, 'Okay tell me, did you do it?'

'No. I was set up, I didn't shoot Alexander. It was my gun, yes. But it was Tony who shot Alexander in the shoulder and framed me for it.'

'So why were you there in the first place? You know he has a restraining order against you.'

'I went there because I was tipped off – by guess who?'

'I don't know. Who?'

'Monica Anton. She told me something was going down last night.'

'And you believed her?' Vince blurted.

'Any opportunity to get this guy, with or without a restraining order, I'll take. You know me.'

'I guess someone else knows you too well also,' Vince replied.

Leonardo hung his head in the passenger seat. 'Good move, Peruggia, you sure did take my queen!' Leonardo whispered.

Putting the car into park, Taylor and Vince had some other bad news to share, news Leonardo was still unaware of. Taylor needed to tell him before he entered the courtroom, just in case someone used it as bait and caused him to react, where the judge would see him in a bad light.

'Hey, Vince, give us a second before we go inside.'

Vince agreed, nudging himself over the seat, exiting the car and shutting the door.

'Leo, I have something I need to tell you, but I need you to stay calm.'

Leonardo stared at Taylor intensely.

'Last night, your house was blown up.'

'You are fucking kidding me!' Leonardo said, clenching his fists and punching the glove compartment. 'Vince, where was Vince at the time?'

'Vince was inside.'

'Mother of God,' Leonardo breathed, his veins rising from his wrists. 'I'm going to kill him.'

'Relax, he obviously made it to safety before the house burned to the ground.'

Leonardo's eyes were now red; tears pooled in them.

Taylor continued. 'After the incident, he came looking for you at the pub, covered in ash. So I organized a patrol car to follow them home.'

Leonardo shook his head and rubbed his eyes. 'Thank you for everything, Luke. You're a good friend.'

'Look, that's all in the past now, let's worry about this court hearing first. We have plenty of time to get Alexander, okay?'

'Okay, fair enough, we better go.' Leonardo stepped out of the vehicle. His judgment awaited.

Chapter 18

Thursday, 8:30 am

The main courtroom to the Los Angeles Superior Court, Santa Monica, was on the second floor, up the tiled staircase to an atrium where sunlight flooded in. A fresh coat of white paint had been applied to the walls and the floors gleamed with new wax.

A large crowd had gathered in the atrium outside the large wooden doors leading to the courtroom. One small group was clustered in a corner, comprised of young men in dark suits, all of whom looked remarkably similar.

The guards opened the courtroom doors at exactly 8:30 am. Detective Taylor escorted Leonardo inside. His was the first case to be dealt with. He sat down in the defendant's chair and waited. The smell of lacquered wood wafted through the cold large space. A young well-groomed lawyer with oily short hair, introduced himself as his appointed lawyer. A deputy burst from the door behind the bench and shouted, 'All rise for the court!'

Everyone in the room jumped to their feet as the Honorable Christian Hawkins stepped up to the bench and asked everyone to be seated. For a judge he was quite young, fifty, slightly overweight with a receding hairline. Speaking into the microphone on the bench, he gave a quick synopsis of the first case in question. Leonardo flexed his fingers, curling and uncurling nervously, listening to the judge speak. He turned to his right at the prosecutor's desk; there was no sign of Alexander. The case had started without the victim, but a team of lawyers was there ready to file suit. Craning his neck to the public gallery seating, he saw Chief Lee Davis, who had just arrived, and Vince, who sat next to a man trying to avoid eye contact. He looked familiar, but Leonardo could not put a name to the face or remember where he had seen him last. The stranger was in his mid-forties, of average height, slender with a fair complexion and wore frameless glasses, behind which his googly blue eyes peered out. He was a man with a forgettable face, with no distinct features other than the glasses he wore.

The man in question always wore a suit and did not speak much, but when he did it was with a raspy voice. Ian Santo kept to himself, a quiet man with a reputation for getting the job done. But his explosives were deadly, making even Osama bin Laden seem like an amateur.

A minute into the judge's introduction, Ian turned to Vince and out of the blue asked a question with a smile. 'Excuse me, do you have two dollars I can borrow?'

'Sorry, sir, I have no money on me,' Vince replied in a soft voice, not realizing the man next to him was responsible for the house explosion last night.

'No, no, no, you don't!' replied Ian, with a slight smile.

The way Vince tilted his head, pursed his lips and lifted an eyebrow, Ian knew he had grabbed his attention, turning now back to the judge who was about to end the summary. Vince shook his head and also turned.

'This looks like a straightforward case,' ended Judge Hawkins. 'The defendant violated Penal Code 273.6pc.'

The young lawyer stood up; he wasn't going down without a fight. 'First, Your Honor the restraining order was handed over the same day as the incident. I'm contesting its merit.'

A man stood up from the opposing table. 'Your Honor, John Peterson from Peterson and Associates. The restraining order took effect yesterday when the defendant was handed the letter drafted by Judge Collins.'

'And when was that letter given to the defendant?' the judge asked.

'I believe it was 5 pm, sir, handed by Chief Lee Davis, who is here today.'

'My client has been a victim of entrapment, set up by the man who's not even here for his own hearing,' said the young lawyer.

'Your Honor, my client is not here because he's in hospital recovering from a gunshot wound.' Mr. Peterson replied in a stronger, deeper voice with a southern accent. 'Your Honor, we have witnesses at the scene who saw Mr. Vancini fire at Mr. Peruggia with the intent to kill!'

The young lawyer stood up with a plea, an even louder voice trying to bombard the experienced Mr. Peterson. 'Mr. Vancini is one of our veteran detectives, loved by his peers and the community. The witnesses have obviously been coerced and threatened. We are dealing with a very dangerous man. I hope you can see what is going on.'

'Your Honor, please – dangerous? Mr. Vancini was the man firing the gun,' said Peterson.

'Okay, okay,' said the judge, ending this tennis match between the counsels. 'This hearing is for the restraining order being violated, anything to do with an attempted murder needs to be dealt with in the Supreme Court.' The judge took a minute, then looked down to where the chief was situated, recognizing his face.

'Mr. Davis, can you confirm you gave Mr. Vancini the restraining order yesterday, making it clear to stay away from Mr. Peruggia? A clear yes or no will suffice.'

Lee Davis stood up and spoke. 'Yes, sir, I did but—'

'No, that's all I need from you, Chief, thank you. You may sit. Okay, Mr. Vancini, can you please stand?'

Leonardo stood up hesitantly, glancing over to Taylor, who ran his fingers through his thick hair. Ian watched and waited; this was the announcement he had been waiting for.

Judge Hawkins's eyes scanned the courtroom. They came to rest on the man in the frameless glasses. A flicker of fear crossed his face as he stared for several seconds. Ian stared right back, unsmiling, his eyelids still, entranced like he was looking deep into the judge's soul. The glare in his eyes reminded the judge what needed to be done.

'I am sorry, Mr. Vancini, but you leave me no choice. You broke the restraining order. The order was clearly given to you and you chose not to adhere to it. You are not above the law and you need to be punished.'

Leonardo sighed in frustration.

'Taking into consideration what you have done for the city, plus the fact this is your first offense, I will fine you five thousand dollars and reduce the standard year sentence to two weeks in a low-risk security facility, starting immediately from today.'

The judge brought his gavel down and the case was closed.

'Jail? I'm going to jail?' Leonardo said, touching the base of his neck. Then he turned over to Vince, who was standing with a blank expression on his face. 'What just happened?'

'I will appeal this, sir,' replied the young lawyer, also surprised with the verdict. 'That was a first.'

No one had expected the judge to hand him jail time. A fine, yes, a talking-to and some anger-management classes to attend, yes. But never jail time. Judge Hawkins was harsh, trying to make an example of the detective.

That was the explanation Judge Hawkins was sticking with, but that wasn't the real reason. Alexander's men had paid him a visit, threatened his life and the lives of the people he loved if he didn't push for jail time. Alexander did not just want Leonardo Vancini to get a slap on the wrist, he wanted him out of the way. Judge Christian Hawkins was yet another puppet in his latest scheme.

Ian's job was to make sure Judge Hawkins went through with it. He was one of the men who had paid him a visit earlier. He was like the devil in his ear, making sure he did as planned, or the death of a loved one would be imminent.

As the handcuffs were slapped on the detective's wrists, Ian walked, expressionless, out of the courthouse, his face a mask. Now he could tell his boss the good news he had been so anxiously awaiting.

Taylor, Lee and Vince stood together watching all this unfold, shocked and speechless as Leonardo was taken away to serve out his sentence. Leonardo dreaded his time in jail, even if it was only two weeks. It was as if you faced a lottery on arrival. What's your new cellmate going to be like? Will he be a serial killer or an unpredictable psychopath, or will he be some poor lad suffering from some kind of mental illness who should be in a hospital? And if you're really unlucky, you could be bunking up with a big bull on the prowl for fresh meat. Occasionally, in prison, homophobia isn't so much a prejudice as a survival instinct. Prison life was about to get a lot more difficult when the word got out that he was a detective. A long journey awaited him and it wasn't going to be easy.

Chapter 19

Thursday, 9 am

Alexander's Beach Club was voted the best fitness center in all of Santa Monica by *American Fitness Magazine*. Alexander was proud of his business: this was his home, his prized possession. No expense had been spared in its construction, overlooking the Pacific Ocean. Not everything was as it seemed, though: after the global financial crisis, even Alexander was feeling the pressure. No matter how many accolades the place acquired, he struggled to pay the mortgage, which had escalated into the millions. With the failure of the first bank robbery, only a couple of blocks away from the establishment, a second heist was in the pipeline. He would rather die than foreclose on the estate.

One of its main attractions was a large gymnasium featuring a full-size boxing ring for members to use, positioned right in the center of a large, open space. Walls of mirrors encircled this multi-levelled gym, with the best machinery money could buy. Aerobics, spin, body pump and many other classes were also held day and night for members.

The lighting above the boxing ring gave off a dim yellow glow, provided by a few bulbs hanging from long wires. Alexander had visited it with his son Phil every Thursday for a sparring match, and it had become a ritual of theirs. Neither of the two had held back once in the ropes. What they had, though, was a love of competition, and that gave them heart and drive, a little extra stamina that allowed them to look in the mirror afterwards and still call themselves family men. Even though Alexander would never admit it, Phil was his favorite son: he was strong, powerful and commanded respect, attributes his father loved and missed dearly. He could never be replaced.

Today was the first Thursday after Phil's death. Alexander walked into his gymnasium, ready to go a few rounds with his youngest son, Joey, even though his wound was still fresh. He wanted to test him, see what he was made of. He stepped inside shirtless, his arm wrapped up tight. His tanned body, well looked after for his age, was lean and as hard as a tree trunk. Scars from knife wounds could be clearly seen, testifying to the type of life he had lived.

Joey's frame was much thinner than his older brother's and father's; he was not proud to show off his gaunt frame in the singlet he wore. Tucking his long blondish hair behind his ears and stretching out his hands, he was ready to fight. He remembered the boxing matches that had taken place in this spot with Phil. He was nervous: his father was a fit man and Joey knew he wasn't going to hold back even with a wounded arm. He prayed that his father was going to take it easy on him.

He needed to be respected. He had always been protected, never having to fight. Everyone knew he was Phil's younger brother and they had kept their distance, even when he'd deserved a beating. Now that his guardian angel was gone, no one was watching over him anymore: he needed to step up and have a stronger presence.

Frank, James and Tony watched on as Joey circled around his father, his blue gloves up in the air. One thing he did have over his father, though, was speed. The boys outside the ring cheered him on.

'Let's see if he can make it past the first round,' joked Frank.

'You're not helping, guys,' said Joey, shaking off the nerves.

'You have no chance, boy,' said Tony. 'Your father's an old-school fighter. He fought against countless boxers and could go the rounds with the best of them. Soon you're going to understand what it feels like to be on the receiving end of one of his punches.'

The bell rang.

'You look really good for an old man,' said Joey, feeling his father out.

Alexander moved left and right like a well-trained boxer. He faked right, then threw a brick-solid left at the unsuspecting Joey. His head had been moving to Alexander's left to escape the right. But the left caught his cheekbone and snapped his head to the right. There, another of his father's rights was awaiting.

Joey wasn't too happy just now.

'Okay, did you see what happened there, son?' Alexander asked with a snide grin, trying to explain what Joey had done wrong. Joey shook his head several times and shifted his jaw from side to side. There was a look of consternation on his glistening features.

'Ouch! I've just lost all feeling in the left side of my face,' sputtered Joey, hurt and upset, but continuing with the spar, wanting to prove to his father he wasn't going to back down. It wasn't about winning. It was about taking the hit and showing he was never going to quit.

'Take it easy on him, boss,' yelled Tony from outside. 'Or you'll have no sons.'

Alexander smiled and said, 'This brings back so many good memories.' He was ready to go in for his next assault.

Joey squeezed his lips together, lowered his strong brow and unleashed a feisty left uppercut. Alexander moved his head to the other side, when Joey followed with a right hook. He lifted his hands in front of his face and took the blow on his red gloves.

'That's it! See, you do have Peruggia blood in you,' Alexander said, protecting his face.

James and Frank cheered as the youngest member of the family stood toe-to-toe with his father.

'You have balls, kid, I'll give you that,' said Tony.

While Joey had his father protecting his face, he managed to sneak in a right, which caught him on the chin. Alexander stepped back. He wasn't laughing anymore.

'Come on, old man,' said Joey with a grin, right into it.

'You like it dirty, my boy. I like that,' said Alexander, his biceps tightening as he raised his arms. 'I won't make that mistake again.'

Alexander faked left. Joey's eyes were on his father's shoulders. He saw a momentary opening and tried to take advantage of it with a right cross. Alexander had enough room to jump back, out of the way, then step back in. As he did, he put everything into a right uppercut.

Joey was trapped. He couldn't get his arm back and gloves up fast enough to protect himself. There was nothing to do but take what was coming. And what was coming was a right uppercut that started just above Alexander's knee and ended on Joey's jaw. Joey flopped back against the cushions, tried to hold onto the ropes with his gloves and landed on the floor. Blood seeped from the corner of his mouth. Alexander stood over him and offered his hand. The fight was definitely over. Tony threw the boy a clean white towel to clean the blood that was now dripping onto the canvas.

'Thanks for going easy on me, Dad.'

'Life was not meant to be easy, son,' said Alexander, taking off his gloves and stepping out of the ring. 'You did alright for our first match. Remember the rules. When the gloves come off, you leave the fight behind. No hard feelings, boy, *capiche*?'

Joey agreed with a nod, dabbing the white towel over his mouth. Today he understood why so many people feared his father.

'So we good for next Thursday?' Alexander asked.

Joey tried to smile.

At 9:30 am, Tony handed Alexander a cell and said, 'It's Ian.'

Alexander took it eagerly. He had desperately been waiting for this call.

'Yes, Ian?'

'Hello, boss, I have news,' said Ian.

'Is it done?' Alexander asked, wanting to hear good news. Bad news didn't sit well with him.

'Yes, sir, he got a five-thousand-dollar fine and two weeks in jail.'

'Bravo, Ian, bravo,' Alexander said, hanging up.

Everything was going as planned.

Chapter 20

Vince caught a lift with Taylor, who was quiet the whole drive home. There was nothing to say. It was what it was. Leonardo needed to do the time. The sentence had been set in stone the minute the judge's gavel had cracked on the sound block.

Pulling up to a parking spot at the campus, Vince noticed a patrol car. The officer inside was bald on top and looked like he had eaten way too many donuts.

'He's here to keep an eye on you,' said Taylor. 'This is his number, call him if you need to.'

Vince sighed and took the police officer's business card.

'Don't judge a book by its cover, he's a good officer,' said Taylor. 'I need to get back to the office and go through the evidence found at your place.'

'What are you hoping to find?'

'I want to see if the same explosives used at the Santa Monica Pier and the Trinity Church are connected.'

'And if they are?'

'Don't you worry about that, just do me a favor and keep a low profile.'

'Hey, by the way, did you guys end up finding the two million dollars at the golf course?'

'No ... That's another thing I have to organize. I'm waiting till the end of the week, let things calm down a little at work, before I give it up to logistics to solve.'

'Why wait?'

'This morning before I picked you up, I received a large damages bill from the Penmar Golf Course for destroying their grounds. When the chief finds out, he's gonna flip and I don't want him to find out as yet.'

'Seems like you have your hands full.' Vince thanked the detective, stepped into his dorm room and dropped on his bed. Mixed emotions ran through his head as he lay still. Today's turn of events had drained him emotionally. He felt like he had run a marathon. Lying there on his pillow, his nostrils flared, the smell of smoke and burnt timber reeked from the linen. On the floor on his side of the room lay his clothes from that horrific night. His once white shirt was now a shade of grey, needing a good wash. In fact, the whole room needed freshening up, as the scent hung in the air.

Gary walked into the room dressed in his sports gear, covered in sweat. He had been hitting the gym hard these past few weeks, trying to get into shape. 'Hey, Romeo, how was your father's hearing today?'

'Not good. He was sentenced to two weeks' jail time.'

'You're kidding me, I don't believe it,' said Gary.

'Me neither, bro. Me neither.' Vince, shook his head and leaned over to pick up his shirt from the ground.

Gary left Vince to take a shower. Sticking his head back around like a meerkat he said, 'Oh yeah, Joseph is looking for you.'

'How come?'

'Who knows? He sounded serious, though. Give him a call.'

Joseph Matter was the college accountant. He was a short man with a husky voice, who wore a hat to cover his bald head. His main role was to make sure all school fees were paid and all budgets balanced for the campus.

'Hi, Joseph, it's Vince. I hear you're looking for me?'

'Yes. Vince, your fees are overdue and have been declined.'

'What do you mean declined?' said Vince, raising his voice.

'Well it seems the direct debit account you designated has no money in it. I tried twice.'

'That's impossible, I have thousands in that account.'

'Sorry to give you this news, Vince, but I've been instructed by the dean that you have until next Monday to pay all your fees, or you'll be evicted from school.'

UCLA was a popular school. There were students out there with money who wanted in. Vince was no special case.

'Hang on, Joseph, let me get back to you.'

'You have until Monday.'

Vince thought to himself: what a heartless wanker; where was the compassion? If what Joseph was saying was true, he was screwed.

Leaping onto his chair, he rolled toward his computer terminal, which was an iMac he and Gary shared. The first thing he needed to do was log into his bank account. After entering his access number and password, he was in. He leaned in closer to see the balance. His eyes widened and his mouth fell open. He blinked a couple of times to see the balance more clearly.

The amount showing was two dollars. 'Motherfucker ... fuck!' yelled Vince. What had happened to all his money?

'What's wrong?' said Gary, entering the room with a towel around his waist. 'Why the cursing?'

'I think my bank account has been hacked.'

'You're kidding me,' said Gary.

'I'm not joking, my balance is only showing two dollars.'

'It's probably just the display, give the bank a call,' said Gary, trying to reassure him.

'Good point, I'll call them now.' Vince picked up the phone again.

A man with an Indian accent picked up the phone at the bank's customer service.

'Hello my name is Arjun, how can I help you, sir?'

'Hello, I think my bank account has been hacked.'

'I'm sorry to hear that, sir. Before I continue can I ask a few questions to verify who I am speaking with?'

After gathering Vince's full name, date of birth, place of residence and mother's maiden name, Arjun accessed his account and pulled up his record.

Vince waited patiently.

'Okay, Vince, thanks for waiting. It shows you have a balance of two dollars.'

Vince cursed again in silence. 'How could this be happening? I had a little over ten thousand dollars. You can see why I'm upset.'

'Let me see. Yes, a large transfer took place yesterday morning.'

'I didn't do that. Someone has hacked into my account. Is there anything you can do? Please, my entire degree depends on that money.'

'Okay, Vince, if it wasn't you who transferred the money, then we have to get the police involved and fill out a form. This kind of thing, believe it or not, is common and usually gets resolved. You should have your money back within a month.'

'A month!' shouted Vince. 'That's way too long.'

He knew Joseph the accountant would not accept any excuse or give him an extension to pay. He was a stubborn man, with strict orders directly from the dean himself. This was not personal; after all, education was a business.

Arjun apologized for his situation and told Vince he was going to speak to the authorities on his behalf, to try to get to the bottom of it ASAP and find out whose bank account the money had been transferred to.

Vince thanked the man for his help and hung up the phone. With a surge of adrenaline he stood up and kicked his chair to the other side of the room. A sudden realization hit him: in the court house, the strange man with the odd question, then his ridiculous answer. 'No, no, no you don't.' Referring to him having no money. Was that a dig? Could he be involved in his hacked bank account?

Vince's superstitious mother had always said that bad things happened in threes. But this was no coincidence. Someone had tried to end his life last night, his father had been framed, and now his bank account was hacked. If you were a betting man, you would put your money on Mr. Peruggia being behind this.

An eye for an eye: he wanted revenge for his son's death.

First he wanted to murder Vince, but after the failed attempt, he realized there were better ways to distribute pain and hardship, such as taking away the one thing he had worked so hard for, his education.

No words could explain how he felt at this very moment. Time was ticking by. If he didn't come up with the money somehow he was possibly going to be homeless.

Chapter 21

Gary was dressed, ready for his Thursday-afternoon art class. Vince stood with a blank expression on his face, staring at a spot on the wall, oblivious to the TV playing in the corner of the room. He could never stand in one place for more than a minute. His friends always laughed at his possible ADHD.

'You okay, man? What happened with the bank?' Gary asked.

Vince was still focusing, like he was about to have a meltdown. 'No, I'm fucked, I have nothing,' said Vince, 'I was told it could take up to a month to get my money back.'

'Okay, that's good, so you'll get it back,' said Gary enthusiastically.

'No it's not. My deadline is this Monday,' said Vince.

'What an asshole. Surely Joseph can give you time to recover the money?'

'Nope, that's exactly it. It's not just Joseph; it's coming from the dean.'

'Vince, you know if I had the money—'

'I know, Gary. I'll find a way. You go to class, you're going to be late,' Vince said, needing the time alone to think.

'Okay. Look, don't worry. I'm sure we can borrow ten-k from some of the rich kids,' said Gary.

Vince smiled as his roommate left the room, knowing this wasn't going to happen. It was easier to borrow money from a poor kid than a rich kid; rich kids stayed rich because they were tight with their money.

He fell face down on his pillow. Thirty minutes passed. Feeling the need to go to the bathroom, he sat up on the bed and glanced over to the TV left on. The nap had helped, but he had not rationalized the fact that he had to prepare himself for what was about to happen in a couple of days.

He rubbed his eyes and found himself staring at a commercial. It was more of a public invitation, to come along and help raise money for disabled kids. A large community event and everyone was invited. The venue was the popular Marine Park, to take place the next day, sponsored by millionaire philanthropist Donald Hemsworth. He couldn't have kids of his own, so he dedicated his life to giving back. The commercial continued with pictures of the park's many attractions: mothers with strollers laughing, kids eating ice-cream, playing on swings, climbing structures, balloons and streamers in the air, ending with a wide angle shot fading to black with the location details in a large bold serif font.

Come on down this Friday
Marine Park – 1406 Marine St, Santa Monica
Adjacent to LA's famous nine-hole golf course,
The Penmar Golf Course

Vince's eyes widened. The commercial had jotted something in his memory. A pattern? Scrambling to his computer, he hit the spacebar to bring it to life. Once the screen came to, he opened Google's home page. He found the maps icon on the far-right-hand side and typed in the address: *Penmar Golf Course Santa Monica*.

Google maps did its thing and zoomed right into large green shapes of the Penmar Golf Course. He noticed its close proximity to the Marine Park and tapped the screen with his finger. His mind swerved with possibilities. He had an epiphany. Now he typed in: *Marine Park Santa Monica*.

A list of search fields displayed, with the very first being the City of Santa Monica, Places, Parks & Beaches. He entered the page and searched through pictures of the park. He then grabbed a piece of paper from his printer and a pen and wrote down:

It lies beneath the third?

<u>*P.ENIMAR*</u> *GC?*

The two clues left behind by Phil Peruggia, shared a couple of days ago by Detective Taylor back at the house. Now a charred ruin.

Vince underlined the second sentence.

<u>*P.ENIMAR GC*</u>

He drew a line through the letter M and wrote it again below. Then another line through the letter A, and wrote it below. He continued with the letters R, I, N, then E. Vince had just written down the word 'Marine.'

The letter P was separated with a period. Was it P for park? Could it be that simple? Could the clue left behind be an anagram, as he had initially mentioned to the detective?

The police analysis had missed a vital bit of information. Penmar Golf course was not spelt with an I. Phil had ingeniously added it to spell the word 'Marine.' He'd no doubt known the police would read, 'It lies beneath the third' and assume it referred to the third hole of the Penmar Golf course. A red herring that seemed to have worked – at least up until now.

Vince had possibly deciphered the location of the two million dollars. A sense of excitement rushed through his body. But what did 'It lies beneath the third' and the last bit 'GC' mean, if it wasn't 'Golf Course.'

He knew he needed to personally visit the park and work it out while he was there. At this point he was willing to try anything. He was desperate and time was running out. He had nothing to lose and everything to gain.

Chapter 22

Friday, 9:30 am

The morning sun hit Joey directly in his bruised and inflamed eye, caused by one of his father's punches yesterday. Moving away from the peering sunlight, he stood up to face the panoramic beach view from within his luxurious bedroom suite at his father's club.

Alexander's Beach Club was not only the place the crew congregated every day, it was their home. Tony, Ian, Frank and James all had bedroom suites, too. Alexander kept the most exquisite suite in the penthouse for himself and his girlfriend, Victoria. All the men lived extravagant lives which had many perks, free accommodation, free meals and drinks, and they had all the facilities at their disposal. That included a garage filled with exotic cars such as the Aston Martin Vanquish, Lamborghini Diablo, Ferrari Testarossa and many other standard vehicles like an AMG Mercedes, Audi R8 and a couple of Range Rovers.

Alexander made sure his blood brothers were properly cared for, that's how he earned their eternal respect. They became his extended family. All of the men would dive in front of a bullet for him, their loyalty was unquestionable.

Joey turned on the shower. It was neither strong nor hot enough to revitalize his sore body or numb mind. But it went some way to wash out his mouth and soothe his weary arms.

Outside in the courtyard, a meeting was being held today to discuss something important. Joey was under-dressed for the occasion, wearing white shorts that came above his knees and a plain blue polo shirt. He greeted a female staff member, as the staircase reached ground level to a marbled foyer flooded with natural sunlight. This was designed with a palace in mind, a royal welcome to all who walked through its lobby.

On the sandy beach sat a dozen white tables and chairs that invited club members outside to have a meal after a workout and enjoy the sun. Many regulars made it their weekend ritual and loved to sit by the beach and have a coffee or two.

On this Friday morning, Alexander, Tony, Frank, James and even Victoria were out enjoying each other's company and having their usual five-star breakfast catered for by the club. No expense was spared as large fruit platters sat on the table. Ian and Monica were the only ones absent from the party.

Joey was the last to arrive, walking onto the sandy beach barefoot. He almost smiled as the sand felt warm and soothing underneath his feet.

'Look, it's Rocky Balboa,' joked Alexander.

Joey sat down in an empty chair. His face displayed for all to see a much bigger swollen eye.

Frank and James joined in on the laughter and teasing. Frank held his fist in the air and yelled out, 'Adrian!'

James and Alexander laughed some more.

'Ha, ha. Very funny,' said Joey.

Victoria ignored the men's constant pestering and poured Joey a fresh cup of coffee. He smiled and thanked her as he lifted the cup to his mouth. Even though he was being ridiculed, he could feel the love within the group. They were a tight unit: they lived together, ate together and took care of each other, as a family would.

Alexander glided into the group with his back toward the club, having something to say. He glanced around and made sure no one else could listen in. He sat down on the sand, his expression dark and enigmatic. Victoria stood behind him, massaging his neck. He seemed not to notice. He had called this meeting to explain the next big heist. Everyone fixated on him, like he was a lord and they were his disciples. In a calm voice he said, 'We're breaking into the downtown LAPD headquarters.'

'What?' said Tony, taken aback.

Frank leaned forward in his chair, knowing the answer. 'Because the six million dollars we lost at Wilshire is there.'

'That's absolutely correct, Frank,' said Alexander. 'All recovered money, by law, needs to be counted and documented before it's returned to the bank it was taken from. It's an insurance thing.'

'How long is it there for?' Tony asked.

'The police must hold onto the stolen item for seven working days, which means we have until Tuesday to get our money back, less the two million that Phil hid, of course. That's gone.'

'I can't believe Phil didn't leave a note or something to the whereabouts of the two million dollars,' said Victoria in her seductive Spanish accent, rubbing her fingers through her man's hair.

Alexander paused, then nodded his head. He seemed to agree with her.

'How do you know all this information, boss?' Tony asked. 'I'm intrigued by your knowledge of police procedure.'

Alexander turned to face Tony on his right and said, 'Tony, Tony, Tony, I'm the hand up the *Mona Lisa*'s skirt, I know and hear everything, my friend.'

Joey and Frank laughed.

Victoria playfully pushed Alexander forwards and said, 'What are you doing with your hand up the *Mona Lisa*'s skirt?'

Alexander smiled and refocused, there was more to tell. 'Do you realize the police have been after me for over ten years, but never had any substantial evidence to arrest me? I have detectives on my ass waiting for me to make a mistake, like Vancini, and look at him now. He's doing time.'

'So who's taking the lead? Phil was irreplaceable,' James said in a deep voice, flexing his biceps.

'How about me?' said Joey, eager to participate, looking the part with his bruised eye.

'Hey, Rocky,' laughed Frank, pointing at Joey. 'Alexander, I think you punched your son once too hard.'

James and Tony giggled.

'You ready for the big league, son?'

Joey nodded, not having the slightest idea what he was getting himself into.

Tony and Frank turned away.

Joey could sense their nervousness and apprehension.

'Why the worried face, Tony?' asked Alexander.

'No disrespect, Joey, but you are no leader. Your brother was a leader. His presence alone demanded respect. You look out of place, like a skinny kid trying out for quarterback.'

Frank laughed.

Alexander said, 'That's harsh, don't hold back, old man.'

'Sorry, Joey,' said Tony, 'I'm just stating the obvious.'

'It's okay, Tony, I understand,' said Joey.

'Okay, hang on, before we all get too excited, you realize the security system is state of the art. It's the police headquarters, for God's sake,' said Frank, the technician who had hacked Vince's bank account in minutes.

Alexander replied, 'I have someone on the inside.'

'Can he give us universal access to all levels of the building?' asked Frank. 'Or will I be needed to do my thing?'

'He'll give us full access, not a problem.'

'Full access – who is he?' Tony asked. 'It's not Tarn Mostrom, is it?'

'No, not using Tarn this time. Think more senior.'

Joey watched the men contemplate who it could be and opened his mouth. It was obvious, it could only be one man.

'Is it the chief, Dad?'

'Bingo, it doesn't get any higher than that,' said Alexander.

'I can't believe you have the Chief of Police on our side,' Tony said. 'This heist might stand a chance.'

'Lee Davis is going to become a wealthy man,' said Alexander. 'His role is simple: shut down all security cameras and turn off the alarm system to allow us into the building undetected. Having him on our side will make this a walk in the park.'

'But can you trust him?' Tony said, scratching his neck. 'It could be a trap.'

'No, it's not a trap. Lee will help us. If it makes you feel any better, this is not the first time I've done business with Lee. He's been a vital player in my reign these last couple of years. I've been using Monica as my direct link with him.'

'I don't know, this one concerns me, boss,' said Tony, the oldest and most cautious of the group. Many of the men looked up to Tony as he rubbed his greying beard. He was considered second-in-charge, Alexander's right-hand man. Tony, like Alexander, never took part in the actual robberies; they were the men on the hill.

'Everything concerns you, Tony,' said Alexander.

James and Frank smirked. He was always worried about something: his cholesterol, the sun, his food – the list went on.

'Look, Lee is retiring soon, it's in his best interests to cooperate. His share is half a mill. Why wouldn't he do it? All he has to do is give up a swipe card, close the security system from the inside and look the other way.'

'I'm just playing devil's advocate here, boss, but what if he jumps ship?'

'He won't,' said Alexander, shaking his head. 'I sent in Monica to make sure of that.'

'What, Monica? I know she was your son's girl, but she can't be trusted either. There's something about her, the way she stares at me with those cat eyes,' said Tony.

'You can trust her,' interrupted Joey, who thought of Monica as part of the family.

Alexander reassured his men, especially plump Tony, that the stars had aligned for this exploit. All the logistics had been planned out with key people playing their role. It wasn't going to get any easier.

Joey knew this job was critical for Alexander to keep his multimillion-dollar beach club. Without this money he would be forced to sell the one thing he had truly built up from scratch. It wasn't just a venue to his father, it showcased his wealth and power. A place he and his men called home. There was absolutely no way anyone was taking it away from him.

'Monday night we go. Joey, you're taking the lead. Make me proud.'

Chapter 23

The backpack strapped to his shoulders was packed with a pair of binoculars, a set of screwdrivers, a cell phone and a bottle of water. Vince was on a mission and the Marine Park was his destination. It was his desperate ploy to solve the clue and find the money, as time was running out.

Gary entered the room while he was on his way out. 'Hey, man, don't forget, my party's on tonight.'

'Can I take your car?' Vince replied. 'I have a few urgent errands to run.' Gary's party was the last thing on his mind. This felt like this was the longest weekend of his life.

'Yeah, just make sure she comes back in one piece.'

Vince snatched the keys and left in a hurry.

He parked Gary's rundown 2002 Ford Mustang in the Marine Park's parking lot. The loud crack of the exhaust as the engine was switched off had people nearby jumping in fright. The original metallic blue had faded, the engine needed reconditioning and the only new thing about it was the white dice that hung from the rearview mirror. It was Gary's project to rebuild her, but it had never amounted to anything.

The park was crowded with people. Children flurried around the perimeter, playing in the sand and on the numerous monkey bars. Mothers pushed their prams, fathers helped with the sausage sizzle. There were balloons and streamers all over the place. The event planner had gone all out to make this fund-raiser a success. No expense had been spared as jumping castles were erected and an ice cream truck was parked offering free treats.

Vince walked into the sandy playground with eyes wide open, wondering where to start. The Marine Park was expansive, the money could be hidden in so many places. He walked through the center and used all his shoulder strength to climb up a tall, well-established birch tree. Its branches were white in color and its huge trunk was seemingly hollow in the middle. The hole was only accessible from a point eight feet above the ground where the first branches reached out from its center. A possible hiding spot. After a near slip to the ground he was disappointed to find nothing in its core except for a bird's nest. Now on the ground, he clutched his right shoulder, as an old injury flared up again caused by the climb. It was his Achilles' heel; every now and then nerves in his shoulder would cause him grief. The only way to fix this problem was to have surgery, but that came at a cost. He chose to live with it and had taken up swimming to help manage the pain.

Hurt and back to square one, the hunt continued. A small bridge was up ahead, no water below, just two palm trees on either side. It was a decorative blue bridge that led to a set of swings. He climbed over the wooden railing, placing all his weight on his left arm, and jumped down to a sandy bed below to find a couple of teenagers kissing. Their intimacy interrupted, they fled a little red-faced, leaving Vince alone underneath the bridge. Looking down at his feet to the soft earth, it seemed like a brilliant spot to bury something. Knees in the sand, he began to shovel around the area with his left hand. First the center, then to his right, then left, hitting nothing but rock in every direction. It was evident this wasn't the spot – another disappointment.

'Damn,' said Vince, picking himself off the ground.

A couple of hours had passed and he was not getting anywhere. Maybe he was wrong: the clue left behind was probably just a scam. His dream of finding the money was just that now, a dream. Giving up and walking back toward the Mustang, a small nine-foot building in red brick could be seen from where he was. It was the park's public restrooms. Could the money be in there? wondered Vince. It didn't hurt to check. He entered the men's toilet and searched under wooden benches and around cavities in the brickwork, searching for a loose brick which might indicate a hollow section beyond.

Nothing but webs.

Next were the female toilets. In the doorway he shouted, 'Hello? Anyone inside?'

No answer.

After a quick glance he ran in to have a look. Exiting, an elderly woman looked at him with a suspicious eye and said, 'What are you doing, boy? This is the ladies.'

'Sorry, ma'am, when you gotta go, you gotta go,' replied Vince, walking out in a hurry toward the back of the building before she made a big fuss. It was time to call it a day. Finding the money in this enormous park was like finding a needle in a haystack. Defeated and with a sore shoulder, he glanced up to the blue sky and stretched his arms backwards and stuck his chest out to ease the stiffness he was feeling.

While looking up, he could clearly see the silver tin roof of the restroom building. As he focused on the roof, he noticed something. It was a stray golf ball. It must have been hit over the bushy wall of trees, planted around the perimeter of the Penmar Golf Course.

Vince, his father's son, had a good eye for problem solving. A thought crossed his mind: he had to retrace Phil's steps after leaving the golf course, if he had indeed entered the Marine Park.

A vast wall of conifer trees encircled the course with no sign of a hole. Or was there? If found, it would give him a starting point to retrace Phil's footsteps, hoping it would lead him to the money.

He stepped over to the small fence that marked the boundary between the Penmar Golf Course and the Marine Park. After jumping over the fence, his hunt led him around the perimeter, searching for a gap. A hole, large enough for a man to squeeze through the bushy wall.

Almost two hundred feet into his search and holding his left hand against his right shoulder, he found a branch jutting outward with police evidence tape stuck on it. He pulled on it to reveal the small gap low to the ground. The branch had been wedged in from the outside to conceal the hole within. It was big enough for an average person to squeeze through. The icing on the cake was when he saw small traces of blood on surrounding leaves, but the blood trail stopped there. It was clear that the police knew he had escaped from here, but what they did not know was where he had hidden the money.

Vince began to visualize the event, with Phil wounded, running for his life from the police and deciding to hide the money somewhere. He turned around, facing the open field and saw a bridge, palm trees, seesaws, climbing structures and various other playing equipment, including five colorful wooden cubbyhouses. The one painted in gold caught his attention. It was the closest one to his position.

Remembering the initials 'GC' in the clue left behind, he wondered if it might simply mean 'Gold Cubbyhouse.' Was the money buried below?

Adrenaline pumped through his veins, as if he had drunk a gallon of coffee. The excitement of finding it first made him feel blessed, like a child on a treasure hunt. He approached the small wooden house with a bounce in his step. Two children were inside playing. Wooden slats formed the base that sat on top of a sandpit. He stood back outside and waited for the children to leave, as their parents were watching.

If the money was buried below, if he wanted to have any

chance of keeping it for himself, he needed to be cautious, patient, not draw any attention to himself. He sat down with his feet in the sand and waited, with his backpack to his side.

'Come on, kids, go,' he said to himself. This was going to be a long wait.

The three-year-old girl wearing a cute pink dress and pink *Dora the Explorer* shirt began to speak to her mother who was listening. She said, 'Mommy house number two.'

'What's that, Kiara?' replied her mother.

'It's number two.'

'That's right, Kiara, that's the number two cubbyhouse.'

Vince rose like a tiger about to pounce, to take a proper look. The child was right: the number two was branded on the side of the house.

'It lies beneath the third,' he said, grabbing the binoculars from his backpack. 'Where are you?'

He searched one house after the other and found number five, a blue cubbyhouse. Four was a red one, until he spotted far in the distance beside a cluster of palm trees the number three house painted in green.

'Shit, that's it,' he said, weak at the knees. He had solved it.

'It lies beneath the third. P.ENIMAR GC' was translated to: 'Buried in the Marine Park, in the number three green cubbyhouse.'

Chapter 24

Vince approached the green cubbyhouse and thankfully, there were no children in sight, just a group of teenagers playing soccer nearby. Too engaged in their game, they were not going to be a problem.

He ducked inside the entrance, his backpack to his side. Inside, his legs stretched out comfortably. There was enough room for someone his size. Even though the day was sunny and bright, the interior was on the darkish side as the timber was painted a dark viridian green.

He took out his iPhone and swiped through his apps to find the flashlight icon. After a few taps on the screen a bright light shone from the phone's camera light. He left his phone on the ground and used a Phillips head screwdriver from his bag to remove the wooden slats one at a time. The screws seemed to turn with ease, as if they were new or had recently been used.

Three timber slats were moved to one side, on top of each other, revealing the yellow sand beneath. The phone's flashlight shadowed the grooves in the sand, like the Sahara desert. Vince felt like Howard Carter, the man who discovered the tomb of Tutankhamun. His fortune awaited. He dug into the soft sand with both hands, until he felt a sharp pain.

He had scraped his arm against a loose nail sticking out from the base. He shook it off and continued. The scratch wasn't going to stop him from digging. Left and right he scooped and dug with his hands. Deeper and deeper.

His fingers touched something. His breath caught in his throat.

Some sort of fabric. A strap. A black backpack was pulled upwards as sand cascaded back down into the hole he had created.

'I found it,' he said, feeling the shape of the bills pushing out against the pack. A shiver ran down his spine as he undid the clips to reveal the loot. A fortune in millions right in front of his ecstatic face.

Vince had found the two million dollars, and had a fist full of hundred-dollar bills in his hand. His mind swirled. This was no imagination or dream, this was reality and it was going to change his life forever.

The time to indulge needed to wait. The first thing was to be smart and leave the cubbyhouse as he had found it. Peeking outside, making sure the coast was clear, he transferred all the bills into his backpack in a hurry. He then squashed the bank robber's backpack inside his own and zipped it closed. He thought about leaving it behind but decided if it was gone no one would be the wiser.

A soccer ball rolled over his way. Vince needed to hurry and not be seen. The timber slats were turned back over and put in place like a jigsaw puzzle. He placed the backpack over his shoulder, held his binoculars in his hand as there was no room left in his bag, and strolled over to the car. It took all his control not to sprint. The old lady he'd bumped into in front of the women's toilets examined him with a suspicious eye. Vince ignored her stare and left.

The late afternoon had come round so quickly. The door to his dorm room was locked in a hurry. The anticipation of seeing all that beautiful green before him again was overwhelming. To find any bag filled to the brim with cash was something out of a movie, but this was no movie or dream, this was real. He unclipped the backpack and tipped it upside down, emptying its contents onto the bed. Bundles of hundred-dollar bills piled up on top of each other, forming a small mountain on his blue duvet, which had now turned green, and what seemed like a thousand Benjamin Franklins stared back at him.

Vince exhaled and picked up a bundle. He tore off the paper banknote strap in its center that held the money together. He wanted to know how much was in each bundle, so he began to count the money in groups of ten, equating to one thousand dollars each. Grouping the money in thousand-dollar piles on the floor, he counted ten piles. So each bundle equaled ten thousand dollars, with a thickness of about ten millimeters each.

Tossing each bundle back into his bag, he kept count. He needed to know what he was playing with. It took half an hour, and the count was one hundred and ninety-five. Total amount: $1,950,000.

Yes, he had in his possession millions, but his life needed to appear to remain the same. This included his work schedule and, most importantly, keeping his spending to a minimum in order to avoid any unwanted suspicion. Keeping a low profile meant no expensive purchases.

He took the money bag off the bed and hid it away in his standalone white wooden wardrobe, which was a gift from his mother. Two blankets and a spare pillow were placed on top to conceal it, until he found a more suitable hiding spot.

Rostered for work soon, he swiftly showered, changed into a black collared shirt and shoved ten or so hundred-dollar bills into his dark blue jeans. Double-checking the front door to his room was locked, he left for work, this time with two million reasons to smile.

Chapter 25

Friday, 6 pm

There was never a dull moment in the club for Joey. Tonight a formal black-tie event was being held in the large Grand Royal function room, designated mostly for weddings. As the guests arrived to the venue, they were escorted to their round tables. Each table was set up with sterling-silver cutlery and fine-bone china. Cotton napkins were folded into swans and perched in front of every seat, the initials ABC (Alexander's Beach Club) embroidered on their side. The center of each table featured a large white candelabra, creating a warm and romantic atmosphere.

The Alexander Beach Club had been awarded Best Function Center three years in a row. His father thrived on having an establishment where his staff members were considered as his adopted family. To be working for the man was a privilege, and the pay was substantially higher than the average wage. Joey loved how at the end of each event his father made it a ritual of his to walk into the function room, introduce himself and have his guests put their hands together for his fantastic staff members. While employed at the club, everyone was respected and treated as equals.

As tonight's events were unfolding in the adjacent room, Joey sat with his father at the bar and drained a bottle of Sullivans Cove whisky. It was good for them to catch up and reminisce on all the great times they shared together as a family. Losing Phil was an enormous loss for them both, and tonight they were going to raise their glasses up high, drink themselves silly and toast to their fallen son and brother.

'Here's to Phil,' said Joey, holding up his glass in the air.

'Cheers to that, my boy,' replied Alexander, knocking his glass.

Joey smiled and poured some more, finally a game he could beat his father at. Drinking came naturally to him. He and his brother would come here every evening for a few shots and a catch-up. Tonight he continued the tradition more out of sadness than relaxation, but today was special: he was sharing it with his old man.

It wasn't long before the first bottle had been knocked back and the second had been opened. They were exceptionally drunk. Alexander more so and he was laughing at anything and everything.

'I'm glad we did this,' said Alexander, raising his glass hand with less coordination.

'Me, too,' replied Joey.

'You know I love you,' said Alexander.

Joey smiled. 'You're not one of those drunks who gets all lovey-dovey, are ya?'

'Maybe.'

Joey, who drank on a regular basis, was feeling the alcohol getting to his head. The room was beginning to spin, like the club had been put on a carousel. He thought about how his father was taking it and helped him upright onto a stool, as he swayed to the left and continued to laugh; this was a moment he wanted to cherish forever. The most powerful and feared man in Los Angeles could not hold still without falling. He was human, after all.

'Dad, I think you should call it a night. You're smashed.'

Alexander regained his focus, grabbed his son's head between his large hands and looked into his blue eyes. 'All this will be yours one day, son,' he mumbled, while trying to balance himself on the barstool.

'Me, I couldn't organize a fuck in a brothel with a fist full of fifties,' said Joey.

Alexander laughed and said, 'I have treasures in this place you wouldn't dream of. One day, my boy, you'll see her face.'

'Dad, you're not making sense.'

Alexander laughed some more.

Joey had the sudden realization of the huge burden placed upon him. He was not ready to take over the family business. He just wanted to surf, party and live the life of a carefree guy. But this part of his life had been expunged the day Phil was killed. Whether he liked it or not, he was trapped.

'Look, son, this is your chance to step up and prove to the boys you're a leader.'

'I'm no leader, Dad, you're talking to the wrong son.'

'You're my only son now, you can do it. We can't let go of this place yet, it's too important.'

'Ahh, stop it!' A female's voice in distress echoed in the outside marbled hallway.

Joey and Alexander turned their stools to listen. There was the girl's voice again, high-pitched this time.

'Stop it, you drunk!'

Two people were causing a commotion in the hallway, verbally abusing each other. Alexander stood up like a man who wasn't intoxicated. It was as if he had turned a switch. Joey saw his demeanor change. He was not drunk anymore but serious and in control of his actions.

As he reached the scene in his black suit, he witnessed one of his waitresses being pushed up against the wall.

Joey wondered what his father was going to do and followed him.

The drunk held both of the waitress's hands above her head with one of his, while he fondled her breast with his other hand, then slid it under her blue dress.

The young waitress was in tears. Alexander immediately grabbed the man from behind his neck and dug his thumb deep into his carotid artery. The pressure dropped the man to his knees instantly, allowing the girl to step free.

'Aw, you motherfucker!' said the drunk, rubbing his neck in pain. Alexander looked stunned and Joey grimaced. Not many people had the audacity to confront and insult his father, especially in his own home. It was a mistake this fool was going to regret. He obviously didn't know who he was dealing with. His bloodshot eyes indicated that he was high on something.

'She wants it, man,' said the stupid guy as he was lifted up to his feet by Joey, who tucked his hand behind his back in a police hold.

'Who said you can touch my girls like that?' Alexander asked. His voice was all menace, like he was about to unleash the wrath of pain onto the man.

'Compose yourself, Dad, people are watching,' said Joey. He did not want another scandal linked to him.

'Everything's okay, carry on.' Alexander reassured everyone watching with a smile. The people did as asked and left the hallway, returning to their event. Alexander then leaned into Joey's ear and whispered, 'Take him out back and dispose of him.'

Joey stood there stunned, his mouth falling open, a sudden shakiness in his limbs. 'What do you mean "dispose," Dad?'

It was the first time he had been ordered to kill someone. If he wanted to take control of his father's business, it meant he needed to get his hands dirty. Joey shook his head; he didn't want to do that. 'Can't we just give him a beating and throw him in the gutter?'

'No, I want him dead,' said Alexander. 'Don't question my authority. This is a chance for you to show your mettle.'

'Who do you want dead?' said the man, realizing he was in a whole lot of trouble. 'Please let me go. I won't do it again, I promise.'

'Joey, if I let him go, what's stopping him coming in tomorrow with a machine gun and killing us all. Look at him, he's a drug addict. That girl is someone's niece, someone's sister, someone's child. I have not made it to where I am just to see it all go to shit because I grew a conscience.'

'Sorry, Dad, I can't do that.'

'Your brother would have done it already.'

'I'm not my brother.'

'Clearly, you ain't.' He poked Joey harshly in the chest. 'You wait here!' He then dragged the man with him by the scruff of the neck into the bar area. They entered the room and the door shut behind them. Joey knew this was not going to end well for the stupid guy.

'I can't be a part of this shit,' said Joey to himself, standing there waiting in the hallway, without a clue what to do.

It only took two minutes. He watched his father walk out alone, fixing his belt back in place. He frowned and stepped up close to Joey and said, 'I need you to man up.' He rested a heavy hand on Joey's shoulder. 'Be the person you were born to be. Now get Frank, he'll know what to do.'

Alexander gave him a friendly slap on the face and went into the function room to do his thing, applaud his staff, business as usual.

Joey walked toward the bar room and opened the thick oak door. Face down on the floor the man lay still. Joey could see choke marks around his neck. He was not breathing.

Joey realized that this was the kind of thing his older brother had protected him from all those years. His father was crazy and dangerous.

Joey wondered one thing standing there with the dead guy at his feet: his father had gone from being plastered, unable to negotiate a stool, to the complete opposite: sober, strong and in control. He was schizophrenic.

Was it an act? Had he truly been drunk, or had he been playing one of his games again? Who knew?

Joey had never realized it before, but now that he was closer to the family business and was seeing things first-hand, one thing was apparent: his father could not be trusted.

Chapter 26

The beat of the bass could be heard outside Terry's Bar, inviting customers to come in and party. Vince strolled inside and greeted Jim, the bouncer, with a friendly knuckle punch. Jim, an African-American, had the frame of a grizzly bear, but was gentle-natured, a big man with a big heart.

'Hey, Jim, what's the count?' he asked, trying to get a sense of how crowded they were going to be tonight.

'Um, so far about fifty. It's going to be busy.'

'Cool, I'll catch you later.'

He walked into the main open-floor arena, where soft ambient light filled the venue. The bar was smack in the center, with dark-mahogany wooden booths, tables and chairs scattered around the perimeter. Terry's Bar could legally cater for two hundred people at any one time. One of Jim's tasks was to monitor these numbers. In three hours' time the bar would be swarming with college students needing a drink or two – or five; their escape from college life and the pressure of study. Once capacity was reached, a line formed outside until others left. The bar's popularity and the shows of skill by cocktail-mixing bartenders brought the crowds in early. No one wanted to wait outside with the possibility of never getting in.

Vince stepped into the main bar. A dark granite benchtop

encircled him and two other bartenders, one of whom was Terry the owner.

Louise and Danielle, two regulars in their mid-thirties, both blonds, clapped and cheered on the drinks master as he entered his domain. The party for them was just getting started. Vince gave his cheer squad a friendly grin and then he continued to grin, as he remembered all he had to smile about.

Terry was happy to see him on time as promised. He was in the middle of pouring six mojitos. He finished with a sprig of extra mint leaves on top for added flavor and decoration. The waitresses at the bar showed off their cleavage, leaning over the counter as they watched on. Blouses too tight, flouncing their assets for all to see. These girls were groupies of sorts. They helped bring in the male customers and Terry liked having them around, as they kept him young in his middle age.

'The prodigal child has returned,' said the waitress Angelina, an ex-girlfriend of Vince's. She eyed him with desire, touching her dark, wavy hair. The fact that he was taken did not seem to concern her.

'And how are the playboy bunnies today?' he asked with a mischievous grin.

'The bunnies are just great,' said the boss, who placed six mojitos on the edge of the bar. 'But their trays are empty.'

Vince laughed.

'Go on, take these to table five,' he said, with a wave of his hand. Angelina blew her ex a kiss and left to serve the table. Veronica followed.

'Looks like it's going to be a good night,' said Vince.

Terry asked. 'So how's your dad, out of hospital?'

'It's a long story, Terry, long story.' If he only knew the truth.

'Okay, then, first up, son. Before we get going, a shot.'

Vince flashed a smile. This was a tradition of theirs before a shift. He accepted the tequila that was poured into a small shot glass, their hands raised high for a toast. In one quick motion the drink was slammed down their throats. Vince finished first, his glass turned upside down on the bar's benchtop. Terry followed seconds later, sticking out his tongue with a gasp: this was not his first tonight.

'Whoo! Let's go,' Vince clapped his hands together; that did the trick. Nothing like a shot to get you pumped.

'Okay, who wants a drink?' he asked in a loud, confident voice.

'We do, we do!' shouted back the relapsed alcoholics Louise and Danielle, up front and center to the action.

'Of course you do, you guys always want a drink.' They drank booze like it was water. Many men had tried getting these girls drunk and failed miserably.

Working at the bar these last three years, Vince had learned many life experiences from Terry, his friend and mentor. Some good, some bad – mostly bad. But one skill he put to good use was the art of being a fantastic bartender with style and flair: the act of flipping, spinning, throwing and catching bottles in the process of producing a colorful cocktail. Soon a reputation had spread around the campus like a virus and Terry was reaping the benefits.

Thirty minutes into his shift, after serving a round of cosmopolitans, a noise erupted to his left. Someone shouted. 'Hey, dickhead! Where are our drinks?'

Vince turned with a grin on his face, knowing that voice, and threw his tea towel onto the benchtop. It was Gary.

'Hey, happy birthday, man!' He reached over for a high-five and a hug.

'Thanks, bro. Fuck, there's a lot of pussy in here tonight.'

Vince continued to smile; he knew his friend was simple-minded. Pussy and cars, not necessarily in that order, was all he lived for. 'What're you drinking? On the house.'

'Hey, by the way, how's your father?'

'I guess he's alright.'

Gary laughed and ran his hand through his curly hair. 'I can't believe your old man is in jail. Who would've thought?'

'Let's not talk about him. It's your birthday. Bourbon?'

'Yeah, why not? But first I need to piss.' Gary slid off the stool and headed for the bathroom.

Wanting to do something for his friend, Vince approached the lushes, Louise and Danielle, who had already spent all their money on booze. A topped-up cosmopolitan was offered to them both, free of charge.

'What's this? I love you, but hang on, why the freebie? Nothing in life is for free,' Louise said, looking like she wanted to wet her lips in the drink.

'Yeah, what's the deal?' said Danielle with a wink.

'Girls, girls, I have a proposition for you both.'

'Does it involves alcohol?'

'It does. It's my friend's birthday today. Show him a good time, dance with him, give him attention, nothing more, and I'll give you both free drinks for the rest of the night.'

Their eyes grew wide, their mouths slightly ajar. He had said the magic words: free alcohol, a gift from the gods.

'Yeah, no problem. Deal,' said Danielle. Louise kept on nodding her head, like she had won the lottery.

As soon as Gary returned to his bar stool, the girls did not waste any time grabbing his hand and pulling him onto the dance floor. He was pinned in the middle like the meatball in a sandwich and looked like he couldn't believe his luck. He had always had a thing for older girls. He began moving his body up against the two girls and they didn't seem to mind.

Seeing the joy in his friend's face was priceless. Every now and then the girls would take turns visiting the bar, and a cocktail would be waiting free of charge. After a couple of hours Terry noticed these transactions. After the next drink, he confronted Vince. He was not happy.

'What's going on with these free drinks? You're ripping me off?'

'Whoa … Whoa … Relax … It may seem like I'm giving them away, but I have a tab going. It's Gary's birthday. I promise you, every drink will be paid for, okay? Trust me.'

Knowing he could cover the cost with the money in his pocket, Vince had no concern. Terry, slightly taller, looked down into his brown eyes.

'Okay, Vince, you've never let me down before. I'll trust you. Don't let me down tonight.'

'I won't, now fuck off, pal,' he said with a smile.

Isabella was aware of Vince's shift and had planned an unexpected visit. She quietly sat herself at the end of the bar. Two college guys sat to her right, discussing how they were going to approach this beautiful creature. Their success rate tonight was zero. Vince walked up to Isabella, pretending they had never met before.

'What are you drinking?'

With a smile on her face, she replied, 'Surprise me.'

'Surprise me? My kind of girl.'

One of the students worked up the confidence and approached Isabella. His body shook nervously, offering to pay for her drink. She smiled and happily agreed, thanking him. Vince tossed the bottle of rum in the air and added ingredients into a stainless-steel shaker filled with ice. Rum, blue liqueur and pineapple juice. After a good shake above his shoulder the drink was poured into a triangular glass. The end result was a beautiful turquoise cocktail which he slid over to Isabella.

'Wow, that's an impressive-looking cocktail,' said the student.

'I love that color,' said Isabella.

'What's the drink called?' asked the student.

'This cocktail is called Bella, named after the girl I'm in love with,' said Vince.

Isabella smiled. It was corny but nice.

The student glanced over at her exotic face and asked her, 'So what's your name?'

'My name is Isabella.'

'Isabella, that's a beautiful name. Hang on,' said the student.

'That's right: Isabella, as in Bella.'

Vince laughed at the poor sucker, as Isabella leaned over the counter to kiss her man.

'I love you, too,' she whispered against Vince's lips.

'Fuck this.' The guy, now embarrassed, shook his head and walked back to his friend, who was bursting at the seams with laughter.

Vince and Isabella had a chuckle of their own.

'That was too funny. So how are you, babe?' he asked.

'I'm okay, considering.'

'Listen, tomorrow I'm taking you out somewhere special.'

'As long as my life is not in danger.'

'I promise, five star from here on.'

Vince had put his girlfriend through a horrific ordeal, and wanted to put what happened behind them and start afresh. What he had was a skeleton key that could open all doors and change their lives forever. The big trick was keeping the secret from her, as she would not accept the risk.

Vince's shift ended. Gary and Isabella had left earlier on. The waitresses were cleaning table spills and tidying up. Jim locked the doors and Terry was counting the day's profits. Inconspicuously, Vince reached into his pocket and pulled out everything he had. The fake tab would not have been more than five hundred dollars in total, but he handed over the entire amount.

'A thousand dollars?' said Terry, surprised.

'Yeah, they left a big tip.'

'Sorry for doubting you, Vince. Thanks for tonight.'

'Not a worry, boss, catch you guys next week.'

Vince waved his hand and left, exhausted.

Chapter 27

Saturday morning arrived in a flash. Vince sat up and stared at his wardrobe as if he was a kid, eager to open up his Christmas presents. Gary's bed was still made, not slept in last night, an indication he had scored with one of the flirting lushes.

Vince didn't waste any time and dived into the wardrobe, removing the blankets and pillows that concealed the backpack. Opening it, he took out two bundles. Then as his hands touched the notes, he decided to take out four. He had said to himself he was going to be careful with the spending, but it was like giving a child a chocolate sundae to hold and not be able to eat it. The paper bands were removed and the money split into two halves, twenty-five thousand into his left pocket and fifteen thousand into his right.

Vince knew his current hiding place was not ideal, but it had to do for now. He thought about securing it in a safe-deposit box, but it was the weekend and not all branches in the area with boxes would have been open. So he returned the backpack into the wardrobe and concealed it again.

Today he was going to have some fun and go on a little spending spree. Number one on his list was to pay off his school fees. He was so close to finishing his bachelor of arts degree and did not want to get expelled. Even though it was Saturday, the campus accountant was working on next year's enrolments, the freshmen. This was a busy time for Joseph

Matter, whose role extended from that of accountant to the lead meet and greeter: the contact who explained to new students about their dorm-room allocations and fee structures – with the emphasis on paying their fees on time or face eviction, just like Vince.

Vince walked into the modern Extension Administration Building, designated for the all-important campus accountant. This was like a mini-bank on campus, the place to pay school fees or organize financial assistance. He stood and waited in the hallway with three other freshmen who were scheduled to meet with Joseph. The high ceiling and tiled floors echoed the footfalls of those walking by.

The door opened. Joseph walked out of his office with a student who had a smile on her face. 'Thanks again, see you next year,' said Joseph to the shy student, dressed as if she was at a job interview.

Joseph scanned to see who was waiting and saw Vince. He curled his index finger at Vince, beckoning him to follow.

'Good morning, Joseph,' said Vince chirpily, knowing it would be taken as cheek.

'Hello, Vince, I've explained your situation to the dean.'

'Okay, what did he say?'

'He told me there will be no excuses, your deadline is Monday. I've been instructed to evict you if you don't come up with the money. Sorry, I don't mean to be the bad guy.'

'I know, you're just doing your job. That's why I'm here. So let's pay it off.'

Joseph laughed sarcastically. 'I had a look at your balance due. You owe twenty-five thousand dollars, and I don't think you have it on you.'

Vince smirked; he had dreamed about this moment. He reached into his left pocket and pulled out a stash of hundred-dollar bills.

'My, you weren't lying!' said Joseph, surprised.

The money was placed on his oak desk, near his black stapler.

'It's all there.'

'What did you do, rob a bank?'

'Something like that.'

Joseph sighed and after five minutes, it was all counted. Just like that, Vince was debt-free and things were looking up. A heavy burden was instantly removed from his shoulders. This meant he didn't need to work at the bar anymore. He could concentrate in class and pass with distinction, having more time to study and arrive in class on time after a good night's sleep – something his teacher had not seen in a long time.

Joseph shook Vince's hand and thanked him. 'Enjoy the rest of your stay, and good luck with everything.'

'Will do, Joseph, thanks again.'

Next stop was the Apple store at Westfield Century City mall. Vince parked his car in Bloomingdale's car park and walked to the Apple store. Entering the cool, white premises, he felt like a child in a candy store. He could purchase anything he wanted. Fifteen thousand dollars to spend was more than enough.

Looking at all the hardware on display, he went straight for a MacBook Pro and checked the specifications. Not long after, a young salesperson who wore thick, dark glasses, approached him. 'Would you like some help with anything?'

'Yes, I have a list of things to buy today. I need two of the latest iPads with black leather cases, one fifteen-inch MacBook Pro with retina display,' he pointed at the one he was playing with, 'a laptop bag, iPod touch and a new iPhone, please.'

The salesperson burst out laughing. 'Is this a practical joke?'

'This is no joke, Steve,' Vince said, glancing at his name tag.

'For real? That's an insanely large purchase.'

'What can I say? I'm a rich kid who loves his toys.'

Steve got all the items one by one, as he discussed the various options while walking through the store. All the products were collected, packed in Apple-branded bags and paid for in cash. The total amount came to a little over five thousand dollars and Steve ended up with a generous hundred-dollar tip in his pocket. For Vince, the feeling of being able to purchase whatever he wanted without a worry in the world was invigorating.

Vince walked back into the shopping center. His shopping spree was not over yet. Up the escalators to his right was a large Tiffany & Co. jewelry store. He had spent $25,000 on school fees and $5500 at the Apple store. He still had $9500, enough to buy Isabella a gift she could wear at tonight's special dinner.

Inside the store he asked the lady behind the counter, 'Do you have any diamond earrings?'

She was thin, perfectly groomed and spoke in a refined English accent. 'We do have diamond earrings, darling, but none with your price tag,' she said, assuming he was too young and couldn't afford anything in the store. Her apologetic smile was equal parts pity and disdain. What an expensive mistake that was.

Vince laughed at the lady as he walked out of the store and said, 'I can't believe I just had a *Pretty Woman* moment!'

He walked a little further and saw a smaller jewelry store. He stepped inside. A woman on the curvy side approached him. She introduced herself with a strong Greek accent.

'Is there anything specifics you are looking for?'

'I'm after some diamond earrings for my girlfriend.'

'I have many, I show you.'

She pulled up a stool for him to sit on, while she brought out an array of diamonds for him to peruse and placed them in front of him. He picked up a beautiful eighteen-carat, white-gold set.

'You have gots good taste, sir,' the woman said with a smile, as he eyed one of the most expensive diamonds she had in her store.

'How much?'

'These earrings cost $5999.'

The single word Vince uttered next made the woman's day.

'Done.'

Chapter 28

Saturday, 6 pm

Vince dressed in a white, long-sleeved summery shirt, the top two buttons undone, tucked into his pressed black trousers. Facing the mirror, he sprayed cologne on his neck and that's when he noticed the brown leather wristband on his right hand missing.

'Shit!' The wristband was a sentimental gift given to him by his mother. A band he always wore that bore his initials on the back.

He could not remember how he had lost it. He looked quickly around his room but couldn't find it. He needed to do a proper search for it later – he was running late. What else was he missing now, he thought. 'Ah yes, money.'

He dug into his jean pocket and grabbed the leftover cash he had not spent, which was more than enough for tonight's dinner. He then slipped the small black velvet box into his pants and he was out the door.

Isabella was waiting outside her place, dressed in a beautiful black cocktail dress that fit her petite body to perfection. He got out and opened her passenger door, every inch the gentleman. His mother had taught him well.

'So, where are you taking me?' she asked in a childlike voice.

'We're going to McDonald's,' he said with a laugh.

'Ha ha, very funny.'

'What? It's a restaurant.' The smile didn't leave his face.

★ ★ ★

Entering the Huntley Hotel's parking lot, a concierge took possession of the vehicle.

'Did you get us a room?' Isabella asked with a cheeky grin. Vince hooked her arm against his and escorted his girl through the side entrance of the hotel to the elevator. Two other couples were also dressed in their best. Smiles were all around. The top-floor button was pressed. When the elevator reached its destination, Vince and Isabella were the first out.

A friendly waitress greeted them.

'Welcome to the Penthouse Restaurant, can I have your name, please?'

'It's under Vancini,' said Vince confidently.

'Oh yes, your table is waiting for you.'

The Penthouse Restaurant was one of Santa Monica's most lavish, upmarket restaurants. It was on the penthouse level, hence the name and the views stretched wide over the Santa Monica coastline.

Isabella squeezed Vince's hand and smiled. 'I can't believe you got us a table here, you must've been planning this for weeks!'

Vince gave her a wink. The truth was, he'd made them an offer they couldn't refuse. After talking to the manager over the phone, he had explained he was going to leave a one-thousand-dollar tip on top of the extravagant meal and fine wine they were planning on having. The only catch was that he wanted the best table in the room.

The waitress walked them over to their own executive booth. A card with their names sat on the table. White embroidered curtains divided each booth that ran across the room's large glass windows. In the center of the table, a thick white candle lit up the booth, emanating a romantic glow. Once seated, the waitress introduced herself. 'My name is Penny. I'll be your waitress tonight.'

Isabella and Vince acknowledged Penny with a smile.

'We have a lovely five-course meal headed your way. First, let's fill up those flutes with a bottle of Moët & Chandon.'

After Penny poured the champagne and left, Isabella whispered, 'Did she just say five-course meal?'

Vince smiled, feeling good about himself. She was getting to see another side of him – an extravagant side, a side he'd always wished for but could never afford, as all his money was funneled into his college fund.

'Hon, did you win the lottery or something?' That wasn't the first time today he had been asked that question. 'Seriously, how can you afford a place like this?'

Vince continued to smile, drinking his second glass of Moët.

'I have a gift for you,' he said, reaching into his pocket.

Isabella's smile was no more. Her eyebrows were now slanting. 'Please don't tell me we're here because you're going to propose.'

Vince pulled out the black velvet box and slid it across the table. She seemed concerned, and noticeable frown lines had appeared on her forehead.

'You look beautiful tonight. I love your dress, but something is missing. Open it.'

She opened the velvet box slowly, to reveal two sparkling diamond earrings. The way they glimmered you could tell they were genuine and seemed expensive.

'Oh my God, thank you!' sighed Isabella. 'I love them.'

She inserted her new treasures into the holes in her ears. He was right: they went fabulously with her black dress and accentuated her neck. She leaned over and gave him a lingering kiss. Soon the courses arrived, one after the other, until it was time to eat dessert.

After a fantastic night's dinner, it was time to leave and pay the bill. Vince excused himself for the bathroom and quietly went to pay it. If Isabella saw the bill, she would know something was up and suspect he was involved in something illegal. The total came to $1625, including the thousand-dollar donation. He swiftly paid the bill in cash, rounding it off to $1700 and left a generous tip for Penny.

Mr. David Salduzi, the owner of the restaurant and a large shareholder of the Huntley Hotel, personally came out to meet and greet him. He was a man who always wore a business suit, a man you felt comfortable with, even though you had only just met him. A dark beard framed his face and his hair was closely cut.

'Nice to meet you, Vince. You're a VIP customer now. If you ever want to dine at the restaurant or need an ocean view suite at the hotel, call this number.'

He handed over a business card with his personal cell number on the back, giving him top priority.

'Thank you so much,' Vince said, shaking his hand.

'No, Vince, it's my pleasure. I arrange this for many of my wealthy clients.'

Vince had entered an elite club and had a taste of how the rich and famous lived and how they were treated. One thing he took from this experience was how money gave you more options in life, and he loved every minute of it.

Chapter 29

Thank God for the weekend. Monica Anton had slept in. Her left arm wandered to the other side of her bed, as she did every morning, hoping to feel a warm body beside her. Phil had been that warm body for her, he was her other half, her partner for life.

There were consequences to being in a relationship with a member of the Peruggia Blood crew, especially the son who was bred to take over. But she had followed her heart and she'd fallen deeply in love with him, until his tragic death.

When Phil had walked into a room, people had feared his hotheaded nature. He could turn in a flash from being pleasant to a monster, unpredictable like his father. A man not to be trusted; everything he did, he did for a reason. But despite all that, she didn't care, she'd seen another side to her boyfriend not many had the pleasure to witness.

He had wanted more in life. He was a passionate man who hated the fact that his life was already planned out, expected to take over the family business. His cold exterior was a front to show his enemies that he was in control and not to be taken for a fool.

Weakness was unacceptable in the family. He was taught at an early age to hold his head up high, even if he was up against someone double his size.

'For people to respect you, son, they need to fear you,' Alexander had told him, planting this seed in his head. This ethos was embedded in his mind early on, growing up in the corrupting influences of the neighborhood and ultimately determining his future.

To make matters worse, Phil lost his mother at an early age. A couple of months after giving birth to Joey, she was found dead, left in the street a couple of blocks from home.

Taking matters into his own hands, and with his father's help, Phil found the killer. He was only ten years old, looking deeply into the man's eyes, the devil himself. His gun fired multiple times. The anger consumed him. His innocence changed from that moment. He lost his gentle nature and became a guarded young man.

Phil was not sure about many things growing up, except one. A pact was formed with his father to exclude his younger brother from any gang activity. It was his one rule: he had had no choice growing up, but his brother did. Alexander had kept his word; the lie about his mother's death was concocted to protect Joey. The less he knew the better.

Monica had also had a tough childhood, and maybe this was the reason she'd accepted Phil and opened up to him. They had shared similar tragic stories and understood each other, having lost both her parents at an early age.

Having no other family to stay with, she had moved in with her grandmother, who cared for her until she finished high school. After graduating, she joined the military and enlisted as an intelligence officer. Her role was vital in the country's national defense. She gathered intelligence to stop any potential terrorist attacks against the United States, looked at photographs and used radar and supersensitive radios.

After five years in the military, she landed a job working for the FBI at the highest level, working in conjunction with the CIA as a counter-intelligence analyst. Her role was to monitor and take down groups or organizations that had infiltrated the state police force, find corrupt cops and agents and bring them to justice.

She met Phil during this period of her life. As one of her first assignments to get her feet wet, she was entrusted with investigating the notorious gangster Alexander Peruggia, a man known to be protected by men with badges who hid in the shadows. No substantial evidence had ever been obtained against him, but he was way too shady to have a clean record. Many agents had rejected the assignment, but not Monica. She believed she could make a difference and contribute. She welcomed the case. The FBI needed an outsider, someone with a fresh perspective to research and analyze all the data they may have missed. She was that person. With a successful military background, she was considered perfect for the job of flushing out the corrupt cops.

Monica, eager to prove herself to her superiors, read dozens of police reports and completed an entire background check on the Peruggia family. She listened to phone recordings and created a diary of locations they visited on a regular basis. The more intel she acquired, the more likely she would find something. Intel was the key. After a month of surveillance, she uncovered a pattern.

Wise guy Tony Giordano helped out at the club's restaurant. He would restock the kitchen every Friday morning with a phone call to their supplier. After rattling off various ingredients – basil, tomatoes, parmesan cheese – he would be asked one final question.

'How about mascarpone cheese, do you require any this week?' An innocent enough question, but Monica thought it was more than that. She believed the last request was a drug-ordering system, disguised as an ingredient.

The problem with her theory was that it wasn't much to go on. She needed stronger evidence if she wanted to use it in court. The other hiccup was that Alexander had never been known as a drug dealer. This was the territory of the Hispanic gangs in the south-west.

So why would Alexander want drugs?

He was more known to be embroiled in armored-guard trucks and bank robberies. Even though there was no real proof of his involvement, he was always documented as the lead suspect. The elaborate getaways were a sign of someone who loved a well-thought-out plan and escape.

Monica decided to send in undercover agents as members of the beach club to keep an eye out from the inside. She continued the phone surveillance, waiting to see if any order was placed for mascarpone cheese. On the fifth Friday, an order was placed. Monica was excited: all her hard work was going to pay off. A team was set up in a van outside the beach club's parking lot.

All who entered the club were scrutinized as possible suspects. After four hours in the van, she got her first break. Three men who did not belong on the premises, dressed in suits, entered the venue. All were distinguished gentlemen in their sixties. They were definitely not here for a workout and there were no events planned for the night. What were they here for? Could it be for the mascarpone cheese, or some other deal?

The first man was identified as District Attorney Steven Kennedy. The second was Judge Carl Burnham and, surprisingly, Chief Lee Davis was the third. On principle, what was he doing at this establishment? she thought.

This was her first insight into the fraudulent nature of the chief and how well-protected Alexander Peruggia was. These influential people had been hired to watch over the gangster, protect his interests and inform him of any threats or dangers he might encounter. He was not a drug user, he just catered for people he needed to use to maintain his lifestyle and status.

Monica knew that all she had to do was raid the houses of these men to find payouts of drugs and large sums of money. An impossible task as they were all respected and considered the elite in their professions. To get a warrant to raid any of these men's homes, under an assumption that they were corrupt, with mascarpone cheese as the only real evidence, was never going to be enough. Monica hit a wall, she needed a new strategy. It wasn't long after her findings that a mole within the FBI outed her.

Chapter 30

The following week in her investigation, Monica realized a change in the restaurant's routine. At the end of a placed order, no mascarpone cheese was ever mentioned again. Someone had tipped them off. She was no dummy, she had spent the last five years studying codes and analytics. Something was wrong; she now understood why Alexander could not be touched. He was too well-informed with moles embedded deep in the system. She was back to square one, with over one month of surveillance amounting to nothing.

The last hour of her shift one Friday afternoon, her phone rang, but no one answered on the other end. Thirty minutes later the same thing happened: someone was keeping track of her whereabouts. She knew she had become a possible target. The last detective who had tried to investigate Alexander Peruggia had ended up dead, found in a dumpster. No substantial evidence had proved he was involved, but you didn't need to be a genius to work that one out.

Monica, in fear for her life, decided to go out in the public eye to a local bar not far from her work, knowing that Peruggia's men would not be far behind watching her every move. She ordered a cocktail and waited alone, ready to confront whoever was going to be sent for her.

When she had first laid eyes on Phil, there was a definite attraction. He walked into the bar, with Victor and Matt following behind like sheep. Everyone in the bar became aware of who it was, with a second look and stare. His reputation was enough to make most men tremble in fear when confronted. The bartender poured him a cold beer as he sat down on the stool beside her.

Monica glanced over to see Phil's powerful dark eyes. His stare was aggressive, but she was not going to let him bully her and stood her ground. She was not intimidated and continued to drink her cocktail, as though without a worry in the world. She smiled and was the first to speak. 'So you know who I am?'

Most people couldn't look into the eyes of a killer, but not Monica. She was not one to back down, coming from a military background – trained for combat, if needed.

'I know who you are,' he said coldly.

'So am I going to be found in a rubbish bin tomorrow?'

Phil smiled slightly. 'You have balls.'

'Are you going to kill me?'

'Maybe. My father's not happy,' he said, waiting to hear her response.

'Let me tell you something: your father doesn't run your life. From an early age you were subjected to this life and it has become you. Don't you want something better for yourself? I know your mom would've wanted that for you.'

Phil's smile disappeared. He gripped her arm tight.

'Ahh, let go of me.'

'Don't you ever talk about my mother, you have no idea!'

Monica had done her homework and knew the mention of his mother was a touchy subject. A former Peruggia Blood member had been beaten to death by Phil when he'd insulted his mother a year ago.

Phil pulled her off her chair. 'You've drunk your last cocktail.'

'Before you kill me, I have one thing I need to tell you, then I'm all yours.' She did not fight his pulling.

'What is it?'

She leaned in close to his ear and whispered something

only he could hear. Victor and Matt stood and watched. This was her one and only chance.

She uttered words into Phil's ear and instantly knew she had grabbed his undivided attention. His frame drooped and his grip loosened. He was paralyzed by her words, his eyes looking glazed. Monica had turned a Rottweiler into a Chihuahua in a matter of seconds.

Victor and Matt glanced over at each other, confused.

What did she say to transform this killer so quickly?

Sometimes in life all it takes is the right person to guide you in a different direction, and that's what Monica had done with Phil.

After that first life-altering meeting, Phil's priority changed. He wanted to keep Monica alive, even if his father disagreed. This was the first time he stood up to his father, and felt empowered. From then on a romance blossomed between them. Everyone on both sides, good and evil, disapproved, especially Alexander. Monica had taken away his son and brainwashed him into leaving the Peruggia Blood family for good. Phil had told his father he wanted out. He wanted children of his own and to start a new life.

Alexander reluctantly accepted his son leaving, but not before one last heist, the California Bank & Trust robbery. A much-needed job for everybody, especially Alexander, who was in trouble with his loan repayments due to the elaborate club renovations that nobody understood.

Phil agreed to help his father one last time and pledged that, after this, his involvement was no more. The rest was history. After Phil's death many had questioned who was responsible. Even on the inside, men had questioned if the big dog himself was possibly behind it. No one could leave the gang once inside – it didn't matter who you were.

Monica could see the men's suspicions were suppressed. If it was true and Alexander had orchestrated the death of his own son, there was no telling what he was capable of doing, and no one was game enough to ask.

Not yet, anyway.

Chapter 31

Monica was collectively hated and feared in the bureau, but somehow she was allowed to continue with her investigations. She was embedded deep in the Peruggia family, had become a part of it. A lamb thrown into the lion's den, promising that, one day, her input from inside the walls would form an uncontested case to put Alexander away for life and throw away the key.

She was an angel, but also possessed a devilish side. Her relationship with Phil Peruggia had caused a stir and panic in the agency, as it had lasted longer than anticipated and had so far borne no convictions. Her loyalty to the bureau was questioned, and many believed she had been turned.

Six months after she had started dating Phil, she was asked by her colleagues how she could be romantically involved with a man who had murdered countless numbers of people in cold blood.

Her answer was simple: 'Someone had to do it.'

'And how do we know you haven't switched sides?'

'You don't,' Monica had replied in a frigid tone, shutting the girl up. Who was this girl questioning her actions? She put her life at risk every day. She felt she deserved a little respect.

Monica had lived both sides of the fence. What her peers didn't realize though, was that it wasn't any better on the good side, the side where you carried a badge. Corruption was everywhere in the force. Men and women were taking bribes to keep quiet and better their own situations. Everyone was bought out; she had seen it first-hand from being inside the Peruggia family.

In her own apartment, away from Alexander's Beach Club, she poured herself a black coffee and sat on her veranda, which overlooked the coastline. Santa Monica was where she chose to live: seeing the aqua-blue waters from her apartment made her feel connected and at home. The lingering smell of last night's Chinese food, left on the dining table, filled the entire unit. She reached for her cell phone and turned it on. Her grandmother, now seventy, would often send her text messages early Sunday morning after church, to catch up with her only granddaughter. As soon as the screen came to life, a message appeared from an anonymous number. It read:

Just received this text, found in Phil's phone: It lies beneath the third, P.ENIMAR GC.

She smiled, a tingling excitement rushing through her body. She knew her boyfriend better than anyone. This was no random message. This was an anagram to the whereabouts of the lost two million dollars. This was meant to be her and Phil's share.

Monica grabbed a pencil and a paper, laid it down on the kitchen table and began to rewrite the clue. She read it over and over in her head. His last words, his masterpiece.

Chapter 32

Three long nights Leonardo Vancini had endured in the Federal Correctional Institution on Terminal Island. All inmates were expected to maintain regular jobs while they were inside, such as cooking, cleaning and other menial tasks. Leonardo knew he needed to do what was required and stay out of trouble. It was only for two weeks, he kept telling himself, locked away in a six-by-eight-foot cell.

Within his first day, first hour inside, word got out that he was a detective, a cop, a pig. Alexander did not want to just kill Leonardo, which he could have arranged by an inmate, he wanted to torment the man. He wanted to teach him a lesson.

The moment he went in, a target was painted on his back; everyone wanted a piece of him, relishing the opportunity. The fact that he had been responsible for incarcerating many of them did not help. Sidelong stares passed by his cell, seeking revenge.

Leonardo stayed focused and sat down on his bunk. The top bed remained empty due to his circumstances. Being a police officer, his protection was the department's first priority. Within the walls of his cell, he felt safe. He even contemplated staying there for the next two weeks but chose not to: he hated confined spaces and needed to get out and stretch his legs.

Early the next morning, a guard appointed Leonardo for kitchen duty. He was to clean dishes, help with the cooking and finish mopping the floors after breakfast was served. He would be the last one out of the kitchen.

Mopping the floors, Leonardo glanced up every so often. His eyes scanning the large hall for any possible threat. While everyone was eating breakfast, one man ran his finger across his bearded neck in a slicing motion, while another blew him a kiss, like he was a piece of meat to be played with.

His eyes fixed upon another three men headed his way. The man in the middle looked familiar. With his jaw set and hard stare the man was closing in on him. This was not going to be a friendly visit. He wanted retribution for his brother, killed in a gunfight by the detective two years ago.

Leonardo found himself alone. The other inmates had hurriedly left the kitchen. His heart pounded in his chest and his body shook with adrenaline. This was it: defend yourself or be killed, he thought, taking a step back.

The men approached him as he held his ground. He was surrounded, with nowhere to run. He tightly gripped the mop with both hands, his only weapon. A fight was imminent. The man in front was overweight, but with a build that suggested immense strength. His considerable height made the ceiling appear closer than it was. The green ink that covered his arms and what skin that was exposed beneath his neck was a pattern of scales like a reptile. Inside, they called him Zilla, short for Godzilla, as he loved to break things, mainly bones, and he was clearly the leader.

Leonardo read the play. The men on either side were going to hold onto him, while the leader planted the blows.

'Hello, pig,' said the leader. The other men smirked: they were smaller, also with tattoos down their arms. Leonardo was outnumbered; he needed to come up with an attack.

'What can I do for you?' he said, fixing his eyes on Zilla's unblinking stare.

'You're a dead man,' replied Zilla, licking his lip like a giant lizard about to pounce.

Leonardo positioned himself sideways, like a fighter. He was a much smaller man and needed to attack first. If he waited for them, it would be over. This way he stood a chance.

He caught the man to his right off guard, grabbed underneath his arm and tossed him over toward the other two, giving him some room to swing his only weapon, the mop. He swung it over his head in a flash, taking out the leader with a deadly blow. The slippery floors helped Zilla fall, with his heavy frame hitting the ground hard. The other men stood back as Leonardo swung the mop like a baseball bat.

Lucky for Leonardo he got a break. The prison guards came running in, as Zilla picked himself up off the floor. They quickly controlled the room and took possession of the mop, pressing Leonardo's nose hard into the cold wetness of the kitchen floor.

'You three get out of here now,' said the guard. Zilla walked away holding his nose. This was not going to be the last time they were to meet.

'Already causing trouble. Throw him in solitary. He needs to understand he's not the law in here,' said the guard.

'I was defending myself,' said Leonardo as he was taken away. The guard didn't care.

After a day in the darkness of solitary confinement without food or water, his door swung open.

'What's going on?' Leonardo asked, as he squinted in the light to identify the man standing beside the guard.

'You have five minutes, make it count,' said the man with the keys.

Zilla entered the dark cell, with intent to inflict pain. Leonardo stepped back, trapped in the confined space.

His small frame was picked up and thrown hard against the brick wall. His back took most of the hit. Multiple punches to his stomach and head followed, leaving him with broken ribs, a bruised eye, a bleeding nose and a cut lip.

This was his worst nightmare come true. He was too old,

too weak; all he could do was try to protect his head from the deadly blows coming his way.

'Time's up,' said the guard.

Zilla kicked him hard in the stomach one last time and left.

Leonardo exhaled, holding his stomach, gasping for air.

'Alexander says hi,' the guard said, slamming shut the door.

The last comment stayed with him and he nodded to himself. Alexander had paid the inmates and guards to give him a hard time while inside. He was now focused. All he could think about was the revenge he was going to unleash when released. The anger was enough to sustain his next eleven days of hell. He was changed. His respect for the law was a thing of the past. How could you appreciate the law when it was bent and shaped so easily by men in power? Those men were not the good guys, they were the criminals, the corrupt, who had the police force and the whole judicial system in their pockets. Everyone was bought and everything had a price.

Leonardo's vision was clear now. He was going after the most powerful man, without a badge or uniform, but as a criminal himself. No arrests were going to be made, he was going to take him out and anyone else who crossed his path. No more good cop. Alexander was going down.

Two whole days passed forgotten in darkness, without a complete meal to eat. It was Sunday morning. The walls had closed in and he could not escape the endless, dark wait to freedom. Sitting in the corner of the chilly room, a small shine of light from the entrance door kissed one of the walls. The dull paint could be seen that carried a burden of memories, where psychotic men drawing closer and closer to their death had been scratching.

The stone floor was covered in small dead insects that were rotting and had been partially eaten by smaller maggots and bugs. Around this speckles of dried blood could be seen, where men had attempted to escape either physically or mentally.

Leonardo screamed out from a little opening in the door for some food, when the outside door to the light opened.

'Please, food, I'm starving,' he said.

'Let's go, you have a call,' said the guard.

Leonardo stretched, digging the back of his fists into his lower back, trying to straighten himself up. He followed the guard out from the darkness into the corridor of the first level of cells. Natural light came in through the tall ceiling windows, bouncing off the green metal bars. The detective squinted, walking into the sunlight, his eyes sensitive from being in the dark for the last two days. He needed time to adjust to the daylight.

'Telephone, you have five minutes.'

Leonardo walked over to the telephone and picked it up. On the other end of the phone was Vince, who sounded chirpy. 'Hey, Dad, have you dropped the soap yet?' he said with a giggle.

'Funny,' said Leonardo, holding his bruised ribs.

'Dad, we have a lot to talk about. I'm coming to visit you.'

Leonardo looked around cautiously, not wanting to be heard by the guard who stood by, and said, 'I'm looking forward to it, son. Can you do me a favor though? Bring me something to eat, the food in here is crap.'

'Will do, Dad. See you in a couple of hours.'

Leonardo hung up the phone and was escorted back to his cold, cramped box.

Chapter 33

Monica almost clipped a pylon as she exited the security complex in her new white AMG Mercedes. She was anxious and she changed lanes without indicating. She was wearing her glasses, which were two sizes too big for her face. With her foot to the pedal, the 6.2-litre engine exceeded the speed limit with ease.

She was on a mission.

Phil's anagram was solved. It had only taken her five minutes to work it out. This was no surprise: she had, after all, taught Phil the technique.

The Marine Park was her destination.

The expensive car was not her doing, she could never afford such a thing. It was an elaborate gift given to her by Phil when they began dating. It was his way of showing his commitment to her, that he was serious, but it was not the only reason.

Phil had secretly installed a GPS tracking device deep within the engine's block. The tracking device was irremovable, wired into the car's computer system and was designed to keep an eye on her movements. A caution insisted by his father, who needed her on a leash, not approving of their relationship.

'She works for the FBI, for Christ's sake,' Alexander said,

confronting Phil when he'd first announced the news. He felt it was a risky move made by his son, but agreed to accept her into the family as Phil was known to be stubborn and he seemed to be truly happy. He had never asked him for anything else, so Alexander accepted their relationship with conditions. The most important being, whether he liked it or not, that she was not to be trusted with knowledge about any illegal dealings or transactions. She was to be treated like Joey, on the outer. Who knew if she was reporting all this back to the FBI. A watchful eye was to be on her at all times, and that included the GPS in her car.

One thing Alexander did like the thought of was having another insider within the FBI. She could theoretically become a valuable asset if turned. He could never have too many informants on the inside.

Monica was not oblivious to the tracking device installed in her car and chose to ignore it. To act any different would be to raise suspicions. There were many downsides to accepting the generous gift, and it didn't sit well with her FBI colleagues, who suspected she had been seduced by the other side. The question of where her true loyalties lay arose constantly in the bureau.

The Mercedes' tires ground to a stop on the gravel road at the entrance to the park. She stepped out and walked into the area. She had worked out the general location, but now she needed to find the actual burial place. It would come to her if she saw it.

'Okay, where are you?' she said, wondering where to start her search. The clue ran through her mind as she scanned, waiting for something to jump out. She took in all the structures and possible hiding places and walked past the basketball courts, to an area where younger kids could play. The ground was covered with sand. This would be the perfect hiding place, she thought. She noticed swings, merry-go-rounds, picnic tables, monkey bars and five vibrantly colored wooden cubbyhouses.

'Could it be?' Monica said, imagining herself in Phil's shoes, wounded and needing to recoup, until the coast was clear.

'But which one?' Four sat around within the same perimeter. One was further away and alone. She decided to inspect the cubbyhouse furthest away, a choice she would have made if it was her trying to evade the police.

Standing outside the dark green cubbyhouse, she couldn't help but smile. She was staring at the numeral that displayed like a street address. It was the number three.

It hit her.

It lies beneath the third, GC, was: It lies beneath the number three, green cubbyhouse.

'You are a genius,' she said, ducking her head through the small opening designed for children. She felt Phil's spirit as she imagined what his last hours would have been like, hiding in this small, confined space. She breathed a sigh of relief and glanced down at the base. The slats were screwed in tight, no movement. She needed a Phillips head screwdriver. A set was resting in the boot of her car, so she left the cubbyhouse in a hurry.

As she approached her car, she saw someone standing next to it. The man was dressed in a black suit, tall and he was dark. Waiting patiently was Alexander Peruggia. He had her followed and wanted to personally be there when she found the money.

'Hello, Monica, did you find what belongs to me?' he asked. His mouth twisted into a sinister smile. Monica caught her breath and looked up at Alexander, realizing he was the anonymous sender of the cryptic message earlier. She should have known: she had been played.

'How come you didn't send me the clue sooner? It's Sunday. Phil's been dead for almost a week now.'

'Because I only received the message an hour ago. The detective in charge kept it a secret, not even the chief knew.'

'And how did your informant get his hands on it?' said Monica.

'He found paperwork that was left on the detective's desk from logistics.'

'And you believed him?' Monica smiled.

'It doesn't matter now. Did you find it?'

'Yes, I have. But if I tell you, are you going to stay true to your word and give me my share?' she asked, flicking her hair out of her face.

He agreed with a nod and raised his hands in a friendly gesture. 'Lead the way.'

Monica opened her boot to find the screwdriver set, then they both walked back in the direction of the cubbyhouse. On the way she explained how Phil had created an anagram that showed the location of the money and fooled the police into thinking it was buried in the Penmar Golf Course.

Alexander flashed a smile. He seemed happy to hear his son was brilliant. 'Like father, like son,' he said.

Monica did not respond.

They arrived at the money's suspected resting place. Alexander stood outside, while Monica dived inside. She kneeled down and began removing the screws, one at a time. Within ten minutes two rows of slats had been detached and placed to the side.

'Okay, the moment of truth,' she said.

Alexander bent his tall frame inside to take a look. She used her hands to shovel the soft sand aside as sweat poured off her forehead.

'It's got to be here somewhere,' she said, tunneling with her hand.

Alexander, excited now, joined her inside, his two-thousand-dollar suit pants scraping the sandy floor. 'Did you find it yet?'

'No.'

'Keep digging.'

'I am, it's not here.'

'Fuck!'

As Monica stopped rummaging through the sand, she noticed something. It was a brown wristband, made of leather. She picked it up and could see it was engraved with the initials V.V. Holding it in her hand she stepped outside, to see Alexander's unhappy face and apologized.

Disappointed that they had come up empty, he did not reply. He turned and sauntered back to his vehicle.

Monica, also upset with the outcome and out of frustration, threw the object in her hand as far as she could. She closed her eyes and took in a breath to calm her nerves.

What she had not realized was two things. She was at the correct burial place and that the fashionable wristband belonged to Vince Vancini, the son of the detective she had helped frame.

Chapter 34

Sunday, 11 am

Vince arrived at the Federal Correctional Institution with a box of Krispy Kreme donuts, a burger with the lot and fries. He was patted down by a prison guard, who then poked a finger around the food to make sure no drugs were hidden inside. 'All clear,' yelled the guard.

He was guided down a safe corridor passage with grey walls to a meeting room where his dad was waiting, dressed in state-issue orange overalls. It was cool and the hairs on his arms stood on end. This was not a comfortable place to be in.

Leonardo looked terrible, tired, like he hadn't slept for days. His eyes were bloodshot, he was unshaven and he had bruises all over his face and a noticeably broken nose. He stood, pushing up off the table. In doing so his expression betrayed the pain he was in.

He approached his dad and shook his hand.

'Dad, are you okay?' he asked, examining the cuts and bruises on his father's face.

Leonardo smiled. He looked happy to see Vince, but most of all the food he brought with him. 'I'm starving, son. You talk while I eat.'

Vince sat down and watched his father devour what was in front of him. Lettuce and sauce fell onto the metal table that divided the two.

'Dad, what's going on? Seriously, you look like shit.'

Leonardo finished the burger and moved onto the fries.

'Don't they feed you in here?'

'Hmm,' said Leonardo, closing his eyes as though savoring every last bite.

A prison guard stood in the back of the room watching. The way Leonardo had glanced over, Vince knew he had been warned not to say a word about the punishment he had endured, or the torture would continue.

He leaned forward and began eating his first Krispy Kreme donut. 'Mmm, now that's what I'm talking about.'

'Dad, if there's anything I can do, name it.'

Leonardo waited to answer. The guard left his post for a moment.

'Okay, Vince, we don't have much time. I need you to do me a favor.'

'What's wrong, Dad? You're scaring me.'

'Listen, I need you to contact the chief, tell him I haven't had a decent meal in days. As you can see, I'm starving. On my second day, I was thrown into solitary confinement for defending myself. I was beaten up by an inmate organized by a guard. Someone on the outside has influence in here as well. Do you understand what I'm telling you?'

'Yes, do you mean …?'

'Yes, shh.'

'How do I contact the chief?'

'He'll be at work.'

'It's Sunday?'

'Trust me, he'll be there. I'm not the only one who's a workaholic.'

The guard stepped back into place.

Vince knew exactly who he was talking about and agreed to go see the chief. He hated seeing his father broken and defeated. The man had never asked for help in his life, so he knew his request was genuine.

He planned to tell his dad about his hacked bank account, but thought he had too much to worry about in here. Money was not an issue for him anyway.

Visiting time was over. Nothing but debris remained of the food.

'Thanks for the meal, Vince.'

'No problem, Dad. About that thing, I'm on it.'

Leonardo smiled and gave his son a quick hug before he was escorted back to his cell.

Vince left the jail with purpose and drove straight to the Los Angeles Police Department. There were no parking spaces on the street so he left his vehicle on the curb. He was in a hurry and didn't care about parking tickets anymore. He was a millionaire: a two-hundred-dollar fine was the equivalent to buying a pack of gum as far as he was concerned.

He entered the building in a hurry and told the receptionist in blue police uniform, 'I'm here to see the chief, I'm Leonardo Vancini's son.' Before she could respond, he barged in and headed for the chief's office.

'Hey, Vince, what's wrong?' the chief said, putting down his gold pen.

'Sir, I need your help, and so does my dad.'

'What do you mean? What's wrong?'

Time was of the essence and Vince spoke quickly. 'Sir, I just visited Dad and he looks like shit. It's only been three nights behind bars and he hasn't been fed properly and thrown into solitary confinement for no apparent reason.'

The chief frowned and cracked his neck. He told Vince not to worry, assuring him he was going to get to the bottom of it. He stood up and immediately picked up the phone.

'Another thing, sir, Dad seems to think Alexander Peruggia is orchestrating this from the outside. Please, Dad is asking for your help.'

'Not that name again,' Lee said. 'Okay, hang on. I have

the number to the Corrections Commissioner somewhere. He's the only man who has the power to overrule the warden if any wrongdoing has occurred. He can move your father to a safe location in the jail to serve out the rest of his time.'

'That would be much appreciated, sir,' said Vince.

Lee dialed the number, while Vince stood by listening.

'Yes, hello, Commissioner, I need your help. One of my detectives doing time is not receiving the protection he was promised. Yes, please, Leonardo Vancini in the Federal Correctional Institution on Terminal Island ... Yes, sir, thank you.'

The phone call ended soon after.

'The commissioner's on it, son. Your dad will be safe now, you can go home.'

Vince breathed a sigh of relief, smiled and thanked the chief with a handshake. Now the commissioner was involved, his dad would, hopefully, get the proper attention he so needed. No more solitary confinement and proper meals from now on – thank God for that.

If in fact the man on the line the chief was talking to was the commissioner?

Chapter 35

Back in the UCLA dorm room, Gary sat on his bed, playing around with the new iPad left to him as a birthday present by Vince. He found it gift-wrapped and hidden under his pillow. He was grateful for Vince's generosity, but at the same time curious about how he could possibly have afforded it. Gary knew his friend. He had barely enough money for himself and the bulk of his earnings went to paying his college tuition.

His suspicious nature took over. The new MacBook Pro left on the desk, in front of his iMac, didn't help, either. It alone would have cost Vince a couple of grand. Where the hell was he getting this money from? Maybe he had come into some money from his parents. Maybe his detective father was corrupt as they said he was, and funneled drug money to his son. It was all speculation for now. One thing was certain, Gary needed to have a big chat with his roommate when he got back.

Whatever the reason though, he could not resist taking a peek at his sexy new laptop, checking out his web browser's history and seeing the sites he had last visited. This could help with understanding his newfound wealth.

He flipped open the screen, which immediately came to life. There was an email notification in red flashing in the dock at the bottom of the screen. He had one unread message.

He felt like a detective, spying on his friend's computer.

'Mail, let's see you.'

After a quick click on the mail program, he was in. Lucky for him no passwords for the computer were set up as yet. The unread email was a tax receipt from the Apple store sent by a Steve Towns with yesterday's date.

Attached to the email was a file containing a purchased list and the individual item pricing.

'Five thousand, five hundred! What the hell?' Gary could not believe his eyes. 'What is going on, Vince?'

He stood up and stared at the ceiling, pondering all the possible reasons for his apparent good fortune. A minute later, while still staring into the abyss, his cell phone rang. He hoped it was Vince: he had some explaining to do.

It wasn't. The words 'debt collector' displayed in capitals on his phone. It was Joseph, the college accountant. He had been labeled 'debt collector,' as the only time he called was when he was after money. This was the last person he wanted to talk to right now, but he knew why he was calling and answered the phone. 'Hello, Joseph what a pleasant surprise.'

'Hello, Gary, do you have what I'm after?' Joseph said.

'How many times do I have to tell you, Joseph, you're not my type.'

'Ha, ha, very funny. Do you have your new account details, so I can debit your college fees or what?'

Gary had changed banks during the year and was meant to inform Joseph of his new account number, but had forgotten to do so.

'Sorry about that, Joseph. I'll email them to you right now. Hang on a second, will you?'

He moved over to the computer on Vince's desk, clicked compose on the email program and began typing his new bank details to send to Joseph, the phone wedged between his shoulder and chin.

'While you're at it,' said Joseph. 'When I receive your

account details, do you want me to deduct just the amount due or do you want me to deduct your entire amount, as Vince did yesterday?'

He stopped typing. His fingers hovered over his keyboard. His breath moved in and out of his chest and for a moment was the only thing that could be heard. 'Did you just say Vince paid off his entire school fees?'

'Yes, I know. Caught me by surprise, too. Yesterday he paid the entire amount in cash. I didn't think he had that kind of money on him.'

'Me neither, Joseph. Me neither.'

'So what would you like me to do with yours?'

'Um, just deduct the amount due for now, thanks,' said Gary. He hit send. 'You should have the bank details now.'

'Got it, thanks for that,' replied Joseph and hung up.

Gary stared at his computer screen. How could Vince afford to pay off his entire college tuition? It would have been over twenty thousand dollars. Did he win the lottery and not tell his best friend? For him to be able to pay off his fees and buy those expensive Apple products, there must be a logical explanation. But what was it?

Did he inherit some money from a dead relative?

Or was he involved in criminal activities like his father? Was this going to affect his safety? So many scenarios.

Enough was enough. He couldn't wait any longer and decided to call Vince and confront him face to face and find out the truth. Why was he Mr. Richie Rich lately, and was there something he wasn't telling his best friend?

Mounted on the front window of his car, Vince's phone rang. He was on his way home after the meeting with the chief. It was a hard day seeing his father like that, battered and bruised and begging for food. He hit the loudspeaker button.

'Hey, champion, what's doing?' he said.

Gary dispensed with the pleasantries.

'Hey, rich boy, what's going on, man?'

'Rich boy?' laughed Vince, not knowing where he was going with this.

'Yeah, where did you get all that money from?' Gary's tone was severe. 'I know, man, so don't bullshit me. Tell me the truth.'

'Fuck!' mouthed Vince silently in the car.

He sat there agape. His eyes wide open but barely focused on the road ahead. His secret had been discovered. Gary had found the money. Why else would he call him a rich boy? Thoughts flowed in a blur through his mind. He had to share the money and his secret now, something he had not planned for.

'I'll be there in ten minutes, Gary. Please just do me a favor and don't take any money out of the bag. I'll explain everything.'

He planted his foot hard on the accelerator.

He had made a terrible mistake.

Chapter 36

The conversation ended, Gary's face turned crimson and he stood frozen. Vince's words rang in his ears. Without wiping the spit from his face, Gary repeated aloud what he'd just heard: 'Please just do me a favor, and don't take any money out of the bag. *Moneybag!* What the hell are you talking about?'

Gary thought he was probably right in assuming Vince's father was involved in a corrupt deal. In this very room could be a bag possibly filled with money, which would explain the elaborate spending.

Now intrigued and with only minutes before Vince would arrive, he snooped under his bed. He noticed a couple of bags with the Apple logo. He pulled the bags out and emptied the contents on the floor to reveal the other purchased items that were on the receipt.

There was only one other place to look, the wardrobe. He opened its doors and picked up the blankets and pillows, piled up on the base. After tossing them onto the floor, he turned back and there it was, a bulging black backpack.

This had to be it. Why else would it be buried under blankets if not to conceal it?

He slowly unclipped the latch and lifted open the top flap. A dark green filled his vision as bundles and bundles of hundred-dollar bills sat atop each other – the bag straining at the sides. His heart pounded. The hairs on the back of his neck stood up, and he blinked twice to make sure this was no dream. This was something he couldn't have imagined.

He was not going to let Vince have all the fun. The money was as much his now as it was his roommate's. Gary liked his girls and his cars. Now one of his true loves could become a reality. He could already hear the roar of the engine in his head as his greedy paws hefted out of the bag a dozen or so bundles, vanishing out of the room as Vince's car screeched to a halt on the campus grounds.

Vince was in a daze as he ran breathless toward his room. His eyes darting left and right, half looking for danger or a sign that something was wrong. His mind swirled with consequences; jail or death seemed possible.

Friends at the campus greeted him as they walked by, but he did not respond. For the first time in his life he was really scared. He desperately needed to talk to Gary: this was a matter of life and death. The men after the bank's money were extremely dangerous, and any whiff that they were in possession of it would end in dire consequences. Gary needed to be sensible and not attract too much attention, a point Vince needed to drill into his thick skull. Knowing his friend, he knew keeping secrets and saving money were not his strong suits.

Vince entered his room. His bed was made, but Gary's looked used. His birthday present lay among his jumbled comforter, but there was no sign of Gary. Vince did not hesitate and went straight for the wardrobe, hoping to find the treasure as he had left it. He saw it as the key to a bright future. He was obsessed. The thought of having to share it didn't fit into his plan. Before opening the wardrobe door, he shut his eyes for a second, his hands shaking.

'Please be there, please.'

He pulled the handle and scanned down. The pillow and blankets were as he'd left them, and underneath, thankfully, after a few shoves, he saw the backpack.

He opened the bag and breathed a huge sigh of relief. It was still there in all its glory. Maybe Gary didn't know about the stash; maybe it was just a misunderstanding. Vince was hoping he had not deduced what he had meant when he'd said, 'Don't take the money out of the bag.' Gary was probably jealous of his roommate's new laptop – he was long overdue for one himself. Who knew why he acted the way he did, but that didn't matter anymore. The money was safe and undiscovered, and he was the only one who knew about it. It was a close call, and he needed to make sure this never happened again.

Vince decided to move the money somewhere safe, under a lock and key. It was Sunday though. Where could he go? Then it came to him, he swung the backpack over his shoulder and left the room. Next stop, the UCLA Student Activities Center.

The Student Activities Center was famous for its eight-lane, thirty-three-yard outdoor pool located at the south end of the campus. The center also ran a large fitness gym with programs to motivate faculty and students to obtain a healthy weight and stress-free lifestyle.

Vince had joined a year ago. His plan had been to do laps in the mornings to help with his shoulder injury and wake himself up for class. But his late shifts saw that the comfort of his bed always won over early-morning workouts. The gym was rarely used.

The day was slipping away. Blue light refracting from the pool danced along the walls and on the ceiling. He swiped his card at the entrance door. It opened and locked itself as he walked through. The lights inside were on and the smell of chlorine filled the air.

He was not alone. Two lanes of the pool were being used, one male was swimming freestyle, while another was doing the breaststroke. They swam up and down continuously, oblivious to his presence. Vince walked away from the pool and entered the men's changing room, which was large and smelled of stale sweat. Wooden seating was placed strategically around the perimeter, and there were hooks on the walls to hang clothes. There was also access to separate shower and toilet areas. But what he was after was mounted on the walls: hundreds of empty white lockers, deep and wide enough to fit a backpack filled with money. This is what he had come for, this was now going to be his hiding spot. It was a lot safer here than in his bedroom.

He chose a locker in the corner of the room and placed the bag inside, closing the door using his membership card by running it over the magnetic lock. It locked with a click and displayed a red light. The only person able to open the locker now was the card bearer.

Locker number forty-nine.

Chapter 37

Gary entered the Felix Chevrolet car dealership in Downtown Los Angeles, thirty minutes away. It was closing time, but the dealership was staying open later than usual, as they had a sale on. The owner had been forced to cut twenty percent on the entire stock as high petrol prices had seen large muscle cars lose their popularity.

He stood over the new Chevrolet Camaro, his dream car. His passion for muscle cars had begun at an early age, when his mechanic father had decided to build their first car together. It was his way of bonding with his son and passing down the trade secrets. By the age of eighteen, Gary was a qualified mechanic but without the schooling.

He appreciated the fine workmanship and kneeled down to take a closer look. While low to the ground, a female salesperson approached him. He turned his head to see a long pair of legs that eventually met a short black skirt. At first glance he pigeonholed the gorgeous blond and assumed she was hired for her appearance and not for her knowledge in cars. Her name was Jessica Myers. She looked down at him as she ran her fingers along the car, as if it was her boyfriend.

'Do you know much about Camaros?' Jessica asked.

Gary stood up, eyeing the way she stroked the car. At that moment he wished he was the car. She was a ten on his personal gauge.

Pulling his focus away from her perfect body he said, 'I believe this is the new 2015 Chevrolet Camaro, a 6.2-litre supercharged V8, five hundred and eighty horsepower and the color is crystal red.' He was no dummy when it came to Camaros.

Jessica smiled and sat inside the display car. Her skirt rose as she sat, attracting his full attention. His initial impression of her was on the money, but he was not complaining.

'Are you in the market to purchase one?' she asked.

'Actually, I'm looking to buy one today,' said Gary, trying not to peek up her skirt.

'As you can see, we have a sale on today, all you need to do is leave a deposit and your new car will be ready in as little as two weeks.'

There was a problem with that scenario. He did not want to wait two weeks, he wanted a car right now. Gary asked, 'How about this one?' Tapping his fingers on the roof of the demonstration car she was occupying.

She stepped out, adjusted her skirt and faced Gary. 'I don't think the demonstration car is for sale. Hang on, let me ask.'

After a quick discussion with her boss she came back with an answer. 'The only way the boss would let me sell you this car, which has all the extras built into it already, is if you pay sixty thousand for it.'

Gary smiled and without any hesitation glanced into her seductive eyes, raised an eyebrow, and said in a cheesy James Bond manner, 'Is cash okay?'

'Yes, of course,' smiled Jessica, touching her hair and directing him into her office to finalize the payment.

'I'll take it on one condition, though, Jessica: you join me for a drink tonight to celebrate.'

Gary could tell by the look in her eyes and the way she was touching her hair that she was into him. Why wouldn't she be, he was young, rich and had just bought the demonstration model at the full asking price, which would have sat well with her boss.

As he exited the dealership, he could not contain himself and revved the engine for no apparent reason. It was like music to his ears. While driving, he decided to call Vince and share the good news.

The phone rang three times, then Vince answered.

'Hey, Vince,' Gary shouted. 'I love you, man!'

'What in the hell are you on, Gary?' said Vince.

'Listen, bro, listen. Doesn't she sound like a beast?' He revved up the 6.2-litre supercharged engine a couple of times.

'What's that noise? Sounds like a V8,' said Vince, leaving the Student Activities Center.

'My V8, Vince. I purchased a new Camaro. I used some of the money from your secret stash.'

'What?' Vince froze in his tracks.

Yes, the backpack had still been in its hiding place, but that didn't mean no money had been taken out of it. When he'd quickly checked it all seemed to be there. He could have never known it had been disturbed without counting it.

It was confirmed: Gary had found his money. This changed everything; he was back to square one. How was he going to manage him? A supercharged Camaro was glaringly obvious to those on the lookout. Vince needed to regroup and stay calm. There was no reason to fight. Starting an argument would only cause more problems; he needed to assess the damage first.

'The car sounds great, Gary. Did you purchase anything else?' Vince asked, taking a deep breath and holding it in.

'Why do you ask? You sound upset,' said Gary.

'Listen, I'm going to be up front with you. We need to have a sit-down and talk about how we'll share the money. We have to be careful. Trust me – if word got out we'll both be serving jail time.'

'I agree,' said Gary. 'I have questions of my own I want to ask you. One being how the fuck you acquired this fortune in the first place.'

Vince shook his head, mentally ordering himself to keep calm and relaxed, not to show his frustration.

'Okay, Vince, meet me at the Zanzibar club in Santa Monica tonight at nine. Let's celebrate and discuss our promising future together. I'm buying.'

Vince laughed. 'You're buying – that's funny. I'll be there. See you then.'

The call ended and Vince's shoulders drooped. This was never going to work. He felt cheated: why should he have to share half the money that he had deciphered and found. Then again, one million dollars each was better than nothing. For this to work he needed to be the distributor, have it locked away and drip-feed Gary cash, as if it was a salary. It was the only way to keep him happy and keep the spending to a minimum.

It was the only way.

Chapter 38

Sunday-night pancakes had become a ritual in the Peruggia household. Alexander would sit in the same booth at the beach club and eat Tony's famous pancakes with a cappuccino. It was a pastime he and the boys had loved until recently. Wise guy Tony was a true Italian, known to dabble in the kitchen. He would always say men make better chefs than women. Phil had nick-named Uncle Tony 'the pancake king.' He had happily served Alexander and the kids for years, because, he said it made Alexander human. Yes, he was a conniving murderer, but also a family man who loved his boys.

'They taste different tonight,' said Alexander, slouched against the bench. His head was bent forward, but his eyes were glaring upward. His voice was laced with menace.

'Okay, boss, I'll make some fresh ones, no problem.' Tony grabbed Alexander's shoulder warmly. 'I'm here for you, Lex, I just want you to know that.'

'No one should ever have to bury their own son,' Alexander said to his oldest friend.

Tony didn't reply. He just patted him on the shoulder as if to say he understood.

Alexander's usual confidence, the demeanor that commanded respect, was absent. Tonight he looked deflated. A hangdog expression on his face.

He wanted to be left alone. Frowning, his eyes fixed intently on the empty bench on the opposite side, the place where his son would have sat. His right leg vibrated with increasing intensity under the table – until, finally, with a wild look in his eyes, he slammed his hand down hard on the table, sending cutlery flying everywhere. He could not believe his eldest son was gone, and the sad thing about it was that he had no suspect to go after – no revenge attack to heal his sorrows. Someone was going to pay, it was the only way the world would be right again.

Ten minutes later in walked the team dressed in black – Ian, Frank and James, who were out scouting alternate routes if things went bad. They had stolen a white van, filled it up with gas, changed the number plates, tinted the windows and left it in the outside parking lot.

As they entered the restaurant, Ian and Frank began ribbing James, punching his massive arms, trying to get a rise. He just ignored them, knowing they were idiots. If he wanted to he could crush them like ants, his biceps were as big as their thighs.

Tony confronted them before they approached Alexander. 'Be careful,' he told them, 'he rejected my pancakes.'

'Maybe they were bad,' joked Frank.

'Nothing's wrong with them,' said Tony. 'I've used the same ingredients for years. He's not having a good day.'

Frank ignored Tony and was the first to face up to Alexander at the booth. The rest followed, including Tony.

'Hey, boss, we've all spoken and we're a little concerned, we're putting all our trust in a corrupt cop,' said Frank. 'The heist we have planned for tomorrow night sounds perfect on paper, but we could be walking into a trap.'

Alexander did not say a word.

James then stepped forward and in his deep voice said, 'The chief is retiring so he doesn't concern us, he's predictable. It's your other informant, Tarn, who knows about the heist. I don't trust him.'

Frank nodded.

Alexander broke his silence; his men needed encouragement. 'You can trust him,' he said.

Frank and James glanced at each other, they were not convinced.

'Tarn was the one who sent me Phil's last message,' said Alexander. 'Not even the chief knew of its existence.'

'Yes, sir, but it's a week late. I don't know, boss. He's too unpredictable, a wild card, in it for the cred,' said Frank, still not convinced. 'If Tarn wants to, he can sabotage our plan. What's stopping him? He has no financial gain in this.'

Alexander stood up. All evidence of his former wretched state fell away from his strong frame. He emanated confidence. All eyes were on him. He looked into the men's eyes. They were concerned, since the last heist had been a catastrophe. 'Don't worry about Tarn. Leave him to me, I have the perfect test to see if he's on our side. Trust me.'

Chapter 39

His name – 'Tarn' – was derived from a Norwegian word, meaning a mountain lake formed from melted glaciers. A peaceful image that belied his true nature, thought Lee Davis reading his file. Detective Tarn Mostrom was the quarterback in his Inglewood High School. He was of Scottish descent, hence his pale features and golden hair. Six foot tall and broad-shouldered. As a young teenager he had bullied other kids and generally made a scene to get noticed. Fast forward to today and nothing had changed, except now he carried a police badge.

He was one of Los Angeles's favorite rogue detectives, known for bending and sometimes ignoring the rules. He was detested within the department for not following procedure. Over ten years in the force he had received five warnings, two suspensions and was under several internal-affairs investigations for fraud and corruption.

The fact that he was a recluse didn't bother the chief. He was good at his job and solved cases. The other reason Lee liked having him around was insurance. If the shit hit the fan or it got too intense, there was a fall guy at the ready.

In Downtown LA, Tarn was about to make a bust on his own. His only problem was that he hadn't acquired a warrant to enter the premises. Like that was going to stop him.

Gritting his teeth, he threw his weight behind a violent

kick to the old wooden door and busted it open, tearing part of the frame with it. With his gun drawn, he found two shocked men and forced them to the ground. One caught an elbow to the head, while the other lay on the ground with fear, shaking, a ring of white powder decorating his nostril. Cocaine, crack and various drug paraphernalia were strewn all over the place.

'What's all this shit?' Tarn said, pointing at the vast amount of drugs on the table. After the men were handcuffed and the room was secured, he helped himself to a bag of uncut cocaine and stashed it in his breast pocket. He could make a fortune with his Latino contacts on the west side.

'Hey, that's mine, *puto*,' shouted one of the dealers on the ground.

Tarn slowly turned around and with menacing calm, asked, 'Whose is it?' Before planting a full-force kick to the man's abdomen, followed by another. 'Whose is it?'

He didn't let up until the man gasped, 'It's yours, it's yours.'

Exiting the building, Tarn pulled out his phone, which was vibrating in his jacket pocket. It was a private number.

'Hello, Tarn.' Alexander's voice was distinctive.

'To what do I owe the honor?' he asked, walking to his car.

'I need you to do something for me, it's important. I need to find out if I can truly trust you.'

'Go on,' said Tarn, wondering what he was required to do now.

'I need you to kill Leonardo Vancini's son, Vince.'

'What ... why?' asked Tarn. Vince was no threat.

'I have my reasons.'

'What's in it for me? I'm not taking out anybody for nothing.'

'You'll gain my trust. Think of it as a test.'

'A test? Haven't you hurt Leonardo enough?'

Alexander ignored the question. 'This needs to be done ASAP, preferably in the morning.'

'Hang on.'

'Call me when it's done, don't let me down.'

'Wait!'

The phone went dead.

Chapter 40

Sunday, 9 pm

The Zanzibar club was a standout place in Santa Monica where you were guaranteed to have a good time. Its true appeal lay in its lounge-like atmosphere, with bedouin-inspired decor, numerous comfy couches and ottomans to relax and indulge in after sweating on the dance floor.

Vince managed to find a parking spot off the main street. It was dark outside. Spotlights dotted the cappuccino-colored exterior walls that shone upwards and downwards. He ignored the small crowd at the front and walked straight into the bar.

The energy inside was electric and the beats of classic hip hop had brought in a plethora of beautiful girls. He remembered the layout from his previous visits; not much had changed. The bar area was still doused in warm reds and browns and the same oversized paintings hung on the exposed brick feature walls.

He approached the bar in the corner of the room. The music was loud, but you could still hear yourself talk. He was determined, and had a clear objective in his head. He and Gary needed to talk and form a unified alliance if they were to get away with the money scot-free. This was no game and this needed to be embedded in his friend's head. Rules needed to be drawn whether he liked it or not.

Vince decided to wait for his friend and ordered a Heineken to calm himself. The cold beer went down quick. It was a warm night and inside was not any cooler. He was perspiring. Keeping it warm was a deliberate tactic by the club to encourage women to wear skimpy clothing and to sell more alcohol.

After finishing his first beer, he spotted Gary in the crowd. He was on the dance floor showing off his John Travolta dance moves to not one but three beautiful women. They were laughing and enjoying his foolishness. How was this possible? he thought. Gary was never this attractive to the opposite sex. He needed another drink.

It all came to him in a flash: the girls were after his money. Gary didn't care, though. It didn't bother him one bit to play the rich-playboy card.

Vince ordered his second drink. Soon Gary noticed him and swaggered over with the three girls in tow. Vince inhaled their perfume and couldn't help but smile.

'Hey, my man!' greeted Gary with open arms, embracing his friend with a hug.

'I see you have company.'

'Yeah, these are the beautiful Jessica, Holly and Vanessa.'

Vince shook their hands. The company of beautiful girls didn't intimidate him; his girlfriend was stunning after all. His curiosity was piqued.

'So tell me, how do you know this guy?'

Jessica was the first to speak. She was the tallest of the girls, 'I met this hunk today at the dealership. I sold him a car.'

'Best day of my life,' chirped in Gary with a wink.

Vince felt frustration but didn't show it. He knew in his heart that there was no way to keep his friend on a leash. He was flashing his wealth around like he was Donald Trump. It would only be a matter of time before the wrong people found out. He knew they needed to have a talk, but now was not the time. Gary was thinking with a different organ tonight. It would be useless bringing it up in this place with the girls present. The talk had to wait and he needed to go with the flow to ensure Gary was onside.

'Gary, listen, tomorrow we need to chat, promise?'

'I understand,' replied Gary. 'Now let's have some fun,' he said, pulling Jessica in close against his body.

Holly, who wore a low-cut white tank top, which showed her cleavage to full effect, was the most flirtatious. She sidled in close to Vince and brushed herself against him seductively. He felt the blood rush through his body and his sexual urges took over. The voice in his head was telling him to go for it, even though he knew it was wrong.

'So, Vince, are you going to buy me a drink or what?' Holly said, touching her lips against his cheek.

He flashed a cheeky smile. He needed to loosen up: it was the weekend, after all and he was only twenty-two. 'Drinks all round,' he shouted.

The girls jumped and clapped.

'That's my boy,' Gary said with a smile. 'Just like old times.'

One shot turned into two, two turned into six. As the night went on the cocktails flowed. Tequila slammers, screaming orgasms, and cock-sucking cowboys – a particular favorite with the girls.

Vince thoroughly enjoyed being on the receiving end of the bar for a change. It was nice to let loose and see how these bartenders stood up compared to himself. At one point he ordered the girls a southern screw cocktail. The bartender had no idea how to make this one, so Vince didn't waste any time.

'I'm a bartender, can I show you?' Vince shouted above the noise. This was a chance to show off his talents.

'He's the best,' said Gary. 'Let him show you.'

The barman hesitantly agreed. 'I'm sick of you ordering drinks I don't know how to make. Talk is cheap. Let's see what you can do.'

On the other side of the bar Vince stood, cracking his knuckles and regaining his balance. The girls cheered him on. This wasn't new to him; this was his territory. He wanted to show this amateur who was boss.

He grabbed the ingredients for the cocktail – vodka, Southern Comfort, peach liqueur and Sunny Delight orange juice. All the ingredients were within his reach. The bartender stood aside and observed. The difference was not his knowledge that impressed him; it was the way he got the crowd fired up as he tossed the bottles up in the air, like twirling acrobats. All eyes were on Vince, including Holly, whose eyes were glued to him. Even intoxicated he was on cue, pouring his friends five beautifully colored creations.

The man behind the bar thanked him for the lesson and Vince clambered back over the counter. The girls couldn't contain their glee and laughed uncontrollably. They were steaming and everything was funny.

'I think I'm in love,' said Holly to Jessica, loud enough for Vince to hear.

'He has a girlfriend,' Jessica slurred.

Vince hugged the two girls from behind, just before Holly giggled and said, 'Like that's gonna stop me.'

After dancing, the pack left the bar hammered out of their minds. At one point Vince fell over and hit his chin on the pavement. Blood poured off his face as the others laughed in amusement. Holly tried to help him back to his feet and she ended up on top of him, partially intentionally. She was a girl who knew what she wanted, and she wanted Vince. They stared deep into each other's eyes. There was an intense attraction that ended with a lingering kiss.

'We can all crash at my place,' said Vanessa. 'It's a walk away.'

Gary quickly responded, 'I like that idea. This is the best day of my life.'

That was the last thing Vince remembered.

Chapter 41

Night had melted away into a majestic sunrise. A red-orange glow seeped over the horizon as if the light itself was being poured from a molten sun. Powerful rays flooded over the landscape, lighting every blade of grass and shining into Vanessa's three-bedroom apartment. Vince felt cheated yet again for not getting enough sleep. He rubbed his hands through his hair, his eyes struggling to open. A throbbing headache welcomed him, so he moved at a slow pace as he felt the room spin around him.

He forced his eyes open. Blurry shapes formed to become an unfamiliar room. He lifted his head off the pillow and noticed traces of blood, and only then did he feel a sudden pain on his chin. He instinctively touched it to feel the rough, scraped surface. The amount of booze he had consumed last night broke his personal best, and that was a lot, coming from a bartender.

Vince felt a tug on the crisp white sheets. He was not alone in the queen-sized bed. His first reaction was to look down under the sheets, to see he was completely nude. Twisting his body to the right, he was caught off guard to see a beautiful, lithe young blond lying beside him. It was Holly. He slowly lifted up the white sheets to see more of Holly's naked body. His eyebrows shot up, liking what he saw, as if registering it for the first time. Her curved backside was a shade lighter than the rest of her, framed by tan lines.

Coming to his senses he slid out of bed, trying not to wake her up. He needed to get out and find Gary. If Isabella found out, their relationship would be over. Great: another secret he needed to keep quiet.

He found his underwear, jeans and shirt in various parts of the room. Last night's escapades must have involved the speedy removal of clothing. He put them back on and left the room, taking in one last glance of last night's triumph. He closed the door behind him and walked to another bedroom door, hoping to find Gary behind it. He still had some talking to do: no more fun and games. Last night was cool, but that wasn't the reason they had planned to meet at the Zanzibar.

He slowly swung the door open, but Gary was not there. Lying alone in bed, among all the sheets and blankets, was Vanessa. Vince quietly shut the door so as not to wake her and walked down the narrow coffee-colored carpeted hallway. The walls were a light yellow, picture frames hung on the walls displaying the girl's love for the ocean. It opened up to a small kitchen, nothing fancy but functional. Next to the kitchen was a decent-sized balcony, overlooking similar façades of opposing apartment blocks.

Jessica was alone, enjoying her morning coffee, her face doll-like and covered in makeup. She was dressed in a grey business suit, skirt and blouse. Vince had interrupted her alone time. His hair stood up like Albert Einstein's. It was evident he was not an early riser.

'I need coffee,' he said.

Jessica, trying to keep a straight face, pointed over to the coffee machine on the granite benchtop.

'Good morning, Vince. Someone had a good time last night.'

He smiled and poured himself a cup. 'So where's the man?'

'He ran out to check on his car. He remembered early in

the morning where his pride and joy was parked off the main road. Let's hope it's still there for all our sakes.'

Vince sighed and nodded. He knew his friend was going to treat this car like it was the crown jewel of Sheba.

'Last night we could hear you through the walls,' said Jessica.

'I was drunk, it was a mistake, I have a girlfriend,' said Vince, upset with himself and now thinking about the consequences.

'That's a shame, you two would've made the perfect couple.'

That was his cue to leave the apartment. Yes, last night was enjoyable, but that's all it was: he loved Isabella and did not want to jeopardize their relationship over a stupid one-night stand. He left the apartment in a hurry before Holly woke up. He hoped that, if he was gone when she woke up, she would realize last night was just a fling and nothing more.

He hoped this night would not come back to bite him in the ass. Karma was a bitch, but this indiscretion could cost him the one thing dearest to him, his girl.

Chapter 42

Gary picked up his unscathed car and parked it on the campus grounds. Two male car enthusiasts observed with envy. A group of girls also stopped for a peek, giggling and wondering who could be inside. He felt important exiting the car, trying to look nonchalant, aware that all eyes were on him, like a celebrity walking down the red carpet. Owning such an exotic car boosted his confidence. If last night's endeavors were anything to go by, he could not ask for anything else. He was living the dream: the surprise fortune was his salvation to a life every man dreamt of and he was loving it.

Early that morning while chatting to Jessica, a thought had crossed his mind. He knew Vince too well; he studied CGI animation, which required systems and processes. One glance at his uber-clean room told you one thing – he was a control freak. Envisioning the future with him as the gatekeeper to the money, taking control and trickling him some sort of allowance, was not what he wanted.

Gary wanted his entire share now. What he did with the money was no one's business, including Vince. So he'd left the apartment in a hurry while Vince was still fast asleep, to take what was his.

The target entered the Sunset Canyon dorm room and went straight for the wardrobe, but he was not the only man in the room. Hiding behind the door, a man dressed head to toe in black, stepped out from the shadows. His jaw was set and he wore a grim expression. The man with the silenced gun was none other than Detective Tarn Mostrom, waiting for Vince, to fulfill his duty and prove his loyalty once and for all.

Tarn was in position. This kill was going to be quick and easy, but something was not right: the male figure in front of him was not the target. Vince was considerably shorter with straight dark hair. The boy in the room was tall with dark curly hair.

Tarn stepped forward, the twenty-something in front of him was unaware of the silencer aimed at his head. His mind seemed to be totally focused on something else. He pulled the blankets and sheets onto the floor behind him. He reached toward the bottom of the wardrobe and punched the wall.

'He fucking moved it,' he said to himself. Ashen-faced, he stood up and ran his hands through his hair, clearly frustrated.

Tarn cocked his gun and the kid in front of him froze. The crisp sound was distinctive and rendered all else silent, except for the sound coming from the boy's breathing. Slowly and hesitantly he turned.

'Please, please be a practical joke,' he said, closing his eyes.

But this was no joke. The cold barrel of a silencer was pressed against the pulsating vein of his temple. His eyes bulged as he opened them. Tarn Mostrom coldly looked back at him.

'Please, please don't kill me,' he begged, holding his hands up and pleading for mercy.

'I'm sorry, kid, I really am,' said Tarn, taking a step back and moving the gun from his head and onto his chest. The noticeable barrel mark could be seen branded on his forehead. 'What's your name?'

'My name is Gary.'

'Why are you in Vince's room?'

'I'm his roommate. Wait, don't shoot. If you're here

because of the money it wasn't me, it was Vince, I swear. Please don't kill me.'

'What money?' Tarn asked with a need to know.

'The millions in the backpack.'

'Millions?' repeated Tarn. 'Where did he get it from?'

'I don't know, please. You can have it, just don't shoot.'

Tarn realized this could be the missing loot from the failed bank heist. Hundreds of police hours, not to mention all of Alexander's men, had been unable to find it, and this idiot knew where it was.

The game plan now changed for Tarn. Yes, he still was going to kill Gary, but not before he knew where the money was. This information was priceless and he wanted to be the man to deliver the good news to Alexander.

'So where is it, then?' he asked, lowering the gun in an attempt to look less threatening. 'Tell me and I'll let you go.'

Gary glanced toward the bed.

'Is it under the bed?' Tarn asked, bending down to take a peek.

Gary sprang. He leapt onto Tarn's back and planted two hard punches into his rib cage. His plan to hit and run to safety backfired dreadfully. Tarn was a man bred from the streets, fighting dirty was his specialty. With a wrestling maneuver Gary was thrown off, hitting the computer desk and breaking it in two.

Now trapped with this imposing figure blocking the exit, Gary had no choice but to fight. The computer keyboard was yanked from the iMac's screen and swung at the head of his attacker. Tarn blocked it with his forearm, shattering it into pieces. He was going to teach this punk some respect.

'My turn,' said Tarn. With a lightning jab he struck Gary's right eye, and he went down hard.

'Ahh!' Gary roared with pain.

Tarn was not finished. He was just getting started as he lifted the boy by his t-shirt. This little shit needed to be taught a lesson.

'Where is the money?'

Gary did not say a word and swung an awkward right punch. Tarn saw it coming and leaned back as his fist flailed past. Then he moved in for a combination of his own, connecting heavy blows to Gary's head, snapping it backwards. The boy flopped to the ground, out cold.

Tarn clenched his jaw. 'Where's the money?'

'Vince has it,' Gary said, struggling to speak.

Tarn picked him up again; blood poured from his mouth. He hung off his arms and his head lolled from side to side. Tarn could see he was defeated.

'Vince, where?' said Tarn. 'I will kill you: speak.'

Hanging there like a rag doll, Gary spotted the lip of a badge sticking out of the man's back pocket. 'You're a cop,' he stupidly spurted, blood spraying out of his mouth.

'Why did you have to do that?' said Tarn, dropping him to the ground like a bag of potatoes. He had to kill him now, there was no option. His identity was at stake.

'One last time, where's the money?'

Gary ignored the question and struggled to crawl over to the door. Tarn knew he was thinking irrationally now, wanting out of this room, but that was not going to happen. He reached up for the door handle, leaving a trail of blood behind on the floor.

'You leave me no choice,' said Tarn.

Gary turned the handle, lifted his body off the ground and that's when Tarn pressed the trigger. A single gunshot had been fired through the gun's silencer that sounded like a small insect. Gary arched forward as if possessed by a demon. Hitting the door, he, too, made barely a noise. He fell to the ground, his hand still gripping the door handle. It was over for Gary, he slumped to the ground, blocking the exit.

Tarn walked over and used his foot to push him onto his back. He was still alive. He waited a few seconds and just to make sure, raised his gun and fired another shot to his chest.

Gary grunted, then said nothing more.

Tarn left, closed the door behind him, feeling bittersweet. Irritated for killing the wrong target, but intrigued at uncovering a secret Alexander Peruggia would immensely appreciate.

Vince had the money.

Chapter 43

Monday, 7 am

Alexander sweated as he threw hard left and right punches into a stern punching bag held by Frank. Young Joey was also in the gym working out. His private lessons with professional UFC fighter Anderson Silva had escalated to another level, taking place center stage in the boxing ring. A crowd of people stood by and watched Joey give it his all. Alexander was happy his son was taking it seriously and he could tell he was a changed man. After last Thursday's embarrassing beating, Joey had practically lived in the gym, focusing on his boxing and lifting weights to boost his aggression. He had told his father that his ultimate plan was to build up his strength, endurance and speed to avoid getting knocked down the next time they met in the ring, or anyone else who wanted a piece of him.

Alexander stopped punching his bag and glanced over at his son's progress. His technique and form had improved dramatically. His combinations were deadly accurate as he punched the trainer's arm pads with a right and then a left, ending with two uppercuts. At the end of the sequence he would duck twice to avoid an incoming hit from the trainer's boxing mitts. The combo would be repeated faster and faster. Right, left, uppercut, uppercut, duck, duck. He had the combination down pat and looked in control.

'Time,' shouted Anderson, 'gloves down.'

Joey regrouped to the corner with a drink of water.

'The kid's improved,' said Frank, walking with Alexander to the edge of the boxing ring.

'You're looking good, boy,' said Alexander. The fact that he was manning up reassured him.

Joey smiled and put his mouth guard back in, ready to go again.

'Alexander, the next time you two fight, I think it's going to be a different story,' said Anderson with a grin. 'He's a machine.'

Alexander sighed with not the slightest concern and said, 'I'm looking forward to it.'

Alexander left the gym, wiping his face on a club towel, and headed for his exquisite rooftop penthouse with breathtaking views of the sea. Complete with SAS-guard bulletproof windows, hidden panic room, outside spa, billiard room and a sunken lounge featuring a magnificent marble mosaic floor. No expense had been spared in the presidential suite.

While opening up the glass doors to his marble shower, his ringing phone echoed from the kitchen, which he'd left on the marble benchtop.

Completely naked, he walked out barefoot onto the heated tiles. Lines of sweat ran down his face, shoulders and back. The wounded shoulder had healed up nicely and blended in among his other scars. While training he didn't perspire much, but now that he had stopped he was sweating like a pig in need of a shower.

'Yes?' he answered.

'Hey, Alexander, it's me,' said Tarn Mostrom. 'I have good and bad news.'

'Is it done?'

'No, that's the bad news. His roommate was there instead, so I had to improvise.'

'So what's the good news?'

'While … questioning the roommate, he revealed something I know you'll like.'

'What's that?'

'The two million dollars, Vince found it.'

Alexander tilted his head to the side, his eyebrows raised. 'Hang on, let me get this straight. You're telling me that Leonardo Vancini's son has my money?'

'Yes, sir.'

'That little shit.'

Alexander was in a desperate financial situation, taking more and more bank loans to stay afloat. He was drowning, with no way out. Time was ticking for him, liquidation was next. The two million would be a much-needed buffer to shut the banks up and offer some leeway until plan B was carried out.

'So, did I pass the test?' Tarn asked.

'No, not yet. I need you to keep a low profile and finish the job you were asked to do. This time I want you to come back with what is rightfully mine. Do you understand?'

'Yes, sir.'

The phone went dead.

Chapter 44

The mist thickened to a dense fog bled of all color at the UCLA campus grounds, as usual a ghost town at that time of morning. It was as if a plague had hit the campus and killed everyone in its wake. Vince felt a huge sense of relief as he saw Gary's immaculate Camaro parked at the gate. Good, he was here. It was time for them to have their all-important chat. His walk down the concrete path was slower than normal. He was still hungover from last night. His clothes reeked of alcohol and cigarettes, not to mention Holly's perfume and lipstick marking his body like a crime scene. He needed a good cleanup, a brushing of the teeth, and a gargle of mouthwash as the booze on his breath was unbearable.

'Gary, it's me, open up,' Vince said, knocking on the door.

No answer. He checked the doorknob. It had been left open, the idiot. He pushed on the door and it abruptly stopped in its tracks and bounced back a little. Something heavy was obstructing it. He thought it was probably something Gary had left on the floor, the slob.

Vince used his shoulder to push on the door with all his strength.

'Help,' he heard from the other side. It was faint, a whisper.

'Help,' said Gary again, this time louder, followed by a cough.

'Is that you, Gary?' Vince stuck his head in the doorway to see his friend lying there, hurt and bleeding. 'Shit! Hang on.'

His dead weight was blocking the door. Vince pushed and squeezed himself into the room and dropped to his knees to help Gary, who had been nudged forward.

'Aww shit dude, you're bleeding everywhere.'

His face was as pale as a ghost, as life left his body, but he was still alive.

'Gary, are these gunshots?'

He did not answer.

His eyes rolled to the back of his head and he faded from consciousness. The blood flowed freely from the wounds to his back and the side of his chest. Vince needed to do something and fast. Picking up the phone, he dialed 911.

'Please come quick. I need help at the UCLA campus. Sunset Canyon dorm room number seven, my friend's been shot.'

'We'll be there in two minutes,' the lady on the phone responded.

Vince then searched for the police officer's card in his pants pocket, who was here to keep an eye on him. He dialed the number, but there was no answer.

Diving to the floor, he held Gary's wrist. 'Your pulse is weak, I need to stop the bleeding.' Time was of the essence. Could he survive another two minutes? That was the question. He leapt up from the ground and saw a thick duct tape beside Gary's bed, used to secure the back of his oil paintings. He snatched it; that would do.

Stopping the loss of blood was his top priority.

He used his teeth to open up the first line of tape. He could see where the bullets had entered his body, just by finding the center of the bloodstains that were rapidly increasing in size. He pulled him into an upright position, and Gary cried with pain.

'Ahh, it hurts.'

'I know, I know, hang in there.' Vince wrapped the duct tape around and around Gary's body, tighter and tighter until all you could see was a blanket of brown tape around his torso. Gary looked like he was about to be mummified. It was not ideal but he was desperate. Whatever worked to stop the bleeding.

'The ambulance is on its way.'

'I'm cold.' Gary shivered, his temperature dropping; his skin was cold to the touch.

Vince pulled his friend in close and rubbed his arms up and down to keep him warm. The blood was pooling on the floor and all over his shoes, but he didn't care.

'Hang in there, Gary.' Vince gently slapped his face a couple of times to keep him conscious. It was obvious he was slipping away and the urge to close his eyes was strong.

'Don't you die on me.'

So many thoughts passed through Vince's mind as he embraced his friend on the floor. These bullets were meant for him. This was the second attempt on his life and his luck was running out. Maybe the next time he would not be so fortunate. Poor Gary had taken the hit and if he died Vince was responsible.

As promised by the operator, within a few minutes, the ambulance sirens were outside. Gary's head fell to one side, his eyes half open.

'They're here, okay, hang on.'

With a sudden movement of his shaking hand, Gary drew through the blood-drenched floor.

'What is it, Gary?'

His breathing was labored, as with every movement he left a mark in blood on the floor with his finger. At the end, the scrawled mess on the floor was obvious – it was a four-digit number: 2426.

'What do these numbers mean?'

He tried to talk, but ended up coughing and spitting blood from his mouth.

'No, no, that's okay, rest. We have time.'

The ambulance officers were in the building.

'We're in here, come quick!' yelled Vince.

The paramedics entered the room and saw Gary wrapped up in duct tape.

'That's a first,' said one of the ambulance officers.

'I tried to stop the bleeding,' said Vince, covered in blood.

'No, you did good,' said the female officer, who checked Gary's pulse and gently slapped him in the face to see his eyes open. 'Hang in there, son, I'm going to give you a shot of morphine to help with the pain.'

Gary was lifted onto a stretcher and carried toward the ambulance. Vince climbed inside and held his hand as they sped toward the hospital. He looked down at his friend's battered face and his damaged and dying body, and gripped his hand.

In thought, Vince ran the numbers over and over in his head: 2426.

They were familiar, but he couldn't pinpoint where he had seen them before.

They arrived at the hospital, Gary was rushed into the emergency ward, leaving Vince to wait it out in the visitors' room. He didn't mind as he needed to clear his head and think. Despite his concern for his friend, he had a splitting headache. He could use another strong coffee, some headache tablets and maybe a bite to eat.

This week was clearly the worst week of his life. How could so much go so wrong? It started with the explosion at the house, his father's incarceration, the hacking of his bank account and now his best friend had been shot and was fighting for his life.

It was blindingly obvious: it was orchestrated by one man. Someone who would do anything to avenge his son's death. Alexander wanted Leonardo to suffer and there was nothing anyone could do to stop him.

Vince took a deep breath. He was alone and up against an impossible adversary. What was next? Ten minutes later, while contemplating his future over a cup of coffee, two messages buzzed from his cell in his pocket. He took it out.

The first message was from Isabella, it read:

Hey, babe, heard what just happened on campus, I'm on my way. Love you xxx

The second was from Detective Tarn Mostrom:

Hello, Vince, this is Detective Mostrom. I've spoken to your father. You still could be in grave danger, don't talk or trust anyone. I'm on my way.

Chapter 45

Monday, 1 pm

Entering the walls of prison could be a daunting experience for many, unless you were Alexander Peruggia. He was well known and respected by the authorities and inmates alike. He did not waste any time. He was fierce in his request to be taken into the facility, expecting immediate compliance; he wanted to meet with prisoner Leonardo Vancini, even if it wasn't visiting time.

Leonardo was not expecting any visitors today, so he was more than surprised when he saw Alexander Peruggia sitting smugly in the visitors' room. He was dressed in his usual expensive suit and tie. The empty chat room was divided into five private cubicles, separated by partitions on either side. A thick shatterproof glass wall separated the visitors from the inmates.

He waited cross-legged, with the posture of someone ever alert, but with the calm poise of control. His Gucci brown leather boots and Rolex were outer displays of wealth and by association, power. He exuded authority.

Leonardo entered the room escorted by a large muscular prison guard and sat opposite him. His face betrayed no emotion and was now covered in an unkempt beard, having not shaved since he'd arrived.

When he saw Alexander sitting calmly on the other side of the glass, one thing struck him like a lightning bolt – the sheer absurdity that, after serving the city for decades as a cop, he should be the one behind bars in an orange jumpsuit, while its biggest criminal roams its streets in freedom. The system was screwed.

How could any possible conviction by this man be accepted in a court of law? Sure, Leonardo had made a stupid mistake by allowing himself to be duped as he was. One thing now was clear: he wasn't going to make that mistake again.

Alexander leaned in and grabbed the white telephone on the small bench in front of him. It was the only means of communicating through the thick glass wall. He placed the phone to his ear and waited for Leonardo to do the same.

Leonardo hesitated, having nothing to say. He despised the man who sat three feet in front of him. All he could think of was how much he was going to enjoy killing him when he was released from this place.

He sat there staring into the middle distance.

Alexander knocked the telephone onto the glass wall a couple of times to regain his attention.

Alexander mouthed, 'Please.'

Leonardo read his lips and continued to stare deep into his dark eyes. Why the sudden visit? he wondered. What was he up to? He reluctantly picked up the phone, his curiosity piqued at his unsightly visitor. He wanted to see what he had to say.

'Good morning, my old friend,' said Alexander with a hint of sarcasm. 'You're probably wondering why the visit?'

Leonardo did not say a word, but just continued to stare blankly ahead, hoping that whatever was coming was not too painful.

'This morning I was alerted to news that blew me away. Fantastic news that I never expected or saw coming.'

Leonardo was not amused. He could not believe this

idiot in front of him. 'And what is that, my friend?' he said, returning the sarcasm.

'Are you ready for it? It's a biggie,' Alexander said as he straightened his tie. He took his time, like a presenter at the Oscars about to reveal who the winner was.

Leonardo wondered to himself what could possibly be so momentous it would bring the so-called 'Alexander the Great' here to tell him personally.

'Do you remember the two million dollars hidden by my late son, that was never found?'

'Do you mean the son I shot, who was blown up at the Trinity Church?' said Leonardo with a smirk on his face.

Alexander frowned a little but otherwise kept his anger in check. 'That's the one.' He leaned in closer to the glass with the phone against his ear. 'This morning I found out that the money has been discovered. Isn't that great?'

'Congratulations,' said Leonardo, shaking his head. 'You came all this way to tell me that? Why?'

Alexander's grin widened.

'Think, genius. I'm telling you this because the person who deciphered Phil's clue and found the money was …'

He didn't finish the sentence; he didn't need to. Leonardo paused, frowned and then his jaw dropped. Wide-eyed he looked at Alexander and whispered, 'Vince.'

'Bingo,' said Alexander, pointing at him like he was holding a gun.

Leonardo wanted to hit something. He stood up, still gripping the telephone, and punched the glass as hard as he could. 'If you touch one hair on my son's head,' he hissed.

'You'll do what? You're in no position to threaten me. It's ironic how your son found his way into our little game. It's beautiful, it's karma. Now I will return the favor.'

'What favor?' Leonardo grunted as two guards slammed him against the wall with his cheek pressed hard onto the glass.

Alexander stood up from his chair and looked him

straight into the eye. 'Now it's my turn to play cat and mouse with your son, chase him down like a little pig, as you did with mine.'

In a rage, Leonardo pushed himself free of the guards and punched the glass wall in a vain hope it might make it through to Alexander's face. It vibrated a little, but that was it.

Alexander stood there with a grin, his face flushed with joy. Coming here today was all he thought it would be. He could see in Leonardo's face the pain he was suffering. Soon he would suffer the same fate with the death of his son, an eye for an eye.

Leonardo was again pushed up against the glass, hands cuffed, but his mouth was free.

'You just wait until I get out, you just wait. I'm coming for you. You're dead! You hear me, you're fucking dead!'

'I'll be waiting,' Alexander said, straightening his tie and leaving the room. His plan to torment him had just begun. He would play on his emotions. Make him endure the last week locked up, not knowing if his son was dead or alive. His son was a target.

The guards walked their prisoner out of the visitors' room. He fell on his knees, making the guards stop in their tracks. His chin trembled. He would do anything to help his son, even if it meant begging, longer chores, whatever.

'Please, sir, my kid is in danger, I need to make one call.'

'Get up off your knees, Leonardo,' said one of the guards pitilessly.

'Don't forget I'm a cop, I'm one of the good guys. Please!'

'Get up!' the guard demanded.

'You have kids, right? What would you do if they were in trouble? You would move heaven and earth, true?'

The second guard's expression softened. Leonardo was right: he had a son, too.

'Please, sir, he's all I have. Please?'

Chapter 46

Leonardo's persistence paid off this time. The second guard reluctantly agreed and allowed him his one call. It was the only way to shut him up. He didn't care how he got the call, his son was in danger.

'You have two minutes, make it snappy,' said the guard, escorting him to the telephone booth. 'Time starts now.'

He thought for a quick moment. Calling Vince wasn't going to make him any safer. He needed more than to be warned, he needed protection. He needed someone with the power to provide a police presence, to keep a constant eye on him and keep him safely away from harm.

He dialed the police department and asked to be connected to the chief.

'Hello, Lee Davis here.' The chief's voice was authoritative.

'Hey, Lee, it's Leonardo. I need your help, I don't have time.'

'What in the hell have you done now? You're behind bars, for Christ's sake.'

'It's not what I've done. It's Vince, my boy, he's in trouble.'

'Trouble, what kind of trouble?'

'Today I was visited by fucking Alexander Peruggia. I don't know if it's true or not, but he claims Vince found the two million dollars his son hid before he was killed.'

'You have got to be kidding me,' said Lee.

'Like I said, I don't know if it's true. He could be playing me again. It wouldn't be the first time, but either way he's in trouble.'

'Okay, so what would you like me to do?'

'If it's true, he's a target. I need your help to keep him safe, move him somewhere, protective custody. Whatever you have to do, until I get out.'

Leonardo's voice was filled with emotion. He sounded desperate, vulnerable and spoke in hurried gasps, worried his two minutes were nearly up.

Lee sighed. 'I don't mean to alarm you, Leonardo, but I think it may be too late.'

'What do you mean too late?'

'There was a shooting at Vince's campus this morning. Officer Michael Brown was gunned down in his car.'

Leonardo gasped.

'A college student was taken to hospital in critical condition. Sorry, I didn't get the boy's name.'

'Please, God, this isn't happening.'

'Look, I'll find out the situation and let you know. I'll send Taylor and Mostrom to investigate.'

Before Leonardo could reply, the prison guard hung up the phone. Time was up. His body tensed. The thought of escaping crossed his mind, but that would be impossible. All he could do was pray his son was okay and hope Lee was a man of his word.

Was he so wrong?

If he only knew Lee was a two-faced lying bastard.

Lee stood up and walked around his room. He stared out from his large glass windows. Alexander had never mentioned anything to him about the money. He didn't like that. If it was Vince who was shot earlier, he was probably already dead. Alexander must have sent someone to retrieve the money and end his life.

Lee dialed the hospital.

'Hello, Ronald Reagan UCLA Medical Center, can I help you?'

'Yes, this is the Chief of Police, Lee Davis. Can you tell me the name of the boy who was brought in this morning with gunshot wounds? Was it Vince Vancini?'

The woman on the phone was the lead nurse who worked in the emergency ward. She asked the chief to wait while she searched through the log book. 'No, Chief,' she said after a few minutes. 'His name was Gary Bronson, but he was signed in by a Vince Vancini. I think he was his roommate.'

'So what's the status on the boy? Will he live?' Lee asked, digging for information.

'He's stable and recovering, pumped with morphine to help with the pain. It's amazing he survived. He was lucky.'

'Good, that's great to hear. Is it possible to speak to his roommate? It's of high importance.'

The nurse agreed and went looking for Vince.

Vince was sitting against a wall with his head between his knees. He was distraught, broken inside. Because of him, his friend was fighting for his life. He was being comforted by his girlfriend, Isabella, who had just arrived at the hospital. Her arms were wrapped around his back and held tight, while his shoulders shook as he sobbed.

'Excuse me, Vince, I'm sorry to interrupt you,' said a nurse in blue scrubs. 'The Chief of Police is on the phone.' She held out the wireless receiver.

Vince grabbed the phone and wiped away his tears with his sleeve and answered. 'Chief?'

'Hello, Vince, how's your friend doing?'

'Better now, I guess.'

'Sorry to have to ask you this, but it's important.'

'Yes, sir.'

'Alexander Peruggia visited your father this morning and claims you've found the missing two million dollars from the bank robbery. Is this true, or is it another one of his lies?'

Vince stood up, rubbing the back of his neck. He had

been caught off guard. He needed to respond quickly or the chief would be suspicious. His body stiffened. He rubbed his nose, then his ear nervously and answered, 'No, sir, it's not true.'

'I didn't think so,' said Lee. 'One more question, son, and I'll leave you alone. When you found your roommate, did he mention who the perpetrator was or did he leave anything behind that might identify him? Anything?'

Vince glanced down at his shoes covered in blood.

'Actually there was something, sir.'

'Yes? I'm listening: anything will help us catch the guy.'

'On the floor in blood Gary wrote the numbers 2426. I think he was trying to identify the killer somehow. I have no idea what it means, though.'

'Okay, I'll look into that. Thanks again for your help, I'll be in touch.'

The chief hung up.

Vince may not know what 2426 was, but Lee Davis certainly did. Those four digits represented a police badge identification number. He was trying to identify his shooter with the last thing he had seen.

Lee immediately knew who was involved, who was doing Alexander's dirty bidding. This wasn't the first time, but it could become a big problem. He was responsible for his men, and if Tarn Mostrom went down he knew he wouldn't hesitate in naming Lee and his involvement in a plea bargain. The feds would have a field day if they found out.

The solution to this problem was simple: Detective Tarn Mostrom needed to finish what he started and clean up all the loose ends.

Chapter 47

Reclining in his high-back black leather chair, Lee Davis could see the police department in full swing. He needed to make sure the college student never left the hospital alive. He breathed in deeply. He had been dealt a double whammy to fix. Tonight the six-million-dollar heist was planned to go ahead and he also had a small but crucial role to play in it.

This last week Monica Anton had opened dialogue with Lee as directed by Alexander to make sure everything was set and all the angles were covered. He needed to stay focused, but first he needed to deal with Tarn.

On the right-hand side of his desk sat three wooden drawers, underneath a small Buddha statue. As he was getting older, his spiritual beliefs swayed toward Buddhism. It calmed him. He unlocked the third drawer with a key. Inside were personal documents, a pistol that looked like it hadn't been used in decades and a cell phone. The phone was clean, untraceable. It was Alexander's direct line, but also used for any other matter that required discretion.

The phone rang twice. Tarn answered. He was in his car parked near the hospital, having a bite to eat. He thought it was better to follow Vince, who would eventually lead him to the money. That was the plan.

No caller ID showed on the phone so he didn't say a word, but put the phone on loudspeaker. Anyone could be on the other end.

'Hey, it's me,' said a craggy, deep voice.

'Hello, me,' replied Tarn, knowing full well who it was. The chief's voice was distinctive.

The chief sighed. 'We have a problem: the boy you shot earlier is still alive. He saw your face and it'll be only a matter of time for them to work out what 2426 is. The boy drew the number on the floor, you idiot.'

Tarn didn't say a word but continued to listen, amazed that the boy had survived after two shots to his torso, at virtually point blank.

'You need to finish this. He's at the Ronald Reagan UCLA Medical Center.'

'I know,' Tarn said. 'I followed the ambulance.'

'Okay, so you would also know Vince is there with him. Do them both.'

Tarn realized this mistake could become a problem. He needed to complete the job, wipe up the mess or end up behind bars permanently. 'I understand,' he said.

'This time, no mistakes!'

Chapter 48

Monday, 5 pm

Monica walked up the front steps of the beach club, wearing her favorite worn-out blue jeans and a dark blue shirt. The jeans hugged her ass and legs, showing them to full effect. Her hair was tied back in a ponytail and her black Versace glasses hid her eyes. She looked sexy yet mysterious, a woman in control. She dangled something in her right hand, something important. It was attached to a white rope that was wrapped around her index finger. She flicked it around like a key ring.

The automatic glass doors opened up wide.

'Good afternoon, Miss Anton,' said a friendly staff member, recognizing her face.

Monica smiled back and asked the young girl, 'Would you happen to know where Mr. Peruggia is?'

'Yes, of course. He's outside having a bite to eat, the usual place.'

Monica understood; it was also Joey's favorite spot. There was nothing better than digging your toes deep into the beach's cold sand, while enjoying some food with a few cold drinks.

She glided down the marble foyer. The clicking sound of her stiletto shoes followed her. The hallway opened up to wall-to-ceiling glass windows, overlooking the aqua-blue Pacific Ocean. She took a moment to observe the sparkling sea, white sand and the atmosphere of people enjoying themselves. She spotted Alexander surrounded by his gang at one of the many tables scattered on the beach.

Everyone sat around the table, their chairs facing their leader. He wore no shirt as Victoria rubbed sunscreen on his back, careful to avoid his wound.

Monica didn't need a reason to show up. She was part of the extended family now, but today she was there to reassure him the heist tonight was good to go. Everything on her end was in place. She'd arranged for the chief to shut down the surveillance cameras and to disarm the alarm when he left the LAPD headquarters.

Alexander looked up at Monica and smiled. She took off her stilettos as she stepped onto the sand. With shoes in hand, she strolled over to the table and greeted Frank, James, Tony, Ian, Victoria and finally, Alexander. As she stood there gazing through her dark glasses, she dangled the missing piece needed for tonight.

It was the entry tag into the LAPD headquarters. The tag belonged to none other than Detective Leonardo Vancini, currently occupied elsewhere. He wouldn't be needing it anytime soon.

Alexander reached forward and grabbed the tag out of her hands.

'Well done, Monica, well done.'

'So where's Joey?' she asked, noticing his absence.

Frank pointed in the direction of the beach. 'He's taking a walk, gathering his thoughts.'

Monica glanced toward the beach and saw him in the distance.

'He has big shoes to fill,' Frank said again, referring to Phil.

Monica knew it was going to be difficult for Joey to lead a team of veteran criminals and murderers with large egos, but Phil was gone and he bore the Peruggia surname.

Alexander stood up. 'It's true, Joey's nervous. He's

concerned this heist might end up like the last one. He needs to realize that if he wants all this to be his one day, he needs to step up.'

After hearing Alexander's last comment, Monica left the group and approached Joey's silhouette.

Tony leaned his bulk toward Alexander and asked, 'She's not doing him, is she?' And burst out laughing.

Frank also laughed and spilled a drink on himself.

'Fuck, if that's true she moves fast. It's only been a week,' said James. 'I might have a chance.'

'No, I have dibs on that pussy next,' said Frank.

'I'll fight you for it.' James laughed, tackling Frank off his chair onto the ground. A childish play fight erupted as they rolled into the sand.

Alexander laughed some more.

Even thirty feet away from the gang, Monica could still hear the sexual innuendos made by the men but continued to walk.

She caught up to Joey, who looked like he was going to have a panic attack, pacing up and down.

'What's up, Joey?'

'Hey, nothing, I'm fine,' he said, walking back and forth over his own footprints already dug in the sand. He didn't look fine, biting on his lip.

'Ah, fine. You know what the definition of fine is?' she said, trying to break the ice.

Joey lifted an eyebrow.

'Freaked out, Insecure, Neurotic and Emotional.'

Joey's frown turned into a smile. 'You always did have a way to make me feel at ease. My father thinks I'm nervous about tonight's job.'

'Are you?'

'No, it's been a week and how many people have been killed? I don't want a life filled with heists and murders. I'm over it.'

'I totally understand,' said Monica.

'I just want to lead a normal life like before.'

'I can help you, if you trust me,' she said.

'Now I know why Phil kept me guarded all those years, to protect me from this shit, and now I've become him. He's probably shaking his head up there.'

Joey faced the cloudless sky.

Monica could see Phil's anguish in Joey, how he'd felt before he died. It came as a surprise to her that Joey felt this way, too. She remembered how excited he had been to rob the bank on Wilshire Boulevard, his first attempt to be a part of the gang. He had begged his older brother to allow him to be a part of the team. Now one week later he wanted out. A perfect example of never judging someone's life until you've walked in their shoes.

'Joey, things will change. I promise you, but for now you need to man up and go ahead with the heist. On a personal note I want out, too, there's no place for me here now. If I'd found the two million, I would've left, but now I'm here until the end.'

'Did you hear about the two million?' Joey asked, changing the subject.

'No – what? Do you have it under your pillow?' she joked.

'Ha ha funny. I overheard Tony tell Frank that Leonardo Vancini's son, Vince, found the money. Dad sent Tarn to pay him a visit this morning.'

'Vince Vancini … that's it,' she said, things suddenly falling into place. 'They were the initials on the wristband. Now that all makes sense. I was in the right place, he just got there before me.' Seeing Joey's frown, she said, 'Listen, you'll be okay, be strong, I have your back.'

'Yeah, I know.'

'Let's get back to the group, but give me a hug first.'

After a quick sisterly embrace, they headed back to the wolves.

Chapter 49

Monday, 6:30 pm

Tarn rolled up to the Ronald Reagan UCLA Medical Center in his freshly cleaned black V8 Chevrolet Impala, a portable police siren stuck on its roof. He parked in the ambulance bay, which was a no-parking zone.

He slammed the door shut while looking over at the valets dressed in their formal white shirts and matching black pants and vests. They shook their heads in disbelief. He didn't care, he was on a cleanup mission. The clumsy work earlier needed to be rectified. He needed to make sure Gary didn't wake up from his induced sleep or risk being identified. It was a chance he could not afford to take and time was running out.

The automatic sliding doors opened to a high open lobby painted white. The floor tiles were white and pale grey, creating a large checkerboard pattern throughout the building. He walked into the lobby passing a large concrete pillar on his left, his eyes inspecting the hospital's modern layout and trendy light scheme, as he entered further into the foyer. To his right was the information desk. He pulled out his badge and showed it to the woman behind the counter.

'Can I help you, Officer?' said the woman in her late forties, rolling her curly locks around her finger. Noticing no ring on her wedding finger, he flashed a smile. He leaned forward onto his elbows and stared deeply into her dark-brown eyes.

'Um, yes, hello. Is it just me or are the receptionists getting prettier and prettier? Your husband is a lucky man.'

The receptionist smiled at the detective. He could tell she was embarrassed but was loving the attention. He continued to smile.

'I'm after the room number of a young boy who was shot this morning at the UCLA campus. Can you point me in the right direction?'

The receptionist's face looked flustered. She continued to smile as she scanned the detective up and down, who gave her a wink. She searched in her log book, to see if she could help.

'Here it is. The boy you're after is Gary Bronson. He's been moved out of the ICU and is now recovering in room twenty, which is on the second floor, down the hall and to your right. Is there anything else, Officer?' she asked with a smile that spoke of her hope that he would invite her out on a date.

The smile had already left his face. He had what he wanted and was moving toward the elevator which had opened. He witnessed the receptionist's sad face as she watched him leave. He stepped inside – he didn't care.

Once the door slid shut, he pulled out his weapon. He twisted on the silencer and made sure the cartridge was full, cocked it and turned off the safety. One thing was certain: Gary and Vince were not leaving this hospital alive.

Before the elevator door opened up to a chime and a level announcement, the gun was behind his back, wedged under his belt and pants and hidden discreetly behind his black leather jacket. He walked down the cold hospital corridor, his eyes darting from side to side in search of room twenty. The first door read number twelve. He slowly continued. Fourteen, sixteen, eighteen, then he found number twenty. With no hesitation he pushed open the door with his left hand, his other tucked behind his back, resting on the handle of his gun.

When the door swung open, he saw Vince and a girl gathered around Gary's bed. Gary was hooked up to an IV drip that was pumping morphine into his body.

Tarn stepped inside and took in the room, scanning for a bag, backpack or briefcase that could be carrying two million dollars, but he saw nothing. The three of them, Vince, Gary and the girl with the perky breasts, were easy targets, but Tarn paused. He knew he needed to be smart and befriend Vince, who was obviously vulnerable. With Leonardo in jail, he could play the older male figure – the confidante to whom Vince might give up the location to the money. After this, and only then, he could dispose of them. He sure as hell wasn't going back to Alexander with bad news.

Tarn's hand left the gun as he stepped into the room and proffered a friendly smile. 'Hello, Vince. The chief sent me over for your protection. I still don't know what all this is about,' he said, pulling up a chair to sit next to Vince and playing dumb.

'I'm pretty sure Alexander Peruggia just put a hit on me,' said Vince. 'It should be me in this bed.'

'Stop it, what are you talking about?' said the girl, shaking her head and touching Vince's arm.

'Sorry, Detective, this is my girlfriend, Isabella. I don't think I introduced you at the pub that night my house was blown up.'

'Nice to meet you,' said Tarn, deep in thought at how he could squeeze out the information he so desired. 'But why would Alexander want you dead? There must be a reason. Do you have something he wants?'

'What in the hell are you caught up in, baby?' Isabella followed.

'All this has happened too fast, I need time to think,' Vince said, clearly not ready to reveal all his cards.

Tarn sighed heavily. He rubbed a hand over his mouth and chin and scratched at his blond stubble. This was going to be harder than he'd thought.

'Vince, enough with the games, don't be stupid, man. I know you have something Peruggia wants. Hand it over, it's the only way to protect you.'

★ ★ ★

At that last comment, Vince peered into the eyes of the detective. An alarm rang in his head. His intuition was telling him not to trust his 'protector.' He turned to Isabella with a troubled expression.

'Are you okay?' Isabella asked.

Vince nodded his head and said, 'Yeah.'

A moment later a phone rang. It was coming from the detective. Tarn stood up and pulled his leather jacket to the side to reach in for his phone.

It was quick, but Vince saw it. He flashed back to the last time he'd spotted it in the bar, just after his house was burnt to the ground. The shiny gold surface was unmistakable. His eyes opened wide. This was no coincidence. The four digits written in blood were the same as those on the detective's badge: 2426. Gary had been trying to identify his assailant, his last act before he'd lost consciousness. His dad was right, no one could be trusted. Tarn had shot Gary and now stood inches away.

Isabella let go of Gary's hand and glanced up at Vince, who was watching the detective talk on the phone. He stared at her intensely, as if to communicate, 'We're in trouble.' She noticed his weird reaction and stood up to face him.

'Are you okay? What's wrong?' she whispered.

Vince did not reply, inconspicuously taking a fork off Gary's lunch tray and slid it in his back pants pocket. He now knew why Tarn was here: not for their protection, but to return the two million dollars to his boss, Alexander. It was the only reason he hadn't finished them already.

The next words uttered by Vince caught the detective by surprise, who had finished his call. He thought there was no point in playing games – Tarn was never going to let them leave the room anyway. 'So was that Alexander Peruggia on the phone?'

Tarn faced him with an intense, fevered stare and forced

out a smile. 'You're a smart kid, I'll give you that, but also stupid. Must run in the Vancini blood.'

Hurt by the last comment, Vince swung a wild right-hand hook, but was forced to the ground with a heavy front kick. He knew this wasn't going to be easy. Tarn dealt with criminals on a regular basis.

Isabella ran to Vince's side. 'What do you want from us?'

Vince knelt on the floor, winded by the kick, and grasped his stomach.

Tarn walked to the door and locked it. He pulled out his 9mm handgun.

Vince turned to Isabella, who eyed the weapon with bleak eyes.

Tarn's hand was steady as he lifted the gun toward them.

'No!' Isabella said, holding back a scream.

Vince held his girl tight and could feel her heart racing, like it was going to explode.

'Vince, it looks like you need more convincing,' said Tarn.

'What's he talking about?' Isabella asked.

Tarn took out his handcuffs and threw them on the floor. 'Vince, handcuff yourself to radiator.'

'No!'

'Was that a no? I don't like nos.'

The gun was redirected to Isabella's head.

'Wait … Wait …' Vince quickly responded, clicking himself onto the radiator in the corner of the room.

Tarn looked down to see Isabella's sobbing face and as he did so, Vince removed the fork from his back pocket and placed it onto his handcuffed hand, careful not to be seen.

'Okay, Vince, what I want is simple: I want the location of the money or everyone in this room dies.'

'What money?' Isabella said, standing up.

'Vince knows what money, don't you, Vince?'

'Just give him the money, babe, please,' Isabella begged.

Vince looked up at Isabella's pained and teary gaze,

knowing the location to the money was the only reason they were still alive. 'I don't know what he's talking about.' He then addressed Tarn. 'You have me mistaken for someone else.'

Tarn just smiled.

At a slow pace he approached a machine beside Gary that was beeping rhythmically. He yanked out the power cord and grabbed a pillow from the lower end of the bed.

'What are you doing?' Vince yelled. 'Don't be stupid.'

Tarn placed the pillow over Gary's head and pushed the muzzle of his gun into it.

'No! Please no,' shrieked Isabella with her hands up.

'Vince?' Tarn said one more time.

No answer …

Without hesitation one bullet was fired.

It went straight into Gary's forehead.

Gary's chest slumped forward. The breath left his body. No flatline and no warning sound. It was a clean kill.

'One down, two to go.'

Chapter 50

In the adjacent room, the hospital was having a celebration for kids with cancer. The party was in full swing with clowns, music and party games. Vince thought to himself while handcuffed onto the radiator, the timing could not have been more perfect for Tarn, as their screams would not be heard. How were they going to get out alive with this psychopath in the room?

Isabella hugged her boyfriend on the ground, digging her face into his shoulder. Vince could feel her trembling chin and lips, as she gasped for air.

'It's okay, we'll get out of this,' said Vince, with tears running down his face. His best friend was gone. All their future plans together after college were destroyed. He was left with no choice. If he told Tarn where the loot was, they would all be dead. He wished he'd never laid eyes on that blood money. Acquiring all that wealth was nothing if it could not be shared with the people he loved, and now his friend was dead because of it.

Tarn was not playing around. 'Okay, now that I have your attention, the money?'

Using his free hand, Vince wiped away his tears before he spoke. 'So how do you think you're going to get away after killing us? You've been recorded by the cameras in the hospital and your gun has been used.'

Tarn smiled. 'Believe me, son, I've gotten off far worse

situations than this. It helps when the Chief of Police is on your side. You should be the one worried right now, not me.'

Vince stared incredulously, realizing yet another of Alexander's puppets went all the way up the food chain. The chief himself was corrupt, this explained a lot. His father's sentence and the chief's address in court made it official. He was behind it all.

'You see, Vince, being a detective I can easily turn this story around, naming you as the shooter. Your motive for killing your friend is easy: he slept with your girl. Plain old revenge.'

He turned to Isabella with a look of disdain and gave her a wink. She looked away and buried her face into Vince's shoulder. Vince did not say a word and stared into Tarn's squinting eyes.

'Now, Vince, you know what I'm capable of: tell me where it is, or I'll put one in your girlfriend's pretty face.'

Vince dug the fork into the handcuff lock mechanism and began to twist and turn, knowing that if he gave up the location he would end up on the six-pm news, portrayed as a murderer due to an alleged affair.

'Hello, Houston to Vince,' said Tarn, pointing his gun at Isabella's head.

Isabella whimpered, shaking uncontrollably.

'My patience is running out, Vince, this is taking too long. I think you need an incentive.' Tarn reached in and grabbed Isabella by the arm, leaving his strong hand prints on her olive skin. He threw her harshly onto the foot of the bed where Gary lay dead. She cried out as her head was pushed over Gary's legs, the gun pressed forcefully into her spine.

'Stop! Please stop, I'll tell you,' sobbed Vince, not wanting his girl to end up like his friend.

Tarn, now in control, lifted up Isabella's summery dress to reveal a yellow G-string up against her taut buttocks.

'Stop, I'll tell you,' Vince shouted again, now jiggling the fork in and out of the mechanism like crazy, trying to set it free. The fork was making a lot of noise, but he didn't care. He knew the pervert he was dealing with and what he was capable of doing if he didn't get free.

Isabella twisted her body around, trying to move away from the leech who was rubbing up against her. 'Get off me, you freak!' she pleaded.

Tarn now seemed to be sexually aroused. He threw the gun onto the nearest chair, as he needed both hands to control Isabella, who was using every bit of strength to stop anything from happening.

'I'm going to kill you,' Vince said, still jiggling the fork.

Tarn laughed. 'Not only am I going to get the money back, I'm going to have me some dessert as well.' He roughly guided Isabella's body closer to the edge of the bed.

'Stop, please stop!' yelled Vince.

'No!' screamed Isabella, trying to keep herself clothed, holding onto her underwear as it was being pulled off.

Vince attempted one more time, this time with more force. It was now or never.

Click ... The handcuffs unlocked. Vince sprang to his feet and reached for the gun, as fast as he could. Tarn saw him from the corner of his eye and tried to react, but was kneed in the groin by Isabella. Vince held the 9mm with a strong grip. He felt comfortable around guns being the son of a policeman and didn't hold back at firing a shot at the corrupt detective, hitting him right in the upper thigh, even though he had been aiming for his chest.

'Ahh, you little shit!' Tarn fell to the ground, holding his ruined leg.

'I will end you,' said Vince.

Tarn instinctively pressed the help service button that hung over the bed, like a remote control and slid under the bed.

'Let's go, let's go,' cried Isabella. Vince wanted revenge and lunged at the enemy under the bed, but the pull on his arm was too strong. Isabella pushed him out the door. The gun was concealed underneath his shirt, as they ran into the open lift.

Downstairs in the lobby he screamed out to the receptionist at the front desk, 'Call 911, there's been a murder in room twenty.'

The receptionist's eyes bulged.

The entrance door to the hospital automatically opened and within seconds Vince and Isabella were out of sight, running for their lives.

Chapter 51

Sprinting out of the building, their feet pounded the tarmac with hearts thumping and rasping throats. They needed to get as far away from the hospital as possible. It seemed like they had run for hours as they reached Wilshire Boulevard, ten minutes down the street. They were running on adrenaline, but Vince knew they needed to keep going and find somewhere to hide; it wouldn't be long before Tarn would come knocking.

Bus number 720 on the metro rapid line, heading south toward the beach, was about to leave. They caught it, panting as they stepped inside and sat down. Now momentarily safe, Vince gave his girl a hug, lost for words and out of breath. She reciprocated, her arms shaking as she held on.

'You have a lipstick mark on your collar,' said Isabella suddenly.

'Do I?' said Vince, deflecting the question, like he had no idea how it got there. 'Can you believe it? That was the second attempt on our lives.'

'Hang on, your phone,' said Isabella. 'Do you have it on you?'

Vince pulled it out from his pants pocket.

Isabella didn't hesitate, snatching it out from his hands and tossing it out of the window into a clump of bushes.

'What are you doing?' said Vince. 'I haven't got a passcode on my phone.'

'That's your stupid fault. At least now we can't be traced.'

Vince shook his head, but Isabella was right.

'Can anyone help us?' asked Isabella.

'Taylor is the only one who I trust, but now knowing the chief is involved, I don't know.'

Daylight slowly slipped away as the bus continued its run.

Isabella leaned back in her seat and said. 'Is it true?'

'Is what true?' Vince replied in a calm, soothing voice, his heart rate now back to normal.

'Do you have the money he's after?'

Vince nodded. 'Yes, I do. Last Friday I worked out the clue, where the bank robber hid two million dollars. I have it locked away. If I knew all this was going to happen, believe me, I never would've gone looking for it.'

'I can't believe you had the money and said nothing, while Gary was killed and I was nearly raped.'

'I had no choice: if I told him, he would've killed us right then and there. You have to understand, it was the only thing that kept us alive.'

'Kept you alive,' said Isabella, averting her gaze.

'Come on. That's not fair.'

She cleared her throat. 'It all makes sense now, how you could afford the expensive jewelry and the Penthouse Restaurant.'

'It's not like that, I want the best for you. Hang on … The Penthouse Restaurant?' Vince had a thought. 'We could …'

'We could what?' Isabella stopped to pay attention.

'We're heading that way, I can get us a room.'

'How are you going to do that, do you have money on you?'

'No, but—' Vince pulled out his empty wallet. Inside was a Huntley Hotel business card, with Mr. Salduzi's personal cell phone number on the back.

'What's that?'

'I have the manager's number. He told me if there was anything I needed, to let him know. Well, we're in need.'

After a long thirty minutes, they both got off the bus on 4th Street and found a pay phone. Stepping inside, Vince dug his hand in his front pocket hoping to feel a coin, but came up empty. He sighed, then watched Isabella walk away to a group of teenagers who were having a smoke and ask for money. The boys smiled at her and were happy to oblige. Vince waited at the pay phone as his girl put on the charm. Not many males, young or old, could say no to her.

'You're amazing,' said Vince with his palm held open.

'Here are your coins, make the call.'

Vince dialed the number on the card. After a brief chat, Mr. Salduzi organized a room, reserved under the alias Vigo Cruise. An account was quickly set up for him as promised, by a man of his word, who was happy to help his new VIP.

'It's all done, we have a place to hide,' Vince said, a semblance of calm returning to him.

Loud music was coming from the 3rd Street shopping district. Crowds of people swarmed in. Hundreds, maybe thousands came to get a glimpse of the parade taking place. Men and women dressed in exotic, skimpy clothing, danced along to the music down the strip.

The music got louder as they walked passed it, and it took some time to get through the crowds, to the traffic lights on 2nd Street.

'Look over there, Isabella, that's the bank that was robbed,' said Vince, pointing to his left. She glanced at it and continued to cross the road, uninterested. The Huntley Hotel was minutes away now.

'We made it,' he said, lifting up her hand in front of the hotel's façade, noticing the relief on her face.

'Thank God, I need a lie-down,' she said.

A déjà vu was felt as they walked through the outside foyer, seeing the same large white curtains on either side, the decorative white bench to the left and the geometric patterns of the large, circular, tiled feature underneath their feet.

'Maybe we can eat at the Penthouse Restaurant again,' said Isabella.

Vince knew she was trying desperately to regain a sense of normality and indulging in the superficial might just block out the murder she had just witnessed, if only for a while.

Vince smiled and held her hand. Reaching the main check-in desk to their left, a man in his fifties waited. 'Hello, I have a reservation for a Vigo Cruise,' asked Vince.

The man behind the desk checked the computer and confirmed the booking.

'Ah yes, Mr. Salduzi has set you up a VIP account. Your room is a water-view room, on level fourteen, number 1410.' Two plastic swipe cards were handed over, as the man behind the counter said, 'Have a nice stay, sir.'

'Let's go.' Vince escorted Isabella to the same elevator that had taken them to the famous Penthouse Restaurant not so long ago. The door opened and she entered. Vince did not though: he stood there, as he heard a girl's distinctive voice from behind him that sounded familiar.

'Hey, Vince, is that you? It is you,' said a husky voice. Her long blond hair flowed over her shoulders, and she had full lips.

Isabella's arm shot out and held open the elevator door. She looked on with a guarded expression.

Vince froze, his eyes shot to Isabella's in front of him. How could this be happening? he thought. Karma was definitely out to get him; this was not going to end well. The stunning girl standing not two feet away from Isabella was Holly, the girl he had slept with last night. He had hoped he would never see her again, a mistake he wanted to keep quiet.

How was he going to explain this to his girlfriend, who had been through hell today? Yes, Isabella had accepted the near-death experience in the bomb explosion at the house, witnessed one of her dearest friends murdered in cold blood, and had almost been raped, but she would never tolerate a cheating boyfriend.

Holly approached Vince and stood within inches of him.

She hadn't noticed Isabella waiting for him in the elevator. Or had she? 'Hey, sexy, what a surprise. I had such a great time last night, but never got to say goodbye or exchange numbers.'

'Um,' he muttered, lost for words. 'What are you doing here?'

Holly moved in closer, running her fingers over his chest. 'I work here at the hotel, silly.'

It was clear this was no friendly chitchat; there was much more going on between them. Then the clincher: Holly grabbed Vince by his shirt and passionately kissed him, while Isabella stood by and watched. The lipstick on his collar made sense now. A hatred she had never thought possible overwhelmed her.

'That's it,' Isabella yelled as she stormed out of the hotel, unable to bear seeing her man in another girl's arms.

Vince pushed Holly away and chased Isabella out the front door.

'She means nothing to me,' he screamed. 'I can explain.'

She was already halfway down 2nd Street, she didn't care for his excuses. A cheat was a cheat. He'd broken her heart and now it was over between them.

'How could you?' she cried. 'How could you?'

Chapter 52

Waiting for the lights to turn green, Isabella stood there, staring vacantly into the distance. Mascara streamed down her face as she continued to weep, waiting for the green stick figure on the lights to display.

'Are you okay?' asked a girl in her twenties standing to her left. She placed her hand on Isabella's back in a friendly gesture.

'I'm okay, thanks,' Isabella said with a smile that didn't show in her eyes.

She turned around and took one last look down 2nd Street, wanting to know if Vince was still standing outside the hotel, but there was no sign of him. He was probably in the arms of his new girl, she thought, distraught with so many mixed emotions going through her head.

As she focused ahead, a strange man caught her eye. The peculiar thing about him was how he acted when he was spotted, stopping and staring the other way, trying to be inconspicuous. The man stood there in his dark, tailored suit, hair short and neat, and the most distinguishing feature were his frameless glasses.

Isabella frowned. What did he want? She continued to stare, even though the lights turned green.

Something was not right about him. She waited; he had to look up sooner or later. Eventually the man in the suit gazed up to see Isabella watching his every move, her arms crossed and legs apart.

She missed the green light, it was red now and the traffic

had recommenced. She had caught the overdressed man by surprise, looking straight into his eyes. He glanced back with a brazen smile; like he had been discovered. She had outsmarted him.

Shocked by his undaunted reaction, she decided to duck across the traffic and disappear. The first thing that came to mind was 3rd Street. She could blend in and hide.

Running through the fashion district, she felt a nervousness tremble through her body as the chase began. The stranger was on the move and not far behind. He seemed fit and flowed through the crowds like the breeze. The Mardi Gras parade was in full swing, but she had never felt more alone. She knew she was being pursued and needed to get to the other side if she was to survive. Her head bobbed up and down as she tried to see where she was going, while furiously pushing her way through the sea of party-goers. She was being jostled and pushed by a merry crowd oblivious to the sinister game of cat and mouse playing out among them.

She lost her sense of direction; the man could be anywhere now. Despite the balmy evening, she felt a chill. She needed to be on guard. She clenched her hands into fists, her only defense mechanism. She would lash out, should she turn and find him in front of her. Her fear kept her alert. Ahead she saw a chance to escape, a taxi sat at the end of the street. She let herself feel a tiny hope as she began to head toward it.

But what caught her eye next caused her heart to race uncontrollably. She was now looking into the cold, dark eyes of her pursuer.

He had caught up. He stood there on her right, waiting out of place, among the semi-naked throng. Time froze and she continued to stare; her next move was critical. In his hand was a razor-sharp six-inch blade. This was it. She had come face to face with a killer. Screaming was not going to help in this raucous crowd and it seemed like only the two of them were here in this space.

She sprinted in the opposite direction, but he anticipated this and leapt at her, grabbing her by the arm. She threw a hard fist that was deflected by his forearm. He swung her around and grabbed her from behind, forcing her arms against her body as if she was hugging herself. He pressed the blade against her neck.

'Let go of me,' she cried out. 'Who are you?'

'I've been following you.'

'Are you going to kill me?'

'No.'

'Where are you taking me?'

'You'll find out soon enough.'

'No! Tell me,' she screamed.

Isabella was thrown into the backseat of a black Mercedes.

The door was shut behind her. The terror she felt was beyond anything she'd experienced before. She didn't know if she was going to survive the night.

Chapter 53

Back at the Ronald Reagan UCLA Medical Center holding his wounded leg, Detective Tarn Mostrom heard running footsteps in the corridor. Four police officers approached room twenty with caution.

Following police protocol, Tarn lifted his badge high in front of him, hoping they would see it before they started shooting as they barged in.

'Police, we're coming in,' said one of the officers. 'Lie on the floor with your hands behind your head.'

The door opened and in entered three officers wearing bulletproof vests with their guns drawn. They saw Tarn on the floor. 'Don't you fuckin' move!' commanded one of the armed men, pointing his gun directly at the chest of the injured figure in front of him.

'I'm a cop, I'm a cop,' Tarn shouted back as they surrounded him. After a quick search and it was declared secure, the detective in charge stepped into the room. He glanced over at the man on the floor.

'Ahh shit, should've known it was you, Tarn.'

'Good to see you, too, Luke.'

'You're lucky my boys didn't put a cap in your ass.'

Detective Luke Taylor looked grim as he walked over to the bed and saw the dead student. He took out the radio from his jacket pocket and alerted base. 'We have a one-eight-seven.'

The police officer who had first entered helped Tarn up from the floor and onto a nearby chair.

'What in the hell happened here?' Taylor asked, pointing over at the dead victim, waiting for an explanation while his team stood by and listened.

'The person you're after is Vince Vancini. He's armed and dangerous.'

'Leo's kid?' Taylor said, scratching his jaw, while his eyes circled the room.

'Yes. When I arrived he had already shot his friend and was about to kill his girlfriend, so I intervened and got one in the leg before I had time to pull my gun.'

Taylor tilted his head to the side inquisitively. 'Why would he want to kill his best friend?'

'Because Vince found out he'd slept with his girlfriend.'

'Ahh yes, that would do it, the classic revenge.'

'I saw it in his eyes, he wanted revenge,' said Tarn, speaking through gritted teeth. 'Now if you don't mind with the questioning, I've just been shot.'

'Of course, let's get a doctor.' Taylor nodded for one of his men to get help. He pulled out his radio again, as a doctor walked in. 'I need an APB out on a Vince Vancini. Proceed with caution: considered armed and dangerous.'

'Ten-four,' replied the female voice on the other side.

The doctor examined the wounded leg and slowly smiled. 'You're a lucky man,' she said. 'The bullet went straight through.'

'What does that mean, Doc?'

'It means that stitches and antibiotics should see you right. Come with me next door where the supply kits are kept.'

He stood up carefully and walked to the adjacent room. He waved goodbye to Taylor, who knelt down to explore under the bed, his hand holding onto the bed rails.

Under the bed was one of the bullets, embedded in the concrete floor. Its vertical trajectory screamed of a cold kill. The only blood splatter was on the back of the pillow. He continued his search and found a second bullet hole underneath the window on the opposite end of the room.

Something didn't feel right; he had never trusted Tarn. Nothing good ever came out of his mouth. He claimed he had been shot as he'd tried to protect Isabella. If that were the case, the second bullet, supposedly shot by Vince, would have ended up on the other side of the room near the door. He was lying; the question was why?

Twenty minutes later Lee Davis stepped into the room. He hid a slight smile as he saw the deceased. At least he did not need to worry about Gary anymore.

'Hey, Chief, you're just in time,' said Taylor, as the two shells were extracted and placed into a plastic sleeve bag.

'Are the shells the same?' asked the chief.

'Looks like it, sir. Only one gun was used.'

'Have you found the gun?'

'No, sir, not yet. I've put an APB out on Vince Vancini.'

'Good, the sooner we catch him the better.'

'If I may, sir, off the record.' Taylor lowered his voice so no one could hear. 'How much do you trust Tarn?'

'Why?' Lee replied bluntly.

'I feel there's more to his story. He's lying. I think he was the shooter, not Vince.'

'Wow, that's a big allegation. You're not the first person to question Tarn.'

'If I'm allowed, sir, a simple swab of his clothing might prove he was the shooter. He said he didn't fire his weapon. Gun powder residue will show up if he did.'

'No!' replied Lee firmly.

'It's Leo's son, for God's sake. Something fishy is going on and you know it.'

The chief stepped forward and stared into Taylor's eyes.

Through gritted teeth he said, 'You don't rat on a fellow officer, period.'

'But, sir.'

'No, that's it, leave it alone!'

Lee left the room with a heavy sigh and entered the adjacent room where Tarn was sitting. His leg was cleaned and bandaged. The doctor had left to organize an x-ray. Closing the door behind him, he walked in and slapped the careless detective in the face.

'What was that for?' Tarn said, caught off guard.

'You idiot, this is the second time you've messed up. Now I have Sherlock Holmes in there wanting fucking hand scans, claiming you could be the shooter.'

Tarn groaned. 'I'll take care of Luke.'

'No, you won't, I will. Listen, before you leave, find some ammonia and drown your hands in it just in case and lose the shirt.'

'Is that all?'

'No, that's not all, smartass. Make sure you dispose of all the surveillance tapes.'

'How come?'

'Because, Einstein, it will probably show Vince and his girl running away together. You don't need to be a genius to work out who they were running from, huh?'

Tarn nodded sheepishly, acknowledging the logic and Lee's help.

'Listen, it's cleanup time. Forget about the money, just kill Vince and his girl. No mistakes this time.'

Lee handed over another gun with a silencer attached, the serial number scratched clean.

'No mistakes,' Lee said again.

'I understand.'

'You'd better.'

Chapter 54

Monday, 8 pm

Alexander sat at the head of the table. The entire Peruggia family, Monica included, was ready to have their last meal before the big heist only hours away. The only one missing was Ian, who had been sent out on a personal assignment and who was not needed tonight anyway. Being as thorough as he could, Alexander had covered all angles, not wanting to emulate the previous catastrophic robbery attempt that had left him with a dead son.

The smell of garlic and oregano filled the room. Tony made his famous traditional spaghetti bolognese passed down by his father, not his mother, a fact he always was proud to share. 'Men are the best chefs, did you know that, Monica?' Tony began his usual banter, proud to be an Italian man.

'I'm sure they are.' Monica smiled, grabbing a serving.

'That's not the only thing Italian men are good at,' said Frank, winking in Monica's direction.

'You're an idiot,' said James, laughing at his come-on.

After eating a generous portion, Alexander stood up and walked over to Joey, who sat beside Monica. The two were inseparable: it was clear to Alexander that they shared a special bond. Joey turned around in his chair while everyone looked on.

'What's up, Pop? Are you going to shoot me in the back?' he asked with a smile.

'No, I need to give you something.'

James, Frank, Tony, Victoria and Monica observed. Alexander reached deep into his pocket and retrieved a beautiful gold necklace attached to a twenty-four-carat-gold cross. By the look on Joey's face and the tears brimming in his eyes, he was familiar with the piece.

'I think your brother would have wanted you to have this,' said Alexander flatly. Sadness overwhelmed him, and even uttering these words emptied him.

Alexander placed the cross over Joey's neck. James, Frank and Monica cheered. It was like being knighted by the king himself. The symbolic meaning of this moment for Alexander represented a new beginning, an awakening. Phil's spirit was to live on through Joey, reincarnated as the next in line to the throne. The youngest member of the family was going to take over his brother's rule as the leader and be the Peruggia he was born to be, even if this wasn't the life he'd asked for.

'Thank you, Dad,' said Joey, who read the inscription written within the cross.

The necklace had been on Phil's neck when he was incinerated. The fact that it had survived in the fire was a positive sign for Alexander, believing his son's death had been orchestrated by a higher power for a reason.

'Tonight you will be great,' he said, as he patted his son on the shoulder.

Joey nodded his head with a slight smile and sat back down, ready for dessert.

'Okay, who's ready for tiramisu?' Tony asked.

Twenty minutes into dessert, Monica's cell phone buzzed. She reached into her pocket and glanced at the caller ID. She raised her eyebrows and peered over at Joey.

'Who is it?' asked Joey.

'Why is he calling?' Monica said, with a puzzled look on her face. All communication was to be ceased until tonight was over. The man on the phone was Chief Lee Davis. No calls twenty-four hours before any major heist was the rule. This was unorthodox of him.

'Find out what he wants,' said Joey in a hushed voice.

'How can I help you?' Monica asked, not mentioning the caller's name.

On the other end there were no formalities. The chief dived straight in with a request. His voice was direct and forward. 'Monica, I need your help.'

'I'm in the middle of dinner, what's the problem?' she said, now worried he was going to bail out on tonight's six-million-dollar event.

'Relax, it's not about tonight, we're still good to go there,' said Lee. 'I have another problem that needs to be eradicated. I need your help to find Vince Vancini. He's on the run.'

'What happened?' Monica asked.

'It doesn't matter now. Tarn was sloppy and he got away. Vince knows way too much and my involvement is compromised. I need someone to clean up Tarn's mess and end him, too. He is a problem now.'

'Look, I'll take care of it. Just make sure you do your part tonight,' said Monica, ending the call.

Joey peered over at Monica with suspicion, raising his thumb up and down as an enquiry to the outcome of the call – was it good news or bad?

'It's all good: he wants my help to find Vince. He's scared he might talk to the press. If word got out, internal affairs would know the robbery was an inside job, naming the chief as a co-conspirator.'

Joey laughed. 'I guess we should find Vince, then.'

'Can I use your laptop? I can access the FBI database and run a trace, maybe get a lock on his cell phone, if he's still carrying it.'

'The laptop's in my room,' said Joey, excusing himself from the table. Monica followed.

'He's definitely fucking her,' said Frank with a smile.

The others laughed and carried on.

'Eat another tiramisu, you skinny piece of shit,' said Tony.

'Yeah, so I can end up like you, you fat bastard,' joked Frank.

Joey pointed to his desk, where a laptop sat. Monica sat down in his overpriced black leather chair and hit the space bar on the keyboard. Joey stood behind her, glancing at the screen. Once the display came alive she didn't waste any time, entering her username and password into the FBI mainframe.

Now inside, she had the power to search for whatever she wanted in the FBI database. She typed 'Vince Vancini' and hit enter. A spinning wheel appeared with the word *searching* beneath it. She sat back in the chair and waited.

'The database will retrieve all criminal records pertaining to Vince, plus bank statements and phone records.'

Joey hunched in closer. The search ended with Vince's file up on screen.

'Okay, his record is clean. No arrests or convictions.'

'What are you trying to find?' asked Joey.

'There's got to be something I can use, a way in. Let's have a look at all his bank accounts and debts.'

She entered into his college fund that was linked to his bank account. A statement was itemized with the amount owing at the bottom.

'Bingo, I can use that.'

'What did you find?'

'Look at the balance owing and the date it had been completely paid off in cash. What money do you think he used?'

'I guess he took some out of the two million.'

'That's right. That means that he has now broken the law

and is going to jail, if he doesn't hand over the money. We have the upper hand.'

Monica knew this could be used as a scare tactic to lure Vince to her and obtain the two million dollars she felt was rightfully hers. It was all about the money for her and now she had an ace up her sleeve over him.

As she dug some more, on the screen appeared the words in a large red font: 'All-Points Bulletin' with Vince's picture and description below. He was wanted for murder.

'What is this?' Monica laughed as she read what had just transpired.

'It appears Vince is on the run, not just from us,' said Joey.

'We need to find him, before the police do,' she said, typing away on the keyboard.

Scrolling down the page, she entered his cell records, hoping he had been stupid enough to carry or use his phone today. After the page refreshed, his latest cell records were in view.

'What an idiot, his phone is still on.'

Her perseverance paid off.

After a quick GPS search, she pin-pointed his exact location. A dot flashed on a map display, with the address to the side.

'I found you,' she whispered to herself, shaking with excitement as she transferred the details onto an app on her phone to be used to track him down.

'So what's the plan now?' asked Joey.

'The plan is for me to take back the two million that belongs to me. This share of the money is mine. Phil and I were going to escape this hellhole with that share. I don't care what anyone says.'

'Why are you talking like that? I'm sure Dad is going to give you a share after tonight.'

'Joey, I have no faith in your father. In due time you'll discover his true nature and what he's done. Only then will you side with me.'

Minutes later the devil himself appeared and entered the room, the door being unlocked. Monica nervously played with her hair and faced the ground, hoping he had not heard what she had said. The last thing she needed was to be excluded from the inner circle she had worked so hard to infiltrate. Not until she had what she was after.

'What are you two up to? You both look suspicious,' said Alexander, easing into Joey's five-thousand-dollar black leather lounge.

'We found Vince,' said Joey, like a good student trying to impress his teacher.

'I can't believe he's still alive, he's a slippery little fish,' replied Alexander. 'Make sure Tarn knows his whereabouts, so he can finish what he started. I want every cent of my money back!'

'Dad, a suggestion: why don't you leave the money Vince has for Monica, her cut in all this? I think she deserves it.'

Monica smiled at Joey. He was genuinely trying to help. Alexander didn't say a word and stared straight into her eyes. Monica could only imagine the negative thoughts going through his mind this very second, but did not budge. She felt Joey's statement was on the money. The two million dollars was hers.

She waited for a response.

Alexander stood up. 'The money is all going to the club!'

'But, Dad ...'

'No buts, that's it!' he said loudly, his eyes bulging. 'Now get yourself ready, you're on tonight. Don't fucking let me down.'

Alexander left the room, slamming the door behind him.

Monica knew in her heart that he was holding back. He needed tonight to go smoothly. She was no dummy: she knew her prospective future within the family was going to end in tears, or her body would be found floating in a river somewhere. That much was certain.

★ ★ ★

Alone in the room, Joey looked dismally at Monica. She was right: his father had been using her this whole time. 'Sorry,' he said. 'I should've known.'

Joey's respect for his father was diminishing with every day. He had seen a side of him that was cruel and selfish. He had decided he wanted out of the gang, but after this last heist. A familiar path was set, but he had learned from his brother's mistake. He wasn't stupid enough to tell his father he was leaving. Who knew what he was capable of doing? In the back of his mind, he'd always thought his father was somehow involved in his brother's death, but he'd never had the balls to ask.

'Listen, Joey, it's not over. I have a plan. Are you in or out?' Monica said, sneaking glances at the doorway. He could tell in her eyes she had devised a strategy that would shake the apple cart, hopefully for the best.

He trusted her. She was always there for him, like an adopted sister. And now it was time to choose a side, just as his brother had done. The decision was easy.

'I'm in.'

Chapter 55

Monica stormed out of the beach club and stepped into her sports AMG Mercedes. The wheels spun, leaving black rubber on the road as she took off to find Vince down Wilshire Boulevard. The app on her phone beeped louder and louder as she pulled up to the curb.

Exiting her vehicle, she glanced up at the buildings that rose around her. Vince could be anywhere, she thought, but her phone continued to beep hysterically. Within a planter box among the bushes, she spotted the cell phone and flashed a smile.

'Smart boy,' she said to herself. Ditching the phone was a smart move. She picked it up, and to her surprise it was without a passcode. She thought, he was a twenty-two-year-old who was in possession of a lot of money. Maybe he'd bragged about what he'd bought or the places he had visited.

She entered his messages, browsed his photos and entered his Facebook account, hoping to find something.

She found nothing.

Vince had not made a Facebook post in months. It was obvious he was not a social-media junky, like most kids his age.

'What about your girlfriend,' she said.

She dived into Isabella's Facebook page, to find she was the complete opposite to Vince. She had posted recently images of them standing in front of the Huntley Hotel. Others of them dining at the extravagant Penthouse Restaurant. Could they have gone there again? she wondered, turning her head down toward Santa Monica.

Vince opened up the long drapes in his hotel room to look over at the Santa Monica mountains that rose above the city of Los Angeles. They met the curve of Santa Monica bay, reaching their highest peaks facing the ocean and forming a beautiful and multi-faceted landscape.

The moonlight reflecting off the beach created enough light for him to see, while he got comfortable on one of the two queen-size beds nearest to the window. Both beds backed onto an olive feature wall and had lavish-cushioned headboards. He needed to rest: it had been a long day and who knew what tomorrow would bring.

As he laid his head on the pillow, his bedroom phone rang. He quickly sprang off the bed and picked it up and said, 'Isabella.'

'Hello, Vince,' said a deeper, more mature female voice.

'Ahh sorry, thought you were someone else.'

'I am, my name is Monica Anton. I work for the FBI. I'm here to help you. I know you're in trouble.'

Vince remembered the name. The day his father was taken to court, her name was dragged through the mud. It was clear his father loathed her. She didn't seem to be a person who could be trusted, but he kept it to himself and played along.

'How did you find me?' asked Vince. 'I was careful to not leave a trace.'

'You didn't, Vince, but your girlfriend sure did.'

'Is she okay?'

'I don't know, isn't she with you?'

'No, we had a fight,' said Vince in a flat tone. 'So tell me, how are you going to help me? Why should I trust you?'

'I know who is after you and why. These people don't stop until they get what they want, so you have no choice.'

'Really, what do you know?'

'Why, is this a test?' Monica asked.

'Maybe. How do I know you're not playing me?'

'Okay, how's this? I know Tarn Mostrom and Lee Davis are corrupt informants working for Alexander Peruggia. Is that enough?'

'No!'

'Okay, I know you have in your possession two million dollars and I know there's an APB on you. It looks like you are being framed for killing your friend and wounding a police officer. Does that sum it up?'

'You seem to know a lot.'

'Vince, if you want to stay alive, you have no choice but to trust me, before they find your location and erase you. You've been lucky this far, but luck runs out.' Her voice sounded sincere and on his side, but why would he trust her? Who was this woman? A woman his father hated.

'Stay where you are, Vince and I'll personally come to retrieve you.'

Vince had no choice: he was vulnerable, he needed to trust someone. Hoping this was not going to be the death of him, he agreed.

Chapter 56

Tarn sat and rested his leg after the meeting with Lee, waiting for the crucial information of Vince's whereabouts. His clumsy mistakes had left Lee and himself in a vulnerable position. Vince was now a liability that needed to be dealt with.

The cell that was already in his hand shook – the message was short and sweet.

It read: *Room 1410, Huntley Hotel. No survivors.*

Chapter 57

Monica quickly stepped into her Mercedes. She was a woman with a plan, acting swiftly. Timing was everything. All her knowledge gained in the military, learning about strategic placement and sequencing, was about to be implemented right now.

She was no saint: her loyalty lay with no one, double-crossing the uniforms as much as the criminals she was in bed with. She didn't care what Lee Davis or Alexander Peruggia thought. All that mattered to her right now was in Vince's possession and she would do anything to acquire it.

She had sent Tarn Mostrom the message. He was on his way, probably twenty minutes or so away. It gave her plenty of time to get to Vince first. The first part of the plan was in motion.

Next was to involve good cop Detective Taylor, who would end up playing a vital role in all of this, even if he didn't know it yet. Even though she did not know Taylor personally, she knew he would do his job and follow up on any potential leads, even if it did come from an untrustworthy source like her.

The old clock on the wall in Taylor's home hit 9 pm. The house smelled of the Chinese food that had been left on the kitchen bench. His children were in bed sleeping and he was sitting in the kitchen with his wife, enjoying his fifth cup of coffee for the day.

'So what time are you on call until?' his wife asked.

'I finish at 7 am. Let's hope it's going to be a slow one.' The graveyard shift was rotated among the members of the unit, and tonight was his turn.

Taylor's work cell rang.

He looked over to his wife with an apologetic glance – a homicide already. Tonight was going to be interesting, he thought.

'Hello, Luke, it's Agent Monica Anton, I need your help.' Her voice echoed on Taylor's end. It was obvious she was on a hands-free device.

'Monica Anton! What an unpleasant surprise. What the hell do you want?'

She was the last person on the face of the earth he wanted to receive a call from. Listening to her voice made him cringe. His guard was up; she couldn't be trusted. Her involvement in the Peruggia family was the reason his good friend Leonardo had been ostracized as a bad guy and sent to jail.

'Listen, I have some important information to tell you. Do you want to hear it or not?' Monica parked her car inside the Huntley Hotel undercover parking lot, reserved for guests only.

'Go on. This better be good,' retorted Taylor. His wife continued to clean the dishes, but was listening.

'Listen, Detective, tonight everything is going down.'

'What do you mean everything?' Taylor asked, frowning.

'Two things are planned to go down tonight.'

'Go on.'

'First will be the murder of a cop. But don't worry, he's dirty, nothing to be concerned about.'

Taylor sarcastically smiled. His services were going to be needed after all. 'Monica, why are you telling me this?'

'I'm telling you this to gain your trust, because of the second thing I'm about to tell you.'

'Okay, and what's that?'

'At midnight tonight the LAPD headquarters holding six million dollars will be robbed.'

She paused, allowing him time to absorb the information.

'So now that I know that, what do you want me to do about it?' he asked.

'What do you mean? You have the upper hand, the element of surprise. They would never be expecting you.'

'You know, Monica, you seem to know a lot for someone who's claiming to be on our side. Sorry, but I don't trust you.'

'I understand that. That's why I've given you two things to earn your trust. Let's start with the first thing I told you.'

'Okay ... How do I know you won't be the one responsible for this supposed corrupt cop's death? Or that you're not setting me up for the fall? It wouldn't be the first time.'

'Look, I understand, but listen to me. You have no idea what danger I've put myself in just by talking to you. If you knew the key players involved, you'd be responding differently.'

'Okay, so why don't you cut the bullshit and enlighten me. If what you're saying is true, I can help you, but I need to know more. Who's involved?'

'You won't believe me.'

'Try me.'

'Okay then: Lee Davis, for one.'

'What?! Come on, you're talking about the Chief of Police.'

'Exactly. Unbelievable as it may sound, this goes right to the top of the food chain. How else has Alexander Peruggia stayed afloat for so long? Think about it, don't be stupid. He's been protected by the big dog himself.'

Taylor took a deep breath. He stared blankly at his wife washing the dishes, trying to rationalize all this. How could this be?

'I've been in the middle of Lee and Alexander for way too long and tonight could be my way out, so please, I need your help.'

Detective Taylor was speechless: the fact that Monica

knew all this was disconcerting. He knew how devious and conniving she was. Could this be another one of her tricks? Most likely.

But what if it were true?

Even though he didn't trust her, he trusted his gut. Something his father had taught him to do from a young age, and it was telling him there was some truth to her story. The claim that Lee was in on all this was far-fetched, but if there was even a hint of truth behind it, it would explain a lot.

Maybe this explained why she had remained part of the inner circle longer than anyone had expected, having nowhere to go, her life threatened by Lee and Alexander. Hostile territory on both sides of the fence.

'Taylor, it's up to you now to decide what you're going to do with the information. I hope you'll keep an open mind.'

'Okay, back to the first thing, about a dead cop,' he said.

'You'll be contacted shortly, stay by your phone.'

She hung up.

Taylor was left feeling stunned and nervous. There was only one thing he knew for sure: it was going to be a long night.

Chapter 58

Tarn walked into the lobby of the Huntley Hotel with a slight limp. The dimly lit foyer was crowded with groups of people waiting for the gold-plated elevator doors to open. Dozens of tea-light candles submerged in small glass cups were placed strategically around the leather seating areas in front of the lifts, lending the place a warm, relaxed ambience.

Five couples and two girls in their early twenties were stylishly dressed. The men wore black single-breasted suits and the women were in glamorous cocktail dresses. It was clear they were here tonight to drink, dine and bask in the atmosphere of the famous Penthouse Restaurant that was on level eighteen.

He stood among those waiting and watched the first group enter the lift, which reached capacity. Any more than six people would have been a tight squeeze. Not long after, another empty elevator arrived to receive another group, Tarn's group. The detective was the fourth person into the lift, followed by two young excited girls who giggled as they stood in front of him. Tonight they were dressed to impress, their breasts pushed up, their hair styled, hoping to find a wealthy Mr. Right. In the lift their perfumes overpowered the confined space. Levels fourteen and eighteen lit up in orange on the elevator console.

As they reached level fourteen and the doors opened, he did not utter a word, but stepped out, keeping his head down. He walked to his left and stopped at the T intersection. Hotel suites ran down both the left- and right-hand sides. A single wooden plaque with a gold font displayed the room numbers in sections: 1400–1420 ran to the left. He absently ran his hand over the plaque and turned left. Room 1410 was only a few feet away to his left.

After a couple of steps, he arrived at the door. Giggles emanated from a young honeymooning couple opposite room 1410, who had ordered room service. Their door was wide open. The maid had just wheeled in their meals. Sounds of joy erupted as they lifted the lid.

'Wow, this is awesome!' the woman chirped.

Tarn was not going to make any mistakes this time. He needed a way into room 1410. There was no way Vince was going to let him enter the room straight up; he needed the element of surprise.

He needed the maid.

He pulled out the untraceable gun Lee had given him and twisted on the silencer. After a few quick breaths, he stormed into the room. From behind he wrapped his left hand over the maid's mouth so she couldn't scream and fired two clean bullets at the honeymooners' heads.

Whoop … Whoop … They were killed instantly, a smooth hit. Their eyes were still wide open as crimson flowed from their head wounds onto the beige carpet. The sound of the TV was still playing in the background.

The maid, in the strong hands of a killer, nodded furiously when asked if she wanted to stay alive. He slowly moved his hand away.

Tarn spoke softly. 'Listen, all I want you to do is take this food to room 1410 and tell the man who answers that dinner has been ordered for him by a Miss Monica Anton. That's it, then you're free to go.' He almost sounded sincere, but there was no mistaking it, he was a cold-ass killer.

'You can do it. Monica Anton, okay?'

She nodded, eyes round and white with terror. Her hands trembled as she replaced the large cover plate on the cooling food. She swerved the trolley outside the doorway and rolled it up to room 1410.

He stood to her right, his gun pointed at her temple. She glanced at it with a wary eye.

'Go!' Tarn directed her to knock with his firearm.

After a few knocks, she spoke loudly with a strong South American accent. 'Hello-a, this is a room service, you have a food for you from Miss-a Monica Anton.'

Tarn prepared himself, his weapon no longer pointed at the trembling woman but toward the door. The shower could be heard inside the room, someone was definitely inside.

'The door's unlocked,' Vince shouted from behind the wall. 'I'm in the shower. You can leave it by the window.'

'Okay,' responded the maid, turning the handle and slowly pushing the trolley inside.

A feeling of excitement came over Tarn. Vince was trapped.

He followed the maid into the room gun first and closed the door behind him. The bathroom door was to his immediate right. It was shut and he could hear the water running. He reached out to turn the handle with one hand while the other firmly gripped the silenced gun. This will be clean and quick, he thought, as the maid continued to push the trolley all the way in and turned around.

Focusing on the bathroom door, Tarn heard a stifled yelp coming from the maid. He looked up to see the woman standing stiffly, her eyes flitting suspiciously to her left. It was clear that she'd seen something.

The events that followed next happened in a flash. To his right, from behind the cube that was the bathroom, dived a figure that rolled deftly on the carpet and came to a halt, low and in front of him. A gun was pointed directly at his chest.

'Shit!' He reacted, but it was too late. Two bullets had

already discharged into his chest, within centimeters of each other. The force sent him flying backwards and on his ass, the back of his head slamming against the door behind him. He had been outplayed. The pain was like an icy wind squeezing the breath from his lungs and choking his windpipe. The savage, bitter blasts had torn right through his heart and he could feel life, like a thing rising to leave him. Yet he could not even lift an arm to claw it back. Like a ghost, he slowly slipped away with one last ragged breath.

Detective Tarn Mostrom was gone.

The maid curled up in a ball on the floor, desperately repeating prayers over and over to herself.

'You can come out now,' said Monica.

Vince stepped out of the wardrobe. The running shower was a distraction and it appeared to have worked. He went over to the lady who was rocking herself back and forth, mumbling in Spanish.

'*Ayúdame Dios, Ayúdame Dios.*'

'It's okay, miss, you're safe now,' he said, putting his arm around her. 'You're safe now.'

The maid looked into Vince's reassuring eyes and stood up. Monica also got to her feet, her eyes shining with pleasure through her golden black mascara, which lent her a feline quality. Her swift and deadly kill only amplifying this.

'Part one of my plan is complete,' she said, holding both hands together, pointing the gun toward the ground.

'What plan? You're a maniac,' said Vince, realizing this was part of a larger scheme of hers. 'I thought you were supposed to be one of the good guys.'

Monica took out her phone.

'Who are you calling?' he demanded, walking over to the slumped body of his would-be killer. He could see the tear in his trousers where he had shot him in their previous encounter. Even though a man lay dead before him, he felt no sympathy; he was simply happy there was one less person to deal with.

'Yes, hello, Taylor, it's me. Huntley Hotel, room 1410. It's all in your hands now. Don't let me down.' She hung up the phone.

'What's going on, Monica? Why did you give away our location?' asked Vince.

'He has his dead cop now,' she said with a smile.

'What? You're talking in riddles!'

'Shut up, you bother me. Just tell me where the money is,' she said absently, while adjusting her ponytail.

It suddenly dawned on Vince that he had been played.

'So this is all for the money? You make me sick. Fuck that, I'm not telling.'

'Did you say you're not telling?'

Monica raised her pistol and shot the maid in the neck. She hit the ground with a thud, the shocked expression still on her face.

Vince's jaw fell open. His knees felt like they were going to give way. This was a complete shock. There was blood everywhere on her face, it dripped down over the long white curtains and spread across the carpet. Now he was trapped in a room with a crazy woman. Her unpredictability was what scared him the most.

'Why ... did you do that?' Vince whispered.

She pointed her gun at him. 'My patience is running out. Where's my money?' Her voice a little louder now.

Vince closed his eyes. He was trapped in a nightmare he could not wake up from. Dealing with criminals trying to kill him was one thing, he could rationalize that. But detectives, FBI agents? What in the hell was happening here? He now understood his dad better than ever before and what it must have been like all these years having to work in this cesspool.

'Vince, the money?'

'Okay, okay. I'll show you.'

He had no option but to take her to the locker at the UCLA Student Activities Center, hoping he could escape if an opportunity revealed itself. His life was now in the hands of a psychopath.

Chapter 59

After flashing his badge, Detective Taylor was handed a spare key to room 1410. He thanked the attendant and asked him to keep it quiet that he was conducting an investigation upstairs. Hovering the plastic card over the door's lock sensor, the red light turned to green and the door unlocked itself. He entered the room with a watchful eye, not knowing what to expect, his gun in hand and at the ready.

He immediately spotted two dead bodies. The smell of fresh blood permeated the room. His first instinct was to clear the room. Who knew if there were any other potential threats inside? The bathroom to his right – clear – the main bedroom – clear except for the dead maid, of course. Lastly, the walk-in closet – empty, except for a small safe sitting on a shelf at the back.

He put away his weapon and walked back to the body slumped in the hallway. Facing him now, he could see it was Tarn Mostrom. Not long ago he had seen him at the hospital and had speculated on his possible involvement. Now he was as dead as a doormat in this hotel suite. What was going on?

He was not surprised, though. He had always suspected Tarn was dirty. He sat on the edge of the bed and took a pause to think this over. Monica had promised him a dead body and she had delivered. Could she be trusted? Hell no, but her first prediction had proved true. Which brought him to the second – the robbery tonight and the accusation that the chief was involved with Alexander Peruggia.

Even though his subconscious was telling him to stop, not to trust her, he could not resist the temptation to find out the truth for himself. He pulled out his cell phone and dialed Lee's number.

'Hello, Chief, it's Taylor. I'm standing over a dead body.'

'Whose dead body?' the chief asked, his speech hurried. 'I never heard anything over the scanner.'

Taylor paused for a second. What was he doing listening to his radio scanner this late in the evening? 'Chief, I'm at the Huntley Hotel in Santa Monica, I need you to come check this out, it's important. But come alone, don't tell anyone. I'm in room 1014. I'll explain everything when you get here. Keep this to yourself.'

'What! Hang on,' said the chief.

'Room 1014.' Taylor hung up.

Twenty minutes passed, and then came a hard knock at the door. Taylor ran his fingers through his straight brown hair as he got up from the bed to answer it. He wished he didn't have to. The man on the other side was his friend and mentor. But things were pointing in an ugly direction and he had to face it. He wished for a second it was room service – who he wouldn't let in anyway. The room was now a crime scene.

'Who is it?' he asked.

'It's me, open the fucking door,' replied Lee in his usual raspy voice.

Taylor closed his eyes as he laid a hand on the door handle. He felt his throat dry up as a single thought filled his mind: Lee could not be trusted. All those years side by side and he was on the take. He unlocked the door.

'What took you so long?'

Lee walked inside. He spotted the figure of Tarn splayed awkwardly on the ground, his shirt soaked in blood. Taylor observed his reaction. Lee's mouth was pinched and his arms were crossed over his chest. Looking through narrowed eyes, he had a look of outrage and disappointment. He had been expecting to see someone much shorter and younger.

'Fuck, that's Detective Mostrom. This wasn't meant to happen.'

'What wasn't meant to happen, sir?'

'No ... no ... you know what I mean,' Lee said, backpedaling.

'Does anyone know you're here, and were you followed, sir?' asked Taylor.

'No, I wasn't followed. What's going on?' replied the chief. 'How did you find out about this murder?' Lee asked, as he paced up and down the room and stared at the blood-drenched maid on the floor.

Taylor looked down at Lee, it was obvious he was anxious. That was because he was a liar: two hundred and nine rooms in the Huntley Hotel and even when given the wrong room number, he still managed to knock on the right door. He had known about this hit somehow. Monica was telling the truth: corruption pervaded the police force to the highest level.

'I received an anonymous call from someone who led me to this room,' said Taylor, not giving away his informant in case it put Monica in grave danger.

'The person on the phone, was it male or female?' Lee asked.

Taylor could tell he was fishing, trying to put the pieces of the puzzle together, and calmly replied, 'It was a male's voice, sir. He told me Detective Mostrom was corrupt, so are others in the department. They'll all be outed soon.'

Lee's mask briefly fell away and he looked terrified. If word got out, he would be one of those people shamed, discharged from the force, stripped of his title and handed over to the courts to be dealt with. This incident needed to be kept quiet, at least for tonight. If Alexander found out about a possible leak, being overly cautious this time round, he would call off the heist. He would never risk Joey's life with a flawed plan.

Lee needed tonight to go ahead; he wanted his share of

the money. He placed his hand on Taylor's shoulder, as if they were old friends and said, 'If what this man is saying is true, we have to be careful to keep this quiet, if we're to find out if there's a leak in the department.'

'I agree, sir,' said Taylor.

'Call Forensics to brush for evidence and catalogue all their findings. Let them know this is a cleanup mission. No one should know what happened in this room tonight.'

'I will, sir.'

Lee left the crime scene and so did Taylor.

But Taylor's next stop was straight for the LAPD headquarters, armed and ready.

Chapter 60

Vince pulled up at the UCLA Student Activities Center's empty parking lot. Monica had sat in the backseat and let him drive. A gun had been pointed directly into the back of the driver's seat the entire way.

As the white Mercedes came to a complete stop, she jammed the barrel of the gun she'd confiscated from Tarn into the back of Vince's seat. He could feel the silencer in the middle of his spine. His back arched forward.

'The money is in there,' he said, resignation in his voice. He had had enough. A week ago he was a happy student with a gorgeous girlfriend, his best friend was dumb but alive. He was getting lucky on his birthday and his father was home for a change. Now Isabella was long gone, his best friend brutally murdered and his father was doing time. The world had spun out of control.

'Get out of the car,' said Monica, slipping the gun under her belt and covering it with her shirt. He got out and headed for the center. Monica followed. Half-baked ideas crossed his mind as they walked through the parking lot. One was to run away. He knew the area well and could possibly make a run for it. With his peripheral vision he kept a wary eye on Monica, but decided that no good would come from running.

'Where in the Activities Center is the money?'

'It's in my locker, in the men's change room.'

'Go on, lead the way.'

Vince reached for his wallet and Monica was quick to respond, with her Glock aimed at his head.

'Relax, I'm just getting my card.'

'Hurry up.'

It was 11:15 pm, but it was a warm night. After swiping his card, the doors opened and all the lights automatically switched on. The lockers in the center worked on a magnetic system that activated when you swiped your card.

'Okay, no funny business. Go get my bag. And remember, I'll not hesitate to use this,' she said, as she took out her gun again and tilted it sideways like a gangster.

Vince nodded. He knew she wasn't lying, having witnessed her cavalier attitude to ending life. He walked ahead past the eight-lane swimming pool and toward the white lockers in the change rooms. They were the only people in the center tonight. The smell of chlorine filled the air. He entered the locker room and Monica followed. There it was, locker number forty-nine. All he needed to do was rub his membership card against the mechanism and the door would unlock.

All of a sudden, the sound of muffled laughter came from outside in the distance. 'Hurry up,' she hissed and went outside to have a look, leaving him alone.

Vince had only seconds before she returned. He thought that, if he had any chance of surviving this, he wasn't going to be left empty-handed. With a quick swipe his locker door was open, then he swiped the locker below.

Locker number fifty-two.

He opened his bag and extracted the original bank robber's backpack that had been wedged in with the money. He then transferred over all the money in a single dump, but left some bundles for himself.

He could hear Monica's footsteps getting louder.

He tossed his bag into locker fifty-two, shut the door and swiped it closed.

In a flash the bank robber's bag had also been closed and he stepped outside, carrying it.

'Here's your money,' he said, tossing the bag between her legs.

Monica knelt and opened it. A smile flashed across her face.

He stood there waiting, his hands clammy and his shoulders tight. She could easily kill him and no one would ever know. She stared him in the eye as she stood up to face him, her cold, feline features hard to read and unpredictable. She had infiltrated the Peruggia family with ease and deceived the FBI. Who knew what she was planning for Vince?

'Are you going to kill me now?' he asked, as sweat beaded on his forehead. It was always much warmer in the pool room and the chlorine was getting to him. 'You wouldn't be so tough if you didn't have that gun in your hands.'

She continued to stare. 'Move, let's go.' She gestured with her weapon. 'In that room.'

He walked into an open space used for aerobics classes. Plastic mats were on the floor and the walls were covered in mirrors. Monica walked in. The next thing she did surprised Vince: she placed her gun onto a nearby table and said, 'Okay, Vince, no gun. Let's see what you've got.'

He realized this was his opening to escape. If she was stupid and naive to think she could take him in a fight, she had another think coming.

'Are you serious?' he stared at her, his expression dark, wrestling with something.

'Let's go. I feel like releasing some tension.'

She shaped up like a boxer and circled around Vince. She attacked him with a jab to his sternum, then with a right swing-kick to his side. The kick was partially blocked by his arm, but the blow still winded him and he winced in pain. He responded with left-right blows to her head. Both of which were blocked and she retaliated with a hard push-kick to his abdomen. At this point it was evident Monica was no ordinary woman.

'Come on, Vince, this is what you wanted, isn't it?'

Vince unbent himself and tried to suck in some air. He stood toe to toe and went for a jab, then another, but both were blocked.

Monica now went on the offensive with a flurry of combinations. Vince copped a right hook to the jaw, causing him to fall to the ground in a daze onto a red mat. She was too good, too strong and too quick. He could taste blood and sharp pain caught him with every breath.

'Stop, okay, you proved your point,' he gasped with a hand up in supplication.

Monica stopped the onslaught and grabbed the gun from where she had left it. Vince had no chance, his time was up. He was going to die in the UCLA Student Activities Center, beaten and executed by a woman.

'Listen, I'm not going to kill you, relax.'

'You're not?'

'It might look like I'm the bad guy here, but believe me, I'm not. I still have unfinished business that I need to sort out. This business does not involve you.' Monica picked up the backpack. 'Let's go.'

'Where are you taking me, then?' he asked, as he stood up gingerly, holding his jaw and ribs.

'I'm taking you to an old acquaintance. You need to trust me.'

'Trust you?' Vince smirked. 'You got what you wanted, it's over.'

'It's not over, Vince, not even close. Now, let's go!'

He began to walk with a gentle nudge from Monica. His face battered and bruised, he entered the car. She was up to something and he was her hostage to command.

Chapter 61

Midnight was fast approaching. Joey dressed all in black: black jeans, black hooded jumper and black steel-cap boots. The rest of the team, Frank, James and Victoria, dressed the same. Joey took time to prepare himself for the main event. In his en suite he splashed cold water onto his face. It was a ritual he had seen his older brother do most nights, leaving the club. He had never understood why until now. It cleansed the soul. It was a rebirth, a communion, before he went out to inflict pain or complete some other dark deed for his father.

As water dripped down his chiseled jaw line, he could see his older brother's reflection in the mirror. He had become him. This was not the life Phil had wanted for his younger brother; he had tried so hard to keep him out of it. Now he was about to lead a team and take his place.

After washing his face, he put on a pair of long-fingered cycling gloves and placed a black knitted beanie on his head to complete the look. He was now ready; the men were already waiting for him outside at the stolen van.

Alexander had given the all-important go-ahead. The team was ready to roll. Frank, James and Victoria were indulging in a twelve-year-old single malt to relax before the big event. Everyone was dealing with their nervousness differently. This particular job was no small bank or armored-guard truck, it was the LAPD headquarters. This was unheard of and yet brilliant and everything needed to go as planned. Key players, including Lee Davis, needed to perform their part for it to be successful.

'Is he ready, boss?' Frank asked. 'Or is he puking his guts out?'

'Give him a chance, Frank,' said Alexander, with his practiced easy charm.

'We have no choice, Frank, this is a four-person operation,' said Victoria, sitting in the van as she cracked her neck side to side. 'Unless you're willing to step in, hon,' she said to Alexander with a cheeky smile.

'You're a comedian,' Alexander replied. He never took part, he always watched from the sideline; he was the puppeteer, not the puppet.

Joey was about to close his bedroom door when he heard the familiar chime of incoming mail from his laptop. He quickly went to check. An image was attached to the email, sent from an anonymous Google account. He clicked on the small thumbnail and a picture of his mom stared back at him. The photo must have been at least thirty years old. She was young. He'd never seen this photo before. The only pictures he had of his mother were those that Phil had kept and given to him. Joey, never having had the chance to truly know his mother, felt a great emptiness. It was one of the reason why Phil was so protective and took on a role much like a mother figure. If he didn't do it, no one would.

Their dad was and always would be a cold and selfish man. It was his nature. He never talked about their mother, and when asked about her, he'd ignore the questions and walk away. Either it was too painful to talk about his loss, or there was something more to her passing.

He gazed at the photo – seeing his mom was not the peculiar thing. It was the man in the picture with her: it wasn't his father. Who was this man? In the photo the two displayed affection, their cheeks touching side by side. They appeared happy together, in love? Joey was confused. How could this be? He was told his mother only fell in love with one man and that was his father, Alexander. The man in the photo was handsome, with a chiseled jaw line, blue eyes and straight blond hair.

Joey paused with a puzzled look on his face.

'Hey, Joey, let's go!' he heard from outside the open window.

He glanced down at his watch. They needed to head off; time was ticking. This would have to wait. He left his room and walked outside into the club's empty car park. His father, Frank, Victoria and James waited by the van. It was time to man up now, channel his brother's confidence. He approached them all enthusiastically. 'Let's fucking do this!' he said.

'Yeah baby,' said Victoria with a smile, pumped up and ready to go.

'Let's do this, man,' said Frank.

Everyone was animated and ready, and Joey appeared confident.

'You good?' Alexander patted him on the shoulder.

'Good as I'll ever be,' said Joey with a nervous smile.

'Okay, listen up. We're on schedule. Be smart, follow the plan and after tonight we'll celebrate in Jamaica,' Alexander joked.

'Yeah, black *putang*!' said Frank, laughing with James inside the van.

'You guys are fucking idiots,' said Victoria, shaking her head.

The light atmosphere and clear starry sky held the promise of a successful night. But the fun and games were short-lived when a white sports Mercedes screeched to a halt at their gate. The car was unmistakable and she was not alone.

Chapter 62

Frank instinctively jumped out of the van at the sound. Armed with a 9mm Beretta he stepped in front of Alexander, his weapon pointed at the passenger's seat. He was an irrefutably devoted member of the clan and would throw his body on the line to protect his leader.

'It's okay, Frank, it's Monica,' said Alexander.

'Yeah, but she's not alone,' said Victoria, also on the lookout.

Exiting the car, Monica scanned the crew with a playful grin.

'Don't shoot, it's me,' she said to Frank with her hands raised in jest. He was yet to lower his gun. He had never liked her. He suspected she was two-faced and untrustworthy. In his mind she was Phil's sexual trophy, nothing more.

'Who's your driver?' Frank asked. The tinted windows did not reveal much detail within, except the vague shape of a driver.

'We don't have time for this, Monica. We're on a deadline,' said Joey, stepping forward with his hands in his pockets.

She glanced over at Alexander and asked, 'Did Ian get the girl?'

Alexander smiled. 'He did. She's in my suite!'

Monica turned to the shape sitting in the driver's seat. 'Get out of the car,' she ordered.

Frank's finger tightened around the trigger of his Beretta. Victoria, who stood opposite, had now pulled out her Glock and had it trained on the young man stepping out from behind the wheel.

★ ★ ★

As Vince got out of the car, his brown eyes were filled with fear, making him appear more like a boy than a man. His heart was pounding so hard it felt like it would tear through his chest as he stood among these killers. How am I ever going to get out of this? he thought.

'Relax, it's only Vince,' said Joey.

Frank and Victoria lowered their guns. He was no threat. Monica gave Vince a shove, forcing him to stand in front of the tall Alexander.

'What's this all about, Monica?' Joey asked.

'He's your fifth,' she said.

'Fifth? Dad, what's she talking about?' asked Joey, thoroughly confused.

'It means, Vince is taking a ride with you all tonight. He's my insurance,' said Alexander.

Vince looked around nervously, his legs shaking. He felt like a soldier sent to the frontline to be slaughtered.

'Is this necessary? Won't he just get in the way?' asked Joey.

Monica answered. 'Joey, your team is entering the LAPD headquarters. Don't you think it's wise having a backup plan just in case something goes wrong?'

'What if I refuse to go?' said Vince, regretting the question the moment he uttered it.

Alexander stepped forward, grabbed him by the neck and began to squeeze. 'You do what I say.'

Vince tried to pull the hand off his neck. He could feel his windpipe crushing and he began to black out, but it was useless, Alexander's grip was like an iron vice.

'Dad!'

'Stop, Alexander,' yelled Monica, 'he's had enough.'

Alexander let go and Vince fell to his hands and knees, gasping for breath.

'Vince is going with you guys. Shit happens and I want to make sure we have a plan B.'

'I don't know, man,' said James, the quiet one of the group, shaking his head.

Alexander launched his body forward, throwing his hip into a violent kick to Vince's stomach. An unpleasant reminder of what he was up against if he didn't listen.

'Dad!' Joey cried out again. 'Stop!'

Vince rolled up in a ball, wounded and winded, struggling to breathe.

'Pick him up. I need to have a word with him,' ordered Alexander. James helped him off the ground and stood him in front of Alexander. Vince looked up, still winded and wincing with every attempt at a breath.

'Tonight you will accompany my men. You will help Joey and do whatever he tells you. You will listen and not cause trouble, and if you don't obey, your pretty little girlfriend will get a bullet in the head. Do you understand me?'

Vince just stood there, staring.

'Here – someone wants to say hi.' Alexander handed him a cell phone.

He held it to his ear.

'Talk, bitch!' He heard a voice say on the other end, followed by the sound of a loud slap and then the scared whimper of a woman.

'It's me,' Isabella sobbed.

'Are you okay?'

'Yes, please just do what they—'

The phone went dead.

'Do we understand each other?' asked Alexander.

'Yes, please don't hurt her.'

'Do as asked, Vince, and everything will be fine,' said Monica.

'Let's get going.' Victoria clapped her hands. 'We don't want to be late.'

'Remember, son, Lee will give you guys a ten-minute window after midnight, good luck. Bring me back my money.'

'Good luck, Joey,' said Monica.

Vince was the last to enter the van, before glancing over to the beach that could be seen from the car park. The sliding door shut and they sped off into the distance.

Standing alone in the empty parking lot, Alexander turned to Monica and said, 'When Vince comes back, kill him. I want no witnesses.'

'Anything else?'

'Lee will be with us shortly after he plays his part. Why don't you come inside and join us for a drink?'

Monica accepted the invitation.

Side by side they walked back to the house to await the outcome of their respective schemes.

Chapter 63

Monday, 11:55 pm

One entire week had passed from the California Bank & Trust robbery on Wilshire Boulevard. Joey, Frank, James and Victoria arrived with new member, Vince, at the downtown LAPD headquarters. It was no ordinary construction, costing $437 million to build, boasting a futuristic design of glass paneling around its perimeter. The five-hundred-thousand square foot, ten-story building was designed by AECOM, the number-one-ranked engineering company in the world. It included a four-hundred-seat auditorium, restaurant and a helicopter pad on the roof. Every level was open plan, which took advantage of natural light, while the offices and conference rooms lined the inner perimeter of each floor. Even though the building had given back to the community, allowing access to the restaurant and parklands, many people believed the money had been wasted and could have been used for a better cause, such as feeding and housing many homeless in America.

The crew advanced onto West Street. In view was the impressive towering structure and its sprawling surrounds. As they drove down the street they passed 'Reflections,' the two-hundred-seat restaurant, open to the public. Then the police memorial site, which included the names of the two hundred and two officers killed in the line of duty.

The street was desolate at this time of night. Past the memorial park to the left was the entrance to the underground garage used for employee access only. As they cruised down the steep ramp, they were blocked by a high–security, steel-reinforced roller gate which prevented their entry to the garage.

Now was Joey's time.

He pulled down the beanie over his face, which became a makeshift balaclava. Holes had been cut out for the eyes and mouth, enabling him to see and breathe.

'Cameras?' he asked Frank.

From behind the van's tinted windows, Frank looked up at the surveillance cameras mounted on the walls. A small red light flashed in the corner of each one.

'Time,' Joey announced, while Vince watched.

Frank flashed down to his digital watch and began the countdown. 'Five, four, three, two, one, time: it's midnight.'

The camera's red lights switched off. So far it seemed Lee had fulfilled his part of the bargain, deactivating all security systems.

'Good to go, cameras are off,' said Victoria, sitting by Frank's side. Her excitement showed. She rubbed her hands together and wore the facial expression of a small child with an especially large Christmas present.

'Okay, here we go. Ten minutes in and out,' said Joey. He started a ten-minute timer on his digital watch, kneeled in position and scouted for any other potential threats.

He drew a breath.

James slid open the van's door, and in a flash Joey leapt out with his balaclava over his head. In his right hand he held Leonardo Vancini's magnetic tag. The tag that accessed a high clearance level, or at least the chief said it did.

With a racing heart, he swiped it across the intercom mounted on a concrete pillar. This was the first access point into the underground car park. Everything relied on this small tag. If it didn't allow them inside, there was no other way in, as the place was like a vault with the best security systems money could buy. In seconds, a small green light illuminated in the stainless-steel plate and the large roller gate started to slowly lift.

The van entered the underground parking lot. Frank drove around two of many support pillars and did a large U-turn, so the van faced the way they had come.

Frank, Victoria and the herculean singlet-wearing James left the van in haste with their hoods on. Vince followed behind like a sheep. No disguise for him.

'Okay, door two.' Joey, at the front, swiped the tag again, this time to a fire-rated door which opened up to a stairwell, giving them access to the headquarters from the fire escape. Another green light lit up on the computer-coded door lock. Not for the first time, Joey was amazed at how many millions of dollars was spent on this building and its security systems. Yet here they were, trotting inside without a worry in the world, without the use of explosive devices or any high-tech computer gadgets.

Now inside, the gang didn't waste any time as they sprinted up the basement's stairwell to ground level. Vince straggled in last position. Reaching the top, they were confronted by a third entry door locked from the inside and decorated with a glass panel in its center. Joey glanced through it to the other side, searching for active cameras. A smile appeared on his face. Lee was on the money, they were all turned off, no flashing red lights anywhere.

'Frank – goggles.'

'Here you go,' he said, handing Joey a pair of infrared goggles.

He put them on, and after a quick peek to his left and right, no laser beams were visible. The coast was clear.

'My turn,' said James, who elbowed the glass and smashed it, creating a decent hole.

Joey moved in and snaked his gloved hand through it, unlocking the door.

The team was inside.

They were the only people in this ten-story contemporary building, but their window of opportunity was small. Ten minutes to get the money and retreat before all systems were back up and running. Joey craned his neck and could see all the levels above them. They seemed to go on forever. It was like being on the ground floor of the largest shopping center in the world. He was amazed at how well they worked as a team, obeying his every command – or at least until they entered the building.

'I can't have this on anymore.' Sweat saturated James's face and clothing. 'It's too hot.' His huge biceps flexed as he removed the hood from his head to take a breather. 'All this running has worn me out.'

Joey knew in the gym James did no aerobic activities, he only lifted weights for size and strength. He went there with the other so-called gorillas to flex and compare muscle mass.

'Ah, what the hell!' said Frank, taking off his hood, too. Without any cameras or alarm systems operating, they could roam the halls freely. Victoria was next.

'What are you all doing? Put your masks back on,' Joey ordered.

James sighed. 'No one's in here, boy. Let's just get what we're after and get out.'

The cracks in the team were beginning to show.

Joey knew he was never really in charge. If it was his brother they would have obeyed immediately. Yes, he was appointed leader, but he didn't have the presence they were used to. He was in his twenties and these men were in their forties and fifties.

Joey kept his mask on as Frank now took the lead and walked further into the room. He was followed by Victoria, with James and Joey behind her. Vince continued at the rear.

'They're stupid,' said Vince quietly to Joey. 'I never would've taken off my mask.'

Joey gave him a hapless smile.

'I can see the door,' alerted Frank, as he walked swiftly across the tiled floor deep inside the structure. His voice echoed through the large empty space as Victoria kept up with his pace. Joey was not as enthusiastic as they were. He trod with more caution, slowly walking with Vince by his side, his eyes roaming the walls and doors for anything out of the ordinary.

'So you know, after this, your father's going to kill me,' said Vince, looking down at Joey's shadow on the floor created by the moonlight shining in from above.

'Just do as you're asked, Vince, and I'm sure he'll let you go.'

'You sure don't know your dad, do you?' said Vince.

To hear this out loud struck something deep within Joey. Upset, he pointed the P99 self-loading pistol he held at Vince's head. 'Shut up and move!'

Approaching the evidence room door, free from police, alarms and surveillance cameras, Joey spotted two cameras that were still operational. Two distinct red lights flashed in the darkened room, an indication they were live, probably running on another source of power that had not been accounted for.

'Stop! Put on your masks, cameras are on,' he said quickly, flattening himself against a wall and pushing Vince with him. Frank, Victoria and James were exposed and vulnerable to the camera's eyes. He knew that even if they got away with the money, the footage captured would reveal their true identities, in turn putting his father at risk and back in the limelight.

Frank and Victoria did not respond.

James was the only one who looked back with concern. Joey pointed vigorously at the CCTV cameras mounted high up on the walls.

'They're on, you idiots,' he shouted.

James understood and turned his face the other way to put on his black ski mask once more.

★ ★ ★

Frank, now at the door, held the handle and waved for Joey to hurry up. He needed his swipe tag to enter. As his anticipation peaked, he pushed down on the handle and was surprised to find that the door was unlocked.

'Fuck, the door's open,' he said to Victoria.

Joey was taking too long.

Victoria smiled. 'Let's go.'

They entered the room one after the other and the door shut behind them.

James, Joey and Vince were now just seconds from opening the door themselves when the unthinkable happened.

Chapter 64

Waiting patiently in the darkness of the evidence room was Detective Taylor. He had gained access to the LAPD headquarters after a few discreet phone calls. Inside he could hear the criminals gradually working their way toward him.

The evidence room was more like being in a large Costco store, framed with rows of floor-to-ceiling shelving units. The facility was vast and the shelves stored hundreds of pounds of confiscated drugs, from marijuana to cocaine and heroin. Weapons ranging from 9mm handguns, shotguns, rifles to semi-automatic machine guns had been separated and laid out in the hundreds. Finally, endless amounts of laundered or stolen money sat in labeled boxes and bags. This included what was retrieved from the Wilshire robbery that took place over a week ago.

As soon as the door closed behind Frank and Victoria, Taylor stepped forward, aiming his Smith & Wesson magnum directly at the suspects' heads.

'Don't move, put your hands up in the air,' he said in a quiet yet menacing tone. He knew there were others yet to come in and wanted the element of surprise.

Frank and Victoria could only see a shape in the darkness of an armed man.

'Motherfucker!' fell out of Frank's mouth and his eyes rolled backwards.

Victoria's hand sneaked down toward the gun tucked in her pants.

'Don't even think about it, missy,' said Taylor, well aware both of them would be concealing weapons.

'How could this be happening?' said Frank, as they both slowly raised their hands above their heads, surrendering to the detective.

'How many more are outside?' asked Taylor. The voices on the other side were about to enter.

Frank and Victoria did not say a word.

Armed and ready with an all-American gun, Taylor had prepared himself for the worst possible outcome. He had the upper hand, though, with key position to take out whoever walked through that door. So he'd waited, with a finger wrapped around the trigger while his other hand steadied his shooting arm. He remembered his history teacher, who had explained how the ancient Spartans forced the Persians to traverse a narrow ravine, slowing their progress. Their huge numbers meant nothing and they were slaughtered as they entered.

That was his plan.

'You're not going to get away with this,' said Victoria with a confident voice. You could tell she was Alexander's girl: tough, direct and not afraid to speak her mind. She probably loved the feeling of being an outlaw and preferred to rough it with the boys. 'We've seen your face, Detective. You realize now you either have to kill us all, or your family will suffer.'

Taylor frowned as he considered the threat. Then he heard the sound of heavy footsteps behind the closed door.

The handle turned and into the darkness stepped a goliath of a man. The silhouette of his large frame was barely contained in the doorframe. The evidence room stretched away from him like an enormous hanger bay lined with industrial shelves.

Taylor faced the Hulk in the doorway. His size would

intimidate anybody and the adrenaline rushed through him. 'Don't move!' he demanded.

Taylor could see James's eyes blinking as he was readjusting to the darkness to see his two cohorts with their hands up.

Frank took a gamble, diving behind the nearest shelving unit to his left.

Taylor reacted, aimed and fired. But the bullets hit nothing but metal, ricocheting in the darkness. All the men dropped to a crouch.

Victoria was not as quick to react, instinctively going for her weapon, while the detective was confronted by James, who began his charge.

He was sixteen feet away.

Victoria's slow reaction enabled Taylor to unload two bullets into her chest. The force sent her flying backwards, her body landing on the cold concrete floor like a rag doll.

'Shit! What the fuck's going on,' said Joey, hearing the gunfire beyond the door. It was too dangerous to step in during this chaos, so he and Vince waited.

'Why do these things always have to go wrong?' he asked himself, hunched down with Vince by his side.

After killing Victoria, Taylor quickly swung back toward James, only a few feet away now.

He was enormous up close. The closer he came, the bigger he towered. Taylor didn't want to stand toe to toe with him: that would be suicide.

He fired twice more.

He hit James in the hip and another bullet smashed into his chest. It slowed the big man but didn't stop him. Taylor could see a rage wash over James, barely aware of the pain that must be making itself known in his side and chest as he pushed forward, randomly firing his shotgun in Taylor's direction, forcing him to retreat and hide.

'Who are you, pig?' James yelled.

Taylor at once edged backwards, while the monster continued to move toward him, dragging his leg behind him.

Frank was now a threat, circling Taylor from behind, so he decided to move back into the darkness, regroup and try to pick them off one at a time.

Chapter 65

'Joey, get in here, I need your help,' shouted James back toward the door behind him. His large shoulder muscles flexed as he reloaded his double-barrel shotgun, ready to fire.

Joey stepped in warily as the smell of gunpowder engulfed the room. Vince followed Joey's every move and stayed hidden behind his back, until they reached James.

'I need you to watch my back, boy,' said James as he spat in the dark.

Cautiously, Joey, Vince and the relentless James, walked past the next shelving unit to their left in search of the idiot in the room trying to foil their plans.

James paused for a moment, still armed, and leaned against the steel shelving unit to take a breather. 'My hip is burning,' he said to Joey.

Joey looked at James as he lowered his head and sucked in deep breaths, sweat dripping from his face and landing on the floor. It was obvious that the big man was hurting.

'Whoever you are, I'll find you and wring your fuckin' neck!' James screamed. 'Come on, show yourself, pig.' His voice echoed and bounced off the walls. He pushed on to the next shelf. Joey and Vince followed. Joey knew they were probably safer standing in James's shadow, obstructed by his larger-than-normal frame.

Suddenly, the sound of gunfire ricocheting off metal rang out from the far-right corner of the room. Then the grunts of men struggling.

'Motherfucker, I'm gonna kill you,' Frank roared.

'I'm coming, Frank,' James shouted, hearing the commotion and stepping up the pace.

Another shot rang out.

'Hey, Frank!' screamed James. 'Talk to me.'

Silence ...

He turned the corner and reached the scene. A body lay face down and it was not the detective's.

As Frank dived on Taylor and knocked the gun out of his hand, Taylor had reached down to the pistol strapped to his calf, buried its barrel into Frank's stomach and pulled the trigger. He had outwitted Victoria and Frank and now had a clear shot at James's head. He was a sitting duck as he leaned heavily on his undamaged leg.

'Go on, pull the trigger, pig.'

'Drop your weapon. Now!' Taylor demanded.

James threw his shotgun onto the floor, defeated. The clatter echoed through the building. Then all of a sudden the sound of a stopwatch beeped in the darkness.

Chapter 66

'Now you put your gun on the floor,' said Joey, stepping out from the shadows. His ten-minute window to get in and out of the building had run out. He shoved his hostage forward, his gun wedged in Vince's back.

'Alright, I'm going,' said Vince. 'Relax.'

Joey was now face to face with a hardened detective, but he had a bargaining chip. Vince was the son of a legend in the department and this was why he had been hauled along on this ride; as leverage in case something just like this transpired.

Monica was two steps ahead of everyone, Joey thought. It was as if she had envisioned all this unfolding. Or even worse: planned for this to happen. The killing of most of Peruggia's men in a single hit.

It was now a standoff, someone had to give. The question was who would drop their weapon?

'Don't do anything stupid, boy,' said the detective, glancing down at the hostage.

Joey dug his gun deeper into Vince's neck, tilting his head over to the side. 'Put your gun down on the ground.'

'I can't do that,' said Taylor.

James stood there on the edge, waiting.

'Okay, this is what we're going to do,' suggested Taylor. 'You leave and I will not come after you, but let Vince go.'

'You're in no position to give orders,' said Joey with a

sudden maturity in his voice. He found he was in control as his father knew he could be.

While this stalemate was taking place, Frank pushed himself off the ground. Blood trickled from the side of his mouth and the red stains on his side and chest had spread. The gun in his trembling hands wavered as, with a final exertion of energy, he squeezed the trigger, sending a bullet into the back of the detective. A smile passed across his face before he collapsed and his body went still.

Taylor fell to the floor, clutching his magnum close to his body. James did not waste any time and went in for the kill, grabbing his head and twisting it with heaving muscles until it snapped. A loud crack echoed as his vertebrae parted. He was killed instantly.

'This was supposed to be an in-and-out job, no deaths,' shouted Joey, searching for the light switch. The lights flickered on, the three corpses came into view, splayed out across the concrete floor. Blood trailed everywhere, leading to the bodies like a macabre joining of the dots.

With the detective out of the way, Joey yelled at Vince, 'Move! I need you to help me, or I swear I'll fucking kill you where you stand.'

'Okay, okay,' replied Vince with his palms raised in supplication.

'Shelf W,' gasped James.

'You heard the man, W,' said Joey.

The police catalogued the bank's money using the street address it had been taken from, W for Wilshire. Within a couple of minutes searching the long shelf, two briefcases were found. A six-digit combination lock had been attached to each case as added security. Joey knew these were the bags, as the yellow sticker on their sides read, 'to be returned' with tomorrow's date. It was the bank's seven-working-day holding period coming to an end.

Joey took possession of the briefcases and handed one over to Vince. He knew they were both going to need their free hand to help carry James to safety. Now all that remained was to escape without getting caught. The main obstacle was helping James back into the van. James struggled as he dragged his leg and held his arm against his chest as blood oozed from his body. Joey could see he was in excruciating pain. He needed urgent medical attention. Time was critical.

'Help me, go on that side,' Joey told Vince.

Vince slung James's arm over his shoulder while Joey did the same on his left. Dragging him back the way they had come felt like carrying a grizzly bear.

And then the LAPD headquarters alarms went off. An extremely loud, ear-shattering siren wailed along the corridors, echoing everywhere.

It was a struggle and Joey felt his shoulders burn, but eventually they got James inside the van. The big man slumped to the floor of the van and groaned in pain.

'Go – drive!' yelled Joey, sliding the door shut.

'The roller door has locked us in,' said Vince.

'Ram it, do it now!'

Vince turned the key and his foot pressed hard on the accelerator. They screeched out of the underground car park and up the ramp, smashing into the gated door, taking most of it with them, as Joey struggled to hold James's head in his lap and watched him gulp his last breath.

Chapter 67

Monica sat with Alexander, Ian and Lee, who had arrived five minutes after Joey and the crew had left. They were all in the club's bistro, enjoying a late-night espresso. The anticipation of the team's return and eagerness for success was felt by all.

Lee swilled his third coffee and continued to shake his leg uncontrollably. The nerves were getting to him, while Alexander looked over and lit up another cigarette, his way of dealing with the stress.

'They should've been back already,' said Alexander, glancing at his Rolex. He squashed his unfinished cigarette into the silver ashtray, where eight identical stubs lay.

Monica finished her espresso and placed the cup back onto the saucer. Alexander's previous statement made her glance over at her own watch. She agreed with him. 'It's true, they've taken a little longer than expected.'

'They'll be here,' said Lee.

'They should've been here twenty minutes ago,' said Alexander, giving Lee a narrow-eyed glare.

'Don't look at me like that, I did my part. I shut down the security systems and gave you easy access into the building.'

All of a sudden Ian reached for his gun and checked to see that his cartridge clip was full. Sixteen in the clip and one in the chamber.

'You backstab me, Lee, or set me up, and I'll cut you up

into small little pieces and toss you into the ocean for the sharks,' warned Alexander.

Monica observed Lee, who sat deep into his chair, rubbing the back of his neck. She knew that when Alexander found out Detective Taylor was at the scene, Lee's life would be worthless. How many of those bullets Ian was checking were going to find their way into Lee's body? He had made a deal with the devil and there was no turning back. He offered a fake smile.

Monica smiled right back as she knew his future.

'The same goes for you, Miss FBI.' Alexander furiously turned to Monica, his jaw clenched. 'Don't you ever fuck with me or I'll leave you in the street with your pretty eyes cut out from their sockets.'

She did not react as Lee had. She slid herself away from the source of anger and stood up against the large glass window, ignoring his outburst. He did not intimidate her; in fact, no one did.

This infuriated Alexander, his presence demanded respect. He loved power and craved the fear it induced. The fact that he could not control her or put fear in her eyes was another reason he could not trust her. She was unknowable and the unknown was dangerous, especially in his line of work. After tonight he was going to see to it, personally, that she was removed from the equation.

Monica stood with her back toward the three men. She took a minute to glance out into the dark ocean, witnessing the gigantic waves relentlessly crashing in the moonlight. Her long, glossy brown hair draped over her shoulders, the hint of a sky-blue rose tattoo showing on her upper-right shoulder.

Alexander must have sensed the wrong in her. She walked both sides of the line, separating good and bad. There was history to this girl; damage. She rode motorbikes, drank with the men and wasn't afraid to break a nail.

Phil had loved strong women, and that's exactly what she was. Her determination had allowed her to join the FBI and infiltrate the Peruggia family with ease, playing both sides against each other. Tonight she had single-handedly wiped out Detective Mostrom, kidnapped Vince, acquired the two million dollars and somehow convinced Alexander to throw Vince into the heist. She had also sabotaged the operation by sending Taylor into the lion's den.

'Something's wrong, I can feel it,' she said, as she sat back down and glanced at her watch.

Alexander bumped out another cigarette. Seeing Monica's reaction unsettled him. He unbuttoned the top of his shirt and rubbed his cigarette-free hand down one pants leg.

'The way you're going smoking those things you're going to get cancer,' said Monica, her eyes darting over to the full ashtray.

Alexander looked her dead in the eyes.

Monica waited for him to speak. She could sense his nervousness. Tonight needed to go as planned for Alexander. His business, his home and his way of life were all being threatened if his crew didn't deliver.

'If I don't hear anything in ten minutes I'm driving down there myself,' said Alexander, standing up then sitting back down.

As time ticked away Lee hauled his body forward, elbows on knees, and ran his hands through his hair then brought them to cover his face.

At 12:48 am a loud, crashing noise was heard from the club's side-gate entrance, the same entrance that allowed customers to enter via the sandy beach, to the rear of the club.

Monica was the first up off the couch, looking out the window. Alexander waited for her response. Lee stood up.

'It's them,' she shouted, seeing the white van's wheels, beached in the soft sand and spinning out of control. The van could not go any further. Alexander stood up and walked over to the window. Ian stood a few feet back to keep Lee and Alexander in his sights.

'Who's that running away?' said Lee, seeing a figure leap out of the van.

'That's Vince, something's wrong,' said Monica.

'Let's go,' ordered Alexander with an intimidating stare.

Chapter 68

'What the fuck, Vince?' Joey screamed as he was thrown around the back of the van like a rag doll. It had wedged itself straight into the sandbank. The tires submerged deep into the soft sand and so did the front end.

Vince's body coiled; he was ready to run. He knew that if he stepped foot in the club he was a dead man. His girlfriend was probably dead anyway: he knew Alexander would eliminate anyone who was a threat. This was his one and only chance to make a run for it onto the beach and head south.

'Don't you even,' warned Joey, who regained his balance and saw Vince bolt out of the van.

Vince was free. His heart pumped out of control as he sprinted for dear life, running as fast as he could on the soft sand. Sweat poured off his face, his mouth was dry, but he kept on going. Moonlight lit up the beach as he kicked up sand that fell down the sides of his sports shoes. He was no athlete; after only a minute of running he was gasping for air and his legs became heavier and heavier. He kept telling himself, 'Keep going, don't stop,' but his body wasn't listening. After a few hundred feet, he could not run anymore. His legs were burning, he was out of breath and a stitch was aching in his chest.

He stopped and held his chest but continued to walk fast, looking back to see Joey jump out of the van to chase him down. He needed to keep moving: the further away from the club the safer he was.

Incapacitated with fear, Vince thought about his father and the sacrifices he'd made in order to fight crime. Only now that he was a part of it, had he truly understood.

Alexander, Monica, Lee and Ian ran to the outside balcony steps to see Joey sprint past, clearly after Vince.

'He's a slippery little fucker,' said Alexander, happy to see Joey in one piece. But where were the others?

Monica brought up her hands to cup them around her mouth and yelled out to Joey, 'Where's the money?'

He turned and called, while continuing his chase, 'The van.'

'Let's go,' said Monica, first down the steps.

The van had the appearance of being abandoned – there was no sign of anyone. Lee pulled out his weapon and took the lead, opening the side door. Lying dead in a pool of his own blood was James, accompanied by two briefcases.

'The money,' said Monica excitedly.

'What in the hell happened here?' said Lee, passing the briefcases out of the van and into Ian's capable hands.

'You set me up, that's what happened,' said Alexander, who grabbed Lee and roughly shoved him up against the vehicle.

Lee grunted as the wind was knocked out of him. 'I don't know what you're talking about,' he said. 'Why would I jeopardize the operation? I'm just as at risk as you are!'

He was backed into a corner. He had no choice but to act. As Ian moved the briefcases to one side, he whipped out the Glock tucked down the back of his trousers and pushed the muzzle into Alexander's chest.

Alexander moved back, staring into the gun's barrel.

'You're not so tough now, are you?' Lee sneered.

'Go fuck yourself, Lee.'

'Relax, boys,' said Monica, stepping between the two. 'Let's see what Joey has to say first, before we all kill each other.'

'You realize I can kill everyone here right now and walk away with the lot?' said Lee.

'And why would you want to do that?' said Monica.

'It looks like you leave me with no choice,' said Lee.

'Listen, don't be stupid. We can work this out: it's just a misunderstanding, that's all. Put your gun down.'

'Misunderstanding my ass,' replied Alexander.

'You're not helping.' Monica glared at Alexander as if to say, 'Shut up.'

She stepped forward, blocking Lee's line of fire. His gun now pressed against the olive skin of her chest.

'I could never understand you,' he said to Monica. 'Why would you defend someone like him?'

Her eyes did not leave Lee's as her placid voice reassured him that everything was going to be okay. Alexander watched on, seemingly fascinated by her calm skill in defusing the situation and manipulating a man holding a weapon, capable of firing seventeen rounds in its double-stacked magazine.

'Look, Lee, everyone is a little on edge tonight, all we need is—'

Before she uttered another word, she grabbed his wrist, twisting it until the gun fell from his hand. An elbow quickly followed, landing and fracturing his nose with a crack.

'Ahh! You broke my nose.' He pinched his nose while kneeling on the sand. He spat out: the bleeding was relentless, running down to his mouth. 'Ahh shit, it hurts!'

'Shut up, you brought it on yourself,' said Monica.

Alexander smiled at the idiot bleeding in the sand. Monica was an impressive woman, with more balls than most of his men put together.

Speaking of which, Alexander now took a couple of steps back as if lining up a field goal, then came running forward to land a kick to Lee's genitals. 'You pigs are all the same.'

Lee collapsed to the ground, his knees up against his chest. He gurgled something unintelligible, which Alexander amusingly imagined had something to do with his nose not hurting anymore. Meanwhile, Monica deftly picked up Lee's gun and tucked it behind her back.

'Ian, take the briefcases to my suite,' said Alexander.

'Yes, sir,' Ian answered, leaving the party.

'Come on, get up, Lee,' Monica ordered with a helping hand.

'You're blind if you think you can trust him,' said Lee.

She looked into Lee's eyes. 'He should be the one who's worried.'

Alexander overheard Monica's hauteur and smiled. Once again he thought to himself that eliminating her was going to be a pleasure. He stepped forward to face Lee, who was considerably shorter standing at only five foot nine, and spoke as if nothing had happened.

'Let's go speak to Joey and find out what happened tonight. I'll then decide if you deserve to live or die.'

Lee nodded and started walking, clutching his groin in one hand and his nose in the other. Alexander was not far behind, followed lastly by Monica, who walked in their shadows.

Chapter 69

'Vince, stop or I'll shoot,' screamed out Joey, now only a short distance away from the beach club. He caught up; he was stronger and fitter. He raised his gun in the night sky and fired two warning shots.

Vince stopped and raised his arms up in the air.

Joey could see his breathing was erratic and out of control. There was no way he was going to escape as Joey approached his position.

He pointed the pistol at Vince's head as he got close. 'I can't believe you made me run!'

'Why don't you shove that gun up your ass?' said Vince.

The smile that flickered on Joey's face wavered: he'd never had it in him to kill anyone. It was not his nature, but this last week certainly had confirmed a darker side in him.

'Do you want some?' said Joey, confident he could take down his opponent, having trained every day in the gym this last week.

'Drop that gun and let's find out,' said Vince.

A showdown between Alexander and Leonardo's sons was about to take place, as they circled each other. Both with something to fight for tonight.

'Let's see what you've got,' said Joey, tossing the gun in the sand and running at Vince. His shoulder collided with Vince's chest, winding him and causing them both to stumble in the sand. Vince grabbed Joey in a headlock and squeezed as hard as he could, as he swung his leg over his back and locked his legs around his torso. Joey's eyesight turned red and started seeing stars as blood was being deprived to his brain.

'Oh no, you don't,' said Joey. He swung an elbow backwards into Vince's stomach, forcing him to let go.

They both pushed themselves to their feet and began to circle each other once more. Joey went in for a left jab and connected. Vince took the hit and through a daze of stars, followed in strong with a right swing of his own.

First was the blackness, followed by an excruciating ringing noise. Joey had been caught off balance and fell to his knees. Kneeling there in the sand, he could see blurry colors flying around his head. This was the second time he had been knocked down this week.

'Is that all you've got?' Vince shouted, satisfied with his handiwork.

Struggling to stand up, Joey could see his father approaching. He closed his eyes for a second, knowing his father would not approve of him losing against a college student, especially Leonardo's son. This was all the impetus Joey needed, who now rose up like a bull.

'That was a lucky punch,' he said.

'What can I say, I'm a lucky guy,' replied Vince, clenching his knuckles back and forth on his right hand.

'You're dead,' Joey threatened. He swayed left and right, as he had been told to do by his boxing teacher, looking for a clear opening. He landed a left jab, then another, followed by a jump-push-kick that threw Vince backwards on the sand. He quickly leapt on him, straddling him like a horse and began swinging blows to his head, one after the other.

He was out of control. Blood poured from Vince's nose and mouth. He was defeated as Joey continued to punch at his head.

'Stop!' yelled Vince, his hands on the ground and unable to cover his face. 'Stop!'

Joey couldn't hear through the red fog of his rage.

'Stop!'

The damage to Vince's features was worsening. Blood now covered his entire face and his swollen eyes.

The emotions swirled in Joey's head as he hammered down. He felt alone: his brother had been torn from him and more deaths had followed. Everything that was familiar was slipping away. This was not the life he wanted. Something was wrong, the world had flipped and now he was the one inflicting pain.

Monica fired a shot into the night sky. Grey smoke rose from the barrel, illuminated by the moonlight.

'Get off him Joey, that's enough,' she shouted.

Joey stopped. Stunned, he looked at his bloody hands and the poor boy who had felt his fury, his wrath.

Who had he become?

Chapter 70

Monica, Lee and Alexander stood around Joey in a circle. Alexander noticed Joey's gun half buried in the sand and picked it up. Monica pretended not to notice as her hand drifted behind her to feel the reassuring hardness of the weapon tucked there.

Joey stood up, his head lowered. He may have been the victor, but he felt terrible. He was upset with himself as he watched Vince struggle to even open his eyes.

Standing there staring at his bloody knuckles, he suddenly had an epiphany: the blood was not his, it was his enemy's – but was Vince really the enemy? He was just an unfortunate kid thrown into the mix. Joey had become rotten after only one week. He had become his gangster brother.

'Come here, son,' said Alexander.

Joey walked over to his father with his head held high, but wished he could go back and change what had happened.

Vince was on his back, facing the stars. The blood he coughed up sprayed everywhere. It would be months before he would resemble himself again. Joey watched Monica drop to her knees to comfort the boy. It was the least she could do after throwing him to the sharks.

'You're okay,' she said, stroking her fingers through his hair, the only place the blood hadn't attached itself to.

Vince mumbled, 'Is Isabella dead?'

'No – she's not,' she said, giving him hope. His eyes opened, or at least partially.

Joey's shoulder was gripped by Alexander, who asked, 'What the hell happened tonight? Where is Frank and Victoria?'

Joey took a deep breath, there was no easy way of saying this.

'They're all dead. We were set up.'

Alexander immediately turned to Lee.

Joey sensed the hatred in his father's eyes. Lee had betrayed him.

Lee stuttered. 'B-bu-bu-but that's impossible.'

'How do you mean?' Alexander demanded of Joey.

'Inside the evidence room, a detective was waiting for us. If I didn't use Vince as collateral, I'd be dead, too.'

'Tarn,' suggested Alexander, positioning the ruthless detective as capable of such a betrayal. His task to kill Vince and retrieve the money was simple, but he'd failed. And after their last phone conversation he had disappeared.

'It wasn't Tarn,' said Monica.

'How do you know that?' asked Alexander.

'Because I killed him tonight. Lee wanted him dead.'

The chief shot a cold stare at Monica.

Joey, too, stared at her in surprise as she revealed this so casually.

'Don't look at me like that,' said Monica. 'If it weren't for me, you'd all be dead. Didn't you hear Joey?'

'You cow. You planned this, didn't you?' said Lee.

'Shut up, Lee. I did you a favor. If it wasn't Tarn in the evidence room, it must've been one of your men.'

Alexander's expression turned cold. He walked over to Lee and looked down his nose at him. His gritted teeth and heavy breathing belied his calm exterior. Someone was about to pay.

'You have to believe me, Alexander. It wasn't me,' Lee protested again.

Alexander slammed the handle of the P99 pistol into the side of his head and Lee fell to the ground, unconscious.

'A general is only as powerful as the men at his disposal and tonight I've lost three,' said Alexander, kicking the sand over Lee's fallen body.

Joey just stood there deep in thought, slowly realizing Monica had to have been the traitor, as Lee had suggested earlier. But the question was why? He knew her well enough to recognize she did not do coincidences. She was strategic, she had organized Vince's inclusion for a reason.

'Okay, Joey, no more games. It's cleanup time,' said Alexander. 'Take this and finish it.' He held out a razor-sharp hunting knife, handle first, and nodded toward the prone figure of Vince. 'He's seen too much.'

Joey stared down at the worn, strapped handle. This knife had been used many times before. He took a step back. 'I can't do it, Dad.'

'Do as you're fucking told.' Alexander moved forward, pushing the handle into Joey's chest. 'Don't worry, we'll make it look like he was mugged.'

'Please, Dad, don't make me do it,' he pleaded, holding his hands up and backing away from his father.

'Leave him alone,' yelled Monica, still on the ground comforting Vince.

'You shut up,' pointed Alexander, 'I haven't even started with you yet.'

He turned back to Joey. 'Do it, or do time.'

'I'll do time, then,' said Joey.

'Do it!'

Joey lowered his head in shame. 'No.'

'Don't disobey me.'

Joey stood there and his heart began to beat uncontrollably. He knew this was unacceptable in his father's eyes. He had warned him before at the club, when he'd choked to death a drunken fool. There was no room in his father's organization for insolence, especially from his own son, who wasn't manning up, who was failing.

Alexander swung his body to land a backhand that sent Joey's head snapping to the side, leaving an angry red handprint on his face. Joey reeled from the shock and pain, and when he recovered his eyes were filled with tears and hatred. His father was evil, vindictive; he was not the man Joey grew up to believe he was.

The slap belittled him. It was like a stab to the heart. He felt he didn't belong anymore and the truth of it all was that he had never belonged. He was a twenty-five-year-old skinny surfer kid who had grown up without a mother. Phil had read the writing on the wall and it took Joey one week in his shoes to understand what he was up against.

'You're too soft, kid, just like your fucking mother.'

'Fuck you, Dad.' Joey swung at Alexander, who saw the wild punch coming. He swayed to his right and easily countered with a stiff jab to his son's jaw.

'Aww come on, son, let's leave the fighting in the ring.'

Joey fell to his knees. His eyes were watering as he adjusted his jaw. The memories of sparring with his father in the gym flooded back. He had no way in hell of winning a fight against him; it was a stupid move on his behalf.

'How dare you try to hit your father?'

'How dare you hit your son?' responded Monica, walking up to stand within inches of the tall, powerfully built man. Even though she was only five foot four.

'I can't take your bullshit any longer,' said Alexander, who grabbed her neck in a bear's grip, his trademark move. His fingers pressed deep into her flesh, making her knees buckle.

'Ahh, let go!' Monica tried to pull away from the vice-like claw, digging into her.

Joey looked at her pained facial expression, as if her muscles and sinews were being crushed underneath her.

Her only option was to go for his groin, and that's what she did. She threw an uppercut to his balls, but it was slapped away by Alexander's free hand. The force of which spun her around, so she was on her hands and knees with her backside facing him. He front-kicked her, sending her sprawling ungraciously into the sand.

'Stupid, conniving dog,' Alexander smirked. 'I've wanted to do that for a very long time. Killing you is going to be a pleasure.'

Joey knew his father was not going to stop; he could see in his eyes that he wanted retribution. In seconds Joey had stepped in his way, stopping any further beating being inflicted on Monica.

'No, Dad.'

'Get out of my way. You're a disappointment, Joey.'

'Why don't you talk about Mom?' cried Joey, changing the subject, knowing the very thought would stun his father.

Then, as memories returned, Joey could see seething hatred pour into his father's eyes.

'Your slut mother.'

'Fuck you.'

Alexander's expression turned evil, his eyebrows met in the middle of his forehead and he bared his gritted teeth in a parody of a smile. He looked possessed. All he needed were horns to complete the picture.

He did not speak, but turned to see Lee waking from unconsciousness. Vince remained on his back this whole time, too injured to move.

'What secret are you hiding, Dad?'

'Yeah, tell him,' said Monica from behind Joey.

'You shut up.'

Groaning, Lee shakily came to his feet, holding his throbbing head and the lump the size of a golf ball that had formed there.

Alexander stood there, looking down at Joey's grey-blue eyes. Joey could see he was wired. The adrenaline was flooding through his father's system.

'Son, this is what's known as getting your sword off.'

Joey closed his eyes.
Five gunshots rang out in the night air.

Chapter 71

Monica screamed as the chief flung backwards like a rag doll, his body cutting a swathe through the sand. By the second bullet he had already landed on his back, but Joey knew his father hadn't finished. He walked to stand over Lee and fired three more times, causing the chief's body to convulse with every shot. Time seemed to stand still as Lee stared blankly into the cloudless night sky. Then his eyes closed.

'No!' Joey shouted. 'Enough killing!'

Lee should have known better. He was never going to walk away with a share from tonight. To trust Alexander was naive. Nothing good was ever going to come from conspiring with the most dangerous man in America. Lee was merely another pawn to be sacrificed when needed, even if it was just to satisfy Alexander's bloodlust. Now he had paid the ultimate price.

'What about the plan?' Monica cried from behind Joey.

'Plans change,' said Alexander, clasping his hands tight.

'What plan are you talking about?' Joey asked, confused, and turned to Monica.

'We were planning to set up the chief,' she said in his ear. 'Frame him as the mastermind behind tonight. We have him on tape manipulating the surveillance cameras. It was our plan until your father over there killed him.'

'Three of my men are dead, I decide when the plans change.'

'So, what are you going to do now, Alexander – kill us all?'

Alexander looked at them with a maniacal smile.

Joey frowned: he had seen this exact smile a week ago in front of the bank, just before the Santa Monica Pier blew up, killing dozens. This wasn't going to be good. His father seemed to be on edge, his eyes darting left and right in thought. His dark features dominated by a five-o'clock shadow. His face grew red as if he were about to erupt.

Joey stepped back, scared he might shoot everyone in sight in frustration, including him.

Monica mirrored Joey's movements as he moved away from Alexander, using him as a human shield.

Vince managed to prop himself up on his elbow and watched everything unfold. He was alone and exposed. There was no use trying to make a run for it. Not without getting a bullet in the back.

'Alexander, you have the money, it's over.'

'I'll tell you when it's over, Monica. Joey, move out of the way,' Alexander ordered.

'No, you're not going to kill anyone else.'

'No?! Say no to me once more and I'll put one in your head.'

'I can't believe it's come to this,' said Joey.

Vince, observing this, could only think that if Alexander's own son was not safe, what chance did he have? Alexander was at boiling point, filled with uncontrollable anger. It would take a miracle for Vince to survive this. He walked over to them and yanked Monica by the arm, while Joey tried to keep her safe by stepping between them.

'No, Dad!'

'Move!'

'If you kill her, you kill me.'

'Move!'

'No!'

'Fuck, Joey,' he yelled.

'It's over, Alexander, go home,' said Monica. 'You have the money.'

Alexander turned to his left with fists that shook. 'Vince.'

'No.'

'You little snake.'

'No!' yelled Joey again.

'Don't do it,' shouted Monica.

Vince lay helpless out in the open. There was nothing and no one to protect him from the psychopath only a heartbeat away. He stared at the face of death through swollen eyes until they fixed on the barrel of the gun pointed at him.

'No!'

A single bullet was fired.

Vince screamed in agony. He immediately felt the cold, sharp pain pulsating around the wound. He clutched his thigh with both hands and sprawled onto his front. He felt like he was drowning and there was no hope of being saved.

'That's enough,' Monica shouted.

Alexander hovered over Vince and aimed his weapon at the back of his neck this time.

'Please don't kill me,' he pleaded. Tears ran down his cheeks. 'Please … please …'

She wanted to be by Vince's side, but knew if she left Joey, her chances of survival were nil. The guilt Monica felt was almost physical. Vince's involvement was her doing. She needed to act fast. Reaching behind her back, she felt the Smith & Wesson revolver tucked away in her pants.

Then Joey felt a hard object dig in his back. 'Monica, what are you doing?'

'Don't you even think about it or your son gets it.'

Alexander's focus now shifted back to Monica, as Vince continued to beg for his life.

'You sure are one clever bitch.'

'I haven't even started yet.'

'And you call her your friend, son?'

By the way Joey kept turning his head over to Monica, she could feel the confusion in him, confronted with the dilemma of who to trust. At this point Vince was the only sure thing.

Monica smiled as she held tight to Joey's shoulder and said, 'I think it's time.'

'Time for what?' asked Alexander, clearly wondering what she was up to.

'Time for the truth to come out.'

'I don't know what Phil saw in you.'

Monica, still hiding behind Joey, lowered her head and spoke into her chest as if she were wearing a wire. A listening device was planted in her bra: someone was listening at the other end.

'It's time,' she said again.

Alexander immediately scanned the beach and the road in the distance, then the large towering cliff face. He assumed she had set him up for a fall. He had been deceived by someone more cunning than himself. Life in jail would be his sentence, having killed the Chief of Police only minutes ago. This was it. His fingers began to tingle, as did the hairs on the back of his neck. But as the seconds stretched to minutes there was nothing; no sirens, no clamoring or barking police dogs.

Nothing but the sound of the waves crashing down and the breeze building, coming up from the south. Only Vince's whimpering betrayed the calm of the situation.

If it wasn't the police, who had she spoken to? thought Alexander, feeling truly vulnerable for the first time.

'So where are your friends, witch?'

Monica gave a hint of a smile.

Alexander, more determined than ever, wanted her dead. She would not live to boast about how she had brought down the notorious Alexander Peruggia. But while Joey was bent on protecting her, he remained an obstacle. He needed to be removed, somehow. But she was stuck to his body like a tattoo. Alexander raised his gun and aimed. Monica ducked her head, using Joey as a shield.

'Watch out now, your only son's life is at stake.'

Bang!

A single shot was fired straight into Joey's right calf.

'Aagh! You fucking shot me!' Joey wailed in surprise as he fell backwards. Monica had no choice but to fall with him or she would be left standing there on her own, leaving Alexander with a clean shot. All this time she could have taken a shot at Alexander, but had held back, waiting for something.

Grasping his leg, Joey landed on top of Monica's small frame, but the momentum sent him a touch over to the right. Her gun fell to the ground as they hit the sand. Alexander had separated the two enough to finish the job.

Step by step and with eyes fixed on her, he approached.

He was in range.

'No, Dad!' screamed Joey. He tried to reach and cover Monica again with his arm.

'Don't do it,' she pleaded.

'Now, you die,' said Alexander.

The gun's barrel pointed between her beautiful green eyes. All that was left to do was squeeze the trigger, but Alexander was suddenly stopped by a deep voice that shouted from a distance.

'Stop! Put your gun down. Now!'

Chapter 72

Alexander looked up, dumbfounded as to who the intruder was. From their knees, both Joey and Monica turned their heads to search behind them. There was something familiar about the timbre of the voice that carried across the breeze. The figure's silhouette became larger with every step toward them. Whoever it was, was muscular and walked with a slight limp. He wore a white singlet, which was the only obvious feature that could be seen in the night, aside from his walk that was purposeful, almost a swagger.

Alexander waited to see who this guy was before he went along with the execution as planned. There would be no loose ends this time; all witnesses would be terminated. That meant Vince, Monica and whoever this faceless person was.

Alexander noticed Vince roll his body over and watched his eyes widen with hope that the man in the shadow was a cop. The only person right now who could possibly help him. His life depended on it.

Joey was another who watched with trepidation as the stranger came closer. Little details became more visible as he made his way into the moonlight. The way his arms swung, Alexander could tell he was unarmed. Joey stood up and placed all the pressure onto his healthy leg, while grasping his other. Monica, on the other hand, did not hesitate and dashed back behind Joey in the upright position and grabbed the gun that she had dropped earlier.

'No, Monica, he'll just shoot my other leg,' said Joey.

'No, Joey. This is it,' Monica said, still using his body as a shield with a firm grip on his shoulder, moving every time his father glanced over.

Alexander sighed. He would, once again, have to separate the two. That had to wait. Right now he needed to know: who was the man approaching them?

'Who are you?' Alexander demanded.

The man didn't respond, and just kept walking. As he got closer, half of his face became visible.

'Oh my God, this is it,' Monica said again, giving up her protection and stepping out from Joey's shadow.

Joey turned to see her expression as she moved to his side. She was beaming. A huge smile replaced the fear on her face.

'What are you doing?' said Joey. 'You're exposed.'

Alexander had a clean shot, but waited. Her gun was lowered and she looked captivated by the newcomer's presence. He decided to wait and see who he was.

'This is it, I have waited so long for this moment,' said Monica, beginning to sob. But these were no tears of sadness: she seemed ecstatic.

'Who is this guy?' Joey asked.

'He's an angel sent from heaven,' replied Monica.

Alexander raised his gun toward the stranger. The target was now close and visible in the light. His face out in the open for all to see.

'It can't be,' Joey whispered, rubbing his hand through his hair.

Alexander blinked several times – he couldn't believe his eyes either. 'Is this a joke?'

The man stood there with a five-o'clock shadow and his hands folded over each other in front of him. His upper body revealed and solid as a rock.

Alexander's gun hand dropped to his side as a tear fell down his cheek. 'My boy,' he said as a smile spread across his face.

'Bro,' said Joey, lost for words.

'Baby,' smiled Monica.

 Phil Peruggia smiled and winked at the last response.

Chapter 73

Monica let out a whimper.

'Hello, remember me?' Phil said in his usual calm, authoritative voice.

Alexander and Joey stood frozen, lost for words in a state of amazement. It was him in the flesh, standing alive before them.

'But you were blown up, I was there,' said Joey. 'I saw you.'

'No, brother. You mean you saw someone who looked like me, wearing my clothes, get blown up.'

Joey left Monica's side to give him a bear hug. 'I missed you, bro.'

'I missed you, too. Blood in blood out, right?'

Joey smiled, happy to hear those familiar words again. They separated, but he kept one hand on Phil's shoulder, not wanting to let go. Phil was everything to him; having him back filled a void that had sat in his heart this past week.

Joey witnessed his father's distance. He was not as welcoming and did not go to embrace his son. He stood there in wonder. The last thing he was expecting to see was his dead son reappear as he did.

'So you're back. You have some explaining to do. Why the elaborate hoax?' Alexander asked with a quaking voice and a glassy stare.

With this question, Phil's demeanor changed immediately. He glanced hard into the eyes that so mirrored his own. His

328

stare was brimming with hatred as he left Joey's side to walk toward his father, until they stood face to face.

'I did all this to destroy you,' he said.

'Destroy me? Please,' said Alexander. 'What did I do for you to hate me so much?'

Joey frowned, unable to understand the hostility coming from his eldest brother.

'You haven't been honest with us.'

'What are you fucking talking about?' Alexander retorted. 'What is this, a goddamn intervention?'

Phil said one word. 'Mom.'

That word sent a chill up Joey's spine. He had always wanted answers about his mother, but was never allowed to bring her up as she was off limits. He shoved between the two and said, 'Mom? What's going on, Phil?'

'Why don't you let your dad explain what he did?'

'Didn't I tell you the truth will set you free?' said Monica to Alexander with a cheeky grin, clearly relishing his comeuppance. Her gun was now aimed at his head. 'Vince … Go … you're free,' she said.

'No, wait,' replied Alexander. 'He's seen too much.'

'Drop your gun, Alexander. I wouldn't be worried about him right now. You have family issues you need to deal with.'

Alexander did as he was told and dropped the gun on the sand.

This was Vince's chance to leave this bizarre family feud. Through the fog of pain, he grunted in agony, pushed himself up to his feet and hobbled in the direction of the road. He struggled, but wasn't going to stop. He knew he needed to escape, just in case they changed their minds.

'That lucky son of a bitch must have a rabbit's foot,' said Alexander. He had survived an almost certain death by the skin of his teeth.

It was now that Monica looked into Joey's eyes and uttered the very same words that she'd whispered into Phil's ear not so long ago that had stopped him dead in his tracks. 'Your dad had your mother murdered.'

Alexander's mouth opened, but no words came out.

'What!?' said Joey, surprised. 'Is it true ...? Why?'

Alexander swallowed, cleared his throat and came clean. 'I did. She was a whore. I caught her cheating on me, that's why.'

'So you fucking killed her?' Joey cried in a voice choked with tears, then pushed his father in the chest.

'Don't you dare lay a finger on me,' he warned as Joey jumped backwards, suddenly aware of what he'd done. Phil did the opposite and stepped in to land a right hook to his father's jaw. Alexander staggered backwards a few steps and shook the stars out of his head as he recovered.

'Or you'll do what, Dad?'

'You planned all this to get back at me, eh!?'

'I couldn't be a part of this no more once I found out the truth,' said Phil. 'I was only ten fucking years old when I killed the man you said was responsible for Mom's death. My innocence was changed from that moment. It was all one big lie and you let me believe it.'

'So you faked your death?'

'People wouldn't ask questions if I was dead, so I disappeared for a week. It gave me enough time to recover from my bullet wound and retrieve all the money!'

'What money? Ian's taken the briefcases to my suite.'

Monica laughed.

'Those briefcases are filled with copy paper, they're worthless. Monica infiltrated the headquarters on Saturday night. I'm currently in possession of all six million dollars, as well as the two million she took from Vince earlier.'

'So you sent us all on a wild goose chase,' said Alexander.

'As a criminal mastermind, Moriarty you ain't,'

Monica said with a sneer. She had outwitted him from the beginning. All his men had been eliminated one way or another by her hand.

'Hey, since when do you take hostages, Dad?' Phil asked.

Alexander didn't have an answer. He could only ask, 'You saw the girl? How could you have known?'

'I climbed through my bedroom window just as the team left for the heist.'

'Tony?'

'Yes, sorry, Fat Tony is dead. He was watching over her when I came in from behind and took him out. A blade in the neck. Don't worry, it was quick.'

'What did you do with the girl?'

'After I saw you all on the beach, I let her go.'

'You don't understand what you've all done. She's probably gone straight to the police.'

'That was the plan, Dad. You're going down.'

'What about Ian?'

'Ah, yes. Ian. You couldn't imagine his surprise when he saw me. I took my time with him.'

'Why?' asked Joey.

'Because, little brother. Ian played a vital role in Mom's death twenty-five years ago. He now hangs from the wooden beams in Dad's suite.'

'I understand why Phil wants revenge for our mother, what's your reason?' Joey asked Monica, who seemed to be enjoying herself way too much.

'Son, don't believe anything she says. Her words are toxic.'

'Shut up, Dad,' Phil snapped.

Monica brought up her free hand and pushed her fingers into her temple and closed her eyes. She could not possibly explain the feeling she had right now. It was pain, but one she was used to. It had been her companion since childhood and now she could feel it rattling loose.

She dropped her hand and peered at Alexander, who

stood there waiting to hear what she had to say. This was the moment, she had practiced many times in the mirror. She took a deep breath then spoke. 'My father was the man your wife was having an affair with.'

Joey's jaw dropped.

This was the second time today Alexander was speechless. Monica watched his reaction as he stood there and the past came rushing back.

'Wha …?' Joey uttered. 'I need to sit down, this is crazy.'

'There's more, Joey, wait,' said Phil, crossing his arms.

'Now I understand why you were so hard to get rid of,' said Alexander. 'You want revenge.'

'Alexander, after you found out your wife was sleeping with my father, you had Ian place an explosive in my house. But at the time of the explosion my father was not alone. My innocent mother, who had nothing to do with all this, was with him. God bless her soul.'

'I only intended to kill your father,' said Alexander.

'Don't lie. You knew my mother had found out about her cheating husband and had her killed, too. No loose ends, that's your motto, right?'

'Where were you when this happened?' Joey asked, bringing a shaky hand to his forehead.

'I can remember it like it was yesterday. I was in my backyard playing and could hear my parents verbally abusing each other. My mother called my father a cheat and mentioned the name Alexander Peruggia on many occasions. That was the last time I ever heard their voices. The house exploded, sending me to the ground with cuts and bruises all over my face. I was lucky to have survived.'

Joey shook his head as it sagged back down to his chest.

'To make matters worse, when I was taken to the police department for questioning, I let them know about the name I had heard. The name that played over and over in my head. They told me they were going to look into it, but they did nothing. That was the day my hatred for the police grew. That was the day I told myself I was going to get my revenge and do whatever it took to get ahead in this godforsaken world. I grew up without my parents and I've been waiting for this moment for a very long time. I could've killed you many times, Alexander, but that would've been too easy. I wanted you to suffer, as I did. I wanted you to have no family, no money and leave you broken from the inside out. Blood in, blood out,' Monica quoted, aiming her gun at his chest.

'Wait,' said Joey. 'You have all his money, killed all his men and now he's lost both his sons. I don't want anything to do with him anymore. You win. That's enough, no one else needs to die.'

Phil laughed. 'Joey, that's not everything. There's more.'

Monica looked Joey dead in his eyes, her back toward Alexander. 'I have one more thing to tell you. Then you can decide if you still want him dead or alive.'

'What else is there?' Alexander asked Monica with a stony glare carved into his dark eyes. 'There's nothing else, that's it.'

Phil's eyes narrowed at the man he'd once called Dad and said, 'You're a liar.'

Chapter 74

Vince felt as if he'd dragged his wounded leg for hours. He had a single-minded focus: to save himself. He was a good distance away, hobbling forwards, but could still hear their muffled voices getting louder and louder above the wind. The small road beneath the cliff face was not too far ahead now, the promenade was also in sight.

'Keep moving. Keep moving,' he kept telling himself. He wasn't on the home stretch yet. Gasping for breath, he continued to drag his leg, leaving a large snake-like furrow in the sand, while wondering whether Isabella was still alive.

'Okay, Dad, tell Joey the truth,' Phil said in a sharp tone.

'What are you talking about? Enough with this crap. We have bigger issues to deal with now. Vince and Isabella have seen too much, they need to be stopped and you're here talking to me about what happened over twenty-five years ago. Come on!'

'What are they talking about, Dad? What else are you hiding?' asked Joey with a pained expression.

Alexander shrugged his shoulders as if his own clothing was creating discomfort. 'I have nothing to tell you. Get out of my way!' He turned to face his beach club in the far distance and began his walk back.

'Don't worry, Joey, I'll tell you the truth,' said Monica, loud enough for Alexander to hear and stop him in his tracks.

'Joey,' she said. 'Alexander isn't your biological father.'

Silence … Joey just stared at Monica. Then his shoulders slumped and he slowly started shaking his head in disbelief.

Alexander hesitated. He wore a frozen smile that turned into a laugh. 'Ha … Ha … Ha … You are something else, lady.'

'Dad, is it true?' Joey asked.

'Of course it's not true. That's absurd. I don't know what drugs she's on. Joey, you're my son, my blood. Phil, how can you let this witch twist your mind like that? I thought I raised you stronger than that.' Alexander swallowed hard. 'They're all lies, Joey.'

Phil kept his composure and kept quiet, offering a watery smile while maintaining a safe distance away from his father.

Monica moved toward Joey to close the gap, then placed her hand on his shoulder. 'Joey, listen to me, your real father's name is Ross Anton.'

'Anton!' repeated Joey, his eyes darting from his brother to his father.

'That's right,' she said. 'He was my father, too.'

'I can't believe this shit!' cried Joey.

'Your mother gave birth to you with my father's seed. Look at you. You look nothing like your father or brother. They're solid and swarthy and you're the complete opposite.'

Joey was speechless. All this information in one day was way too much to handle, but it did explain why Phil was always the favorite. He was never in the running to be considered to take over the family business.

'Joey, you're my half-brother,' she said.

Joey had always known that information about his mom was off limits. But he'd thought it was because her death was too painful for his father to recount. His heart pumped furiously as he scanned left and right. How could he escape this nightmare? He felt as if he didn't belong. He was lost and alone. His whole existence was a lie. Tears fell down his cheeks and his hands began to tremble.

★ ★ ★

'What a load of bullshit.' Alexander stepped in. With clenched fists and gritted teeth, visions of ripping Monica's head off swirled in his head.

He wasn't going to stand there and do nothing while this rubbish was rammed down his son's throat. It was amazing how he had kept his composure all this time. He looked over at his eldest son with disgust and disappointment. This wasn't the Phil he'd known and raised. This imposter was too pussy-whipped and brainwashed to know where to stand. It was as if a spell had been cast over him.

'So you're my sister?' Joey said in a whisper. 'So tell me, why was I raised by Alexander? This doesn't make any sense.'

'Alexander didn't want to be laughed at and ridiculed. So to hide the embarrassment, he named you as his own and had both your mother and real father murdered,' said Monica hurriedly, as Alexander edged closer.

'Don't listen to her,' yelled Alexander. 'She's manipulated your brother and now is trying to do the same to you.'

Joey stood there in a daze. 'How could this be?'

'Now do you understand, Joey, why I did what I did?' said Phil, standing behind Monica.

Joey responded, 'So you're not my brother?'

'Yes, I am. We share the same mother, just different fathers. Half-brother or not, you will always be my baby brother. Blood in, blood out forever, right?'

The term Phil had spoken and used so many times before had been explained.

Alexander approached Joey. The others took a step back. 'Yes, I admit it, I had her killed. I'm sorry, son, but it had to happen. Any woman that cheats on her husband is not worthy to stay alive. She broke my heart, but what Monica's saying isn't true. I'm your real dad.'

Monica went to talk, but hesitated as Alexander's glare

bore a hole into her skull. She gulped and continued, 'The photo I emailed you is your real father.'

'What photo? Show me,' demanded Alexander. Enough was enough. He gripped her by the neck: her death would fill him with pleasure right now.

'Stop!' yelled Phil.

Alexander held Monica in a headlock. The pressure to her neck was immense. Her airways were blocked and she began to suffocate. Phil leapt toward them and began pulling at his father's arms, trying to release his grip before it was too late. Monica's hands clawed at his wrists weakly and her eyes rolled back into her head.

'Dad, stop!' cried Joey.

'Ohh – I *am* your dad now?' replied Alexander. 'She's too dangerous to be allowed to live.'

Monica's face was crimson. Her hands were barely tapping the vice around her neck as she gargled for air. Death was not far away.

Chapter 75

The promenade was in sight. Sweat poured into Vince's eyes, blurring his vision. But it was his wounded leg that had searing pain shooting through his body, slowing him down to the point he thought he would never reach it.

'Stop, you mother—' Sounds of a brawl carried on the breeze coming from behind him.

He turned around and with a sigh of relief, realized he was a safe distance away now.

'Let go.' Phil threw vicious blows to his father's stomach again and again. Monica was suffocating. Finally, Alexander could not take it any longer and let go, holding his bruised ribs.

On her knees Monica took a colossal breath of air, then another.

'You okay?' Phil asked.

She did not reply and Alexander smirked, clearly happy with himself. The way he had squeezed her neck she would have felt like a scuba diver on an empty tank, desperately trying to reach the surface.

'Monica, you okay?' Joey asked again.

She was still unresponsive, her head hung down and her urgent breathing sounded unnatural.

'I'm going to kill you!' Phil lunged at his father, tackling him onto the ground. He landed two blows to Alexander's head, leaving a trail of blood that ran out from his nose.

'Is that all you've got, son?' Alexander retaliated with a brutal combination of his own and grunted, 'You'd betray your own father!'

It was like old times, but now there were no gloves to prevent knuckles from causing severe damage. This was for real, with an inevitable outcome: only one man would walk away from this.

'Stop!' Joey pleaded. 'You are family.'

No one listened.

The fight escalated. Both men grunted as they took handfuls of each other's clothing as they wrestled each other to the ground. Elbows were thrown as well as knees. Alexander released a hand and used it to start bashing Phil in the ribs. Phil grabbed his father's hair and yanked his head down sharply onto his bent knee. Blood flowed from Alexander's broken nose as he staggered backwards. Neither was holding back, even though the same blood ran through their veins.

Alexander idealized Phil. He was his favorite son and was now fighting for his life, throwing everything he had at him. He could not believe his son was trying to destroy him over a woman who had sought to tear his family apart. The family that was thick as thieves, who would die for each other, was now shattered and lost.

'You're dead to me,' he kept telling Phil. He needed to believe the person he was fighting was no longer his son. His son had died in the explosion a week ago. It was the only way he could take it to its logical conclusion.

Phil's punches came at him like tomahawks to his sixty-one-year-old body. He was younger, stronger and his pain threshold was much higher. Alexander's defeat was inexorable as he tried to cover up in a defensive position to avoid being knocked unconscious. Coming from the streets, he was a man who could take a few punches.

He needed to try something else. Standing toe to toe against Phil, who was fighting with the singular purpose and fury of revenge, would not work. He dropped to one knee while holding an arm up to block the blows, scooped up a handful of sand and threw it into Phil's face.

'Ah, you fuck!' Phil yelled, as he staggered backwards and tried to rub the sand out of his eyes. He shook his head and blinked furiously in an attempt to clear his vision.

'I'm going to kill you, old man.'

Alexander slipped out the deadly pocket knife Joey had refused earlier on.

'No!' yelled Joey, seeing all this unfold in slow motion.

It was only a split second, but it was all Alexander needed. He charged with a mighty cry, his knife up over his head.

Phil had just managed to open his eyes, but it was too late. The knife entered his chest in a downward blow. Deeper and deeper it sank, right into his beating heart.

He stared into his father's regretful eyes in shock, his mouth agape.

'I'm sorry,' Alexander whispered.

Phil's hands instinctively reached for the source of the searing pain. They wrapped around his father's hands, still holding onto the hilt of the blade. The pain was too much to bear and he shut his eyes.

Everything slowed down for Alexander at that moment. He realized what he had done and wondered how he was going to live with himself, knowing he had killed his own son. He stepped backwards on weak knees, taking the knife with him. Blood gushed from Phil's chest. The front of his white singlet quickly changed to a deep red. He dropped to his knees, then fell on his back to face the sky. His hands still clutching his chest.

'No!' screamed Joey, running to his brother's side and pushed his father away.

Monica crawled over and kneeled beside Joey, having

recovered from her near suffocation. Her first reaction was to put pressure on his wound, but Alexander knew her efforts were futile. Phil coughed blood and inhaled in quick, short breaths. His face was pallid and his lips were now a purplish blue. It was only a matter of time.

Monica closed her eyes and turned her head away. When she reopened them they were filled with tears. 'This wasn't supposed to happen,' she said, shaking her head. 'Honey, stay with us.'

Phil turned to face her, coughing up more blood. 'I love you.' With his last bit of strength, he grabbed his brother's hand and placed it in Monica's. 'Take care of my brother,' he said in a soft, croaky voice. Death was seconds away.

'I will,' she replied, 'I will.' Nodding her head toward Joey, whose face was filled with anguish.

'I love you, bro.'

Phil took a rasping breath, then another. They seemed to be coming faster and faster as he gasped for air. His eyes looked up into the night sky one last time, then closed. Phil Peruggia had died for the second time, but on this occasion he was never coming back.

Chapter 76

There was silence for a time. The southerly wind picked up to lift and gather the loose sand around the two dead bodies of Lee and Phil.

After saying goodbye, Joey stood up. His fists were clenched and his face was twisted with rage. He turned and faced the man he had called 'Dad' for all these years and said in a voice that started as a guttural whisper and finished in a roar, 'I hate you!'

'I know,' Alexander replied resignedly. He looked down at the knife in his hand and watched the blood run down the blade and drip off the end. He imagined he could hear the drops landing in the sand below.

His eyes seemed vacant as he stared around at the carnage he had wrought, the wreckage of his ego. Thoughts of suicide crept into his mind. As if involuntarily, he brought up the knife and rested the sharp edge against the skin of his neck. There was nothing but darkness and despair swirling within him now.

'Go on, do it,' said Monica. 'Save us all the trouble.'

Alexander was stripped of his persona and had become a frail man, with no will to live anymore. Phil's death had built a deep depression that made him feel bare and vulnerable inside. His soul didn't deserve to live in this world. Despite the medications he took daily, the realization of what he had just done reawakened the bipolar disorder he had been diagnosed with many years before.

Joey faced Alexander and said, 'Look what you've done, to my life, to me. My parents, now my brother.'

'I know,' Alexander said once more, the only words he could speak.

Letting go of Phil's hand, Monica reached for the only loaded weapon. The clip was full. She aimed it right between Alexander's eyes. 'So, are you going to do it or am I?'

Feeling dread and hopelessness, Alexander did not answer.

'There is no escaping death for you tonight, Alexander. All I need is one shot. My parents will be avenged one way or the other.'

'No, don't shoot,' Joey said, jumping in front of his dad and holding up his hands. 'Look at him, he's defeated.'

'I don't care.' Monica readjusted her stance, trying to get a clearer shot. 'He's going down. Move, Joey.'

Head faced down the entire time, dejected and regretful, Alexander slowly raised his head to look at Joey. Tears ran down his unshaved face as his hair blew in the wind.

'I love you, son,' he said with open arms, waiting for Joey to reciprocate with a hug. He had a weak smile on his face and his eyes begged for forgiveness.

Joey took a step backwards.

'Before she shoots me, I need to tell you something.' Alexander's hands dropped to his side.

Joey hesitantly walked over.

Monica stood waiting.

He raised his head and stared deep into his father's dark eyes, with nothing but hatred. 'What is it?'

Alexander's voice was soft but clear. He placed his unarmed hand on his son's shoulder and leaned in to speak in his ear. 'This is probably the end for me, but when I'm gone, you'll find out other truths, son. Truths not many people know about our family, especially your great-grandpa. In the bible, you'll find your answers.'

Joey raised his eyebrows in confusion. 'Dad, you're talking nonsense.'

'What's he saying?' asked Monica, still staring down the barrel of her gun.

Alexander's grip remained firm on Joey's shoulder. 'Don't trust her, son, it's all lies.'

Joey rolled his eyes, but Alexander shook him a little. 'You need to believe me.'

Monica stepped closer. 'Enough, move away.'

'Just remember, son, it's in your hands now. Take care of her for me.' His grip tightened with every step Monica took.

'That's enough!' she shouted. 'Move away, Joey.'

Alexander could see she was directly behind Joey. Her shadow was now cast under his son's feet.

'Joey, I'm—'

His knife flashed in his free hand.

'Your FATHER!'

He propelled himself forward, using Joey as a shield. His knife hand punched outward, seeking Monica's neck. The forlorn, depressed act had merely been a ploy to lure her within striking distance. His expression changed to something new, truly crazed now. The madness held back in check so long had been let off its leash. His eyes and mouth were wide open as he thrust himself over Joey, seeing his target in plain sight. She was going down.

Monica dived to the side in one fluid motion in the nick of time. Her arm caught the brunt of the blow as she continued to roll out of the way. She landed on her backside with both her hands outstretched, gripping the gun.

She could see Alexander's menacing eyes.

She squeezed the trigger and emptied the entire cartridge.

Alexander was hit several times in the chest, causing him to fly backwards with his arms flailing into the air. He hit the ground on his back. His hands clenched the sand at his sides and his back arched in a spasm. His legs shook a moment before he collapsed back down and exhaled his last breath.

Her war with Alexander had come to an end. After decades in the making, she had her revenge. Alexander Peruggia was finally dead.

Chapter 77

On the main road, five police cars raced to the promenade where Vince had just stepped foot. Sirens blaring, red-and-blue lights flickered as they skidded to a halt just inches away from his feet. Through all the noise and confusion he was barely aware of the black helicopter hovering behind him, until the wind blew him forward a step. A bright light shone down on him.

Where had that come from? he thought.

Looking up, he could see the pilot wearing a helmet and a microphone covering his mouth, hunched over the controls. It swung around over him, its blades beat the air and parted his hair down the middle. Seconds later it advanced toward the beach, still low to the ground, its LED floodlights sweeping across the sand.

Vince pressed his lips tight to keep from smiling. His palms pressed together as if he was praying. He breathed a sigh of relief and then grinned. He was safe and grateful to be alive.

A familiar face stepped out of one of the patrol cars. His grin widened and tears ran down his face as he recognized the scruffy, unkempt man, covered in bruises before him. It was his old man. He was the one in command, telling fellow officers where to go and what to do. Leonardo beamed back at Vince, happy to see he was safe. He opened up the back door to his vehicle and spoke to someone inside. 'He's all yours.'

Her face made his heart beat out of control. She'd made it; she'd survived. Isabella exited the car and bolted down the promenade toward him. Vince thanked the Lord once more that she had survived the night and held his arms wide open, waiting for her warm embrace to reach him. She slammed her lips into his and nearly knocked all the wind from his lungs. It was like they had not seen each other in years.

'I love you so much,' she said.

'You made it,' said Vince, caressing her hair. 'How did you get free?' he whispered in her ear with a happy cry.

'A man let me go, so I ran to the police.'

'I guess that explains why Dad's here?'

'Yeah, I heard an officer at the police department mention the commissioner's name. I told them about my kidnapping, the chief's involvement and the location on the beach, where I saw you running.'

She told him that after her statement the commissioner had received a call, even though it was in the early hours of the morning. Soon after, Leonardo's release was expedited, to take effect immediately – a direct order made by the commissioner himself, who felt enough was enough already. He was dealing with two dead cops, Tarn Mostrom in a hotel room and Luke Taylor, who was found inside the LAPD headquarters evidence room. His body was accompanied by two others, identified as part of Alexander's crew.

Now, with Isabella's statement citing the Chief of Police was corrupt and Vince was in danger, the commissioner reinstated veteran Leonardo Vancini. Screw the restraining orders, he said. A go-ahead was given to take down Alexander Peruggia.

Leonardo approached Vince, who was still in Isabella's arms. She moved to the side and Leonardo pulled him into his arms like a child. He hugged him as he had never hugged him before. This was new for Vince, who had never had much of a connection with his father. He liked it and smiled, cherishing the moment. Now safe, Vince had a deeper respect for his father. All the times he had complained as a kid were now justified. He had seen how dirty and corrupt the world really was, and how hard his father had worked to keep him away from that.

'Are you okay, son?' Leonardo noticed the blood coming from his leg. 'You've been shot.' He shouted to Detective Joanne Brown to call an ambulance. 'Sit down, Vince.'

'I'm okay, Dad.'

Suddenly his radio sparked to life. 'Detective Vancini, come in, over.'

He unclipped the radio from his belt. 'Yes, go ahead, over.'

'We have three down, two standing, over.'

'Keep your lights on them. Don't lose them,' he ordered. 'I'm on my way.'

'Roger that.'

'Vince, I need to know, is Alexander out there?'

'Who do you think shot me?' said Vince, as Detective Brown placed a medical kit in front of his leg.

'I'm going to fucking kill him.' Leonardo's eyes filled with venom.

'Get a ticket, Dad. Listen, there's something else you need to know, if you don't know it already. The chief, Lee Davis, is corrupt.

'That's what I hear,' said Leonardo.

'And Phil Peruggia is still alive.'

'Phil! What? Stay here, don't move. Chris, Steve, Craig, come with me.'

Leading the way, Leonardo started jogging to where the helicopter shone its lights. His gun was in his hand and he picked up his pace. Three men ran behind him as backup, one on the left and two on his right.

'It looks like the boys in blue are coming,' said Monica. She turned to Joey, whose hands shook with nerves. 'Come here, you. It's okay. Give me a hug.'

The helicopter continued to hover, blowing sand onto the three dead bodies. Joey, sheltered in Monica's arms, glanced down at his father, brother and the Chief of Police and said, 'How are we going to get out of this? I can't go to jail.'

'You won't, don't worry, I have your back,' said Monica, wiping a tear from his eye. 'Just follow my lead. I promised your brother I'll take care of you and that's what I'll do.'

'What do I say when they ask me questions. Do I lie?'

'Just tell them nothing, no one saw you.'

'What about Vince? He saw me.'

'Don't worry about Vince, I'll take care of him. Trust me.'

The team of armed men was upon them.

'Get down on your knees, place your hands on your head,' demanded Leonardo. 'This could be a trap, be careful. Eyes to the ground,' he warned his colleagues. He kept the two suspects in front of him in his sights, while his men stood above the three figures on the ground who may have been pretending to be dead. Each of them had their guns trained on a body.

'This is no trap, Leonardo. They're all dead,' Monica said with her hands held over her head. 'We're lucky to be alive.'

'Check their pulses,' said Leonardo to his team.

'No pulse, sir.'

'No pulse.'

'Same here. All dead, sir.'

He rubbed his eyebrows. 'Don't you fucking move,' he yelled.

'Relax, Detective, it's all over,' she said, pointing at the dead corpses. 'I'll have a full FBI briefing to your department explaining all this first thing. If you don't mind, I've had a rough day.'

'I don't trust you,' he said.

'Geez, I haven't heard that before,' said Monica with a grin.

'You're like an octopus with tentacles in everyone's business. How can anyone believe you? I did time because of you, so don't expect me to be on your side.'

'I can explain that.'

'No, don't bother. Arrest them and keep them locked up. I want statements. Something is wrong here and I don't like it.'

'Yes, sir,' Chris replied. 'Let's go.'

After a pat-down, Joey and Monica were handcuffed and escorted off the beach. The helicopter followed them with lights blinding them from above. Joey could only wonder how this was going to go down. How was he going to be painted, being the son of a man who was a well-known criminal and killer? But the big question that was on his mind was: will Monica rat him out?

He could only hope she was true to her word, as that was all he had. She was the only one who could help him now. He had no one else, they were all gone.

Now the helicopter was gone, the only light came from the full moon. Leonardo knelt down on one knee to take a closer look at the man who had been the bane of most of his police life. He smiled to himself, realizing fate had intervened and killed Alexander before he could do it. The universe had better plans for Leonardo than rolling in a cell for murdering a monster.

For years he had tried to net Alexander and failed. The man was too cunning, too influential, and now he was dead. He closed his eyes and breathed the fresh, salty air deep into his lungs as relief washed over him. It was finally over.

'Leonardo,' the commissioner said from behind him. 'We got him?'

'Yes, we did, sir,' said Leonardo, nodding emphatically.

'Who's this guy?' the commissioner asked, pointing at the third body.

'That's Phil Peruggia, his son.'

'Wasn't he killed a week ago?'

'I guess he rose from the dead.' Leonardo looked at Lee Davis's body. 'There's nothing worse than a dirty cop, and you know there are probably more lurking around.'

'Too true, Leo.' The commissioner nodded. 'That's why I need someone like you to weed them out. I want you to be my next Chief of Police. How do you feel about that, Captain Vancini?'

'Captain Vancini,' Leonardo repeated. 'I like the sound of that.'

Chapter 78

The new chief sat back in the chair, draped his laced fingers over his chest and eyed Joey Peruggia from across the steel table. It was two in the morning, but he had questions. The room set up for interviews and interrogations had no pictures on the walls, nothing to break up the unpainted grey brickwork except the two-way mirror, which sat directly behind Leonardo's head.

He set his feet flat on the floor and leaned forward, placing his elbows on the metal surface that separated them. He had been chasing Joey's father for years, and though happy with his demise, there were still more pieces of the puzzle to uncover.

'So, Joey, it's been a long night. Tell me what happened.'

Joey's posture was one of disdain. He sat with legs apart, arms draped over the chair as he looked down his nose at the new Chief of Police. He had been raised to believe the police were from the other side; the enemy.

'What do you want to know?'

'What's your role in all this?'

'What role are you talking about?'

'Don't play games with me.'

Joey looked away, shaking his head. Then he turned back to Leonardo and said, 'The only role you need to know, is that I saved your son from certain death tonight.

I was the one who stood in a bullet's path for him. The rest don't matter.'

'It does matter!' The chief slammed his fist hard on the table, causing the water in a Styrofoam cup to splash over. 'It's as if someone went on a killing spree. I have a college student dead, a maid, three cops, including the Chief of Police, and a bunch of your crew, including your father.'

'I didn't kill anyone, if that's what you're asking.' Joey squirmed in the silver chair and began to fidget, clasping his hands together and rubbing his thumb into his palm.

'Tell me what happened, or I'll charge you with murder.'

'Murder? I told you, I didn't kill anyone.' Joey hesitated for a second, not knowing what possible evidence he had on him, but he had a sudden feeling that he might not make it out of this room without a brand-new set of bracelets. 'You're fishing, you've got nothing,' he said with a doubtful smile.

'I have a witness. You're looking at life.'

Joey shifted forward. 'When you say "witness", do you mean your son, Vince? He's the only one I can think of. The rest are dead. If that's all you have, Chief, I don't like your chances.'

'Why do you say that?'

'No one is going to believe a kid who committed fraud by withholding two million dollars over an FBI agent.'

'You sure sound like your father, Joey.'

This seemed to sting Joey. He sat there as if he had lost his train of thought. Finally, he spoke. 'I think I'd like my lawyer now.'

'Just tell me, did Monica kill your father?'

'It's all over, Chief, the good guys won, let it go.'

'What about the money, who has it?'

Joey smiled. He glanced at the mirror over Leonardo's shoulder, hoping a video camera was recording on the other side and said, 'Maybe you should ask your son, he's the schemer.'

'That's funny,' replied Leonardo coldly. He stood up slowly before roaring 'funny' again as he swung a vicious backhand across Joey's jaw, knocking him off his chair. 'Is it still funny? Is it?'

'What do you want from me?' Joey darted his eyes up, to see a crazed man looming over him.

'Where is the six million? As you can see, your last answer didn't impress me.'

'I don't know.'

'Don't play games with me.' Leonardo took a step back, then lunged forward to deliver a hard kick to Joey's ribs. Joey grunted in pain as Leonardo gave him a moment to get his wind back. Just as he opened his mouth to tell the chief to go fuck himself, Leonardo sent another kick to the same spot, then another.

'Stop, stop, alright! I heard Phil took it. He said he took it.'

Leonardo grabbed Joey by the ear and pulled, stretching the skin, while he was still on the ground. 'Where did Phil put the money? Six million dollars is still missing.'

'Phil said tonight's heist was a ruse. He'd deceived all of us. He'd taken the money already with inside help.'

'Was his inside help Monica? Tell me.'

'No, it was Lee Davis.'

'That's bullshit. I don't believe you.'

The door to the interrogation room swung open and in walked the chubby commissioner, followed by three FBI agents and the FBI Assistant Director himself, who had initially assigned Monica Anton to the Alexander Peruggia case over a year ago.

'Let him go, Leonardo. We're taking over now,' said the Assistant Director, brushing crumbs off his sweats.

'What are you talking about? We made the arrest, it's ours,' said Leonardo, stepping away from the curled-up figure of Joey.

'No, we made the arrest. Don't forget, Ms. Anton is one of ours. We appreciate all your help, but it's now in our jurisdiction.'

'Come on, Commissioner, do something. Don't let them pull this juristic-shit. You know this case is personal. I was thrown in jail, for Christ's sake.'

The commissioner faced the beseeching chief. 'Sorry, Leo, it's their case now, they have rank. You need to hand over Joey and Monica.'

Leonardo shook his head while the FBI agents picked up Joey and escorted him outside, where Monica was already waiting.

'Look, Leonardo, it's in good hands. I wouldn't be here this early in the morning if it weren't important.' The Assistant Director reached out and shook his hand. 'Thanks again for your cooperation and please tell your son we'll be in touch in the next couple of days for his statement.'

Leonardo nodded. There was nothing he could do about the FBI taking over. The sad truth to all this was how the FBI would deal with Monica if she was found guilty. To this day no one in the FBI had been publicly branded a traitor. It looked bad for the agency. At most a slap on the wrist and a forced retirement would ensue. In due time all will be revealed and the six million dollars retrieved, thought Leonardo, hopefully.

Chapter 79

Tuesday, 7 am

The start of the new day arrived in a flash. The new Chief of Police sat back in his leather chair while drinking a hot cup of coffee. He'd barely slept a wink the night before. It was early in the morning and the first shift of officers were entering the building. Some smiled as they noticed Leonardo Vancini sitting behind the desk that had had Lee Davis behind it only yesterday, unaware of last night's events and his new appointment.

'What's he doing in there?' asked one under his breath to his partner.

'Isn't he supposed to be in jail?' replied the other, pulling up a seat at his cubicle.

Last night the commissioner had organized an email to be sent to all staff, addressing Leonardo's promotion as the new chief and commander. The police officers who had checked their emails via their smart phones were happy with the new appointment, as they walked by his office.

'Congratulations, sir,' a young officer stuck his head through the door.

'Hey, boss, congrats,' said another, his thumb up in the air. Leonardo smiled right back with an appreciative nod.

'Looks like he's our new boss,' said the officer from earlier, overhearing the congratulatory wishes.

It didn't take long. The news swept through the department like a flash flood, bringing with it a renewed positivity with the bonus that Alexander Peruggia was dead. Leonardo was the perfect man for the job.

By 9 am, the station was a hive of activity. Printer machines churned out paper with a rhythmic hum. Telephones rang as if barraged by a Delhi call center and the sound of the coffee machine gurgled in the background. Leonardo paused for a moment to take a look around the floor and take in all the craziness that was his second home. He loved it.

Not many people could handle the role he had been entrusted with. He was going to make sure that, under his command, there was going to be no leniency toward corrupt cops. Wearing a badge was an honor, you were a good guy.

His eyes told a story of a man who had lived through hell, wrongly accused and with first-hand knowledge of how flawed the judicial system was. This was never going to happen again, not under his command.

He walked back to his sturdy wooden desk, where a brown manila folder had been left open. He took another glance at the large surveillance photo taken of Alexander Peruggia. Though Leonardo knew he was dead, even through the photograph the man's black eyes possessed a chilling stare. He took one last peek, before closing the folder shut. That chapter in his life was now over and in the hands of the FBI.

He placed the file on top of another closed case, and noticed in the corner of his eye a framed picture of Vince. This particular photo he had carried with him in jail to keep motivated, stay strong and fight the odds. Now it sat on his desk. Vince was only seven years old, dressed up as a police officer like his father. It was Halloween and his mother was taking him out for trick or treating. He picked up the frame and smiled at the fond memory; it was an innocent time.

Last night Vince could easily have been a fourth person

dead on the beach. He had witnessed a darker side of life. A side people seldom see, and yet his father dealt with it daily. On a positive note, Leonardo knew this terrible experience had united and brought them closer. For the first time Vince understood why his father was the way he was. It had been his duty to keep scum off the streets and now, as chief, he had to keep it out of the department as well.

Leonardo did learn one thing about his son, though. During his ordeal, alone and on the run with killers on his heels, he proved he was a survivor. He was tougher than he realized. This was an exceptional trait if he decided to become a police officer like his old man. It was in his blood, or that's what Leonardo told himself as he continued to smile at the photo with pride.

At midday Leonardo stepped up and addressed the entire floor, explaining his position as the new chief. All the department heads, detectives, officers and the commissioner himself stood by and welcomed him with open arms. He spoke of how his predecessor had unfortunately succumbed to the influences of all that was wrong with the city. He explained, generously, that Lee Davis was merely human in his flaws, but that no such tolerance would be shown from now on for any officer discovered to be corrupt. And for those whose behavior might be considered shady, now was the time to stop.

He received a rowdy applause at the end from everybody, including a few who clapped coldly while looking at their shoes.

'Okay, now back to work. You all bother me,' he said with a cheerful smile that was met with a roar of laughter. He turned and walked back into his office with the commissioner, who closed the door.

'You did well, Leonardo,' he said, 'but we can't always have the victories we want.'

'What are you talking about?' Leonardo said, sitting behind his wooden desk.

The commissioner pulled an envelope from his jacket. It appeared to have been opened already. 'I have Monica's report.'

'You've read it, I assume?' asked Leonardo.

'Yes, I have. Just remember, you're on top now and you need to choose your battles. I'll leave this for you to read. And please, after you have, let it go.'

'That bad, huh?'

The commissioner just shrugged and walked out of the room, leaving the envelope sitting on the desk. Leonardo picked it up, pulled out its contents and began to read.

Chapter 80

Monday, July 21, 2016
Submitted by Special Agent Monica Kate Anton

After being assigned to the case by Assistant Director Kallis on April 26 2015, it was my job to investigate and uncover evidence linking Alexander Peruggia and his associates to criminal activity. The bureau needed eyes directly on the man himself and, knowing I could be of assistance, I volunteered.

After months of surveillance, I worked out the code for their drug-ordering system. It was a breakthrough, but they got word they were being monitored and changes were made instantly. That was when I first realized there were leaks in the department, so I decided to change tactics in order to get closer to the family.

Three months into the investigation, I began a sexual relationship with Phil Peruggia, Alexander's eldest son. I made it clear from the start I was an FBI agent. There was no need to lie, as I knew it would be leaked anyway. Me being an agent didn't bother him. I had convinced him from the beginning that I was a dirty cop who took bribes. I gained his trust by giving the family access to personnel files that were non-damaging to the bureau.

Alexander Peruggia did not appear convinced of my loyalty to Phil and was always mindful of what he revealed in front of me. It took six months before he seemed to trust me, but he remained cautious.

As part of the Peruggia family, I witnessed many violent crimes, but I was never able to collect enough evidence to convict Alexander of any substantial crime. He always covered his tracks and seemed to know when the police were otherwise occupied.

I soon came to realize he was receiving information from within the department and that source was the Chief of Police himself, Lee Davis. I then discovered that not only was he protecting Alexander, but that he was responsible for setting up the codes and systems that kept their operations invisible.

Lee played a pivotal role in setting up Detective Leonardo Vancini to do time with his testimony in court. Lee organized Detective Tarn Mostrom to eliminate Vince Vancini and retrieve the two million dollars he discovered he had. While tracking Vince, Mostrom killed Vince's roommate, Gary Bronson, the couple Louise and Kayden Smith and Consuela Sanchez, the maid at the Huntley Hotel. It was at this point I intervened and shot him dead, while protecting Vince.

Lee was instrumental in the LAPD headquarters heist, knowing the six million dollars was kept in the evidence room. He had complete control of the security system and its surveillance cameras.

All of Alexander's gang members that night were killed: Victoria Hughes, who was Alexander's girlfriend; Frank Hopkins, known as the gadgets man; James Johnson, known as the Hulk; Tony Giordano, known as the wise guy; Ian Santo, known as the explosives expert; the Chief of Police, Lee Davis; and Alexander Peruggia himself.

I was shocked to find out that Phil Peruggia had faked his own death to avenge his mother. She had been murdered by his father when he was only ten years old because of an alleged affair. I witnessed Alexander kill Lee Davis, then his son, Phil, before turning the gun onto me, so I didn't hesitate to shoot him.

Also killed that night was Detective Luke Taylor, who put his life on the line at the LAPD headquarters. He had apparently gone there on a tip-off, to prevent the heist from taking place.

Concluding my report: After a year on this case I'm happy it has come to an end, helping take down the most wanted man in America. The FBI had been after this man for years and I feel grateful for being a part of it. The $1,800,000 I confiscated from Vince is now in police hands and will be returned to the bank a week from now. The amount is $150,000 shy, due to Gary Bronson's elaborate spending and is the reason why he was murdered. The bank will be claiming back its lost funds through insurance.

The six million dollars taken from the LAPD headquarters is still unaccounted for and it is believed Phil Peruggia has hidden it. We are currently searching for it.

While on the inside, I spent much of my time dealing with all the gang members, including Joey Peruggia. He was instrumental in saving my life, placing himself between me and his father, who was trying to kill me. He never took a life and I urge that leniency be shown to him.

Monica's report was leaked to the press, becoming the top news story on every TV station. The report, underlining everyone's involvement, became gospel to the events that unfolded, and one of the crucial reasons why Joey Peruggia was allowed to walk free. The FBI painted her to be a hero, giving her the FBI Medal for Meritorious Achievement, awarded for extraordinary or exceptional service in the line of duty.

In her acceptance speech, she thanked all her peers and superiors and announced to everyone that she would be stepping down and resigning from duty. She ended her speech with, 'After a lifetime of serving my country, it's been a pleasure and now it's time for me to move on. God bless and thank you.'

Chapter 81

A week went by. Vince returned to the routine of college life, but he loved every minute of it. Having come so close to death numerous times made him appreciate life a lot more than usual. He was going to make an effort this year, study hard and graduate college at the top of his class. There was no time like the present to pursue his passion as a 3D artist and get himself employed at a big studio production house.

Having his tuition paid for allowed him to concentrate fully on his studies, but more importantly, it allowed him more quality time with the one person who meant the world to him – Isabella.

Losing her had been hell, she was his rock. He hadn't realized how much he loved her until she was gone. After begging forgiveness, she'd agreed to take him back, as she still loved him. But he had one promise to fulfill: to never be unfaithful again.

If there was one thing he'd learned through this misadventure, it was no matter what you did or did not have, all that mattered was being around the people you loved. Money was not everything if it meant ending up in a body bag or having no one to share it with. And that's why Vince had made a deal with his father to help him rebuild their new home together and make an effort to also rebuild their relationship. Gary had paid the ultimate price and was going to be missed. He was a good friend, but as sad as it was, life had to go on.

★ ★ ★

Heading for the campus swimming pool, Vince and Isabella held hands. Their days were hectic with back-to-back classes, so this was a chance to stretch their legs that had been crammed in a student's chair and get some laps in. As they entered the facility, Vince looked into Isabella's warm eyes.

'I love you,' he said candidly.

She smiled, knowing he meant it. 'I love you, too.'

Isabella, eager to jump in the pool, threw her bag and towel over Vince's arm like he was a coat stand and said, 'Can you put my stuff in your locker?'

Vince froze. He mumbled, 'locker' as a memory came rushing back to him. His heart began beating furiously as a mixture of fear and excitement flooded his body.

Could it still be there? No way – could it?

'You okay?' Isabella touched his hand, startling him.

'Yeah, I'm good,' Vince spoke softly, as if barely in the present. 'I'll be right back,' he said and did an about-face, heading toward the locker room.

He walked in carrying the two bags and wearing his black swimming trunks, shirt and flip-flops. The familiar smell of sweat hit him in the face. He stood in front of locker forty-nine, the same locker he'd used throughout the year. Its door was left open. He then drifted his eyes south to the locker beneath it. Number fifty-two.

This locker was still shut. A good sign.

Could the money still be inside?

There was only one way to find out. His hand shook as he ran his magnetic membership card over the silver panel.

There was a click and the red marker disappeared. The hairs on the back of his neck stood on end as he glanced around, making sure he was alone.

'Hey, is everything okay?' Isabella yelled from the pool's edge.

Vince took a deep breath, opened the door slightly and

took a peek. His eyes lit up as he turned to yell back to Isabella, 'Everything is perfect, just perfect.'

Chapter 82

The day after Monica's report hit the news headlines, Joey was released from FBI custody and left to go back to the Beach Club that now had six vacant rooms. No father, brother, Tony or Ian. No Frank or James. Just him. As the only heir to his father's fortune, the venue was now his.

Knowing the club was due to be liquidated in the next couple of months, he planned to enjoy his last weeks there. Yet only days after his father's death, he learned Alexander had taken out a substantial life-insurance policy.

With this unexpected windfall, Joey had enough money to pay off all the debts, take the reins of the business and make it his own. His first change was the name: it became Joey's Beach Club.

He leaned on the railing of his enormous balcony and drank in the view. He thought about his freedom and how its architect was a most unlikely source. It was not his newly discovered half-sister who could have put him away for life.

When Vince Vancini was brought into the FBI for questioning and asked to write down a statement regarding his involvement in the events that had taken place, he had left the paper in front of him blank and took the Fifth Amendment. He still feared for his life and those he loved. Who knew if other corrupt cops were lurking in the department? At least that is what he'd told them.

The truth of it was Monica had got to him first, as she'd

told Joey she would. It was her last act before she left. Vince and Joey were two men from very different backgrounds, but they had one thing in common: overbearing, distant fathers whose approval they desperately sought.

Back on the beach, Joey could have easily killed Vince if he had listened to his father, but he'd chosen a different path. It took a lot of courage to say no to a man like Alexander. It was due to this act that Vince had decided to take the Fifth and let Joey walk free. A life for a life. Now Joey had the chance to start a new life. One without crime or corruption.

With Monica's report, Vince's silence and no other witnesses, the FBI had let him go with the warning: 'We'll be keeping our eyes on you.'

Early in the morning, Joey took a long walk down Venice Beach. The sea air smelled sweeter than usual. He relished his freedom, from jail, from his father's control and a life he didn't want to be a part of. He was his own man and could decide his own future. He was wealthy and he was in control of his own life. He dug his toes into the hard, wet sand.

He closed his eyes and breathed in the breeze. He thought about his father, his brother and his new half-sister, who had disappeared without a goodbye, handshake or kiss.

The day after he was released, he saw her on TV being handed a reward for her take-down, regarded as one of the biggest of the century. She told the press she was resigning and going on a much-needed holiday.

Joey sat there, shaking his head, knowing she was on no holiday. She was gone permanently with millions in her pocket. He felt it was suspicious how she didn't even call to say goodbye. He thought they were friends – they were family, after all. He wanted to at least thank her for keeping the promise she'd made Phil. True to her word, she'd helped him to his freedom.

Joey strolled over to the promenade, which was filled with

souvenir shops, eateries and throngs of tourists. He spotted a souvenir shop with a fridge out the front. He helped himself to a sports drink. As he approached the counter to pay, something stopped him in his tracks. Though his mouth was dry, he stood frozen to the spot, staring over the shop clerk's shoulder. He smiled slightly but it did not show in his eyes, as he slowly cursed.

On three shelves behind the clerk sat countless photo frames of various sizes. 'Special, save fifty percent on all frames,' read a sign.

Inside each frame was a picture identical to the next. The same two models were smiling at the camera, a man and a woman. It was the man who'd caught Joey's eye. He was handsome, with fair skin and blond hair. The flash of familiarity lasted only seconds before he realized he was staring at the same man Monica had sent him a picture of previously. In fact, he was in the same pose.

Joey reached into his pocket and took out his phone. He found the email she had sent with the attachment image and took a closer look. It was confirmed, aside from a subtle difference in hue, he was looking at the exact same photograph. Only the woman was different.

Monica had organized a Photoshop artist to superimpose his mother's image in place of the female model. The color was retouched and balanced, shadows adjusted. It was seamless and completely unnoticeable to the eye. She had fabricated a new father for him.

Joey stood there with a five-dollar bill halfway out of his wallet, staring at the shelves lined with rows of his fictitious father. The clerk looked at Joey expectantly, waiting for him to hand over the money. This meant Alexander had been telling the truth the whole time and his dying words, 'I am your father,' were not a lie.

Joey blinked out of his trance. 'The bitch,' he thought. Monica had fooled him: she was not his sister; not even close.

The truth of his mother's murder, as it was told to him by Monica, was the bait that had convinced him to swallow the hook that Alexander was not even his father. This had severed any real connection to the tyrant who'd raised him and allowed Monica to kill him with impunity.

She had also turned Phil against his father with the same lie and she had gained an all-important ally.

They had planned Phil's fake death together to throw his father off guard. But it would not be revealed as a ruse until the six million dollars was in her possession. It was always about the money for Monica. Phil was merely a pawn, and she had never truly loved him. She would have inevitably killed him if Alexander had not done it for her.

Two days before the heist of the LAPD headquarters, she had personally extracted the six million dollars unseen, before she'd orchestrated the blood bath in the evidence room that had killed half of Alexander's men. She knew most of them would die that night, leaving Alexander till last.

Joey paid for his drink and walked out.

What was he going to do now with this knowledge?

Finding her was going to be like finding a needle in a haystack.

Chapter 83

The relentless rain fell without a break down the steep San Francisco roads like shallow rivers. The lightning and thunder continued as dark clouds rolled over Union Square, where Monica Anton was enjoying a no-expense-spared shopping spree in Victoria's Secret.

Months had gone by; it was now winter. Monica had vanished into thin air and was enjoying her freedom. With numerous shopping bags in each hand, she left the store and ran to her Mercedes, which she had left in a no-parking zone.

Outside it was cold, wet and windy and the rain battered the roof of the car as she stepped inside, drenched. She smiled; it was as if she was a child again running to her mom's car after school.

The white sports Mercedes was the only possession she had kept from her previous life, using it to drive up and down the California coast.

As she placed the bags on the passenger seat, a call came in through the car's telephone system mounted on the dashboard. She wondered who could be calling. Who had her number?

She wiped her dripping face with the dry patch of her sleeve and hesitantly answered the call by pushing a button on the steering wheel. Craning forward, she could not see anything through the waterfall that was on her windscreen. She did not speak a word and just waited for a response at the other end.

'Hello, Monica, I know you're there,' said Joey quietly.

Shocked, she did not reply.

'You lied to me.'

Monica opened her mouth to speak but quickly shut it, thinking it was better to stay quiet and see what he had to say, as water from her limp hair ran down her face.

'I know Alexander was my real father.'

Monica was now concerned. Joey's tone was firm and direct, like that of a man beyond his years. This was not the insecure boy she'd known as Phil's younger brother.

She continued to listen.

She could hear rain and thunder pounding in the background at Joey's end of the phone, as if he was outside her car. From nowhere, flashing red lights and a loud siren flew past her, kicking up water which sprayed over her side window. It was an ambulance on the way to an emergency. A second later Monica heard the same siren through the phone.

She realized Joey was there, outside somewhere. He had tracked her down somehow.

'You lied to me!' Joey said again, sounding as though he was gritting his teeth.

Monica could not contain herself anymore. 'Where are you, Joey? Show yourself,' she blurted.

'I'm going to make you pay,' he said, just as Monica heard a sharp crack, like breaking glass through the phone.

'What was that noise?' she said.

Joey laughed malevolently. 'That was my fist slamming into the glass window of the phone booth I'm in.'

'Which phone booth?' Monica demanded as the rain continued to pound the roof of her car. 'How did you get this number?'

'I have lost everyone I loved,' said Joey. His tone had softened.

'Your father deserved to die.'

'Yes, he did, but so do you.'

Monica could just see through her window down the empty street now that the rain had stopped.

Joey was only a hundred feet away, standing inside a phone booth like he said he was. He was unshaven and dressed in black.

'Now it's time for my retribution,' he said. He stepped out of the phone booth, holding the phone in one hand and another peculiar object in his other. 'Never fuck with a Peruggia!' He let go of the phone and placed both hands on the detonator.

Monica's eyes bulged and her jaw dropped. She was sitting on a bomb. She gasped as her hands pawed desperately at the door handle to get out.

'See you in hell, bitch,' said Joey, one last time and flicked the switch.

'No!' Monica screamed.

The car exploded in front of his eyes. The hood blew off and the windows shattered like they were nothing, as debris rained down on the wet road. Joey shielded his face from the blast. When he finally lowered his arm, all he saw was a burning shell beneath a huge plume of black smoke.

Punishment had been meted. This was a justice surely even Leonardo Vancini would have appreciated, if he had known the true extent of her crimes.

She had fooled the Chief of Police, Alexander and Phil Peruggia, used Detective Taylor as a pawn and manipulated the lives of Leonardo and Vince Vancini. The last person she ever saw as a threat to her plans was the young surfer kid, who had wanted nothing more than to be respected by his father.

After taking over his father's assets, Joey had received an email regarding an upgrade to the GPS tracking device, still active, attached to Monica's Mercedes. After some due diligence using a search engine, he had tracked her movements and pin-pointed her exact location.

The rain began to fall again.

Joey smiled as he watched the fire burn uncontrollably. The rain turned his blond hair to a darker brown. He took his father's sunglasses from his front pocket and put them on, displaying his bleeding knuckles and the new Vitruvian man tattoo on his wrist.

He had a glint in his eye, a darkness. The fire reflected off the dark lenses. He looked like a reborn Alexander Peruggia.

A hint of a smile appeared on his face.

Joey had enjoyed it a little too much.

He was a Peruggia after all. It was in his blood.

Chapter 84

The rain continued to pour. She sat back in a dark BMW and put her phone down. It was the last time she was ever going to hear his voice again. She was one hundred yards away from the blast site and had watched Joey take his revenge. He stood for a while and watched the gift his brother had given her go up in flames. A gift she'd known would come back one day to bite her in the ass, if she continued to drive it.

She had sent Joey an anonymous email regarding the tracking device and knew he would take the bait. When Alexander was alive, she drove it only to maintain the façade that she was on his team. But now, Monica used it to lure Joey in. Her final masterpiece.

Needing a body double to fake her own death, she had hired a personal assistant, who resembled her in many ways. She had given her the keys to her Mercedes with a list of chores to do and followed her from afar this past week.

Her plan once again had worked to perfection.

Now that Joey thought he had outsmarted and killed her, she could finally disappear. It was her last act before she vanished out of sight for good. She glanced over to the passenger seat and smiled at the six million dollars concealed in two large duffle bags.

She had all the money in the world at her disposal. She could start a new life anywhere she wanted.

Maybe this time a life without corruption and death.

Maybe one with a family and a home with a picket fence.

Also by Phil Philips

FORTUNE IN BLOOD
MONA LISA'S SECRET
LAST SECRET CHAMBER
LAST SECRET KEYSTONE
GUARDIANS OF EGYPT

ACKNOWLEDGMENTS

I owe so many people for the realization of this lifelong dream. First and foremost, I would like to thank my beautiful wife Marie, who supported me and put up with me, throughout this amazing journey.

And to my boys Alexander and Leonardo, who are too young to read this book now, for your unconditional love. This book is a testament, you can do anything, if you put your mind to it.

Next I want to thank my extended family, parents and friends for their loving support and always believing in me.

A special thank you goes out to my good friends Ian Townsend and Tarn Mount for being my beta readers. Ian was one of the first people to read the novel in its infant stage and offered me some invaluable advice. Tarn helped shape the story you hold in your hands today. Tarn I will always cherish the discussions we had at Max Brenner, Bondi Junction, that always started with a coffee stain on the manuscript, to make it official. *The Pacino mark.*

A huge thank you, to my genius editor Alexandra Nahlous for giving this book life and making it the best it could possibly be. Alexandra you were a pleasure to work with and I can't thank you enough. I'm looking forward to our next project together.

I also want to give a big thank you to Bonnie Wilson for doing a fantastic job with the proofreading.

Last of all to you, my dear reader, for picking up my book. I truly hope you have as much fun reading it as I did writing it. I would love to hear from you. I can be contacted via social media, or on my website **philphilips.com**

ONE MORE THING ...

If you loved the book and have a moment to spare, I would really appreciate a short review where you bought the book. Your help in spreading the word is gratefully appreciated, as it helps other readers discover the story.

MORE FICTION FROM PHIL PHILIPS

Mona Lisa's Secret

A Joey Peruggia Adventure Series Book 1

Joey is the great-grandson of Vincenzo Peruggia, the man who stole the original Mona Lisa in 1911. Along with his girlfriend, Marie, an art connoisseur, he stumbles across his father's secret room, and finds himself staring at what he thinks is a replica of da Vinci's most famous masterpiece.

BUT IT IS NO FAKE ...

The Louvre has kept this secret for over one hundred years, waiting for the original to come to light, and now they want it back at any cost.

With Marie held hostage and the Louvre curator and his men hot on his trail, Joey is left to run for his life in an unfamiliar city, with the priceless Mona Lisa his only bargaining chip. While formulating a plan to get Marie back with the help from an unexpected quarter, Joey discovers hidden secrets within the painting, secrets which, if made public, could change the world forever.

In this elaborately plotted, fast-paced thriller, Phil Philips takes you on a roller-coaster ride through the streets of Paris and to the Jura mountains of Switzerland, to uncover a secret hidden for thousands of years ...

MORE FICTION FROM PHIL PHILIPS

Last Secret Chamber

A Joey Peruggia Adventure Series Book 2

Where is ancient Egypt's last secret chamber, and what is concealed within?

When an archaeologist is murdered in his Cairo apartment, an ancient artefact is stolen from his safe – one believed to hold the clue to the last secret chamber.

When Joey Peruggia discovers that the dead man was his long-lost uncle, he travels with his girlfriend, Marie, and his friend Boyce, who works for the French intelligence, to Egypt, on a mission to find answers.

But once they arrive, they are lured into a trap and become hostages to a crazed man and his gang of thieves. This is a man who will stop at nothing to discover what lies in the last secret chamber.

All bets are off, and only the cleverest will survive this deadliest of adventures.

In this elaborately plotted, fast-paced thriller, Phil Philips takes you on a roller-coaster ride through Egypt's most prized structures on the Giza plateau, to uncover a secret hidden for thousands of years …

MORE FICTION FROM PHIL PHILIPS

Last Secret Keystone

A Joey Peruggia Adventure Series Book 3

When a cargo plane carrying an ancient vase crashes into the Atlantic, the DGSE – otherwise known as the French CIA – immediately suspect it's deliberate. The vase is believed to hold a key that gives entrance to a hidden cave on Easter Island: a site connected with ancient Egypt and an otherworldly portal discovered deep beneath the Great Pyramid of Giza.

Joey, Marie, and Boyce are once again caught up in a dangerous adventure, forced on them by a trained assassin who is on his own spiritual quest for answers ... A ruthless man who will stop at nothing to get what he wants.

His objective: to find the last secret keystone, and with it activate the portal once again. Joey and his friends must stop him – at any cost.

In this fast-paced thriller, Book 3 in the Joey Peruggia Adventure Series, Phil Philips takes you on a roller-coaster ride from the giant Moai statues of Easter Island to the Greek island of Santorini and back to Egypt, where the fate of humankind once again rests with the most unlikely of heroes.